SEARCH FOR
THE SWAN MAIDEN

SEARCH FOR THE SWAN MAIDEN

A SAM LONDON ADVENTURE

TODD CALGI GALLICANO

PERMUTED
PRESS

A PERMUTED PRESS BOOK

ISBN: 978-1-68261-987-2
ISBN (eBook): 978-1-68261-988-9

Search for the Swan Maiden:
A Sam London Adventure
© 2021 by Todd Calgi Gallicano
All Rights Reserved

Cover and illustrations by Kevin Keele
Design by Chris McClary

PERMUTED
PRESS

Permuted Press, LLC
New York · Nashville
permutedpress.com

Published in the United States of America

1 2 3 4 5 6 7 8 9 10

Kazuya To Gohiki No Yōkai Ni Sasagu

和哉と五匹の妖怪に捧ぐ

AUTHOR'S NOTE

The following account is based on case files that originated with the Department of Mythical Wildlife (DMW). In an effort to inform the public of this previously unknown government agency, my sources have provided me with copies of files from the DMW archives. As far as I can determine, Sam London's third case was nearly designated "Rise of the Mongolian Death Worm" but was ultimately classified as "Search for the Swan Maiden."

As always, DMW case files consist of witness interviews, investigative notes, research materials, and reports offering comprehensive explanations of the events that transpired. Due to the often dry, fact-laden nature of this information, I have created a dramatic interpretation of the file's contents. All the details have been maintained, but the narrative has been enhanced for the reader's enjoyment. I have also included several references to the source material within the text and have appended a legend of abbreviations, codes, and terms to assist in decoding the DMW's distinct classification system.

Since these files are classified, dates have been omitted and some names have been altered to protect the identities of witnesses and individuals still in the department's employ.

—T.C.G.

PROLOGUE

For intrepid San Francisco news reporter Cynthia Salazar, the greater the secret, the greater the thrill of exposing it. Of course, the most worthwhile secrets didn't simply offer themselves up to be revealed to the masses. Rather, it took considerable effort to mine these hidden truths from the cavernous depths of human minds. Cynthia prided herself in possessing the patience and perseverance required to unearth the gems buried deep within those caves. She found fulfillment in this quest—a sort of "secret" spelunking that satisfied her self-worth.

The secret Cynthia recently stumbled upon would no doubt change the course of human history. It was crazy, impossible, inconceivable...but it had been consuming Cynthia's every thought. Her journalistic instincts blindly pushed aside her rational mind. Dig deeper, these instincts told her, and so down the jackalope hole she hopped.

Her first hint that this secret even existed came in Death Valley, California. She was covering the explosion of a gas station that had miraculously resulted in no fatalities. The woman who had run onto the highway and triggered the events that led to the blast was a San Francisco native named Gladys Hartwicke. When Cynthia interviewed Gladys on live television, the woman claimed she had seen a mythical creature known as a gryphon. She also said there was a boy with the creature—a boy Cynthia later learned was named Sam London. Cynthia was mocked and derided for giving Gladys the airtime to make her ridiculous claim, and she was certain that the embarrassing episode had cost her the nightly anchor chair.

A few weeks after the Death Valley fiasco, Cynthia was at a fashion show in San Francisco, reporting on model and social media star Pearl Eklund. As the teenager was whisked away to a waiting car, she was accosted by a mysterious man—the same man who earlier that day had popped onto a platform at Pier 39 in what eyewitnesses described as a seal suit. Not only did this man act and speak strangely—exhibiting remarkable strength and referring to Pearl as a princess—but when he touched the model, Cynthia saw a bluish mist erupt from Pearl's skin. Before the reporter could speak with the mystery man, he ran off.

Intrigued, Cynthia sought to interview the witnesses of the incident at Pier 39. She was shocked to find one of them was Gladys Hartwicke. She went to Gladys's apartment to ask her about the stranger's appearance in a "seal suit," but the woman was evasive and unnerved by the reporter's questions. When Cynthia asked about Sam London, Gladys said she was much too busy for "this nonsense," then slammed the door in the reporter's face. This was a common tactic among individuals who were hiding something and only fueled Cynthia's suspicion that there was more to the story. Several days later, Cynthia confronted Pearl Eklund on a street in Miami, Florida. The young woman was guarded, and the moment the reporter inquired about Sam London, Pearl immediately cut off the interview and escaped into her limo.

All roads seemed to lead to a twelve-year-old boy who Cynthia learned was living in Benicia, California, with his mother and attending Benicia Middle School. Cynthia was preparing to visit the London household when she received an anonymous tip that the answers to her many questions could be found in Washington, D.C., at the Department of the Interior (DOI).

The DOI had begun its mission in 1849 to protect and manage the natural resources and cultural heritage of the United States. It had often been dubbed the Department of Everything Else, given its wide-ranging purview. Cynthia wondered if the "Everything Else" moniker was hiding something truly extraordinary. She hopped on a plane and headed to the nation's capital, intent on finding out.

* * *

As Cynthia Salazar sat on a park bench across from the DOI building on C Street, she nervously checked her watch and her surroundings. For the past several days, she had staked out the DOI building and recorded every individual who passed through its doors, cross-referencing her list with a roster of government employees. All visitors could be accounted for, except one—a man in his late thirties with perfectly round glasses and a receding head of hair parted right down the middle. Every day he wore the same light blue short-sleeved dress shirt, steel grey tie, and beige khaki pants. Either he had several of the same outfit in his closet or he was doing laundry on a nightly basis. Each morning right before 8:30 a.m., he approached on foot from the northwest side of the building holding a homemade reddish-pink smoothie in a clear bottle. He didn't associate with anyone and didn't emerge from the building until 5:00 p.m.

On this day, Cynthia was planning to make contact with the man by "accident"—she would bump into him as he turned the building's corner on his way into work. She waited anxiously for her moment; then, at 8:29 a.m., the reporter crossed the street and rounded the northwest corner of the building to meet her mark...but her mark wasn't there.

She quickly scanned the faces of the pedestrians walking towards her, but the man was not among them. Confounded by this wrinkle in her plan, Cynthia sidled over to the building and leaned against the outside wall. She pretended to play with her phone, all the while keeping a close eye on the passers-by. Several minutes ticked away and there was still no sign of him. Perhaps he was sick? Or on vacation?

"Looking for me?" a voice called out a moment later. Cynthia spun to her right and found the mystery man standing a few feet from her, dressed in his usual outfit with his smoothie in hand. "Miss Salazar, am I right?"

"How did you—?" Cynthia began to ask, before he cut her off.

"We know," he answered with a smirk, then slurped up some of his smoothie. Cynthia eyed him.

"We? And who are you, exactly?" Cynthia asked.

"The name's Bob Ferguson. And your investigation ends now."

Chapter 1
THE MEMORY REMAINS

Doctor Vance Vantana of the U.S. Department of Mythical Wildlife died on a Sunday evening in late spring. It was an angry death. A violent, bloody, and gut-wrenching demise. The ranger battled tooth and nail until the bitter end, but his body simply couldn't battle any longer. He didn't blame himself—forty to one were terrible odds. As he watched his world close in, Vance recognized that he had made some poor life decisions of late—the worst being dying at this particular moment in time.

Up until recently, Vance had never been concerned about the consequences of something happening to him, because he didn't believe there were all that many to be concerned about. Sure, his parents and relatives would be upset to hear of his passing. Doctor Knox would probably be sad, that is, if gryphons even got sad. And there would be the smattering of friends who would grieve his death by swapping fun stories about him after the funeral over burgers and french fries. But he didn't have a family of his own, relying on him. He didn't have a child or a wife, and so Vance Vantana never thought twice about taking chances with his life—it helped him do his job well and made it infinitely more interesting.

But Vance's world had changed in the last few weeks, and he'd forgotten to change with it. He wasn't a lone wolf anymore. He was a father. Sam London, the son he never knew existed, was back home, still reeling from the death of his mom, Odette, the wife Vance never knew he had. It was complicated and tragic...and Vance had been so consumed by his fury at the hand that fate had dealt him, he forgot his actions had more serious ramifications. His death would devastate Sam, a realization that became clear to him in those final moments.

Aw nuts, he thought, as the lights went out.

Memories are the foundation of a human being's existence. At least, that was what twelve-year-old Sam London had come to conclude after recognizing the role memory played in his life. Without his memories, Sam wouldn't be Sam. For one, he might suddenly think he was good at baseball and try out again, only to completely humiliate himself a second time.

Memories connected individuals to their truths and the world around them. And although they were protective and comforting, they could also be oppressive and suffocating. Losing a loved one was the most heartbreaking example of the negative effect of memories. In the wake of the loss of his mother, Odette—or Ettie as everyone called her—Sam found that his memory was a double-edged sword that he had been parrying with for weeks. He cherished his recollections of his mother now more than ever, but he felt the overwhelming pain of her death each time he remembered her.

Sam was now living with the knowledge that his mother had been returned to Gaia by the Maiden Council for the simple act of falling in love with Doctor Vance Vantana. Her punishment for this so-called "crime" came more than twelve years later and was witnessed by Sam and Vance at Lake Baikal. The memories of that tragic day haunted him daily. There was a time when Sam might have thought that was the price that came with being human. But now? He wasn't so sure.

In his time with the DMW, Sam had become aware of several examples of memories manipulated by magic and, in some cases, erased entirely. This is what had happened to his mother, Vance, Ranger Penelope Naughton, and Pearl Eklund, the mermaid princess who had forgotten who she was in Sam's previous case. But Sam wasn't interested in deleting his memories to avoid his sadness—rather he wanted to know: If magic could be used to eliminate memories, could it also be used to restore them to make that person whole again?

This was the question Sam London had been asking himself since the moment Doctor Henry Knox, the human form of the mighty gryphon, Phylassos, winked at him in his room a few weeks earlier. Sam believed it to be a signal that Sam's mother had been reincarnated. Mythical death, otherwise known as "returning to Gaia," was different than human death— Gaia absorbed a creature's life force. Sam had come to learn that this life force, once absorbed, could reappear in other forms, even forms that were similar to the original being. His teacher, Mr. Canis, was once Chriscanis, a cynocephalus who wished to be human. Mr. Canis's human appearance was not all that dissimilar from his previous incarnation, minus the hair, whiskers, and snout, of course. This led Sam to conclude that, like Chriscanis, his mother was now human somewhere in the world. So all he had to do was find her.

* * *

It was a quiet Saturday morning when Sam London sprung out of bed with purpose. But his ebullient start came to a sudden halt when he realized he wasn't alone. He yelped, then leapt back onto the bed.

"Tashi?!" Sam exclaimed, his heart having skipped two beats. Tashi was a Guardian of the Gryphon's Claw, who had become Sam's protector. She had healed him in her village of Kustos and ever since, their life forces had been intertwined. She had even moved to Sam's hometown of Benicia, so she could keep a watchful eye on him. She lived right next door with Miss Bastifal, the crazy cat lady who had turned out to be a half-feline mythical creature.

"I'm sorry if I startled you," Tashi said in her stoic tone.

"You scared me half to death," Sam told her. "I thought you were supposed to be making sure I didn't die, not causing it to happen." Tashi eyed him from his desk chair, across the room from the bed. She frowned.

"You are being dramatic, Sam London."

"I'm being dramatic?" Sam asked. "Dramatic is sneaking into people's bedrooms and watching them sleep. That's dramatically creepy."

"I can assure you I have better things to do with my time than watch you sleep and listen to your strange snoring." Tashi proceeded to exhale in a series of quick puffs of air. *Pft. Pft. Pft.*

"I don't sound like that!" Sam insisted, feeling both defensive and embarrassed.

"You most certainly do," Tashi assured him. "And my reason for being here is simply to remind you that when Nuks is away, you must take certain precautions to protect yourself. Like making sure your window is closed before you go to sleep." Nuks was a shapeshifting raccoon dog who posed as Sam's pet but was currently on a two-day berry and nut gathering trip.

"What's it matter, Tashi?" Sam inquired.

"It matters a great deal," Tashi asserted. "There are creatures who could enter this room and do you harm."

"Who wants to harm me now? I think everyone knows I'm not exactly a fan of Phylassos at the moment," Sam told her. "I probably don't even need guarding anymore. I am a shapeshifter, remember?" Sam was referring to the fact that his mom was a mythical creature and that made him part mythical creature. This meant he would likely exhibit certain powers, the most probable of which, given his pedigree, would be shapeshifting.

"You are not a shapeshifter, Sam London. And if you do manifest such abilities, it may not be for some time." She paused and gave him a sideways glance. "Are you saying you wish me to return to Kustos?"

"Of course not," Sam replied quickly. "You're my friend. My best friend, actually. My only best friend."

"I thought Nuks was your best friend."

"Nuks is a raccoon dog," Sam reminded her. "Our relationship is different."

"What about Nerida Nyx?" Tashi asked, referring to the girl Sam had known since he was little—and had a crush on. He had recently learned Nerida was a sea nymph who had been stationed in Benicia with her mother at the behest of Phylassos. Their mission was to ensure Sam's mom did not discover the truth about her mythical nature. Unfortunately, they happened to be out of town when Sam's mom found her swan maiden feathers and returned to the sanctuary. Sam had noticed that Nerida had been spending more time with him of late. He figured she'd felt a tinge of guilt for not being able to prevent Ettie's death. Though Sam enjoyed hanging out with

Nerida, he often became self-conscious in her presence. But that wasn't the case with Tashi. With her, he could always just be himself.

"She's a friend—a good friend," Sam responded, adding, "but that's different too…"

"How so?" Tashi asked innocently.

"It just is," Sam offered, trying to avoid further explanation.

"I see," Tashi replied with narrowed eyes. "Well, thank you. I consider you to be a 'best' friend as well. And to answer your question of who wants to harm you, the fact that you are related to Vance Vantana could put you in danger."

"Why?"

"Because he has made many enemies in the mythical world, not least of which is Cernunnos. As his offspring, you would make a valuable bargaining chip."

"I guess," Sam replied skeptically.

"There is also an aswang on the loose who isn't particularly fond of you," Tashi reminded him.

She had a point there. Miss Capiz, Sam's former teacher, was actually a ghastly Filipino mythical creature known as an aswang. She had tried to kill Sam on two occasions, then escaped punishment from Phylassos when the traitorous cynocephalus, Chase, was defeated.

"And perhaps you've forgotten that when I healed you, I made a life oath to protect both you and the gryphon for as long as you both live," Tashi said. "I hope to have that job for quite some time."

"Me too," Sam said, smiling. He climbed out of bed and started towards the door. "Are you coming to the meeting today?"

"Are you going to tell me what this meeting is in regards to?"

"I guess you'll just have to show up and find out with everyone else," Sam teased.

"Is it about your mother?"

Sam stopped and looked back, "And if it were?"

"I have been reading into human grief to better understand what you are going through," the Guardian explained, "and it appears you may be in—"

"I'm not *in* anything, Tashi. I know what I'm doing," Sam snapped back at her.

"I did not intend to upset you," she replied.

Sam softened. "I'm sorry," he offered. "It seems like everyone has been trying to tell me how I should feel. Just come to the meeting, okay? You'll see."

The meeting Sam was referring to wasn't scheduled to start for another two hours, so Tashi returned to Miss Bastifal's to do whatever Tashi did when she wasn't in school or hanging out with Sam. Sam didn't know what that was, exactly, but speculated it involved learning new kinds of martial arts techniques, meditating, and playing with Miss Bastifal's cats. Sam, meanwhile, showered, got dressed, and headed downstairs to grab some breakfast and prepare for the meeting, which was set to take place in his living room.

Since returning home, Sam felt the sting of his mother's absence every time he ventured downstairs and didn't find her flitting about, although he had gotten better at pushing those thoughts aside and focusing on what he could do to fix the situation. When Sam got to the bottom of the steps, he looked around but didn't see Vance. Sam had already checked upstairs, so he touched his Department of Mythical Wildlife badge, which acted as a communication device for DMW rangers.

"Ranger Vantana?" Sam said aloud into the device, which automatically routed his message to Vance's badge. No answer. Sam considered that for a moment and was about to try again when there was a knock at the front door. Sam walked over and peered through the peephole—it was Vance. Sam unlocked and opened the door.

"Hey, I just tried reaching you on the badge," Sam told him.

"Oh, I didn't have it with me," the doctor answered, as he stepped past Sam and walked to the kitchen. "I picked up some breakfast," he added, holding up a rucksack that Sam recognized as the bag Nuks used to gather berries.

"Berries? Did you go with Nuks?" Sam asked.

"Nuks? No, no," Vance replied. "I just went for a walk to get some morning air and saw an opportunity."

"Why'd you knock and not use your key?" Sam inquired.

"I left it at home with the badge. Ready for your big meeting?"

Sam eyed him, unsure. "Yes, are you?"

"What do you mean?" Vance responded, seeming puzzled by the question.

"You said you didn't want me to do it, remember?" Sam reminded him. "Does this mean you're okay with it?" Vance had been trying to dissuade Sam from holding this meeting, believing it best if they kept their intentions to themselves and did not involve anyone else.

"Oh. Well, I'm not okay with it, but I figure you're going to do it anyway." He was right about that, Sam thought. "I'm just going to be there and listen. You'll be doing all the talking."

"Me? I don't know this stuff like you do," Sam replied. Vance was an expert in mythology and this discussion was going to require his knowledge, especially given the subject matter and the audience.

"You'll be fine, and I can't look like I'm too much of an influence," Vance explained. He emptied out the rucksack and began sorting the berries. His hands moved quickly, and Sam was impressed by his speed and dexterity.

"Someone's been taking lessons from Nuks," Sam observed. Vance stopped and looked up to Sam.

"What? Oh, right. He's way faster. Human hands are limiting. According to him, I mean," Vance said, then added, "C'mon, let's rearrange the furniture to make room for our guests."

* * *

Ninety minutes later, the meeting's attendees began to arrive. The first guests at the door were Ranger Penelope Naughton of Redwood National Park, Trevor the Troll, and Carl the Bigfoot. Ranger Naughton and Trevor traveled down in an Interior Department SUV, while Carl hitched a ride with Trevor's sister, Bernice, in her minivan. She had removed the seats to better accommodate him, but he still had to scrunch up.

"Thanks for coming," Sam told them as they entered. "I can't imagine it was all that comfortable of a ride," he added, looking towards Carl. The bigfoot shrugged.

"It sounded *muy importante*," he said.

"We're all awfully curious to hear what this is about," Penelope told him.

"Where's Nuks?" Trevor asked, as he glanced around the living room.

"On an extended berry-gathering trip," Sam answered.

"He didn't tell me about it," Trevor replied, appearing surprised. "And I told him I wanted to go with him the next time he went out to pick berries. They're a great food to share." Trolls believed friends were made by sharing, and sharing food was an easy way to gain new friends.

"Maybe he forgot," Sam suggested. A disappointed Trevor ambled over to the couch and sat down. The sofa's wooden frame creaked under the creature's weight. He took up two whole seat cushions—Penelope barely squeezed in on the end. Carl settled on the floor, but even when sitting the bigfoot's head was only a few inches shy of the ceiling.

Miss Bastifal arrived next, along with Tashi, who was giving Sam her suspicious stare. Tashi might not have been telepathic, but she always knew when Sam was hiding something...and he had been hiding something from her for weeks. Nerida Nyx and her mom, Nola, followed. Nola had stopped by soon after Sam's return from Lake Baikal. She had intended on consoling Sam in the wake of his loss, but her visit backfired—she had reminded Sam so much of his own mother that he was an emotional wreck at the sight of her and retreated to his room, apologizing through his tears.

Once all of the guests were present, Sam directed them towards the snacks he had set out on the kitchen table. They mostly consisted of items he liked, specifically cookies and other sweets. Trevor ate nearly all of them before being quietly scolded by Ranger Naughton. After a few minutes, everyone took their seats and Sam decided it was time to begin the meeting. He couldn't help feeling apprehensive about talking with the group, but he knew that if he wanted their help, he would need to ask for it.

"You're all probably wondering why you're here, so let's get right to it." Sam took a deep breath and slowly exhaled. "I believe my mom—Ettie London—is alive." A hush fell upon the room and the crowd's attention was now entirely on Sam. He continued, "I can't tell you how I know, but I can promise you my belief is based on information I received from a very credible source." Ranger Naughton's hand sprung up, but Sam figured he knew what she was going to ask so he had his answer ready. "I know what you're thinking: How can I know for sure? Nothing is certain, but I do know that across the street lives Mister Canis; he is the reincarnation of Chriscanis."

"We don't know that," Tashi interjected.

"Of course he is, Tashi," Sam responded. "I knew Chriscanis, and that human out there is him. Believe me. He just doesn't know it."

"And never will," Miss Bastifal added. Sam nodded.

"Right," he agreed. "If my mom is alive like Chriscanis—and I know she is—then we have to find her, and we have to bring her home." Gasps erupted in the audience at the suggestion, including Miss Bastifal and Nola Nyx. Sam didn't stop to check out anyone else's expressions, he just kept going. "How can we do that? I mean, where do you start? There are billions of human beings on this planet and she could be anywhere. But I have an idea. I've been reading about psychopomps—"

"You mean the creatures that are death omens?" Ranger Naughton interjected in an incredulous tone.

"Some of them are death omens; others are guides that help the living transition to a new plane of existence," Sam explained. "Now I've narrowed down the list to several creatures that I think might be able to point us in the right direction. That's where you all come in—"

"I'm going to have to freeze you right there, Sam," Penelope said, holding up her hand like a stop sign. She peered over to Vance in the kitchen. "Vance? How could you let Sam get this far?" Before the doctor could answer, Sam spoke up.

"He had nothing to do with it. I insisted. And if you just let me finish—"

"I can't do that, Sam. What you're talking about, I can't be a part of," Ranger Naughton told him. "I'm a ranger with the Department of Mythical Wildlife. I am sworn to protect humans and mythical creatures. I can't interfere with the mythical world, especially like this. Just being here and listening to this is highly inappropriate and borderline unethical. It could undermine the legitimacy of the DMW. I don't think I need to remind you, but the trust we currently have with the mythical world is tenuous at best."

"You don't have to be directly involved, Ranger Naughton," Sam tried to assure her. "I just need some input. Advice. That's all. You know these creatures—"

"I don't know the creatures you're talking about," Ranger Naughton quickly clarified. "These psychopomps are a different breed. Neither mythical creatures nor humans mess with them, Sam. Unless they're dead, or want to be."

"The ranger is right," Miss Bastifal chimed in. "The creatures you seek are among the most dangerous in our world. They do not fear the gryphon or abide by his laws; they serve Gaia. They have a very particular purpose and this sacrilege you speak of is not it."

Nerida raised her hand and Sam gestured for her to talk.

"I understand what you're trying to do, Sam. I totally do. I'd probably do the same thing if I were in your shoes," she said in a gentle, sympathetic tone. Sam smiled slightly as he watched her speak, pleased someone finally got it—and that it was Nerida. "And let's just say that somehow you contact these psychopomps and convince them to help you and you find your mom, then what?" she asked. "She won't be who you remember her to be. She won't know who you are; she'll have new memories. Look at Mister Canis."

"You're right, and I'm fully aware of that, but I have some theories that—" Sam began before being interrupted by Miss Bastifal.

"Your theories will not matter," she said, firmly. "Any attempts to circumvent the intentions of Gaia are monitored by creatures known as the bennu."

"Yes," Sam said. "I've read about them. They're like an Egyptian phoenix, right?"

"In a way, I suppose, but their purpose is much different," Miss Bastifal explained. "They are sensitive to the energies of rebirth. If they sense a disturbance in this balance, they will come for those who seek to disrupt the aims of Gaia…and they will punish those who are guilty without mercy."

"That sounds pretty bad," Trevor the troll said, before popping an entire peanut butter cup into his mouth.

"Real bad," Penelope confirmed. She stood up. "You can go ahead and finish your talk, Sam, but I'm going to wait outside until it's over." And with that, Penelope headed for the front door.

"I am also leaving," Miss Bastifal declared as she got to her feet. "To even speak of this would make me a conspirator."

Trevor was next to head for the exit. "It sounds like helping you would lose me a lot of friends. I don't want to lose friends, Sam," he explained.

"I'm sorry, but we can't get involved either," Nola said, as she took Nerida's hand and led her to the door.

Nerida peered back to Sam and mouthed "Sorry."

Vance had warned Sam weeks ago that this outcome would be a distinct possibility, but Sam didn't expect this strong of a reaction. He scrambled to try and salvage the meeting.

"Wait. Just—" Sam started to say, but didn't know what he could tell them to keep them from leaving. As the group reached the front, Sam noticed Carl was still sitting on the floor. He hadn't moved or said a word, but he was the oldest and wisest among them. "Carl?" Sam said. "You always know what to do. Do you have anything to say?" Sam hoped that maybe the bigfoot would tell the crowd something that would put their minds at ease, something that would make it all okay. Maybe he even had some information that would be crucial in Sam's quest—anything that would change the direction this meeting had suddenly taken. Carl looked to Sam thoughtfully, as the guests paused to hear from him.

"I have to admit I'm confused, Sam," the bigfoot began. "I've been confused since the moment we arrived. I imagined my confusion would merely be a temporary state and that an explanation would be forthcoming that would clear it up."

"An explanation?" Sam asked, unsure. "About what exactly?"

"About why Nuks is in the kitchen masquerading as Doctor Vance Vantana."

Chapter 2
GOING ROGUE

Several days before his death, Doctor Vance Vantana was contem-plating a cluster of coincidences. Among them was Sam's teacher turning out to be an aswang, and Ettie finding her feathers after all these years. Vance found it difficult to believe events like these occurred solely by chance. He didn't need his enhanced bigfoot olfactory senses to smell a rat. What Vance knew about mythology and swan maidens told him that Ettie would never have purposely sought out or opened the trunk that contained her feathers. However, that wasn't driving his suspicions—it was something more elementary. From speaking with Nola Nyx, Vance learned that the trunk was not only locked but also well hidden in the attic. It was a way of meeting the requirements of the maiden council without making it too easy for Ettie to find her feathers—they didn't want her stumbling onto the trunk by mere happenstance.

But when Vance went to the attic to investigate the circumstances of Ettie's discovery, he found the trunk unlocked and near the attic opening. Yet, Nola still had the key...so how did Ettie open it? Anything she would have used to pick the lock would have still been sitting right next to the trunk. That's because as soon as she caught sight of her feathers, she would have forgotten everything else and immediately returned to the sanctuary. That meant someone had unlocked it for her and moved it so she would find it. But when did they do it...and more importantly, who was responsible?

These questions nagged Vance in the days since Ettie's return to Gaia, so he decided to head back to Lake Baikal and speak with the swan maiden, Lynnae. She was the maiden who helped guide him and the others to the council's meeting place. It was there that Vance and Sam tried to prevent Ettie from being punished for a past of which she had no memory. One that involved falling in love with Vance, fleeing the sanctuary, and becoming pregnant with Sam.

Before leaving, Vance had given Nuks permission to pose as him at home, as he wanted to avoid an explanation to Sam—or the kid's insistence that he join him. Sam had been obsessed with the idea that he could find Ettie, believing that Doctor Knox's wink was proof positive she was alive. Vance didn't dispute this, but he did know that finding her would be near impossible...and then what? She wouldn't be Ettie, she would simply be someone who looked like her. But Vance wasn't interested in that search at the moment, he wanted to determine who led Ettie to those feathers and sealed her fate.

According to Lynnae, who met Vance at the sanctuary's boundary, the maiden council did not know of Sam's involvement with Vance until they were told by Cernunnos, an arrogant creature who despised Phylassos and believed himself to be the real "king" of mythical creatures. Cernunnos also happened to be behind Chase's betrayal of the gryphon in Sam London's first case, and that likely meant he was responsible for setting up the aswang as Sam's teacher. Vance concluded that after Cernunnos had his plan to eliminate Phylassos and the curse thwarted, he turned his attention to Vance and Ettie. He likely saw it as another way to undermine the gryphon and stoke division among his supporters. When Vance learned that Cernunnos had alerted the council to a violation of an agreement they had with Phylassos concerning Odette, he was furious. He knew he had to confront the creature...but that was about as far as his plan went. He'd figure out the rest along the way.

As Vance stepped out from behind the Tor waterfall in Killarney National Park in Ireland several hours later, he remembered back to the previous time he was in this place. He had been here with Sam, Princess Iaira, and Tashi, to speak with the Salmon of Knowledge about the location of Ta Cathair. Luckily, Vance wouldn't have to talk with that irksome fish this time, but he did have a meeting arranged at a pub located along the Ring of Kerry, a circular driving route around the Iveragh peninsula in Southwestern Ireland.

The pub was connected to a hotel and had become a tourist hot-spot, offering Irish cuisine, along with a nightly show featuring traditional Irish music and dancing. Vance arrived just before closing, so the evening's entertainment had concluded and the place was relatively empty. He entered the dimly lit pub inconspicuously, having left the ranger uniform at home. He didn't want to appear to be operating in an official capacity for this particular mission. The building was old, with creaky wood floors, stone walls, and beamed ceilings. He scanned the pub and spotted a stocky man sitting at a table near the fireplace—the man's feet barely touched the floor. He had a bushy red beard and was dressed in a worn black suit with a dark, maroon-colored vest and a white shirt with no tie. He had on a pair of black shoes with silver buckles that were so shiny they couldn't be missed. There was a black felt hat sitting on the table, which looked to be a stubbier version of a top hat. He smoked a long pipe and had a tall glass of milk that he sipped between puffs. The floor squeaked under Vance's feet as he stepped over to the man's table.

"Mister Darby?" Vance asked. Darby peered upward and Vance gestured to the other chair at the table. "May I?" Darby nodded and Vance sat down. "I'm mighty glad you agreed to meet."

"I always answer when the DMW calls. I'm a big supporter of the gryphon," Darby said in a thick Irish brogue with less than total conviction. "So what can I do for ya, lad?"

"I need a guide of sorts," Vance told him.

"A guide?" Darby asked, narrowing his eyes. "And where pray tell are we goin' now?"

"A very particular place. One that's not easy to get to for a man of my... background," Vance replied, then leaned forward and quietly added, "A place where one might find a certain horned creature with an unhealthy God complex."

"And yer wishin' me to help you? Yer coddin' me? Do I look as mad as a box of frogs?" Darby asked, rhetorically. Vance appreciated the colorful metaphor and filed it away in the back of his mind for later use.

"You don't, and I assure you I'm not kidding," Vance informed him.

"Well, I have ya know, I din't get to be a hundred and thirty-seven bein' an eejit. What yer suggestin' could get me returned to Gaia." Vance knew Darby was an older leprechaun, but a hundred and thirty-seven was impressive, even by their standards. They were a type of fairy from Irish folklore, who loved gold almost as much as the gryphon and lived among humankind, often as shoemakers. The stories about them granting wishes were false, unfortunately, but they did believe heavily on the power of luck.

"I just need a way in, that's all. You can point me in the right direction and be off. I'd consider it a personal favor. One that you could cash in on when needed."

"Favors won't keep me alive when that divil comes callin', or that witch of his. Nevermindin' the banshees..."

"They won't know you're involved," Vance assured him.

"How are ya so certain of dis now?" Darby asked. Vance pulled a small jewelry box made of wood out of his pocket and slid it across the table.

"You'll have luck on your side," Vance told him. Darby snatched up the box in his stubby fingers and cracked it open. He smirked, then pulled out a clear crystal square. Inside the square was a brilliant four-leaf clover. Darby shifted his eyes from the clover to Vance.

"How old?" he asked.

"That one there is two hundred years young," Vance answered. Darby eyed it a few more seconds.

"You know, I hear yer DMW has one that's even older, locked away somewhere. One that goes all the way back to before the curse."

"I can't comment on that," Vance informed him. "But two hundred years is a heck-of-a nice vintage. That'd garner you at least a few days of extraordinary luck, am I right?" Luck could be drawn from a four-leaf clover by anyone who had not yet possessed it, but this was particularly true for leprechauns. The older the clover, the stronger the magic. Hence, the vintage of a clover was a critical element of assessing its value.

"Indeed it would," Darby confirmed. "Quite a price to pay for a point in the right direction."

"A point and your silence. Will it do?"

"Aye, lad, it'll do. But will you? I'm not playing Dullahan in the Cóiste Bodhar this evenin'," the leprechaun said, in reference to the headless driver of the death coach from Irish folklore.

"I appreciate the concern, but don't worry about lil' old me," Vance replied. "Do we have a deal?" Darby eyed Vance a long few moments and nodded.

"Leadin' a wee mouse into the lion's den willingly. That's a first."

Darby and Vance hiked back to the Tor waterfall and caught a dvergen subway to Smoo Cave in Durness, Scotland. The previous time Vance had been to Smoo Cave was when Cernunnos hijacked the subway on Sam's first case with the DMW.

Instead of getting off the subway and exiting the station, Darby led Vance back into the subway tunnel. He followed as Darby continued into the darkness on foot with a small flashlight in hand. They had gone about two hundred feet in when the leprechaun stopped, then shined the light against the rock wall. There was a narrow crevice that was just large enough to fit Darby. He slipped through with ease.

"Watch yer head," he told Vance. Vance crouched down and squeezed through the crevice and into a tunnel. The ceiling was only a few inches taller than Darby, so Vance continued his crouch and followed. "A long time ago, these tunnels were used to trade in mythical objects and information." He looked back to Vance with a smile, adding, "Leprechaun spies workin' for the gryphon, can you imagine it? Nowadays we keep our heads down and try to blend in. We've all heard of the massacre in Herault." Darby was referring to an incident in Sam London's first case, where Phylassos had returned hundreds of mythical creatures to Gaia as punishment for their involvement with an attempt to overthrow and kill him.

"It wasn't a massacre," Vance interjected, defensively. "Those creatures knew the consequences of attempting to murder the gryphon and end the curse. There was no other way. Phylassos had to do it. He had to send a message."

"Aye, he sent a message, all right," Darby remarked. "In some ways, I t'ink it did more harm than good."

That wasn't comforting to hear. Vance was under the impression that his travels in the wake of the incident in Herault had helped assuage any feelings of fear and discontent in the mythical world. He had gone to several national and international parks to speak with the local mythical wildlife and assure them that Herault was an isolated case and they had nothing to worry about. But if creatures were referring to it as a massacre, the die had already been cast and the perception did not endear the gryphon to his subjects.

Darby continued down the tunnel with Vance practically crawling on the ground behind him. The passageway finally opened up to a cavern and the path extended over a small lake that sat about forty feet below. A slow trickle of water ran down along one of the cavern walls and emptied into the pool. The path opened up to an area with another tunnel entry, but this one was larger and—based on the perfectly carved archway—appeared to have been purposely constructed. When they got to the second tunnel, Darby stopped.

"This is as far as I go," the leprechaun said. "You keep headin' in that direction and you'll find what ya shouldn't be lookin' fir. But you'd be doin' yerself a favor if ya waited a bit before goin' anywhere."

"All part of the plan, but thanks for the reminder," Vance replied. Darby was no doubt referring to the after-effect of relinquishing a four-leaf clover. Although the new recipient would enjoy good luck, whoever gave it up would experience a brief, albeit significant spate of bad luck. The older the clover, the more extreme the misfortune. Vance had remembered this caveat and had taken it into account when planning his mission. Darby nodded, then headed back towards the dvergen subway tunnel and disappeared into the darkness.

Once Darby was gone, Vance retrieved a compact jet injector from his pocket. It was a type of syringe that used a compressed burst of air to deliver medicine through the skin. He then took a small vial of purplish liquid out of another pocket, shook up the contents, and attached the vial to the jet injector. It was an experimental serum he had "borrowed" from Ranger Naughton's lab, which was based on the mythical creature known as a chimera. The chimera possessed an impenetrable exterior and Ranger Naughton had devised the serum to provide human rangers with the same—potentially lifesaving—attribute. Of course, chimeras were particularly nasty beasts and mixing their blood with a human's was not wise. That's why Penelope had come up with this jet inject method that would deliver the serum directly into the ranger's muscular system. It would then fortify the ranger's muscles and make them impenetrable for a short period of time. The transformation of the muscle would take about an hour from the moment of injection, so Vance would be waiting for the serum to take effect, while also waiting for the spate of bad luck to run out. It seemed smart and efficient, but the real-world result was anything but that.

Vance pulled his sleeve up and prepared to inject the serum into his arm, but the trigger in the jet injection gun jammed. As he tried to readjust his grip to help with leverage, the injector slipped from his hand and dropped to the cave floor. The impact caused the serum bottle to pop off and roll away. Vance reached out to catch it but missed. To his horror, the bottle tumbled over the edge of the path and plunged into the water below. In an infuriating rush of hindsight, Vance realized he should have injected himself with the serum before relinquishing the four-leaf clover.

Vance was now forced to reconsider his plan. He could wait out the hour of bad luck here and confront Cernunnos without the help of the chimera's magic skin or he could scrap the entire escapade and try again at another time—and with a better plan. He considered his options and decided to head for the exit, yet when he stepped towards the passageway that led to the subway, his leg got caught on something. He struggled for a moment, then looked down to see what the problem was.

It wasn't just one problem, it was thousands of them.

A massive swarm of ant-lions were covering his entire foot and working their way up his ankle, towards his knee. These were not the insects that humans referred to as antlions; rather, these were a mythical hybrid that had been known but never encountered by human rangers. The bizarre creatures were about two inches in length and had the body of an ant and the miniature head of a male lion. Unfortunately, Vance was encountering them en masse at a terribly inopportune time. He tried to lift his foot to shake them off, but they were too strong. He used his hands to brush them away, but they wouldn't budge. As he was focusing on removing them from one leg, they quickly swarmed the other. Then, once they had covered both legs up to his thighs, they forced him to his knees, likely working in tandem like a massive game of tug of war. Vance expended every ounce of energy trying to resist the little monsters, but there were just too many. The ant-lions continued their march past his thighs and up his torso. The ranger fell onto his back and attempted to roll along the cave floor to rid himself of the creatures—it didn't work.

The swarm of ant-lions were soon enveloping his entire body below his neck and began constricting his chest, like a Burmese python. Vance had tussled with large snakes before and he wished this situation were as simple—fighting off one snake was easier than battling a thousand ant-lions. As the critters constricted his ribcage, Vance's breathing became increasingly labored until he couldn't breathe at all. Vance spotted them heading towards his face, as the lack of oxygen finally caught up to him and he lost consciousness.

* * *

Vance awoke in a familiar, yet uninviting place. When his eyes slowly opened and the world came back into focus, the first thing he saw were the murals on the ceiling above him. They depicted great battles involving a large green creature with antlers fighting human soldiers. Vance immediately knew where he was, and the voice that spoke confirmed it.

"You survived," the voice said in a mocking tone. "The ant-lions can sometimes get carried away, but I'm pleased they showed restraint. If only to satisfy my curiosity as to why you would be trying to sneak into my home. Certainly not to try to do me harm, I hope." The voice chuckled at the thought.

Vance rolled over and spotted Cernunnos sitting lazily on his throne. His advisor, the sorceress Marzanna, stood next to him. That woman always looked like she smelled something awful, Vance thought. She would have been quite pretty, if not for the constant scowl...and the fact that she was pure evil. Vance climbed to his feet and tried to ignore his pounding head-ache; it was so intense it made his sight blurry. Vance took a look around Cernunnos's expansive underground lair and saw that there were several dozen redcaps standing in formation behind him, their long axes at the ready. These goblins had been operating as Cernunnos's private army for centuries. They sneered and snarled at Vance when he looked their way. The doctor turned back to Cernunnos.

"You know why I'm here, green bean," Vance snarked. If there was one thing that annoyed Cernunnos to no end it was disrespect, especially from a human—a species he considered a lower life form. The creature waved off Marzanna, who appeared ready to respond to Vance with dark magic—her hands starting to swirl.

"Not yet, Marzanna," Cernunnos told her. "Humor me, or should I let the ant-lions finish the job?"

"I know what you did in the sanctuary. You told them about Ettie and me. And I know your witch made sure Ettie found her feathers. It's because of you that she was returned to Gaia," Vance said, the anger rising in his voice. Cernunnos leaned forward.

"And it is because of me you learned you had a son!" the creature bel-lowed. "Don't you think you should be sneaking into Phylasso's cave and confronting him? He was the one responsible for all that has befallen you, and yet you still pledge loyalty to that loathsome beast?"

"It was my own fault. He was simply cleaning up my mess as best he could. I might not have liked the outcome, but my boy's alive because of it."

"His mother isn't."

"Yeah. And that's on you," Vance told him with an icy glare.

"I simply told the maidens the truth. I don't believe that is criminal in Phylassos's world. At least, not yet."

"Too many coincidences, Cernunnos. Too many," Vance maintained. "We know what you've been up to, but now? You messed with my family. I take that personally—and I'm here to deal with it in my own personal kind of way."

"Are you threatening me, human?"

"I'd say threat isn't a strong enough word."

"Thank you, Doctor Vantana," Cernunnos said. Vance wasn't sure why the creature was thanking him, but it didn't matter. Cernunnos stood up from his throne and approached Vance. The doctor reflexively reached for his knife, but it was gone. Cernunnos revealed it in his hand and tossed it to Vance, who caught it and quickly took a combat stance. "We have to give you a fighting chance."

"We? This is about you and me, pal," Vance told him.

"Not anymore." The creature gestured to his army of redcaps. "Kill him," he said matter-of-factly. Vance didn't wait for an invitation, he lunged forward and slashed with his knife, catching Cernunnos in the torso and drawing blood. Cernunnos grabbed the wound and roared. By that point, the redcaps were already converging. Vance engaged with the horde of enemies, raising his knife and running towards them with a deafening war cry.

Upon realizing Nuks's ruse and then questioning the raccoon dog, Sam London was both stunned and angered to learn that not only was Cernunnos involved in Ettie's death, but Vance had gone off to confront the creature by himself. Nuks apologized profusely for trying to trick Sam, but it sounded as though Vance took advantage of the raccoon dog's guilt in relation to Ettie finding her wings. Sam, Tashi, Ranger Naughton, and Carl the Bigfoot were on a dvergen subway within hours of the revelation, hoping they could stop Vance before he did something irreversibly stupid.

Once they got to Durness, Carl called upon the elusive Am Fear Liath Mor, also known as the Big Grey Man. The giant humanoid with dark silver fur was an ancestor of the bigfoot. Carl called him Ben, a shortened version of the word Beinn, which translated to "mountain" from Scottish Gaelic. He appeared much older than Carl, and fiercer, with fangs that hooked over his bottom lip. Ben led Sam, Tashi, Penelope, and Carl to the entrance of Cernunnos's lair and walked them inside.

What they found when they entered made Sam's heart drop.

Vance was being attacked by dozens of redcaps, but he was no longer fighting back. He lay on the ground, lifeless, with bloody axe wounds across his body. Carl roared and the redcaps froze.

"Enough! Call back your little monsters, Cernunnos!" Carl demanded. Cernunnos looked surprised by the bigfoot's appearance in the cave.

"Carl? Far from home, I see. And out of your element."

"You heard him, Cernunnos. Do as he asks," Ben said in a deep, firm voice as he stepped forward and made his presence known.

"You are taking the humans' side?" Cernunnos asked the Big Grey Man. "After everything you've seen?"

"I take no sides," Ben replied.

"The day will come when everyone will have to choose a side," Cernunnos informed them.

"The day will come when you will beg Phylassos for mercy," Carl told him.

Cernunnos chuckled. "That reminds me of an old Scottish proverb...'When pigs fly.'"

"So be it," Ben said, as he reached into the worn canvas bag that was slung over his shoulder. When he pulled his hand out and opened his palm, a dozen tiny white creatures took to the skies. But the creatures didn't stay tiny for long, they began to grow, exponentially, until Sam recognized them as pigs. But these weren't just any pigs—these had wings! Tashi's eyebrow arched upward in surprise and Ranger Naughton was dumbstruck.

"Arkan sonney?" the ranger wondered aloud. Sam noticed Ben catch her eye and nod. She leaned over to Sam and Tashi. "Pig fairies from the Isle of Man. They're really fast."

Indeed they were, Sam observed. The pigs moved lightning quick and descended on the redcaps, tossing them about with ease. Marzanna attempted magic to halt the creatures but they swarmed her as well and she flailed about, trying to swat them away. Sam and Tashi both raced to Vance's side. Sam quickly checked his breathing then his pulse, but there was no sign of life. He looked up to Tashi, hopeful.

"Please tell me you can heal him."

"He is already dead, Sam," she replied. "But..." She leaned down and listened to his chest. "It is recent. Step back." Sam did as he was told and Tashi rested the tip of her shekchen to Vance's chest, right above his heart. She sent a bolt of blue energy into the ranger's body. He convulsed, lifting off of the ground a few feet and dropping back down. She fired off two more shots and on the final one, Vance sucked in a breath and began coughing. Tashi knelt down and put her hands on Vance's shoulders. Sam watched as the Guardian absorbed Vance's wounds, her own skin mirroring his injuries for a moment before quickly healing itself. Once all of Vance's wounds had closed up, the ranger opened his eyes and found Tashi looking down on him.

"I'm guessin' I lost that one," he said. She nodded.

"You died."

"There's a first time for everything," he quipped.

"Dad!" Sam exclaimed and embraced Vance, who hugged him tight.

"Hey ya, kiddo. Thanks for the rescue."

"I thought I was the one who did stupid things. But this beats all of mine put together times a thousand," Sam said.

"I reckon you're right about that," Vance replied. He struggled to get to his feet and eyed Cernunnos. "Coward."

"Your gryphon is the coward. And you are his slave. Remove yourselves from my sight before I finish what I started," the creature said. "Remember, my actions today were within Phylassos's law. Yours, however, were not. I'll be filing a formal complaint."

"You do that," Vance chided. "Let's blow this pathetic pop stand."

Ben whistled and the arkan sonney shrunk and flew back into his hand. He deposited them into his sack and the group headed for the exit, walking in reverse to keep an eye on Cernunnos. They each entered the passage that led to the surface, when all of a sudden Sam felt a tug at his leg. A vine wrapped around his ankle, lifted him and pulled him back into Cernunnos's cave.

"Tashi!" Sam yelled.

"Sam!" She exclaimed reaching out, but it was too late.

A massive stone door dropped between the passage and the cave, separating Sam from Tashi and the others. The vine carried Sam—upside down—to the throne where Cernunnos was waiting. Sam struggled to break free, but soon found himself staring face-to-face with the sneering monster.

"Let me go!" Sam demanded, as he struggled against the vine.

"We need to talk," Cernunnos told him, gruffly.

"I don't want to talk to you."

"Well, that's a pity. I'm the one who can help you find your mother."

Chapter 3
NORTH TO THE FUTURE

CLASSIFICATION 480 (Medical Records)

Vantana, Vance

Doctor Vance Vantana's murder at the hands of redcaps and his revival by the Guardian Tashi afforded the Department of Mythical Wildlife a unique opportunity to determine if a human being's death was affected by the involvement of a mythical creature.

During his debriefing for case #SL003-720, Doctor Vantana relayed his experience following what would have been considered clinical death. Upon feeling the fatal blow, the doctor described a sense of separation from his physical body. This sensation was visually confirmed when Vance saw his body from above, as he floated up to the ceiling, passed through the rock, and emerged on the surface, where his movement stopped. Vance immediately found that he was not alone on this moonlit grassy hillside—there were several redcaps present, who he recognized as having met the operating end of his knife during the battle. According to the doctor, these creatures appeared confused by their state and quickly began rummaging through the grass, presumably searching for their axes.

The doctor's attention was pulled away from the redcaps by something he spotted approaching in the distance. It took form as it grew closer and Vance could see it was an old-fashioned horse-drawn carriage. The vehicle was black as soot and was pulled by horses with sable-colored fur that didn't entirely cover their skeletal structure, exposing both muscle and bone in several areas. Their hooves struck the earth like flint striking steel, sending out explosions of sparks that occasionally ignited the brush. The effect left a scattered trail of fire in the carriage's wake. The being that drove this nightmarish vehicle was a tall, impossibly slender man in a long, black coat. He lashed out at his steeds with a whip that looked to be fashioned from a human spine. It should also be noted that the driver lacked a head between his shoulders; rather it sat on the seat next to him. Doctor Vantana described the scene as one that would give even the most lionhearted man a serious case of the "jim-jams, willies, and the heebie-jeebies, all at once."

The skull-adorned carriage door, which included a jaw for a door handle, swung open. The wind suddenly swirled around Vance and the redcaps, and howled with a haunting, bone-rattling resonance. Doctor Vantana reported that it was akin to being in a whirlpool. The redcaps were quickly sucked into the vehicle; then, Vance felt pulled towards the carriage by the force of the wind. He frantically tried grabbing onto the ground, the grass, anything to stop his momentum, but his ethereal fingers passed right through the living, physical world. The driver's head suddenly spun to face Doctor Vantana and it spoke in a deep, calming voice. "Come, come. It's a lovely ride."

Vance Vantana was pulled back to a standing position, his toes up as his heels dragged across the ground towards the carriage. Vance had already concluded that this being was Dullahan, a psychopomp from Irish folklore. The doctor lamented not having brought a gold object with him, since, according to some accounts, the precious metal could ward off the creature. Just as the doctor reached the carriage door, a blue spark erupted over his skin and his physical form leapt back a few feet. Dullahan narrowed his eyes. When the next blue spark appeared and spread across the doctor's body, he was instantly yanked back from the carriage and he awoke on the floor of Cernunnos's lair.

Dullahan filed a complaint with the Agency for the Welfare of Mythical Beasts within twenty-four hours of the incident, believing it constituted illegal interference with the mythical world. The complaint was relayed to the DMW, where it was forwarded to the internal affairs division. Given the jurisdictional issues involving human and mythical death, the doctor did not face any penalties for his actions related to this particular psychopomp interaction.

The dusky green vines that ensnared Sam London in Cernunnos's lair eased up as they carried him away from their master and placed him on the ground. Sam shook them off and they retracted into the cracks and crevices of the stone floor. As soon as he was free of the rope-like vines, Sam wondered if he should try and make a run for it, but it didn't seem like a promising venture. The cavern had been sealed off, and there was a horde of redcaps between him and where the exit used to be. Realizing he was trapped, Sam turned his attention to Cernunnos.

"I don't believe you," Sam declared with defiance. The monster wasn't exactly trustworthy—how could Sam believe anything he said, especially about his mother whose fate the creature helped seal?

"That is your choice," Cernunnos replied. "But I thought you would be willing to do whatever was needed to get your mother back. I can assure you I'm not lying. I can help you find her. I will, if you let me."

"Why would you help me?"

"Not everyone is loyal to your gryphon, Sam. They have vision. They can see a time when Phylassos's rule ends...and they wonder who will take his place," Cernunnos explained.

"Let me guess, you think that's going to be you," Sam surmised. The monster shrugged.

"Perhaps. Perhaps not," he mused. "That is a question for another day. The question for us in this moment is posed to you. Do you want to find your mother, or should I rescind my generous offer?"

"What's in it for you?" Sam inquired with discerning eyes.

"I want you to retrieve something for me."

"Will this something help you harm humanity or the gryphon?"

Cernunnos smirked, then rose from his throne and walked towards Sam. Sam reflexively backed away, until he heard snarls from the redcaps behind him and stopped. He was trapped between the green monster and his axe-wielding minions.

"Sam, I want you to consider for a moment what the gryphon has done for you that inspires such mindless devotion. Look around, boy. You've lost friends. You've lost your mother. You lost years you could have spent with your father." Cernunnos was now directly in front of Sam and leaned forward to meet his eyes. "And now?" he whispered. "Now you are lost, Sam London. Lost to a world you don't understand, and on a mission to put back what never should have been broken. I could have helped you. I still can."

"Lord Cernunnos, they have nearly breached the final wall," Marzanna announced in an anxious tone, her hands outstretched towards the cavern's blocked entrance. "The Guardian is interfering with my magic."

Sam peered back at the entrance and spotted blue energy seeping through the cracks in the rock.

"Tashi," Sam said to himself with a smile. Then he heard pounding against the wall that caused the entire cavern to shake. The redcaps spun around to face the sound, axes at the ready. "My friends are coming for me," Sam told Cernunnos, who appeared unfazed by the news. He turned and headed for his throne, waving his hand in a nonchalant gesture.

"Go. Join them. I am finished with you," the green monster said. He reached the throne and settled in. "I suggest you give some further thought to my offer. I'll be in touch." Cernunnos nodded towards his redcap army and they split down the middle, creating an aisle that led to the rear of the cave. Sam beelined for it, and when he reached the wall, it opened like double doors. Another wall crashed down behind him, blocking entry into Cernunnos's cave. He found Vance, Penelope, Carl, Ben, and Tashi standing in the narrow passage. Tashi was wielding her shekchen, which glowed and sparked with the blue energy of Gaia. The others appeared to have been busy clearing away rubble. The sorceress must have dropped several walls of rock between him and his friends, Sam concluded.

"Sam!" Everyone seemed to shout in unison. Vance rushed over.

"Are you okay?" the doctor asked, grabbing Sam and pulling him in for an embrace. "What did he do to you?"

"Nothing. He just wanted to talk," Sam revealed. This spurred curious glances from the group so, as they all made their way back up to the surface, Sam relayed the conversation and Cernunnos's offer. Everyone agreed that Cernunnos couldn't be trusted. Penelope belabored this point with Sam as if she was somehow concerned he might actually entertain Cernunnos's offer. Once back on the hillside, Ben the Big Grey Man bid them farewell and headed off into the night, while the remaining five started towards Smoo Cave to catch a dvergen subway home.

"What the heck were you thinking, Vance?" Ranger Naughton finally asked. The question had no doubt been on the tip of her tongue since they learned of Vance's audacious plan from Nuks.

"I suppose I wasn't doing a whole lot of thinking," he replied, sheepishly.

"No, you sure weren't," she retorted.

"It was a foolish, foolish thing to do, Doctor Vantana," Carl added.

Vance nodded in agreement. "I guess I should be right thankful Nuks didn't fool ya," he said, before shifting his attention to Sam. "That reminds me, Sam. How did your meeting go?"

"Don't ask," Sam responded.

"Yes; please don't," Penelope echoed, walking quickly ahead to show her disapproval. They continued their trek in silence until Sam found himself alongside Carl.

"Thanks for coming and bringing Ben," he told the bigfoot.

"You're welcome," Carl replied. "About your presentation, Sam. I have some advice." He stopped and Sam hung back, excited to hear what Carl had to say, but also slightly worried that it might be critical. "If you truly wish to seek out these psychopomps—"

"I do," Sam interrupted, emphatically.

"I must tell you it won't be easy, but you have proven the impossible possible. However, for this journey," Carl cautioned, "you are not just risking your life, you are facing death, itself. And I mean that in the most literal of senses."

"I know."

"Okay, then," Carl said. He leaned down and spoke in a whisper, "To find these creatures you must travel to the valley of ten thousand smokes beyond the river of forgetfulness and into a forbidding land, through the gates, and to the lights of the afterlife. But be warned, the creatures you encounter from this point forward are not to be trusted and if you do find your mother, Miss Bastifal is correct. You will put yourself and everyone around you in grave danger. Pun intended." He smirked slightly, as he stood straight.

"Why are you telling me this?" Sam asked. "I mean, I appreciate it, I do. But I thought you were going to react like the others."

"I could," Carl admitted. "But I am not the type to interfere in another's destiny. You must choose your path, Sam London. And the choice is never easy." Sam nodded, understandingly.

"Thanks," Sam said. He left Carl's side and hurried to catch up with Doctor Vantana. Sam passed along Carl's words to his dad and Vance nodded.

"Remind me to thank him...if we survive."

When they reached the dvergen station, Ranger Naughton eagerly stepped on board the subway, followed by Carl, who squeezed into the back. She noticed Vance wasn't following.

"We'll catch the next one," the doctor told her. Penelope flashed a judgmental glare.

"Vance—" she began.

"Don't worry. I know what I'm doing."

"Just like you knew what you were doing when you decided to confront Cernunnos by yourself without telling anyone?" Penelope asked, sarcastically. "I don't know if you remember this, but you died. I don't think that could have gone worse."

"It was a just a spot of bad luck," Vance contended.

"Making stupid decisions isn't a matter of luck," Ranger Naughton countered. "It's a matter of stupid."

"Maybe so, but we're doing this nonetheless. I'll make sure if things go south—"

"Again?" she posited.

"Again," he allowed. "They won't, but if they do, I'll make certain the powers that be know you tried to stop us and that you had nothing to do with it."

"That's not why I'm protesting, Vance. You know that," Ranger Naughton responded, a bit annoyed by the insinuation.

"I know," Vance said in a softer tone. "I just want to give you some plausible deniability."

She relaxed and nodded. "Not that I'm offering any help in this illegal and dangerous search of yours, but if you need anything..."

"We know where to find you," Vance said and she nodded once more.

"I am available as well," Carl noted.

"I do not approve of this course of action," Tashi suddenly chimed in.

"Sam," she said, then grabbed him by the shoulders and turned him to face her. She looked into his eyes and wore an expression of compassion and caring that Sam had yet to see from the Guardian. "If I could heal a broken heart, I would," she said softly. "All I can tell you is that just because your mother is not physically here, doesn't mean she is gone." Tashi placed her hand on Sam's heart. "She is right here," she told him, then gestured to his head. "And here. And she always will be. Her presence is beyond simply seeing her in the form you are most familiar. She never left, Sam. And she never will. To find someone who simply looks like her will not bring her back."

"Maybe that's true, but I can't let this go. I can't let her go," Sam explained. "And maybe it won't work, but I have to try, Tashi. You don't have to come. Vance and I can do this."

"I am bound to you, Sam, you know this."

"Can you unbind yourself? Maybe just for a few days?" Sam asked, earnestly. He was met by a disapproving glare. "I don't mean to sound ungrateful. I just don't want you to do something you don't believe in."

"If you are going to embark on this foolish mission, you will need a voice of reason and a protector from the trouble you both will inevitably get into," Tashi said. "I will go, not because I support the mission, but because I support you, Sam London. Despite your stubbornness."

"Thank you?" Sam replied, unsure.

"Good luck," Penelope said, as she settled into the subway with Carl. She set the navigation console and switched on the jets.

"By the way, my apologies," Vance yelled over the engine's roar to Penelope. She looked to him, confused.

"For what?" she yelled.

"For borrowing and losing your chimera serum," he replied.

"You did what?!" Ranger Naughton exclaimed angrily. Vance didn't have to answer; he timed his confession perfectly. The subway launched and disappeared into the tunnel.

"What chimera serum?" Sam asked his dad.

"Long story," he answered. "We best get a move-on."

"Do you know where we're headed?" Sam asked.

"You mean, where do we begin?" Vance countered. Sam nodded. "Where Carl told us to go."

"Where's that?" Tashi asked.

"Someplace cold and vast," Vance replied.

"Outer space?" Sam guessed.

"Nope. I'm talking about the last frontier."

"I said outer space," Sam reiterated.

"That's the final frontier, Sherlock," Vance teased with a smirk. "The last frontier is Alaska."

Doctor Vance Vantana hadn't visited Alaska in quite some time. It was not exactly around the corner, and dvergen stations were few and far between. But there were also aspects of this northernmost state that made it particularly dangerous for rangers with the DMW. The danger wasn't due to weather or terrain—though that was a contributing factor—rather the real threat stemmed from the local mythical wildlife. In Alaska, the folklore of the indigenous people came alive, and given the numerous monsters it included, Vance's anxiety level was cranked up to eleven when they arrived. The station they used was behind the two-hundred-foot Thunderbird Falls in Chugach National Forest, a forest located in south central Alaska, which was roughly the size of the state of New Hampshire.

Vance, Sam, and Tashi hiked down from the falls, then, headed to Eklutna Lake, where Vance had arranged to have a floatplane waiting. It was a small propeller type aircraft with floats, which enabled it to both land and take off from water. They climbed inside and Vance settled into the cockpit. Vance considered himself a decent pilot, having learned on crop-dusters when he was in his teens. Seaplanes weren't much different—once you got them in the air, that is. It was the taking off and landing that was the tricky part. Fortunately, the wind direction was steady and so Vance turned the plane into the wind, lowered the flaps, and applied the necessary propeller thrust to get them up and away. Vance did his best to point out some of the sights on the flight: lakes, bears, and a few volcanos—inactive, of course. The ride was bumpy but short, and an hour later Vance touched the plane's pontoons to the surface of Naknek Lake in Katmai National Park and Reserve. The plane floated to maneuvering speed and Vance taxied the craft to the shallow, rocky shoreline.

SL003-720-10

SOURCE: PR

DATE: ▮▮▮▮▮▮▮

Katmai National Park and Reserve in Southern Alaska was established in 1918 and encompasses over three million acres of wilderness and active volcano landscape. Its designation as a national monument relates to the preservation of the area following the eruption of

Novarupta volcano, which collapsed the summit of Mt. Katmai and created the Valley of Ten Thousand Smokes. The unofficial reason for the park's establishment remains classified.

Once they had landed at Katmai and pulled up to the shore, Sam stepped onto the rocky beach and took in the majestic views surrounding them. Alaska was breathtaking, and Sam was about to comment on the sheer beauty of it when Vance spoke up.

"Thanks for meeting us and arranging for the plane," the doctor said, while looking past Sam and Tashi. Sam's eyes darted around, but he didn't see anyone else on the shore.

"Are you talking to us?" Sam asked his dad.

"He's speaking with me," another voice answered. It was deep, and sported an unfamiliar accent. Sam scanned the beach once again, but saw nothing. Tashi had spun towards the voice but appeared unconcerned by the invisible stranger in their midst. He was obviously not a threat or she would have already charged her shekchen and pounced. Sam squished his eyes, looked this way and that but still didn't see anyone.

"You've got the sight now, Sam. That means you will see mythical creatures in their true state," Vance explained. "In this case, the tariaksuq are a type of shadow people from Inuit folklore. They can't be seen straight on."

"Then how am I supposed to see them?" Sam asked.

"Look to the sound of my voice," the invisible stranger said. Sam obliged. "Now begin shifting your eyes away from my voice. Do you see me? In your peripheral vision?" the man asked. "I'm waving."

As Sam looked away, he caught a glimpse of something, but his eyes reflexively shifted back and it instantly disappeared. He tried again and this time resisted the urge to avert his eyes to the figure. He could see that the Tariaksuq was indeed waving.

"I can see you!" Sam exclaimed. He couldn't see the stranger clearly, but he could definitely tell the man was standing there and he could make out what he looked like. He was in a ranger hat and uniform, including a heavy park-issued green jacket. He appeared to be several inches shorter than Vance with a bronzish skin tone and facial features that resembled Tashi. He had almond-shaped eyes and a broad nose with short, straight black hair and a closely cropped moustache and beard.

"This is Ranger Inuksuk, Sam," Vance revealed. "He's the ranger here at Katmai. He'll be taking us part of the way."

"I went ahead and issued a local weather alert to keep any visitors out of the valley, just to be sure," Inuksuk informed them. "Though we don't have much time."

"Why?" Sam asked. "Nightfall?"

"Quite the opposite, actually," Inuksuk replied. "We are chasing the moon in this case."

"I don't understand," Sam said.

"You are in the land of the midnight sun. Did you not notice the time of day right now?" Inuksuk inquired. With that mention, Sam immediately glanced at his watch. It was nearly 10:00 p.m. Alaska time, but the sun was shining as brightly as ever. "Our nights become shorter as summer approaches, until they disappear entirely. Your timing could not be worse for what you seek."

"Let me guess," Vance chimed in. "Tonight is your last night?"

"I'm afraid so. You will have but several minutes to see them."

Before Sam could ask the inevitable question, Vance preempted, "We'll talk about it later. We have to move."

Inuksuk led the trio to a white school bus that had been converted into a tourist vehicle, and modified to sit on high struts.

"This bus is really tall," Sam observed. "Like a monster truck."

"That's because we'll be driving through a river," Inuksuk informed him, as everyone took their seats. The Katmai ranger sat behind the wheel.

"No bridge?" Sam wondered.

"No bridge," Inuksuk answered, then started up the bus and pulled away. Sure enough, a few minutes later the bus came to a narrow, rushing river. Inuksuk forged ahead and the bus bumped and wobbled over the riverbed, but easily made it to the other side. It wasn't much further past the river that Inuksuk brought the bus to a squeaky stop.

"This is where I must leave you," he said, hitting the lever that released and opened the door. "You'll be able to hike down into the canyon from here. Just follow the river to where it meets the Ukak. Good luck."

"Thanks," Vance replied. "I owe you one."

"You owe me several ones," the Katmai ranger responded. "Any chance you'll tell me what this is all about?"

"Trust me, Inuksuk, you don't want to know."

The bus ambled away, back down the rocky road, and Vance walked ahead, with Sam and Tashi following close behind. The park's vegetation soon gave way to a barren, otherworldly landscape. They were in a massive valley, the expanse of which Sam couldn't completely process. He was surrounded by mountains and the ground he stood on was unfamiliar. This wasn't dirt, as he knew it. The light, chalky grey sediment appeared almost sand-like in texture, but with finer grains. They made their way to a roaring river, which cascaded over steel-colored rocks that were jagged and jutted out in haphazard directions.

"Welcome to the Valley of Ten Thousand Smokes," Vance announced. "This is what happened after the biggest volcanic eruption of the twentieth century. That dirt under your feet isn't potting soil. It's ash and pumice— the same stuff that blew out of the Earth for nearly three days straight."

"Carl said something about going beyond the river of forgetfulness," Sam said, recalling the bigfoot's riddle-like words.

Vance nodded. "The river Lethe."

"Isn't that from Greek mythology?" Sam wondered.

"It is," Vance confirmed, "but the botanist who was first on the scene after the eruption looked upon a valley with steam pouring out of it and must have thought it looked like Hell on Earth. This here river was cutting right through it. He named it accordingly," Vance explained. "Stay close, this terrain isn't kind and if you fall in the river it could be two feet deep or two hundred."

Sam nodded and followed extra close to Vance as they made their way along the rushing waters.

The river carved its way through cliffs of ash, peppered by charred, broken tree limbs and striated rock. Once Sam was comfortable with the terrain, he slowed down and joined Tashi, who had been following behind in her protective mode.

"You seem awfully quiet. I mean, more quiet than usual, which come to think of it is pretty quiet," Sam realized, before concluding, "Never mind."

"I am concerned," Tashi replied after a few moments.

"Concerned? About the danger we might face?" Sam asked.

"I am always concerned about that, but I am most concerned about you, Sam London," Tashi explained.

"Me? I'm fine," Sam insisted. "Nothing wrong here."

"But will you be fine when our mission is unsuccessful?" the Guardian asked. "Will you be able to move on?"

Sam bristled at the thought.

"Our mission will be successful, so don't say that or even think it," Sam warned her, the irritation clear in his voice. The last thing he needed was a negative Nellie on this trip—the deck was already stacked against them.

"Success—if attainable—will come with a price," Tashi informed him.

"I'll cross that bridge when I come to it."

"You are not taking my words as seriously as you should," Tashi said. "You do not seem to understand the way our world works."

"It's my world now, too, you know," Sam quickly responded, reminding Tashi that he was not entirely human. "And you're starting to sound like Cernunnos."

"Cernunnos may have nefarious aims and be a loathsome creature, but he does understand the power of Gaia and the need for balance," Tashi countered. "The balance of Gaia must be kept...and is *always* kept." Tashi emphasized that last part.

"Okay?" Sam responded, unsure of her point.

"Doctor Vantana," the Guardian called out. Vance looked back, as he continued forward.

"What do ya need, Tashi?"

"Why was Gaia angry with this place?" she asked. Vance stopped and turned to face them.

"Excuse me?"

"The eruption you spoke of—the one that did all of this," Tashi gestured to the area surrounding them. "It was a punishment from Gaia, was it not? Why was she angry?"

"Smart cookie, this one," Vance told Sam as he hooked his thumb towards Tashi.

"I thought volcanos were caused by shifting plates in the ground," Sam contended.

"That's what volcanologists say and they're mostly right," Vance revealed. "But some believe that there was a great battle here. According to the native folklore, the indigenous people co-existed with a mythical race known as the tornit. This was before the curse. These tornits were giants and they got along with the native people just fine until those natives believed the creatures had stolen from them. They hunted down and killed a tornit as punishment. Tensions ran high and it was decided that the two races would keep their distance. The tornits were driven from their homes and settled here, but that didn't go over so well with the creatures who were already living here—the adlet. Things came to a head in the early nineteen-hundreds. Their battles shook the ground and left many mythical creatures dead, so many at one time that it caused an imbalance. Gaia rectified that by, well, blowing her top."

Sam noticed Tashi glancing his way, her eyebrows raised in an "I told you so" sort of way. Sam sighed and shifted his eyes back to Vance, who continued his story.

"Now all this was before the DMW, before this place was even a national park. But it was uninhabitable. So Phylassos allowed the survivors to escape to another area—a more remote area, given their aggressive tendencies. Speaking of which—"

Vance stopped at the edge of the river. Sam noticed the sound of the rushing water had grown in volume. He looked ahead to see they had reached a fork in the river—a three-pronged fork where one of the "prongs" was a steady, cascading waterfall of modest height.

"A dvergen station?" Sam concluded.

Vance nodded. "It'll take us where we need to go."

"Why didn't we just take a subway there?" Sam inquired, puzzled by the need to go by foot.

"Because it was cut off from the other stations after the eruption," Vance explained. "And it's the only way we can get to where we need to go without hiking for days."

"The forbidding place Carl talked about?"

"That's right," Vance answered him. "Gates of the Arctic National Park. The name is a little misleading. The 'gates' aren't welcoming us—they're keeping something in to protect us. This subway will take us to that part of the park, a part that humans do not see and the DMW rarely enters."

Great, Sam thought to himself, as he followed Vance across the shallow river, stepping on stones where possible. When they reached the other side, Vance moved to the edge of the waterfall, spoke the words of the dvergen, and the station's entrance slid open. Inside appeared like any other dvergen station and there was a subway car waiting on the platform. They climbed inside and Vance switched it on. The subway sputtered and choked, then suddenly shot forward. It was only a few seconds later when it came to an abrupt halt at another platform, but Sam could tell much of the trip was an ascent.

After exiting the station, they found themselves near the top of a thin, but strongly rushing waterfall that emptied into a river that wound through another expansive valley. They carefully stepped down the steep mountainside to the uneven, rocky ground. Vance froze and sniffed the air. Tashi grabbed Sam and pulled him behind her.

"What? What's the problem?" Sam asked.

"It appears someone knew we were coming," Vance replied and pointed to his left, where the ground sloped upward. At the top of the slope were dozens of monstrous giants, who were ten feet in height and dressed in animal skins.

"Tornits," Tashi concluded. Vance nodded in agreement.

"Maybe we can outrun them," Sam suggested.

"I don't think so," Vance said. "'Cause we'd have to run that way—" Vance gestured to his right. Directly facing the giants were humanoid creatures who had the lower half of canines and the upper half of humans.

"Adlets?" Sam posited.

"Adlets," Vance confirmed with a sigh.

The adlets let out a tremendous roar and began their charge toward the waterfall. That must have been the signal for the tornits, since they also launched from their positions and headed right for Sam, Vance, and Tashi.

Panicking, Sam searched for an escape route and saw that the only way out was to follow the river that flowed from the waterfall and through a narrow, winding canyon. But that wasn't all he saw—a female figure was standing on a large rock in the middle of the water. Sam blinked several times, disbelieving his own eyes. But the figure was Sam's mom and she was beckoning him toward her with a frantic wave.

Sam didn't hesitate, he immediately took off running, sloshing through the shallow river.

Chapter 4

DEAD ENDS

"**Mom?!**" **Sam exclaimed in disbelief as he ran towards Ettie London** at the Gates of the Arctic National Park.

"Sam!" Vance called out. Sam peered back briefly to find his father following close behind.

"Are you seeing what I'm seeing?" Sam asked, now just feet away from a reunion he couldn't quite believe was about to take place.

"Yes," Vance confirmed. "But—" The rest of his statement got lost amid the roar of the adlets and tornits, as well as the rushing waters.

Sam reached the stone, scrambled up onto it, and embraced his mother. Sam London had no problem showing his affection—he wouldn't have cared if it was smack dab in the front of school with everyone watching. She wrapped her arms around him, but didn't say anything. For a moment, Sam wondered why she was so quiet, but decided it didn't matter. He didn't want to let go. Not now. Not ever.

"I missed you so much," he told her as tears of joy streamed down his cheeks. The mythical world was a strange place and maybe, just maybe, things were going his way. Did Phylassos do this for him, he wondered? Was it the gryphon's way of making things right once again?

And then something strange began to happen. Sam was overcome by a pins and needles sensation that rippled across his skin from head to toe. As this numbing feeling spread, Sam noticed that the world appeared to be growing bigger only to quickly realize that he was shrinking. Before Sam could comprehend what was happening, he was sliding off the rock and into the water. He looked down at his body and was stunned by what he saw.

Sam London wasn't human anymore. He was a sea otter.

Tashi of Kustos was so busy trying to strategize how she would face the horde of creatures bearing down on them that she didn't entirely process Sam London's words. She thought she heard him say the word "mom," but perhaps she misunderstood. It wasn't easy to hear anything over the storm of noise created by the approaching monsters. Tashi had an idea: She would send Sam and Vance toward the river, while she remained in place. As soon as they were far enough from Tashi's position, she would shoot an enormous burst of Gaia's energy from her shekchen into the sky. It would act as a warning to the attackers and perhaps compel them to stop their assault long enough for her to communicate with them.

She was just about to execute her plan when she saw that Sam was already making a run for the river and Vance was right behind him. Apparently, they had come to the same conclusion and were attempting their getaway. But what did Sam call out that prompted him to run? And why didn't Vance or Sam signal their intentions beforehand? Vance rarely let her just take care of things herself, even though she was more than capable.

There was no time to dissect the situation—the creatures were still on their way and the sound was deafening. Tashi plunged her shekchen into the ground and the blue energy of Gaia began pouring into it, crackling around the staff as it continued to a full charge. With the adlets and tornits nearly upon her, Tashi thrust the staff into the air and released a blast of energy that rocketed upward and webbed out in zigzagging streams across the sky like horizontal lightning. The life force of Gaia bathed the valley in a blinding blue light. Both sides instantly froze. They gazed up, awestruck. As the energy showered back to earth like indigo raindrops, Tashi was set to address the two armies...and then she spotted the unthinkable. Sam London had climbed onto a large rock in the middle of the river and was currently embracing Ettie London.

This simply couldn't be possible, Tashi thought to herself. Finding Sam's mother couldn't be this easy. She immediately concluded that whoever or whatever Sam had his arms wrapped around was not Ettie, rather it was some kind of shapeshifting creature. Was it the aswang known as Ms. Capiz? Disguising herself to wreak her vengeance on Sam? Vance was almost at the rock and Tashi wasn't sure if he realized what was happening or was also caught up in the false notion that Ettie had miraculously returned from Gaia. Tashi had to protect Sam, and she had to move quickly. She had no idea what this creature might do to him. Unfortunately, Tashi's view of Sam and her path to reach him were suddenly blocked.

The adlets and tornits had turned their attention from Tashi's light show and charged head-on, colliding in the river with a thunderous boom. And that meant the tornits stampeded right passed Tashi toward the adlets.

Apparently, the giants were not coming for her, Sam, or Vance. In fact, they created a protective line in front of Tashi. Several of the giants carried large boulders over their heads and hurled them at the adlets, who leapt and dodged the rocks as best they could; though, many were immediately taken out of the fight. The wall of giants in front of Tashi was a problem—she could no longer see Sam and Vance and was blocked from reaching them.

"Tornit!" Tashi exclaimed as she poked her shekchen into the back of one of the giant's legs. The tornit glanced her way.

"Stay back. We will drive them off," the creature assured her.

"Tell your army to fall back to the river's edge and get out of the water," Tashi ordered. "I will take care of these adlets."

The tornit eyed Tashi discerningly, then nodded. He called out to the army in a native language and they immediately fell back and out of the river. Tashi slipped between the giants, charged her shekchen, then dipped the tip into the water. A massive rush of energy flowed from her staff and into the river, until the adlets were surrounded by glowing blue water. The creatures didn't know what to make of it before it was simply too late for them to react. The energy swirled and converged on the adlets, then used their bodies as conduits to return back to Gaia. The result was immediate and effective. The adlets were consumed by Gaia's life force and hurled out of the water to the other side of the river. Outmatched and licking their wounds, the creatures scurried away in retreat. The tornit army let loose with a roaring cheer. The tornit who Tashi spoke with caught her eye.

"We had come to guard you and your friends, but you guarded us," he told her. "We are grateful. My name is Amaqjuaq." Tashi nodded in acknowledgement and was about to reply when the words the giant spoke suddenly reminded her—

"My friends!" She turned toward the spot she had last seen Sam and sprinted to it. When she reached the rock, she found no sign of Sam or Vance or the creature that was pretending to be Ettie London. Her eyes scanned the area for a clue. "Sam!" she called out, her voice echoing through the valley. "Vance!" she tried. But the world was quiet now, except for the water trickling over the river rocks. Amaqjuaq joined her at the stone.

"The others are gone?" he asked, an expression of concern washing over his enormous face. He resembled the native peoples—just a giant-sized version.

Tashi nodded. "There was a creature on this rock. A shapeshifter."

"The kooshdakhaa," the tornit said gravely.

"Kooshdakhaa?" Tashi confirmed.

"An otter-man," he replied. "He lured your friends close, then transformed them."

"Into what?" Tashi asked, growing more alarmed by the moment.

"Sea otters," Amaqjuaq said, matter-of-factly. "He does it because he is lonely. May you find peace in their loss."

Tashi was certainly not ready for that. She was becoming angry. She was annoyed that she allowed Sam to come here on this fool's errand and put himself in danger, but she was more irritated that she did not anticipate what they would find waiting for them.

"How did you and the adlets know we were here?" Tashi asked. "And this otter-man, he knew about my friend's mother. How is that possible?"

"The adlets can smell fresh meat from miles away. As for us, Ranger Inuksuk let us know you would be on your way and to look out for you," the tornit explained. "But the kooshdakhaa...it has an ability to sense that which a person most desires and uses it to manipulate them."

"So I must find the creature and ask him to change my friends back to their true form," Tashi concluded.

"He will not do it," Amaqjuaq said, assuredly. "He is not just collecting companions, he is gathering souls. Once the sun sets on the last night of the year, their souls will be his forever."

"I will simply have to convince him before nightfall then," Tashi replied firmly. "Where can I find this kooshdakhaa?"

"You don't," he answered. "It finds you." He gestured ahead. "Follow along the river's edge. Do not trust your eyes or your ears, and do not let it touch you."

Tashi nodded. "I am grateful for your help," she told him and bowed her head in respect.

Amaqjuaq nodded once, then turned and headed back to the other tornits, who were watching from afar.

* * *

It wasn't long before Tashi found a stream that branched off from the main waterway. The stream ended at a large shelter made of leaves, dead branches, and rocks—an oversized otter den. With daylight growing scarcer by the moment, Tashi took in her surroundings, then approached the den for a closer look. She paused halfway when she sensed she was no longer alone.

The Guardian froze in place and her eyes went to the ground. The last remnants of sunlight were casting long shadows, but her shadow was not the only one that could be seen. There was something rising up from the river behind her. A human-shaped silhouette began to take form. She spun to face it, shekchen at the ready, and found her own mother staring back at her.

"Hello, little one," her mother said in a soft voice.

The form the kooshdakhaa chose surprised the Guardian. Was it her mother she most desired to see, Tashi wondered, or was it what her mother represented, namely, home? When the kooshdakhaa spoke again, it was revealed to be the latter.

"You can return to Kustos," Tashi's mother added, warmly, then beckoned to her. "Come, I will take you home. Your father will be pleased, as will Yeshe and the others."

The unexpected nature of the kooshdakhaa's appearance had caused Tashi a momentary loss of focus and the creature took advantage. Tashi was contemplating the notion that she desired to return to Kustos for a millisecond longer than she should have and the kooshdakhaa lunged forward. It attempted to grab her—no doubt in an effort to transform the Guardian—and the creature got within inches before Tashi spun and arched back, deftly avoiding its shapeshifting touch.

"You cannot fool me, kooshdakhaa," Tashi said, her shekchen charged and pointed squarely at the creature.

The creature responded by transforming once again, but this time it shifted into its natural form and it was exactly as its name suggested: an otter-man. The creature was approximately six feet tall and covered in short grey fur that was still slick from the water. His head was human-shaped, but his features were all otter. It had whiskers that sprouted above his beady eyes, his upper lip, and chin. When he spoke he exposed short, sharp teeth.

"You could see me?" the creature asked, puzzled. Tashi ignored his question.

"I am here for Sam London and Vance Vantana," she told him. "The humans you transformed a short time ago—in the river by the waterfall."

"You mean Balto and Nanook?" the kooshdakhaa said. "They are my friends. They are playing over there." The creature gestured to the river. Tashi spotted two otters rolling along the river's edge and frolicking in the water. "Aren't they cute?" The otter-man asked while eyeing them adoringly.

"They are not your friends," Tashi informed him, "and they are not otters."

"They *are* otters. Look at them—do you not see otters?" the kooshda-khaa asked, seeming genuinely confused by the Guardian's assertion.

"They are only otters because you changed them into otters," she clarified.

"And now they are otters!" he declared proudly. "I will make you an otter too," the kooshdakhaa said, as if he would be doing Tashi a favor.

"You will do no such thing," she told him in a firm voice, her patience dwindling. "And you will return my friends to their natural form."

"They are otters now and otters they will be forever."

"Change them back, kooshdakhaa, or I will do it myself," Tashi warned.

The Guardian's shekchen had the ability to disrupt magic, so it could theoretically reverse the transformation. Of course, it could also return them both to Gaia if Tashi wasn't careful. It was risky, but the kooshdakhaa wasn't cooperating, and she had no other options.

"I don't like you," the otter-man admitted. "And my friends don't like you either." Upon making that statement, twenty or so otters poured out of the river and swarmed around the kooshdakhaa in a protective manner. Tashi was now officially done with diplomacy: it was time for action. She fired her shekchen at the otter-man, dazing the creature and sending him reeling back. Tashi quickly located one of the two otters that the kooshda-khaa identified as Sam and Vance. She aimed her shekchen carefully at it, then released a short, controlled burst of energy—hoping to mitigate any harm if her attempt didn't work. Luckily, the otter instantly transformed back into Vance. The other one must be Sam, she concluded.

"Get back, Doctor Vantana!" Tashi called out. A groggy Vance crawled quickly away from the otter-man and took cover behind Tashi.

"Where's Sam?" he asked, his voice strained.

Tashi didn't answer. She had her eyes trained on the Sam-otter—it was hard to tell the creatures apart, and she didn't want to lose sight of him. Tashi fired, but the Sam-otter purposely dodged the blast and scurried up the side of the narrow canyon. It scampered to the edge and Tashi immediately realized what the kooshdakhaa had planned. The creature had regained his bearings and was going to force the Sam-otter to jump to its death.

"Don't!" Tashi implored.

"You must go!" the kooshdakhaa insisted.

"Let him go and I will allow you to touch me," Tashi offered.

"Tashi—" Vance protested in a weakened voice, as he slowly got to his feet.

"Why would I want to?" the creature asked.

"I am a Guardian of the Gryphon's Claw. Phylassos's blood runs through my veins," Tashi revealed. "It means my soul is unique."

"Phylassos?" the creature replied, intrigued.

Tashi nodded. "I am immortal. Strong. And brave. I would make a great companion. The best companion."

"Then come closer," the otter-man instructed. Tashi complied.

"You will let me change him back first?" she confirmed. The otter-man nodded.

Tashi had a plan to avoid living the rest of her days as an otter, but it was dangerous. She would counteract the creature's touch by channeling the energy of Gaia through her shekchen and into her body. This would reverse the magic, but it could go terribly wrong. When a Guardian receives their shekchen in a ceremony attended by the entire village, they are warned about the perils of wielding such a weapon. These staffs were carved from trees that lived deep within the Earth, in a place called Agartha. They are living objects that grow with the Guardian to match his or her height.

Guardians are taught how to channel Gaia's energy through the shekchen and resist absorbing it. This is why other creatures cannot touch the staff without being instantly jolted. Although Guardians have a high tolerance for Gaia's life force, they cannot resist it for long periods. Once their bodies begin to absorb the energy, they risk becoming one with it. If that happens, when the energy eventually returns to the earth, the Guardian will be returned with it.

Tashi shot at the otter at the edge of the cliff and it instantly transformed back into Sam. Unfortunately, his position and size caused him to immediately tumble over the side of the cliff and plummet to the ground. Doctor Vantana must have seen this coming, because he was already in motion. He wasn't able to catch Sam, but he did manage to break Sam's fall with his own body. They both wound up in a pained, groaning heap on the ground. Tashi's eyes were on her friends when the kooshdakhaa latched onto her wrist and her body began the transformation.

When Sam's eyes opened, he was surprised and thrilled to see that he was human once again. He found himself on top of Vance, but his dad's attention was elsewhere. Sam followed his gaze and spotted Tashi allowing herself to be touched by the creature that had transformed Sam in the river. He had seen the true form of the shape-shifter when it turned him into an otter. Sam couldn't recall all of his time as an otter—it was as if the longer he spent as one, the less of a connection he had with his previous human form. It was an odd feeling—knowing what he should be, but suddenly not caring anymore. He had been tricked into believing the creature was his mother. Vance had attempted to rescue Sam before it was too late, but in the melee, the otter-man managed to grab onto Vance and transform him, as well. Considering what had happened, Sam couldn't understand what Tashi was doing.

"Tashi! Don't!" Sam exclaimed, aghast.

"It is okay, Sam. You are safe. That is what matters," she said, as the creature gripped her wrist, her body already beginning to transform.

"We have to help her," Sam insisted as he scrambled to his feet. Vance stood back up and put a hand on Sam's shoulder to keep him from interfering.

"We're not in any shape to tussle with a kooshdakhaa," Vance told him. "We'll all wind up otters and forfeit our souls."

Forfeit our souls? That statement lingered in Sam's head. Was that what would have happened if they hadn't been rescued? The thought terrified Sam. What made it even more disturbing was the fact it was about to happen to Tashi. Sam felt responsible for this horrific turn of events. He wracked his brain, trying to come up with a way to rescue her. As he scanned the scene, he noticed the Guardian was still clutching her shekchen. She was allowing the energy of Gaia to pour through her staff and into her body.

Sam hadn't seen her do that before, and, though it had the effect of slowing down the transformation, it didn't appear entirely safe.

Soon, the surge of energy consumed Tashi and she was glowing with the blue energy of Gaia. She was halfway through her otter transformation when it began to reverse itself. The creature grew angered by this and grabbed onto the hand that was holding the shekchen. It was a bad move, since the kooshdakhaa was now completing the circuit, in a sense. All of the energy pulsing through Tashi instantly streamed into the otter-man. He tightened his grip and the energy of Gaia enveloped both of them.

Then something disturbing began to happen.

The otter-man and Tashi appeared to fade in and out of sight. The blue energy was so overwhelming that their bodies became indistinguishable from the light. In his gut, Sam knew this was bad. Real bad. The energy of Gaia would be pulled back to Earth—he knew this from all of his experience with it. Would Tashi be pulled in with it?

Sam shot forward, not willing to take the chance, and pushed Tashi to the ground, separating her from the kooshdakhaa. When the two split, there was a blast of energy that rippled out from the spot like a shockwave. The resulting rings were quickly absorbed back into the Earth.

The kooshdakhaa reappeared and slumped to the ground. Sparks of Gaia's energy leapt off his skin, as the creature's otter minions scurried over and surrounded him. Sam rushed to Tashi's side. She was lying on the ground, her eyes closed. Her shekchen beside her.

"Tashi!" Sam exclaimed, trying to wake her. Just like the otter-man, the energy was sparking off her skin. Sam didn't know if it was safe to touch her, but he did it anyway. He grabbed her shoulders and attempted to jostle her awake. His own skin tingled when he made contact, like a low current of electricity. "Please be okay," he said repeatedly. After a few agonizing moments, Tashi's eyes opened.

"I am okay," she answered in a weakened voice. She slowly got to her feet. Sam tried to help her, but she brushed him off. "You could have been injured, interfering in that way."

"It looked like you were the one who was going to be injured," Sam replied.

"Sam's right," Vance said. "That was a heckuva charge running through you. It looked like you even disappeared for a moment."

"Yes, I'm sure I did; that was the risk of my gambit," Tashi explained. "My body could have become one with Gaia."

"And you'd what? Disappear forever?" Sam questioned her.

Tashi nodded. "In a sense, yes. I would be returned to Gaia instantly."

"Why would you do that?" Sam asked anxiously.

"To save you," she answered, as if obvious. "It was an easy decision. I had a plan. And it worked."

"But what if it didn't?" Sam challenged her. "You wouldn't be standing here right now."

The thought of Tashi risking her life for Sam was difficult for him to accept. Sure, the Guardian had come to his rescue countless times before, but not since the healing of Sam in Kustos had she put her life on the line so brazenly. It also happened in the shadow of the loss of Ettie, which had been—and still was—causing him so much pain. In fact, the experience of thinking he found his mom then losing her again just exacerbated his hurt. He couldn't bear to go through more of it. Sam was thankful for Tashi's protection, but their relationship meant more to him than just having a bodyguard. He couldn't shake the guilt of what he nearly caused. He didn't see himself worthy of this act of self-sacrifice. And he certainly didn't want to be the reason for her return to Gaia or her misery—in the case of spending her life as the otter-man's companion.

"You don't have to do that, Tashi," Sam said. "You don't have to save me if it means risking your life."

"Yes, I do," Tashi replied. "It is my purpose and my commitment."

"I know, but I don't want you to do it for me anymore, okay?" he pleaded. "You can do it for Phylassos, that's fine. But don't do it for me."

"That is not something that can change," she responded, firmly.

"It has to be. There must be a way," Sam told her. "We'll figure it out," he added with determination. Sam didn't know the answer, but he was certain one existed. Perhaps he could convince Phylassos to unbind Tashi from this commitment. Maybe if Sam grew strong enough to prove he no longer needed protection, Phylassos would release her. Sam held out hope that this was the best path to his goal and he also felt confident that it was achievable. His experience transforming into an otter, while scary and downright bizarre, was also life-changing. Sam got a glimpse of the power he would be wielding when his abilities finally manifested themselves. He would be able to change into anything or anyone at will. Sam would no longer have to settle for being average Sam ever again. He would be able to protect himself without relying on Tashi or Vance or anyone, for that matter. Sam would be special. Powerful.

"We're all safe and that's what counts," Vance chimed in. "No need to over-think it. We don't have time for that. The sun is about to set and that gives us less than an hour to get to Xanadu."

"Xanadu?" Sam asked.

"It's a mountain peak—it will give us our best chance to see them."

"See what?" Tashi asked.

"The aurora borealis. The northern lights," Vance revealed.

"The lights of the afterlife," Sam realized, aloud. It was just as Carl had indicated. "And once we see the lights, then what?"

"Tashi has to kill me."

Chapter 5

THE PSYCHOPOMPS

SL003-720-20

SOURCE: PR, AR

DATE:

In Roman mythology, "Aurora" is the goddess of dawn, hence the term "aurora borealis" can be translated as "dawn of the north," aka the "northern lights." This colorful light display is caused by the convergence of gaseous particles and charged particles in the Earth's atmosphere. The color of the aurora depends on the type of gas involved, which is determined by the altitude of these particle collisions. The northern lights, as their name suggests, are best seen in areas of higher latitude, especially within the arctic circle. The southern counterpart to the display is known as the "aurora australis" and is most clearly viewed within the Antarctic circle. In addition to the colorful manifestation, there is often a crackling or popping noise that accompanies the appearance of the aurora. It should be noted that the science behind the cause of these auroras is not settled. At this time, the Department of Mythical Wildlife has refrained from sharing with the scientific community its own conclusions regarding the origins of the aurora and has no plans to do so, in accordance with Phylassos's law.

By taking into account the folklore of a great many cultures who live in areas impacted by the aurora, the DMW has determined that they act as a window into a spirit world or dimension, a passageway for the souls who have returned to Gaia to enter a new realm of being.

The words of the esteemed American anthropologist Ernest William Hawkes hold more truth than he might have realized at the time he wrote them:

> The ends of the land and sea are bounded by an immense abyss, over which a narrow and dangerous pathway leads to the heavenly regions. The sky is a great dome of hard material arched over the earth. There is a hole in it through which the spirits pass to the true heavens...the spirits who live there light torches to guide the feet of new arrivals. This is the light of the aurora...The whistling, crackling noise which sometimes accompanies the aurora is the voices of these spirits trying to communicate with the people of the earth...

Although the Department forbids human rangers from communicating with those who exist beyond the northern lights, it has never been determined if such communication is even possible, as it would require the death of the human participant, which would effectively eliminate the participant's ability to file a report of the encounter.

Sam London stood on the shoulders of giants...well, more like rode on them. After Vance made his ominous declaration about Tashi having to kill him, a group of tornits showed up. The one called Amaqjuaq had grown concerned for Tashi's safety and had come to check on her well-being. The giant was pleased to find everyone was unharmed. When Vance explained that they needed to reach Xanadu before nightfall, Amaqjuaq offered to take them. With their long strides and knowledge of the landscape, the tornit argued they could reach Xanadu in a quarter of the time it would take Vance, Sam, and Tashi. So they each climbed aboard a giant's shoulders and off they went.

Sam had experienced many modes of transportation through his experience with the Department of Mythical Wildlife. Some had been thrilling, others terrifying, many puke-inducing, but they could all be categorized as strange and unusual. Riding on a giant was no exception, and though it wasn't terrifying, it was much too bumpy to be of any fun. Sam felt like a milkshake on a trampoline. But at least he didn't feel an urge to throw up...yet.

According to Vance, Xanadu was among the Arrigetch Peaks of the Endicott mountains in the Brooks range. As the giants bounded across the Arrigetch Valley, Sam could see Xanadu looming in the distance, soaring thousands of feet in the sky and shaped like a fin at its zenith. It appeared to be nearly all rock, and Sam had no idea how they would reach the top. Sam also felt anxious about Vance's statement regarding Tashi killing him. His dad assured them it wasn't as bad as it sounded and to hold their questions for later. Though skeptical, Tashi and Sam knew they were losing time to get to the peak, so they put their concerns on hold.

They reached the base of the peaks just as the orange glow of the setting sun had disappeared entirely, and a glimmering silver moon began its slow, methodical rise.

"Hold tightly!" the tornit Sam was riding suggested, apparently not realizing Sam had been doing that the entire time. He clutched the giant's massive head with all of his strength, as the giant grabbed onto the rock face with its oversized hand and began the ascent of Xanadu.

Vance Vantana grew up learning about the power and symbolism of animal omens. Nature—or Gaia, as Vance later came to understand it—spoke to the living through wildlife instead of words. It was a language for the eyes and ears, and as he ventured across the Arrigetch Valley on a tornit with the others, he was sure as shootin' that Gaia was giving him quite a talking to. First thing Vance spotted were blackbirds circling overhead, indicating the magic and power of the moment.

The owls Vance sighted on the trees they passed were another signal from Gaia. The creatures were known to represent a connection to the spirit realm; in fact, in some cultures they were considered a type of psychopomp. Here, they were watching Vance, likely acting as the eyes of those beyond the human world, following Vance's progress towards this forbidden goal. In much the same way, the lynx Vance noticed was also connected to the spirit realm. The wild cat could not only see that which was invisible, it could also read the human mind and soul. This was an important element, since it was known as a symbol of caution—a warning to Vance that what he intended was fraught with danger. At least the sight of the male moose was encouraging, Vance thought. These animals symbolized strength, courage, and bravery. Of course, the caveat was that the creature's determination, while admirable, could also lead to severe injury or death.

Vance's mind was so distracted by these omens, he was surprised when he found himself being hoisted into the air by the tornit. The giant lifted Vance up off his shoulders and placed him on a flattened area of the Xanadu ridgeline. Sam and Tashi were already waiting there, with Sam huddled as far from the edge as possible. They were up mighty high, though nightfall made it difficult to appreciate what must be a spectacular daytime view. And then the night brightened...

The ridge was suddenly bathed in a cascade of colored light. Vance looked to the northern sky and could see the aurora forming. It was like the opening of a tear in space, a tear that erupted in bands of green, blue, and violet that stretched across the Alaskan sky. Vance could hear the crackling of the lights and knew it was time to make contact.

"Tashi?" he called to the Guardian. "It's time." Tashi and Sam shifted their gaze from the lights to Vance.

"If you are referring to your declaration earlier involving my participating in your death, then, no, it's not time," the Guardian said.

"I don't think he was talking about literal death," Sam offered, then turned his attention back to his father. "The only reason why we agreed to come here was because you said it wasn't as bad as it sounded."

"It isn't as bad as it sounded," Vance confirmed. "But I was talking about literal death."

"How could anything be worse than that?" Sam responded, dumbfounded.

"Just listen. Tashi will touch her shekchen to my chest. The jolt of Gaia's energy will stop my heart," Vance began to explain.

"What?!" Sam interjected, incredulous.

"Briefly," Vance qualified. "That's the key word here. It'll just be for a few seconds. Luckily, time slows down on the other side. I'm guessin' I only need to be dead for thirty seconds, tops."

"Do you not hear yourself, Doctor?" Tashi asked.

"You revived me before."

"But that does not mean it'll work a second time."

"It'll work," he told her, confidently.

"Um. This sounds pretty sketchy," Sam chimed in. "And really dangerous. Are you sure about this?" Vance looked Sam in the eye.

"It's the only way, Sam," Vance replied. "We have to talk with the psychopomps, you know that. We have to find your mother. You're just going to have to trust that I know what I'm doing."

Sam nodded, reluctantly.

"This is absurd," Tashi declared. "You are going to risk your life for this? Sam could wind up losing both of his parents."

"If memory serves, you just risked your life with the kooshdakhaa," Vance reminded her.

"That was to save someone," she responded.

"That's what I'm trying to do," Vance countered.

"No, you're not," Tashi replied. "This is not the same. I came on the mission to protect Sam, not to deliberately bring harm to his father. I'm sorry, Doctor Vantana. But this is madness and I won't be a part of it."

"Too late," Vance told her, as he leaned down and allowed the tip of the staff to touch his chest right above his heart. As soon as it did, Vance immediately felt his body seize up. Tashi tried to pull it away as a surge of energy leapt off of the staff and onto his skin. There was a blinding flash of white light and then Vance was suddenly alone on the ridge.

Vance shifted his gaze to the aurora, eager to make contact before Tashi tried to resuscitate him. The bands of color were more vibrant now and appeared to be moving toward him. He noticed an opening within the bands, a pure white window amid the ribbon of colors. He could discern a few figures inside—a large wolf-shaped creature, a woman with flowing hair who appeared to be on horseback, an unkindness of ravens with wings flapping in slow motion, a being that looked to be made of pure light, and a tall figure in a cloak holding a scythe. Vance concluded that the latter one was Ankou, a well-known psychopomp from Breton folklore. He had become the personification of the "grim reaper." Vance hoped Ankou would not be the one that he would have to talk to. An old Irish proverb claimed that the creature never went away empty handed, and Vance didn't want to take any chances. Fortunately, it appeared that none of them were coming forward. Vance was going to call out to the figure on the horse, who he believed was Epona, but then a female voice with a native accent spoke softly from behind him.

"I see the man who cheated death is playing another round."

Vance spun to face his visitor and came to find a beautiful young woman in a fur-lined coat and hood. Her blue eyes sparkled like sapphire. Vance noticed her appearance seemed to change at random, transforming from a young woman to an elderly woman in an instant, though the twinkle in those impossibly blue eyes remained constant. Vance recognized her as Pinga, "the one above"—a powerful being from Inuit folklore.

"Did you believe you would be able to return so easily?" she asked, narrowing her gaze. Vance shrugged.

"I reckon my ticket isn't ready to be punched quite yet," he answered.

"There are consequences to such offenses, Vance Vantana," she told him. "Inescapable consequences that will be felt in time."

"If that's the price..." Vance replied.

"I can assure you the cost is higher than you think. And the universe will come to collect," Pinga said.

"It always does. But the thing is, I need your help more than I need to be right with the universe."

"Help in your search for the swan maiden?"

Vance nodded. "I imagine you know the circumstances around her return," Vance told Pinga. "I don't believe justice has been done."

"And do you believe fate is always just?" she wondered.

"Frankly, I've had my fill of fate and the universe and all of it. Nothing is gonna stop me from fighting for what I believe. Or for those I love," Vance asserted. Pinga studied him a moment, then nodded in acknowledgment.

"I respect your determination, but it is wasted here," she revealed. "I can be of no help to you in your journey. Odette's soul remains in transition."

"And her body?" Vance inquired.

"It walks the Earth. But I possess no knowledge of the whereabouts of that incarnation. And why would I? It is not my realm. You know this."

"I do," Vance replied. "But I also know you're not bound to the same laws as the living, nor are you ruled by the gryphon. In other words, I think you know who can point me in the right direction. Please."

Pinga studied him for a moment, then responded, "There is a creature. A creature who feels every ripple that passes over the Earth. When the swan maiden's body returned, this creature would have sensed it, instantly."

"What creature is this?" Vance asked. He was not familiar with one that would have such ability.

"It is called the leshy."

Vance recognized the name. "The Taiga forest?" he asked.

Pinga nodded.

Vance knew little about the creature, except that it was a forest-dwelling ogre from Russian folklore. He certainly didn't know it had this unique ability.

"But the leshy will prove far more dangerous than cheating death," she told him.

"Great," Vance sighed.

"He is a shapeshifter, a rogue, who will try and lead you astray. But he knows where your Ettie is. He may not be willing to share it, however."

"I'll have to convince him."

"You can try. But you don't have much time," she said.

"What do you mean?" Vance asked.

"Ettie's soul is still in transition, but it won't be forever," Pinga revealed. "Her spirit will join with Gaia and be scattered across the heavens by the start of the new moon."

"How many days in this cycle?" he asked quickly.

"Twenty-seven," she answered. Vance had a momentary sigh of relief. Twenty-seven days was plenty of—

"Twenty three have already passed," Pinga added.

They only had four days to find her.

"Now just supposin' we find her in time—" Vance began.

"How will you restore her soul? Her memories? Her...pneuma?" Pinga replied. Vance nodded. "You will have to bring her to Gaia herself. Only she can do what you ask. But once you find the swan maiden, you will be interfering with the will of Gaia. And that will not go unnoticed."

"But if we make it...it's possible to bring her back?"

"Possible, yes. Probable?" She shook her head. "A balance must be kept. It *will* be kept."

"How?" Vance asked, unnerved by Pinga's tone.

"A sacrifice would need to be made. A sacrifice that would change the destiny of—"

There was a flash of blinding white light and Vance suddenly found himself lying on his back. Sam and Tashi were peering down at him. Their expressions grave.

"You couldn't have brought me back a second later?" he grumbled, his chest feeling heavy.

"Tashi didn't bring you back," Sam revealed. "He did."

Sam moved out of Vance's eyeline and gestured to the sky. Against the backdrop of the aurora borealis, Vance took in the surprising sight of a gryphon—Phylassos. His golden wings flapping as he hovered above Xanadu. The creature's unexpected appearance stunned Vance, but what he found even more astonishing was the figure who was riding on the gryphon's back—Marzanna, the sorceress who served at the behest of Cernunnos. Almost as shocking as her presence was her expression: she was smiling.

"Doctor Vance Vantana," Phylassos bellowed. "You stand accused of making threats against a mythical creature and carrying out your threats with an attempted murder. This is a clear violation of your oath and the law. You are hereby placed under arrest and will face trial for your crimes."

Vance sighed. "Aw, nuts."

In the interests of authenticity, the following source document is presented in code. Although this is not the same encryption used by the Department of Mythical Wildlife for highly classified communications (due to secrecy concerns), the document has been encoded in the spirit of the original source. Please refer to the cipher for translation.

Emergency Dispatch
TO: Doctor Vance Vantana/ Bob Ferguson/ Authorized Staff, U.S. Department of Mythical Wildlife
VIA: Ministry of Environment, Green Development, and Tourism, Mongolia
Immediate—Classified
Location: Gobi Gurvansaikhan National Park
Reporting Ranger: Jaran (Species: Kinnara)

Shu Skbodvvrv'v ghfuhh, dqb dqg doo fkdqjhv lq wkh ehkdylru ri wkh Rojrl-Nkrunkrl (PGZ) duh wr eh lpphgldwhob uhsruwhg wr wkh jubskrq. Khqfh, lw lv zlwk prvw xujhqfb wkdw L pxvw uhsruw wkh frqwlqxhg dwwhpswhg euhdfk ri wkh sdun erxqgdulhv eb wkh PGZ, iru uhdvrqv wkdw duh dv bhw xqnqrzq. Wkh eduulhu lv fxuuhqwob kroglqj, dv lqwhqghg, wkrxjk pb shuvrqdo vdihwb uhpdlqv dw judyh ulvn. Li L vkrxog ehfrph frpsurplvhg, wkh eduulhu frxog zhdnhq dqg euhdfk lv srvvleoh—dqg suredeoh—jlyhq uhfhqw hyhqwv.

Ixuwkhu (dqg olnhob uhodwhg wr deryh frqfhuqv), lq wkh sdvw ihz krxuv L kdyh ehfrph dzduh ri pxowlsoh ylrodwlrqv ri wkh jubskrq'v odz. D jurvv ylrodwlrq ri Fodvvlilfdwlrq 210 lv lq surjuhvv. Lghqwlwlhv ri vxvshfw kxpdqv duh nqrzq djlwdwruv wr GPZ dqg dsshdu zhoo suhsduhg dqg lqiruphg. L kdyh dovr ylvxdoob frqiluphg ylrodwlrqv ri Fodvvlilfdwlrq 220, dv zhoo dv srvvleoh ylrodwlrqv ri 230. Lqyhvwljdwlrq lv rqjrlqj, exw wkh vlwxdwlrq kdv ghwhulrudwhg dqg frqwdlqphqw pdb qrz suryh xqihdvleoh.

Sohdvh dgylvh dqg vhqg vxssruw. Hawuhphob gdqjhurxv vlwxdwlrq lq surjuhvv. Hasrvxuh dsshduv lpplqhqw. Brxu xujhqfb lq wklv pdwwhu lv lpshudwlyh wr surwhfw wkh fxuvh, wkh [UHGDFWHG], dqg kxpdqnlqg.

TRANSMISSION FAILED

Chapter 6

THE TRIAL OF DOCTOR VANCE VANTANA

RELEVANT EXCERPTS FROM THE PHYLASSOS ACCORDS OF 1945

SEC: ███████████

The threat to commit a crime of violence or threat(s) to cause injury to a creature of mythical origin with or without provocation by a human being is a level 2 violation. Punishment for level 2 violations is subject to the will of Phylassos.

SEC: ██████████

The attempted murder of a creature of mythical origin by a human being with or without provocation is a level 3 violation. Punishment for level 3 violations is death of convicted human offender.

Sam London was dying to find out what his dad had learned while dead; but unfortunately, his questions would have to remain buried for now. Sam had never seen Phylassos as angry as when he appeared above

Xanadu. The terrifying sight was compounded by the shocking presence of Marzanna. She was no friend of the gryphon, that much was certain, yet there she was, riding on his back and grinning like a Cheshire cat.

"Return to the valley at once for transfer to your trial," Marzanna ordered. The tornits appeared a second later and carried them swiftly back down the mountain where Phylassos and Marzanna were already waiting. The giants dropped off the trio then quickly retreated from the scene.

"What's happening?" Sam whispered to Vance.

"Silence, child," Marzanna ordered.

Sam didn't much appreciate being ordered around by one of Cernunnos's minions, and he looked to Phylassos for some modicum of support, but the gryphon seemed to purposely avoid eye contact. He raised his massive paw and Marzanna raised a hand. A beam of silvery white energy erupted between them. The shimmering ribbon of light stretched above them and down to the ground, forming a large archway. Within this arch of energy, the air wrinkled like invisible waves crashing on a shore.

"Enter the gateway," Marzanna instructed.

"Could we inquire as to—?" Vance began.

"If you do not wish to add to your alleged crimes, Doctor Vantana, I suggest you follow Marzanna's directions," Phylassos interjected in a curt, commanding tone.

Tashi reached out and grabbed Sam's hand. When he looked to her, she nodded and stepped forward. Vance followed close behind.

"What is that thing?" Sam asked in a whisper.

"Human scientists would call it a wormhole. But in the mythical world it's known as a gateway of Gaia: an ancient and rare form of travel. It can only be opened by two very powerful magical creatures," Vance revealed.

"Is it safe?" Sam asked.

"I'm assumin' it is, since they probably aren't looking to kill us right now," Vance conjectured.

That was reassuring, Sam thought as he and Tashi paused at the gateway. He clenched her hand and they both stepped through. It felt as though he was walking beneath a thin drape of cloth that glided delicately across his body as he crossed the threshold. With a flash of blue light, Sam suddenly found himself in a pure white room within a massive domed building. The layout was like that of a courtroom. Two long tables—likely for the defense and prosecution—were placed in front of a platform, presumably set aside for a particularly large judge.

Unlike the courtroom movies and shows Sam had seen, the audience here was loud and boisterous and filled up all available space. The spectators were comprised entirely of mythical creatures and beings, many of which Sam didn't recognize. But he did notice yetis, cynocephali, scorpion men, and others. They were seated in the rows behind the defense and prosecution tables, as well as along the walls and all the way up to the ceiling. Within the dome were mythical creatures perched on short platforms, while creatures with wings simply hovered above to view the proceedings.

Carl the Bigfoot suddenly stepped toward him. He had a bucket in his hand, which he offered up to Sam.

"Carl? Why are you holding a—" And then an unstoppable urge took control of Sam's body. He sprung forward and threw up into the bucket. Puking was never fun, but this brought it to a whole new level. It was easily the worst Sam had physically felt in his life. No flu, cold, or food poisoning came close.

"A human side effect of traveling thousands of miles in just a few steps," Carl explained. Sam finally stopped heaving and Carl offered the bucket to Tashi.

"I'm fine," Tashi said, falteringly. She looked green, Sam thought, but the Guardian swallowed, steeled herself, and the color quickly returned to her face.

Vance entered right after them and a deafening chorus of boos and hisses rained down, along with growls, squawks, and other bizarre sounds that didn't seem positive or supportive in nature.

"Aren't you going to offer him the bucket?" Sam asked the bigfoot.

"Nah. He's got my blood inside him. He might just get a little dizzy." And with that, Vance lost his balance and went down hard on the floor. Carl helped him back up. "Take it easy, Doctor. Traveling through a gate of Gaia tinkers with your equilibrium."

"My head is spinning like a top," Vance said, his hands on his temples.

"Where is this place?" Sam asked, as he took it all in.

"Atlantis, I believe," Tashi answered, gesturing to the dome. It was open at the top and Sam could see the Tower of Atlas rising in the distance, the fire crystal gleaming at its peak.

"The Guardian is correct. Welcome back," Carl said.

"Not again," Sam sighed. Last time they were here, things didn't go very well. At least getting to the "city that never stops" was not as complicated as their previous visit, which involved a dvergen subway rocketing into the air and landing in a volcano. That proved slightly more comfortable than stepping through a gate and becoming a fountain of sick.

"Please, sit down," Carl said, as he ushered them over to the defense table. They all took their seats and Vance looked over to Carl quizzically.

"What's this all about, Carl?"

"To borrow a phrase, you're in a heap of trouble," the bigfoot answered. "I have volunteered to act as your advocate. The law requires you to have mythical counsel, and there were few creatures qualified and willing to take your case."

"Few?" Vance wondered.

"None," Carl confirmed.

"Silence!" Phylassos bellowed as he and Marzanna stepped through the archway and into the room, closing the portal as they passed. The crowd instantly went quiet. Marzanna walked to the prosecution table where she was joined by Cernunnos, who emerged from the audience dressed in a long black robe. It reminded Sam of the kind that judges wear, but this had a high neck and a red stripe that ran down the back.

"What's with the outfit?" Vance whispered to Carl.

"Cernunnos loves his traditions," the bigfoot answered, rolling his eyes.

Cernunnos and Marzanna conferred with each other quietly. He then nodded to the witch and she stepped backward, spun around, and quickly exited the building.

"Where is she going?" Sam murmured to Tashi.

"She didn't tell me," Tashi replied seriously.

"I wasn't—never mind," Sam said.

A large boom reverberated through the room and immediately captured everyone's attention. The gryphon had stomped his front paw to the floor like a gavel. He gazed upon the gathered crowd, his eyes passed over Vance and Sam, then settled on Cernunnos.

"Cernunnos, you claim that crimes have been committed against you by the human, Vance Vantana?"

"I do, mighty Phylassos," Cernunnos said, bowing his head.

"And you have called this inquest to present evidence of these crimes?

"I have. I will prove that the human has engaged in multiple violations of the Phylassos Accords."

"I remind you that exploiting this process or the law's deference to mythical creatures will result in a harsh penalty."

"I am fully aware of this and would not dare distort these most serious charges."

"Very well. Proceed."

Sam leaned over to Carl. "Deference to mythical creatures? What does that mean?"

"Humans are generally considered an untrustworthy, deceitful species, so mythical creatures are always given the benefit of the doubt in criminal matters."

"But Cernunnos isn't exactly innocent. He'll lie and cheat and do whatever he needs to—"

"Cernunnos is not a friend of the gryphon, that much we know, but I don't believe he will risk returning to Gaia over a petty dispute. We will see," Carl told him.

Cernunnos walked into the space directly in front of Phylassos. He raised his voice, as he addressed both the gryphon and the audience.

"The human you see before you violated my rights and the rights of all my mythical brethren. He did not just violate them, he trampled upon them. He invaded my home without cause in official capacity with the DMW. That means he did this under your authority," Cernunnos looked to the gryphon for emphasis. Phylassos leaned his head forward.

"That is inaccurate. Doctor Vantana was not on any operation sanctioned by me or the DMW. He acted alone," Phylassos clarified.

"That was not clear to me and it would not have been clear to any other creature in my position," Cernunnos contended. "Obviously, human organizations like the DMW must do a better job of controlling its rogue employees. This one confronted me while armed, and he threatened my life." The crowd reacted with a flurry of shocked whispers. "But that was not enough for this human.... He also tried to murder me!" A collective gasp erupted from the audience.

"Now hold on a hot minute," Vance said, as he stood up. "You're not the victim here. You doomed Ettie London to return to Gaia for revenge. Phylassos—" Vance began, directing his attention to the gryphon.

"Quiet!" Phylassos bellowed at Vance. "You, Vance Vantana, are a ranger with the Department of Mythical Wildlife. As such, you took an oath to uphold the laws I established and to adhere to the system that was put in place to protect mythical creatures from exploitation, and humanity from the dangers they could face. I suggest you remain silent and reacquaint yourself with your pledge."

Carl eyed Vance, disapprovingly.

"My apologies, mighty Phylassos, I got emotional. Won't happen again," Vance assured him.

"If it does, I will consider it evidence of your dereliction of duty and your guilt. Do you understand?" the gryphon asked pointedly.

"Yes, I sure do. May I have a word with my counsel for a moment?" Phylassos nodded his approval. Vance leaned over to talk with Carl in a hushed voice, "I shouldn't have shouted like that, I know. But we need to make everyone aware of why I was there in the first place—"

"It is irrelevant," Carl interrupted.

"How isn't it relevant?" Sam asked, listening in. "If Cernunnos committed a crime then—"

"He didn't," Carl responded. "And even if he did, Vance's crime cannot be justified by what he alleges the victim to have done, no matter how heinous."

"Fine," Vance capitulated. "But is there a way to hurry this all up?"

"Why? Do you have someplace to be?" Carl asked, surprised by the request.

"Yeah, we sorta do," Vance replied.

That got Sam's attention.

"You know where she is, don't you?" Sam asked, excitedly. "Did you find out from the psychopomps? What did they say?!"

"I'll fill ya in later," Vance told him, before shifting back to Carl. "Can I just confess to the threat and get a deal of some kind?"

"I am aware that you are not familiar with the processes that govern trials involving humans and mythical creatures—"

"That's 'cause there's never been one. It was all just hypothetical."

"That's not entirely true," Carl responded. "But the point is, things work differently here. You do not hold the same rights as mythical creatures. Now, I need you to remain quiet before you get us all held in contempt." Carl then addressed Phylassos, "Our apologies for the delay. We can continue."

"Thank you," Cernunnos said sarcastically. He faced the crowd, "I ask you all, sitting here today. For those who have put their trust in this system, have kept your heads down in a noble and selfless gesture for the good of the world and the humans we share it with. Is this what we can expect in return? Treated as common animals? Disrespected? Should we allow them to try once again to dominate our kind and kill us? Like Alexander, when he butchered those majestic gryphons to feed his human ego? Did we not accept the curse to avoid their violence and subjugation? This brazen attack on me is not an isolated incident," Cernunnos declared. "No. It is yet another example of human arrogance that cannot be reined in by laws alone." Cernunnos walked back to the prosecution table and Carl stood.

"Mighty Phylassos. I have conferred with Doctor Vantana and he is willing to admit to making a criminal threat with some extenuating circumstances that we would like to submit for consideration at the time of sentencing."

"And what of the charge of attempted murder?" Cernunnos inquired.

"That is a serious accusation that my client denies."

"In this court, my word holds greater value than the words of a human."

"I am aware of this, but given the severity of the penalty, we believe that it would aid Phylassos to see proof of this particular crime."

"Then proof I shall provide," Cernunnos replied with a smirk. "Mighty Phylassos, I call upon the human ranger Penelope Naughton of the Department of Mythical Wildlife to come forward."

Sam turned towards the main entrance and spotted Penelope in full uniform heading down the center aisle toward the gryphon. As she passed Vance, she surreptitiously mouthed "Sorry."

"Step into the circle of candor," Phylassos told her.

"Circle of candor?" Sam whispered to Carl.

"An enchanted circle from which the witness can only speak the truth," Carl explained.

Penelope took three steps up a small circular dais that was just off to the side of the gryphon—the spot where one would find a witness stand in a human court. Once inside, her face became expressionless and she stared forward, as if in a trance. Cernunnos approached Penelope. He was holding out a small vial filled with a purple-colored liquid.

"Do you know what this is?" he asked. Penelope eyed it a moment and nodded. "Care to inform the rest of us?"

"It is an experimental serum I created. Synthesized from the blood of the chimera," Penelope said in a monotone voice.

"What is its purpose?"

"It was intended to make the recipient impenetrable for a short period of time."

"Please note, Mighty Phylassos, that I found this in my home after the human's illegal visit," Cernunnos said, directing his statement to the gryphon, who nodded in acknowledgment. Cernunnos shifted back to the ranger. "Did you give this serum to Doctor Vantana to help him kill me?"

"No," Penelope answered.

"Then how did it end up in my cave?"

"It was taken from my lab," she answered.

"Vantana stole it?"

"Yes." The audience erupted into more whispers and Cernunnos turned to address them and the gryphon.

"I wonder why he would have thought he needed such magical protection?" The creature asked rhetorically. "Vantana came seeking a fight. He was prepared to act upon his threat."

"May I question Ranger Naughton?" Carl asked, as he stepped out from behind the defense table.

"Be my guest," Cernunnos replied.

"May I see the vial?"

Cernunnos handed it to the bigfoot and walked to the prosecution table. Carl approached Penelope, holding the vial up.

"Has this been used?" he asked, then passed it to her for closer inspection. She examined it.

"No."

"How can you tell?" Carl inquired.

"The vial is still sealed," she explained, as she pointed to the rim at the top of the container. Phylassos peered over and Penelope displayed it for him. The gryphon snatched up the vial in his claw to get a better look.

"This example rises to the level of threat and nothing more," Carl announced, directing his words to the gryphon. "We have already stipulated—"

"What about this?" Cernunnos asked in a booming voice. The creature pulled back his robe to reveal a partially healed slash wound across his torso. Shocked gasps reverberated throughout the room. "Does this rise past the level of threat, Bigfoot? The human's knife will show traces of mythical blood. My blood!"

"Please relinquish your knife, Doctor Vantana," Phylassos requested. "If there are traces of Cernunnos's blood I will be able to detect them."

"You don't have to look, I'll admit it," Vance said to more shock and awe from the audience. Sam couldn't believe it; his dad just confessed to the crime.

"Doctor Vantana!" Carl scolded him.

"They would have found out," Vance said with a shrug.

"It's not that black and white," Carl told him. "We were trying to avoid the charge of attempted murder."

"Why? What's the difference in punishment?" Sam asked, his concern growing.

"Attempted murder carries an automatic death sentence, according to the law," Carl revealed.

"Oh," Vance said, somberly. "And that'd be my third time.... Doesn't sound like a charm."

"Is this really the moment to jest?" Tashi asked, annoyed by Vance's flippant demeanor.

"Just reflex," Vance replied sheepishly.

"The suspect has confessed to the crime of attempted murder of a mythical creature," Cernunnos declared. "The punishment is clear."

"Doctor Vance Vantana, please stand," Phylassos ordered. Vance slowly rose to his feet. "As a ranger with the Department of Mythical Wildlife, you hold a special position in the mythical world. A position of authority and, by extension, our trust. Your actions against Cernunnos have violated a sacred oath that empowers the mythical and human worlds to co-exist on this earth. It is with great regret and extreme disappointment that I must sentence you to the punishment required by this crime. Death."

Sam had been too busy thinking about Vance's joke to fully absorb the gryphon's horrifying sentence. As Vance mentioned, this would be his third time dying and that gave Sam an idea.

"Phylassos?" Sam called out as he stood up next to his dad. "I'd like to request a short recess. I may have information that will have an impact on how you carry out this sentence."

"The law is clear, Mister London," the gryphon told him.

"Yes, of course, and I'm not arguing that the punishment shouldn't be death," Sam explained. "Please. Given the lifetime of service Doctor Vantana has given to the mythical world and all the times he has risked his life to save it, I think he deserves this one, last consideration."

"I will allow you to present this information before the sentence is carried out and I will grant Doctor Vantana a short time to say his farewells, but that is all."

"Thank you," Sam said, before turning to Carl. "I'm going to need your help."

Chapter 7
A NOT-SO-SLIGHT DETOUR

Vance Vantana was a dead man sitting. He had spent the better part of an hour waiting for Sam and Carl to return, contemplating potential escape routes and avoiding Tashi's judgmental glare. He was still in a state of shock from this entire surreal episode. The gryphon appeared unwilling to help him, despite the knowledge that Cernunnos was actively seeking to undermine his rule. Was he really prepared to send his friend and longtime mentee to his death over this?

Vance had faced death numerous times during his tenure with the DMW and even died...and now he'd die again. He obviously couldn't allow it to happen, but his options were few. Even if he could manage to slip past a scorpion-man guard and out an exit, how would he get off the floating invisible island without being caught? The mayor of the city, the legendary hero Gilgamesh, would certainly not help him, as Vance had nothing to offer in return, and old Gil didn't do anything for free.

Maybe Sam would find a way. Before leaving with Carl, his son had interrogated him about his time in Cernunnos's cave and appeared confident he was onto something—what that something was, Sam didn't say. But Vance couldn't simply rely on his son to save him—he needed to have a Plan B, C, and D through Z. He was wracking his brain, when Sam finally returned. He entered the courtroom accompanied by Carl and Ranger Naughton. The crowd grew quiet as they noticed his arrival. Ranger Naughton and Carl sat behind the defense table, while Sam stepped to the area in front of Phylassos.

"Mighty Phylassos, we believe it is illegal for you to carry out the sentence of death on Doctor Vantana."

"Mister London, I believe we went over this."

"Yes. And I fully accept that the sentence is the legal punishment for the crimes he has been found guilty of, but can a criminal be sentenced twice for the same crime?"

"I am not sure I follow your logic," Phylassos told him.

"He is a child. He does not possess logic," Cernunnos quipped. "He should not even be allowed to speak in front of you, Mighty Phylassos."

Phylassos eyed Cernunnos.

"Need I remind you that Sam London has done immeasurable good for the mythical world and is he, himself, part mythical creature? He deserves the same rights you enjoy," Phylassos said in an admonishing tone. Cernunnos backed off and nodded.

"According to Doctor Vantana, Cernunnos ordered his redcaps to kill him," Sam explained. "Does he deny this?"

"You can address me, directly, boy. And no, I do not deny. He threatened and tried to murder me."

"So you took justice into your own hands and convicted him of these crimes yourself?" Sam confirmed.

"I realize you are not old enough to understand the complexities of the gryphon's law," Cernunnos chided. "But I was within my rights to convict Doctor Vantana. Perhaps the gryphon can explain that to the child."

"Sam, Cernunnos is correct. He was acting within the law," Phylassos revealed.

"I am not saying he wasn't, I'm just trying to figure out what happened. I accept that Cernunnos rightly convicted Doctor Vantana of the crime," Sam conceded, then shifted his questioning back to Cernunnos. "And when you ordered your redcaps to kill Doctor Vantana, you were sentencing him as well, is that right?"

"Yes, and as we have seen, I made the proper ruling."

"Of course. And did the redcaps, acting on your orders, carry out the sentence?" Sam inquired.

"What are you asking?" the creature replied, his irritation growing. Vance had to hand it to the kid, he knew how to make old green bean's blood boil.

"I'm asking if Doctor Vantana was executed," Sam clarified. Cernunnos scoffed.

"What do you think, boy? He is sitting right there!"

"I didn't ask if he was sitting there," Sam countered. "I asked if the redcaps carried out the sentence. Was Doctor Vantana put to death?"

"That is an idiotic question," Cernunnos declared, then turned to Phylassos. "I implore the gryphon to end this mockery of the court."

"Sam, do you have a point to all of this?" Phylassos asked.

"I do," Sam said. "The Guardian Tashi is willing to testify that Doctor Vantana was killed that day by the redcaps under Cernunnos's orders."

"If they killed him, why is he here, breathing?" Cernunnos asked. "Or is that his corpse you've dressed up and sat in the chair?" The crowd laughed uproariously.

"You didn't let me finish," Sam shouted over the laughs. "Tashi is also willing to provide details on how she brought him back to life using the life force of Gaia."

"Tashi of Kustos, does Sam speak the truth?" Phylassos asked. Tashi stood up and nodded.

"He does. I was there. Doctor Vantana was indeed deceased."

"Absurd!" Cernunnos proclaimed. "Is the Guardian a physician?"

"I am not," Tashi replied.

"Then this entire point is moot, boy," Cernunnos retorted. "Not to mention, irrelevant."

"Can the living see a psychopomp?" Sam asked Cernunnos as he stepped toward him.

"What?"

"Can a living creature see a psychopomp?" Sam repeated.

"I don't know why—"

"Can anyone help Cernunnos out? He seems to be having memory problems," Sam snarked. The crowd chuckled.

"No, to answer your question. They cannot. Phylassos?" Cernunnos made another appeal to the gryphon.

"I must echo Cernunnos's concerns. The relevance of your questioning is unclear and I'm afraid I am going to have to—"

As the gryphon spoke, Sam walked back to the defense table where Ranger Naughton handed him a piece of paper. Sam took the opportunity to smile and wink at his dad. *What did this kid have up his sleeve*, Vance wondered. Sam turned and headed back to Phylassos, holding the piece of paper aloft.

"I submit to you a complaint filed with the DMW by one Dullahan of Irish folklore: the headless carriage man and psychopomp. In this complaint, Dullahan states that the human known as Vance Vantana escaped him, which proves that Doctor Vantana did die that day at the hands of Cernunnos's redcaps."

"What does it matter?!" Cernunnos roared. "He is alive!"

"It matters because I'm pretty sure you can't sentence someone to the same punishment twice for the same crime," Sam explained. "I mean, if you sentenced a man to ten years in prison for a crime, could you re-sentence him to another ten years for the same crime after he served his time?"

"He is clearly not dead," Cernunnos said with a snarl.

"I'm sorry, but did you specify how long Doctor Vantana had to be dead, or if he had to remain dead forever? I don't think you did. You chose to be judge, jury, and executioner. You set the rules."

"He violated the law—the gryphon's law!" Cernunnos shouted. He then addressed the gryphon. "Mighty Phylassos, you are our leader and our king, your ruling must be honored."

"That it must," Phylassos responded. "But this is a unique situation. As king of mythical creatures, I give the mythical world more...latitude. I believe you were well within your rights to charge and sentence Doctor Vantana, but Sam London is correct—"

"This is outrageous!" Cernunnos declared.

"Had you come to me immediately with this information or handed the human over to me for judgment, I would have enacted the sentence myself and it would have been permanent, I can assure you of that," Phylassos told him, his voice rising. "But you took matters into your own hands. I cannot sentence any creature to die twice because of your incompetence."

"So you will allow this human to threaten us?" Cernunnos asked. "To try and kill us?"

"Doctor Vantana will still be punished for his crime," Phylassos replied. "However, I cannot put him to death nor imprison him, so I hereby declare him dismissed from the DMW. Stripped of his rank and authority, and the sight shall be removed from him, so he will never look upon another mythical creature again."

"What?!" Vance, Sam, and Cernunnos all said at the same time.

"The curse was meant to protect your creatures, not imperil them!" Cernunnos declared defiantly. "This is a travesty."

"This is your doing!" Phylassos proclaimed. "If any other creature expressed this sort of insolence toward me, they would be sent to Gaia immediately!" The crowd murmured in agreement. "I have given you special consideration because of the respect you hold in our world. But let me be clear. You are not king. You do not hold dominion over my creatures and you do not have a right to challenge my authority. Do you understand?"

"Yes, Mighty Phylassos," Cernunnos said, as he bowed his head. Vance could tell Cernunnos realized he had overstepped his authority and was now attempting damage control. "My apologies for this usurpation. It was not my intention."

"That is the only reason why you are still breathing," Phylassos informed him. "This trial is concluded. Guardian? You will see that the criminal is returned to his home and the sentence is carried out?"

"I will," Tashi answered.

"And let it be clear, Doctor Vantana. Whatever you do from this point forward is no longer under the auspices of the Department of Mythical Wildlife and will not be subject to the terms that govern employees of the organization. Do you understand?" Phylassos emphasized those last three words...and suddenly, the brightest bulb lit up inside Vance's head. Vance immediately recognized what the gryphon had done—why he chose the sentence he did. He was freeing him to finish the mission. It absolved the DMW and allowed Vance to see it through to the end.

"Yes, Mighty Phylassos. I understand," Vance responded with a firm resolve. And with that Phylassos nodded once in acknowledgment, then took flight from the platform and disappeared through the open glass dome. Vance was still watching the ceiling when he was nearly bowled over by Sam, who threw his arms around him.

"We did it!" the boy declared. Vance scooped him up and spun him around.

"You did it!" he told him. "Thank you," Vance said as he put him back down.

"I wasn't about to lose both parents," Sam explained. That jarred Vance back to reality.

"That reminds me, we have to get off this island," Vance whispered to Sam. He realized that Tashi could no longer know the plan, since she would be adamant about carrying out the gryphon's orders. "We only have three days to rescue your mom."

"The psychopomp told you that?" Sam asked.

"She gave me a lead," Vance revealed. "We'll have to take a detour on the way home, but it's best if we keep this between us for now." Sam nodded.

"You all must think you're quite clever," Cernunnos said, as he stepped past the defense table and toward the exit.

"Oh, come on now, Cernunnos," Vance replied. "Don't be bitter just because your little plan failed."

"On the contrary, Doctor Vantana," the creature said. "My 'little' plan turned out to be more successful than I could have wished. You'll come to realize that in time." Cernunnos shifted his attention to Sam. "As for you, Mister London, I am sorry to inform you that I must withdraw my earlier offer. Turns out, I won't be needing your help, after all. I'd wish you luck, but that would give you false hope. And I was your only hope to finding her."

"Don't you worry about us, now, green bean," Vance said. "We'll do just fine."

"No, you won't," Cernunnos replied assuredly. "You most certainly won't."

Cernunnos laughed as he continued toward the exit. It was a knowing laugh, as if tickled by ignorance. Vance didn't like it. Not just because it was obnoxious—which it unquestionably was—but because it triggered a sense of unease in the doctor. It was the animals earlier trying to give him a message, and now it was the hair on the back of his neck standing at attention and looking to capture his attention. What exactly did Cernunnos know that Vance didn't? Time would tell, Vance concluded. Hopefully it wouldn't tell too late.

As Sam London settled into the dvergen subway car in the Atlantis station, which lay behind a waterfall in a dormant volcano, he thought back on Cernunnos's words and, more importantly, his demeanor. He appeared supremely confident that Sam's only chance to bring Ettie back rested with him and was now out of Sam's reach. What if Cernunnos was telling the truth? What if he had the only solution? After all, they just had three days, according to the psychopomp, and that left scant room for error. Could Sam live with the fact that he had been given the chance and didn't take it? He had to keep reminding himself that the price was much too high.

Sam didn't know where Vance was taking them, but he seemed convinced it would work. Tashi would not be pleased about the detour when she realized it. But he hoped she would forgive him for his mild deceit and perhaps see to it to delay her duty a few days, which is all they had, anyway.

"Hang on!" Vance announced, as he activated the subway.

The metal capsule tipped downward and the rockets ignited. They blasted off from the station and into a black abyss that Sam hoped contained an entrance to a tunnel. The vehicle plummeted into darkness and Sam could feel an intense pressure building against his chest. They were shooting deeper and deeper into the volcanic rock, until they were suddenly diving through water towards the ocean floor. Fortunately, the ground opened up just as they made contact with it and the vehicle slipped down into a passageway, righted itself, and shot forward. It only took a few seconds of the vehicle's breakneck speed to dry Sam off completely.

The subway had been moving for only a few minutes when a wave of blue energy passed over the vehicle's exterior. It looked like a cross between a shot from Tashi's shekchen and sparks from a downed power line. Fingers of blue electricity spread throughout the subway car and into the navigation console, which appeared to short out and smoke. That sent the subway spiraling at top speed. Sam couldn't catch his breath long enough to scream in terror, but that was probably a good thing, since opening his mouth might have unintended consequences of the regurgitating kind. Strangely enough, Sam thought he saw daylight in the distance. Considering they were deep beneath the earth, that couldn't be a positive sign.

The subway car reached the intruding daylight and it was as if the dvergen tunnel had been split in half. The car shot across a chasm, spiraling as it leapt to the other section of the tunnel. Sam caught a glimpse of the pitch-black hole beneath them—a hole that cut through the dvergen tunnel and led to what he concluded was the surface. The subway made it to the other side of this fissure in the earth, but just barely. The rear of the car smashed against the lip of the opening of the other side of the tunnel. The impact sent the subway hurtling end over end, until it finally came to rest upside down in a diagonal position; its nose dug into the tunnel floor. Dust and dirt that had been stirred up from the crash clouded Sam's view.

"Everyone okay?" Vance asked in a strained voice.

"I'm okay, I think," Sam replied.

"I am fine," Tashi added.

The dust settled and Vance hit a lever on the control board.

"Hang onto the car and climb down," he directed, as the restraint system retracted. "Slowly," he cautioned.

Sam followed Vance's orders and extricated himself from the subway car. He dropped down onto the ground and was quickly joined by Tashi and Vance.

"You didn't fire that shekchen, did you?" Vance asked the Guardian. She shook her head.

"That did not come from me," she assured him. "Although it did appear to be a form of Gaia's energy."

Vance walked back towards the chasm, "Looks like something shot up and out. Something big. Real big." He gestured to the hole in the earth—the shaft was almost entirely vertical, except when it hit the dvergen tunnel; at that point it curved and shot out to the surface at a near horizontal angle. The daylight poured inside and the sun was so bright it was difficult to see what lay beyond the opening. "We might as well head out there. I'll go first," Vance told them, as he climbed into the tunnel.

"Doctor!" Tashi exclaimed. "Watch out—"

It was too late. Vance reared back and quickly wriggled out of his jacket, which was now smoking and disintegrating. The coat was gone in just a few seconds.

"Acid," Vance concluded, gesturing towards the stream of reddish liquid that ran down the inside of the tunnel. "Now that is odd," he said. "Stay extra close and watch your hands and feet." After witnessing the acid eat Vance's jacket, Sam didn't have to be told twice to be careful. He studied every inch of the tunnel before placing a hand or foot on the surface.

When Vance reached the opening, he leaned out to get a look around, muttered something to the effect of "aw, nuts," then tumbled over the side and disappeared from view. Before Sam could readjust his position and get some space between him and the edge, the lip of the cave collapsed, sending Sam sliding down a towering sand dune—though it probably looked a lot more like falling uncontrollably. He coughed and hacked as sand shot up his nose and burrowed into his mouth. He reflexively scrunched up his face, shutting his eyes and sealing his lips, but the sand still found a way to creep in. Down and down he went until finally—thankfully—his momentum slowed and he came to a sputtering, thumping stop.

Sam could feel sand in places on his body that he didn't even know existed. He imagined he would need to rinse off with a fire hose to get totally clean again. But he could worry about that later; right now he needed to get his bearings. He spotted Tashi already on her feet—she must have followed him. Then he scanned the terrain and was stunned by the other-worldly surroundings. There were dunes that looked to be the size of skyscrapers. Massive domes of dark, golden sand dotted the landscape and resembled the surface of Mars. There was also something else that contributed to the alien feel of this place...a sound. It was a low reverberating hum that felt as if it was enveloping Sam, bombarding him from all sides.

"Do you hear that?" Sam asked.

"The singing sand dunes," Vance answered, as he trudged over to join them. "I think that puts us in the Gobi desert."

"Where is that?" Sam asked.

"Mongolia," he replied. "Great," he added, sounding deflated.

"Is this close to where we need to be?" Sam asked Vance quietly.

"It's on the way...but we don't have time for hiccups."

"Doctor Vantana," Tashi called out. They looked her way and found her pointing towards something in the distance. "There appears to be a situation unfolding in that village." Sam followed her gesture and spotted a small group of round huts inside a fenced perimeter. Several streams of black, acrid smoke billowed up from the village.

"Looks like a resort compound for tourists," Vance said.

The strange sounds of the singing sand dunes were suddenly interrupted by human screams—they were coming from the compound. Vance immediately took off. Sam and Tashi were quick to follow, racing to the village. When they got closer, Sam could clearly see that many of these round shelters were destroyed. Some had collapsed and others were ablaze. There were people screaming amid the chaos, and many were injured.

"What the—?" Vance began, when he was cut off by a deafening rumble that shook the ground beneath their feet.

A monster erupted out of the earth like a geyser. It was the most terrifying creature Sam had ever seen, bar-none. That included the shark-octopus that Sam tangled with in Biscayne Bay and the leviathan that nearly killed him in Ta Cathair. This beast was massive—a long, segmented creature that Sam immediately recognized from his books on cryptids. It was the dreaded Mongolian death worm.

And it was currently raining death on everyone.

Chapter 8
THE OLGOI-KHORKHOI

Tashi of Kustos always believed that she could win every battle she fought in, no matter the odds. This was more than just a matter of being overly self-confident; rather it was an intentional tactic taught to every Guardian. This unyielding faith had a direct, and positive, effect on their prowess as warriors. A fighter who saw failure as an option and invited doubt into their minds took the chance of creating a self-fulfilling prophecy. That being said, Tashi's tussle with the Mongolian death worm in the Gobi desert was stretching the limits of this technique.

Tashi had fought large and dangerous creatures before, but nothing quite like this. The giant worm was a rage-filled monster that appeared bent on death and destruction. Tashi didn't know enough about the creature to determine if this was an aberration in its behavior or its normal state. The latter could certainly be the case, she concluded, since the creature hadn't been named the Mongolian peace worm. But she believed she owed it to the worm to attempt communication. Once the creature had breached the ground at the edge of the encampment, Tashi called out to it using her mind.

The response she received was swift—and it wasn't in word form, it was a flash of color. A blinding, searing red light that blocked her sight and gave her an instant, excruciating headache. She was sent stumbling back by the strength of this vision and immediately cut off telepathic contact, though the dizziness remained.

Once the worm was halfway out of the earth, it twisted its body and slithered toward the village where it continued its attack. The creature wasn't just flattening the shelters with its monstrous body, its tail end was whipping into people and tossing them around like dolls. The screams of victims echoed through the valley. It was like no battle she had seen. It wasn't a fair fight; this was a slaughter.

"Protect Sam!" Doctor Vantana shouted. "I'm going to try and help those people." Before Tashi could protest, Vantana bounded forward into the fray. The death worm's attack grew more dangerous by the second, as the creature hit a propane tank that instantly exploded and caused another fire to erupt.

Protecting Sam went without saying for Tashi, but the problem was there was no cover to be had. Unless she could make Sam levitate or he could grow wings, he would remain—like her—a sitting duck. They were standing in the middle of a flat grassland with towering dunes on one side and equally towering mountains on the other. The only semblance of cover that Tashi could see was a small grouping of boulders near the camp.

It was better than nothing.

"Head to those rocks!" Tashi announced, while gesturing for Sam. "Climb onto the largest one and remain there."

"What about you?" he asked.

"I will try and help your father, but this situation is far more perilous than he may realize." Tashi had noticed that Doctor Vantana had a tendency to act on impulse rather than with thoughtful consideration. She now knew it was a familial trait, as Sam suffered from the same flaw. Wanting to help was a noble aim, but Vance was not prepared to fight a creature of this sort—no human was. Tashi was about to remind Sam to run, when a pick-up truck with two passengers peeled out of the village and headed right for them. Tashi threw Sam out of harm's way, then deftly avoided being hit by leaping and somersaulting over the vehicle as it drove beneath her. She landed in a crouch and located Sam, who was safe and just getting back on his feet.

The people in the truck were attempting a getaway, and Tashi couldn't blame them. It was the right idea given the circumstances—and the Guardian was not someone to shrink from a fight. Unfortunately, the death worm noticed and turned towards the fleeing car. It reared back and expelled a reddish glob from its mouth toward the truck. Tashi recognized it as the same substance they found in the tunnel—the stuff that ate Doctor Vantana's jacket. The humans inside the vehicle never stood a chance—it disintegrated in seconds. Sam screamed in absolute terror at the grisly display.

"Go to the rocks, now, Sam!" Tashi ordered. The boy was in a state of shock.

"It spits acid, Tashi! Acid!" he shouted hysterically. "Those people!"

"Go! Do not look back. You do not need to see this."

Sam did what he was told and ran toward the boulders. Tashi had hoped the creature could be talked out of its behavior, but this was a mindless, sickening rampage and people were dying. Tashi had to act and quickly; she just wasn't sure she would be enough. There was something about the wave of energy that had shorted out the dvergen subway that was gnawing at her. She tried to shake off the tinge of self-doubt, just as she was trained to do.

Tashi charged her shekchen and released a short, but powerful blast of energy, over the head of the creature. A warning shot. The monster paid it no mind. Tashi shot another blast and this time hit the worm, but the creature didn't react. Tashi tried again with a full charge. A massive surge of Gaia's life force poured out of the tip of the shekchen and rocketed toward the monster. A direct hit. The creature finally noticed and twisted back to confront its attacker.

Tashi immediately recharged the staff to full strength and fired, hoping to at least slow or paralyze the monster. The energy struck the worm, but simply rippled out across the length of its segmented body, like a rock tossed into still water. Its skin undulated as the concentric waves of energy spread out from the point of impact. And then something unsettling began to happen. The waves of energy that she watched get absorbed into the worm's skin returned, but now they were rippling up from its tail towards the creature's head. The blue rings increased in speed as the head of the monster began to glimmer with the light of Gaia's energy. The now glowing worm tipped its head down, angling it toward Tashi.

Tashi realized a moment too late that all of the charge she had sent into the creature was about to be turned against her. An immense burst of blue energy exploded out of the worm's head, hurtled through the air, and struck Tashi in the chest. She didn't have a chance to leap out of the way—it came on fast and her mind was blinded by another flash of red. The monster had clouded her mind just long enough to slow her reflexes. Tashi had never taken a hit like this...her body was instantly and violently thrust backward. She watched the village grow more distant as she was propelled across the landscape for what seemed like an eternity. Was it the doubt that had crept into her thoughts, or were there just some battles she couldn't win? This question crossed her mind for a brief moment, as the energy webbed out over her skin and seized up her muscles. She never even felt herself hit the ground. At some point, while her body was in mid-flight, Tashi the Guardian lost consciousness.

Sam London had seen mythical creatures get returned to Gaia—the equivalent of death in the mythical world—but he had never witnessed the death of humans before. He had seen it depicted in movies, of course, but this was much, much different. Watching the pick-up truck disintegrate and realizing there were humans inside was a horrible, awful, near-paralyzing experience. But the more he tried to push the visual from his thoughts, the more the images lingered in his mind's eye. If he wasn't so terrified of suffering the same grisly fate, he'd probably stop running long enough to throw up. But for now, his focus was on moving his feet as fast as he could, all the while worrying about Tashi and his dad. They should be running with him. They should be trying to escape or they might wind up like those poor people in the truck.

The boulders were coming up quickly and Sam wasn't all that hopeful they could do much protecting; after all, the death worm could spit acid. But Tashi was right, it was the only semblance of cover in the area. As Sam approached the rocks, he suddenly noticed he wasn't the only person heading that way. Though he had done his best to avoid looking toward the village—as Tashi had suggested—Sam caught movement out of the corner of his eye: a man running from the village toward the same spot. Sam reached the tightly knit group of rocks first and scrambled up and over a large round boulder to get to the biggest of the cluster—one with a wide base and a flat but sloping top that jutted out from the group. The rocks were a light red in color and covered in grit from the sand blowing off the dunes.

The man that was running for the boulders was carrying a long case and had a camera around his neck, which he was holding in place with one hand. He had a scarf covering his mouth, a baseball cap on his head, and was wearing a khaki cargo vest and pants, each with a copious number of pockets. He made it to the boulders and pulled himself up on the same rock as Sam, panting heavily, and looking shocked to see he wasn't alone.

"Who the heck are you?" the man asked, still trying to catch his breath. He pulled down the scarf and revealed himself to be in his late twenties, Sam would guess. He was scruffy and spoke in an accented English that Sam later learned was South African.

"Sam London. Who are you?" Upon hearing this, the man smiled wide and chuckled.

"Sam London? You're that kid from Death Valley." Sam was stunned by his response.

"How did you—"

"Know? Oh, we know all about you," he said, still amused by the situation. "The boss is gonna love meeting you." He offered up his hand and Sam shook it tentatively. He was about to follow up on the man's "boss" and how he knew of him, when the man continued, "The name's Hennessy. Rick Hennessy. But my friends call me 'Shooter.'" He raised his camera to his eye and started snapping pictures of the death worm. "My pictures are going to change the world. And the video I got? Mind-blowing. I've been to every god-awful war zone in the world, been shot at, taken hostage, and nearly killed, but this here? This is going to get me a Pulitzer." The camera fired off a flurry of snaps that was shortly interrupted by a loud crackle of static noise, followed by the sound of a muffled voice.

"Shooter? Can you hear me? Copy?" The man that was talking was nearly drowned out by the sounds of screams, but Sam could detect a slight southern drawl similar to Vance's accent. Hennessy pulled a walkie-talkie from one of his many pockets and hit the talk button.

"Go for Shooter."

"Status report?"

"You're not gonna like it—we just lost Morris and Chen," Hennessy informed him.

"The pick-up?" the man's voice responded.

"Yep. Your lady friend never told us it could do that," Hennessy remarked.

"She told us enough to get us this far. If it wasn't for Morris getting us lost in that sandstorm, we would have avoided this whole mess."

"I've got another surprise for you," Shooter said with a smirk. "I've got Sam London here. Sitting right next to me."

"Well, how about that? When it rains..."

"Do you have the package?" Hennessy asked.

"Of course, but I need you to distract that thing so I can get away. I'll pick you up and we'll head for the mountains."

"Ten-four, Wildman," Hennessy replied. "We are gonna be so filthy rich," he added, a smile from ear-to-ear.

"And *right*. Don't forget that. They'll see I was right all along. I told you it was true."

"I always believed," Hennessy assured him. "Be ready to move. Shooter out."

Hennessy pulled the case toward him and opened it. Inside was a long rifle, as well as a scope and several accessories, including a small tripod, which he set up on the rock. He lifted the rifle out of the case and set the water bottle-sized barrel down on the tripod. He attached the scope, then carefully loaded the gun with bullets that looked like miniature missiles. No wonder the rifle's barrel was so big, Sam concluded.

"I shoot more than pictures. I bought this special, just for big critters like that. But I've never been able to use it before," Hennessy revealed. "I'd cover those ears if I were you, this can—"

Hennessy's attention was pulled away by a flash in the distance. They both looked to the spot and Sam was stunned—and horrified—to see Tashi firing her shekchen at the death worm. What was she thinking, Sam wondered, aghast.

"What the—?" Hennessy reacted, bewildered by the sight. "I've seen a lot of weird stuff in my time but I've never seen a weapon like that."

Sam watched as the creature fired Tashi's energy blasts back at her in one massive burst that sent the Guardian flying.

"Tashi!" Sam yelled. She finally crashed to the ground several hundred feet from the spot she was hit. She wasn't getting back up right away and that worried Sam. He had seen her take the best hits Gilgamesh had to offer on their last case and she kept going back for more.

"Is she a friend of yours?" Hennessy asked, but Sam wasn't about to answer. He scrambled toward the edge of the rock, prepared to race to her side. "I wouldn't try that if I were you. Open grassland like that? When that monster spots you—and it will spot you—you'll wind up a side dish."

Sam swallowed down his terror at the thought of being eaten and digested by that thing. He knew Tashi would agree with Hennessy. He also knew Tashi was not easy to hurt or kill. In fact, it was theoretically impossible, as long as the gryphon's claw remained under the Guardians' protection or she didn't allow herself to be consumed by Gaia's energy. There was a good chance she was just temporarily out of the fight, like when she was struck by the fire crystal in Atlantis. Plus, the worm had apparently lost interest in her and turned back to the village.

"My turn," Hennessy said, as he lowered himself to a prone position and aimed his rifle at the death worm. "Let's see how you like a seven hundred caliber round."

Sam's hands went to his ears, just as Hennessy squeezed the trigger. The weapon fired with a deafening blast that echoed through the landscape. Sam's hands were no match for the loudness of the gunshot. His head felt like a bell that had been rung. The creature was struck in its mid-section and shuddered, then let out a groan that sounded like a whale call.

"Hah!" Hennessy shouted in glee. "That was for Morris. This one's for Chen."

Hennessy fired off another round and the worm trembled again from the impact. Hennessy continued firing, striking the creature with the projectiles three more times. The worm twisted this way and that as the massive bullets tore into its flesh. The groan turned into a screech before the worm dove back into the hole just beyond the village's entrance. A satisfied Hennessy smiled wide and pumped his fist in victory.

"Now that's how it is done!" he exclaimed, then petted his rifle like it was a kitten. "I knew this little cap gun would come in handy one day." Hennessy pulled his walkie-talkie out of his pocket and clicked the button. "This is Shooter. Worm's down. Let's make tracks before it magically heals."

There was a sudden, earth-shaking rumble beneath the pile of boulders, powerful enough to send Sam sliding back across the rock and nearly over the side. He was barely holding on as the vibrations grew in ferocity. The walkie-talkie flew from Hennessy's grasp and then the unthinkable happened. The Mongolian death worm erupted out of the ground in front of the boulders. It caught the flying walkie-talkie in its mouth as it shot up into the air, then turned its body toward Hennessy, who was scrambling to get to his feet and make a getaway.

It was too late.

One second a living, breathing human being was there and then *gulp...* he was gone. Sam was horrified. He fell off the back of the boulder and onto the ground with a painful thud. He couldn't scream and his body seized up in shock. His fight or flight instinct finally kicked in and Sam sprung to his feet and sprinted toward the village with all of the energy he could muster. He heard another rumble and briefly looked back to see the worm had re-entered the tunnel. The ground leading from the tunnel began buckling upward.

The worm was burrowing right below the surface.

Right for him.

Sam turned back to the village and ran for his life.

Doctor Vance Vantana had been involved in many cases with the DMW that had gone south, but never this far south. From what Vance understood, the Mongolian death worm was a creature of the under-earth and was never supposed to tangle with humans in any way, shape, or form. Like mythical creatures of the sea, creatures of the under-earth were not covered by the curse and were, therefore, visible to humankind. But that required them to be extra careful or risk Phylassos changing his mind. Although Vance knew the death worm existed, most everything else about the creature remained classified, even for someone at his level of security clearance. It had struck Vance as unusual when he learned about the extra secrecy surrounding the worm, but he didn't dwell on it. Unfortunately, it was this lack of information that put Vance at an immediate disadvantage in this circumstance. He had no idea what to expect and, right now, the creature appeared to be one of the most dangerous that Vance had seen in the mythical world. The fact that it was on the loose and actively harming humans could have devastating repercussions on the mythical and human worlds.

Vance had just instructed the Guardian, Tashi, to keep Sam safe as he headed toward the village to be of some assistance. He was pretty certain they were in Gobi Gurvansaikhan National Park in southern Mongolia, and the village appeared to be a kind of tourist resort—one that acted as a launching point for visitors looking to embark on one of the park's many adventures. It consisted of a loose collection of a dozen or so yurts, a traditional round shelter of the region's nomadic people. Although they were originally built using felt, wood, and animal hair, these modern incarnations were constructed of wood, metal, and more contemporary—and weather-resistant—fabrics. The group of yurts was encircled by a fence made of chicken wire and wood logs. It had an opening for cars to enter the compound, and Vance assumed there were other breaks in the fence to the rear—this would be important if Vance's plan was going to work. There were a few vehicles within the enclosed area, along with a motorcycle, and Vance planned to use one of them to lure the creature away, as the tourists escaped to the mountains through the back.

With the worm making a beeline for the gate, Vance tacked to the side and leapt over the fence. He didn't immediately see a ranger on scene—if one was here, he or she was either incapacitated or doing a terrible job of following protocol. Vance might not technically be a ranger anymore, but he still had his badge, so he tapped it.

"Gobi Gurvansaikhan park ranger, this is Vance Vantana, what is your twenty, copy?" He waited a moment, then added. "Can you hear me? Copy?" Still nothing. He was on his own.

Vance took stock of the situation and quickly spotted an old Mongolian woman struggling from under a collapsed yurt. Her leg was trapped beneath a metal pole. Vance rushed over and found that she was conscious, but bleeding.

"I'm going to move the pole, just hold tight," he told her. She looked back, eyes wide with fear. He lifted the pole and hurled it to the side. Her leg was badly wounded—she desperately needed medical attention. He spied a young Mongolian man dragging a woman from another collapsed yurt. "Over here!" Vance called out to him. The man pulled the injured woman over. "You understand English?" Vance asked. The man nodded. "This woman needs serious medical help. You got any doctors or someone with medical training stationed here?"

"No, I'm afraid there is not," the man answered in a thick Mongolian accent, which sounded like a blend of Russian and Chinese-accented English.

"Great," Vance responded with sarcasm. He knelt down and grabbed some fabric from the smashed yurt's debris. He used it to tie a tourniquet around the woman's leg, right above the wound. "That'll hold you for a spell," he told the woman. "What in Sam Hill happened here?" Vance asked the man, who was now tending to the woman he had rescued.

"We do not know. The worm just appeared and it was so angry," the man said. "I had heard stories, but never believed they were true."

"The men...the men like you. They did this!" the old woman declared in a pained voice, as she pointed at Vance.

"Like me?" Vance replied, quizzically.

"She means there are other Westerners here," the man explained. "They came with cameras. The elders believe they are responsible."

"Where is the ranger?"

The man shrugged. "We sent a distress call to Ranger Jaran, but she has not come."

A propane tank suddenly exploded not far from their position and they all hit the ground.

"We gotta get you all out of here A-SAP," Vance announced. "Do you have keys for any of those vehicles?"

"The keys for the cars are in that yurt," the man said, gesturing to a collapsed shelter. As Vance considered the pile of wreckage, two men dashed for a pick-up truck and climbed inside. Vance leapt to his feet and waved his arms, attempting to get their attention.

"Over here! We need to evacuate these people now!"

"Sorry, pal. They're on their own!" The passenger shouted through the open window as the truck peeled out of the compound, barely avoiding the rampaging worm. But the worm simply turned and spat at the escaping vehicle. Its acidic saliva consumed the car in seconds, along with its human contents.

A few more survivors had joined the group; many had injuries and had to be carried. Getting away on foot would not be easy, but they had little choice. The worm shifted its attention to the remaining vehicles and was destroying them one by one. Maybe they could make their escape now, while the monster was distracted, Vance considered.

"Is this everyone?" the doctor asked the man from earlier, who scanned the area.

"All of our people are here," he reported. "Besides those two Westerners in the truck, there were two others and a woman, but she is already gone."

"What two other westerners?" Vance asked. The man pointed to the far end of the resort, where a figure could be seen ferreting through the wreckage of a flattened yurt.

"There's one, the other ran off," he said.

"All right, I'll go talk some sense into him. Is there a break in the fence in the back?" The man nodded. "Get your people together and head to it," Vance instructed. "I'll distract the worm and y'all get to those mountains as fast as you can."

Vance left the group and set out for the other survivor. He darted from yurt to yurt, staying low, as to not draw the worm's attention. When he got closer, he found the Westerner was tall and dark haired with a scarf covering his mouth. He was dressed in a beige outfit, the sort of which you'd find on a big game hunter. He spoke into the walkie-talkie in his hand, while he sifted through the yurt's wreckage. Vance hooked around another yurt and watched as the man pulled a large silver case out from the debris. Before confronting the stranger, Vance looked to the rear of the compound. The group had reached the back entrance. Vance needed to distract the worm so they could escape, but luckily the creature had already turned away from the village. Vance seized the opportunity and waved to the Mongolian man to go. The man nodded, then quickly led the group out of the fenced in area.

Vance shifted back toward the westerner, who was now checking the silver case for damage.

"Excuse me, fella, but we need to get you to safety right quick," Vance said, as he approached. The man whipped around and pulled the scarf from his face, revealing his identity. "Boone Walker?" Vance said in surprise.

The man responded with a smirk. "Hello, Vance. I've been waiting a long time to do this."

And then Boone Walker clocked Vance in the jaw.

Chapter 9

DON'T FENCE ME IN

FD-204

FILE #: ███████

DATE: ███████

SUBJECT: WILDLAND FIRE OF SUSPICIOUS ORIGIN

OVERVIEW: Forest fire in the bigfoot habitation zone of Great Smoky Mountains National Park, which resulted in one human death and was caused by arson via liquid accelerant. The investigation into this criminal act is intended to ascertain the motivations of the arsonist, assess possible ramifications for the department, and gauge the public acceptance of the government's official account of the events that transpired.

DETAILS: The following investigation is based upon information provided by Ranger Orry Avskogen of the Great Smoky Mountains National Park; Vance Vantana, a ranger-in-training and friend of the department; as well as testimony given to the ███████

police department by cooperating witnesses. As associates of the DMW, Ranger Avskogen and Vance Vantana have the sight— Ranger Avskogen of natural origin and Vance Vantana through a department serum.

For the purposes of establishing a historical context to the events of ██████████, Vance Vantana attends ██████████ school with Boone Walker, the son of Daniel Walker, who resided at ██████████. Boone is a longtime rival of Vance and the two often compete against each other in local sporting events and contests. Mr. Daniel Walker was known as a very adept hiker and survival expert. Much like Vance and his father, Boone and Daniel spent a substantial amount of time in Great Smoky Mountains National Park. It should be noted that the Walker lineage does not contain any evidence of mythical ancestry; therefore, the Walkers do not possess the sight.

Although the two fathers had been friends in their youth, according to several sources, the animosity between them had developed from a rivalry involving Vance's mother. Given the small size of the town of ██████████, their animus did not go unnoticed by their neighbors. Fortunately, this friction had not turned hostile. The two families simply avoided socializing and it has been determined that their existing strained relationship *did not* contribute to the incident of ██████████.

In an interview with the DOI investigator a few days after the incident, Ms. Genevieve Walker, spouse of Daniel Walker, stated the following (excerpt taken from 302 Form, attached):

GENEVIEVE WALKER: "I don't care what the doctor or the police said about him hallucinating because of stress or whatever. That wasn't Dan. He was always on top of things. Always clear-headed. I was the one with my head in the clouds. No, this was something else. I saw a change in him on ███████. He came home that night and was acting real funny-like. He said he saw somethin' in the woods, but he couldn't explain it. That I'd think he was crazy. But he said he was going to figure it out. Now I didn't know what that meant at the time. But after that day Dan wasn't the same. He got obsessed with spending time in that park alone. He used to bring Boone along with him all the time, but after the incident he forbid him from going into those woods ever again. It took a toll on all of us. I pleaded with Dan to go to the police or get counseling, but he refused..."

The day Ms. Walker indicated the shift in her husband's behavior coincides with the thirteenth birthday of Vance Vantana—these two events were not without correlation. According to department records, it was on that particular day that Vance tracked down and encountered one of the bigfoots residing in the bigfoot habitation zone of Great Smoky Mountains National Park. This unlikely meeting surprised Vance and led him to flee the scene; unfortunately, Vance was not paying full attention to his surroundings and wound up running straight into a tree. The collision instantly knocked him unconscious. The bigfoot Vance had successfully tracked (identified as Rupert) picked Vance up and carried him to another area of the park, where he soon regained consciousness and spoke with Doctor Henry Knox and Ranger Avskogen. It was during this conversation that Vance was informed about the Department of Mythical Wildlife and invited to join the department's mentoring program, which he did.

In the weeks and months that followed, Ranger Avskogen had been forced to call authorities on Daniel Walker multiple times, after it was found that Mr. Walker had placed bear traps, trip-wire activated cameras, and engaged in other activities that could have proven harmful to the local wildlife (mythical or otherwise). When questioned by police, Mr. Walker stated the following (excerpt taken from a transcript of an interview conducted by ████████ police department):

POLICE OFFICER (PO): "You're saying you saw the boy...floating? Is that correct?"

DANIEL WALKER (DW): "Yeah, that's right. I was on the ridge near the ████████ stream. I had my binoculars out and I caught sight of him. I heard a scream and a growl—it wasn't a bear. I know bears. The boy spun like a top and ran smack dab into a tree. He went tail over tea kettle and was out cold. I was about ready to go down there and help the kid, but then somethin'—somethin' big—picked him up and carried him off like a sack of potatoes."

PO: "And you can't describe what that something was, Mister Walker? Any information at all would be helpful."

DW: "No, I can't. I told you before, I couldn't see the darn thing. But that boy was...floating. Right through the air. I don't know what had him. It was some kind of camouflage, but like nothing I've ever seen, that's for certain. Maybe it was some sort of new-fangled military tech or some giant chameleon critter. Heck, I don't know. But it was there, I tell ya. You need to talk to that Vantana kid."

PO: "We did. He said he remembers hitting the tree and getting knocked out for a few seconds, but that he didn't encounter anything unusual."

DW: "Then he's lying through his teeth! And that ranger—the one with them black eyes? He's lying too. I know it. I've spent my life in those woods and I always knew there was something there—watchin' me. The kid found it. And it's big. Y'all need to do something about it. And quick. As long as whatever it is is out there, we're all in danger. The whole lot of us! So why don't you stop asking me stupid questions and go do your job!"

PO: "Calm down, Mister Walker."

DW: "I'm not calming down until you people get off your rear ends and protect our town. Where's Sheriff ███████? Why isn't he here? ███████ has known me since preschool for goodness sake. He knows I'm no liar."

PO: "Sheriff ███████ had other matters to attend to and wanted me to tell you he was sorry he couldn't be here."

DW: "He's a coward. I'm telling you, I'm not making this up!"

PO: "We aren't saying you are, Mister Walker."

DW: "You're condescendin' me, kid. You don't think I see that?"

PO: "Is there any chance your eyes were playing tricks on you?"

DW: "Ain't nothing wrong with my eyes. You know what? Forget it. If y'all aren't going to do anything about it, I will. I'll prove it to you and everyone."

Three days after the questioning by ██████████ police, Mr. Walker entered the Great Smoky Mountains National Park with a box of matches and a five-gallon gas can filled with an accelerant the arson investigator confirmed as gasoline. Mr. Walker distributed the gasoline in a perimeter around the area he believed held the creatures. This circular boundary did in fact encroach on the bigfoot habitation zone. According to sources, Mr. Walker could be heard calling out to the "monster" in the woods, demanding it make itself known. His voice carried hundreds of yards, but was not answered. Phylassos's law prevented any creatures in the vicinity to make contact; unfortunately, the lack of response further frustrated Mr. Walker and he decided to "smoke" them out. He ignited the accelerant with a match and it spread quickly. It was the drier part of the season, so there was more than enough fuel for the fire to burn rapidly and encircle the area. This appears to have been a miscalculation on the part of Mr. Walker, as the arson investigator believes he was inside the perimeter when he started the fire and became trapped.

Despite his location when initiating the blaze, Mr. Walker's body was found just outside the perimeter. The ██████████ Coroner found the cause of death to be smoke inhalation. The DMW, through the auspices of the Department of the Interior and National Park Service, issued a public statement disclosing that the fire had begun due to a windswept campfire and that Mr. Walker was heroically attempting to contain the blaze to save the surrounding forest. Unfortunately, he became trapped within the ring of fire and perished. Media coverage of the incident remained local and contained. The DMW—through cooperating charities—provided an undisclosed sum of money to Mr. Walker's family to help compensate them for their loss. This donation also helped to reinforce the hero narrative that has been presented by authorities.

Although the truth of this incident was successfully concealed from the public, the episode was tragic and nearly exposed the secret. It is strongly recommended that the DMW undertake a thorough review of the policies, protocols, and departmental failures that led to these events and a human death. There does not appear to be any evidence at this time that there will be additional consequences related to this incident that could jeopardize or impede the department's ongoing operations and/or threaten to expose the secret.

The unexpected punch from Boone Walker sent Vance reeling backward. Fortunately, he caught himself before his head slammed onto hard earth. Vance wasn't used to taking a punch like that. He had a sense about these sorts of things, a reflex that had kept him from taking the first punch in any altercation. Vance liked to think it was a family trait, but it might have been the result of his bigfoot-enhanced blood.

In this instance, the shock of seeing Boone had paralyzed Vance. This was the last person he expected to see in Mongolia. Boone and Vance had history together. Tragic history. They hadn't seen each other since they were kids—at least, not in person. Vance had seen Boone on television, where he masqueraded as a so-called monster hunter on his own reality television show. He had even given himself the nickname "Wildman." Boone "Wildman" Walker would travel the world, scouring parks and wilderness for monsters. Of course, he never provided any actual proof of the monsters he was seeking, but that didn't stop people from watching and speculating about these creatures' existence. Boone had become a thorn in the side of the DMW, but had yet to threaten the secret in any meaningful way... until now.

As Vance was climbing back to his feet, gunshots rang out.

"Perfect timing," Boone said with a smile. Vance spotted the worm diving back into its hole, a momentary respite that Vance took immediate advantage of. He tackled Boone and the silver case came loose from Boone's grip and slid across the ground. The two wrestled for a few seconds and Vance clearly had the upper hand—just as he did when they were in elementary school together. But just like those days, Boone always found a way to play dirty. He snatched up a piece of metal from a collapsed yurt and swung it, nailing Vance in his temple. His head rang like a cowbell in a stampede. Vance rolled off of him and squinted from the pain.

"What are you up to, Boone?" Vance asked him, wincing.

"Proving him right," Boone replied with air of satisfaction. "I knew it all along. And now the world will know."

"I can't let you do that," Vance informed him, as he stood back up to face him once again.

Before they could resume the fight, they were distracted by a distant rumbling. They both looked to the noise and saw the death worm rise up in front of a group of boulders. Whoever had fired those shots at the creature had just become its lunch.

"Shooter," Vance heard Boone say to himself with a sigh. Boone had lost another of his crew, Vance concluded. He was poised to try to subdue his old rival once more when he spotted a figure running from the group of boulders.

"Sam?" Vance yelled in horror.

The death worm was now following close behind Sam. It was tunneling just barely below the surface and sending the ground buckling upward. There was no way Sam would make it to safety if he continued in the same direction. Vance frantically waved his hands to the side, indicating that Sam should turn. He knew the creature was too big to make a quick course correction.

"Hook right!" Vance hollered, even though Sam was too far to hear. Fortunately, the kid must have sighted his dad's hand signals, because he banked to his right and stumbled as he moved off from the worm's trajectory. He managed to clear the buckling earth; the worm didn't bother to follow. Unfortunately, that meant it was now heading for Vance and the village.

Like a fountain of death, the giant worm sprung out of the ground directly in front of Boone. Boone had just managed to retrieve his case only to have the quaking earth send it flying from his possession once again. An unsteady Boone turned to find the worm rearing upward, preparing to enjoy another human snack. Vance sprinted forward, dove, and tackled Boone, throwing both of them out of the way. Boone smacked his head on a rock and was out like a light. The worm, having missed its meal, rose back up and shifted to their new position. Vance grabbed hold of Boone, attempting to drag his limp body to safety. The worm opened its mouth wide and Vance knew he was done for. He winced as he pulled on an unconscious Boone with all of his might. *What a way to go*, Vance thought.

Then something unexpected happened.

A singular sound cut through the noise of raging fires and crumbling earth: a beautiful, angelic voice.

This high-pitched vocal was abruptly joined by another voice—this one sounded guttural and impossibly low. Two distinct voices singing in a strange, other-worldly harmony...and to Vance's utter shock it was somehow calming the worm down. The creature didn't make another attempt to eat Vance or Boone, rather it turned away, toward the origin of the voices. Vance's eyes followed and he spotted a figure approaching, a half-bird, half-human creature with wings that extended from its back, an angelic human face, and feathers instead of hair. Vance recognized the singer as a kinnara. He had heard of this phenomenon before; it was known as Mongolian or Tuvan throat singing. Practitioners of this ancient art form could sing in multiple tones at the same time. It was both haunting and soothing and, most importantly, it was calming the death worm. The monster slowly slid back into its tunnel and disappeared.

The bird woman stopped singing, then collapsed to the ground. Vance rushed to her side.

"Are you all right?" Vance asked as he cradled her head in his hands. He could see from the patches on her camouflage outfit that she was a park ranger with the Mongolian government. She looked up and nodded, her big brown eyes blinking with surprise. They weren't like human eyes. Instead of having white surrounding a colored iris, the entire eye was brown except for a large black pupil.

"Yes. I am Jaran," she said, as she carefully climbed to her feet. "You are a DMW ranger?" she asked.

Vance nodded. "I take it you're the ranger here," Vance replied. Now was not the time to explain his current status with the DMW. It was immaterial—he was here and could help.

"I was trapped in my cabin. Someone had gone to great lengths to seal me in while I slept," she revealed.

Sam arrived, panting, and rushed to Vance, immediately embracing him. Vance held his son close and could feel the boy trembling.

"It killed those people," Sam told him, his voice cracking with distress. Vance had never seen the boy so frazzled before and tried his best to console him.

"I know, buddy," Vance said, gently. They separated and Vance looked his son in the eye. "But you're okay now." Sam nodded, slightly, as if not entirely convinced. Then his eyes widened.

"Tashi!" The boy said anxiously. "She was—"

"I am fine," a voice spoke out. They both turned to find the Guardian stepping over debris and heading toward them. She appeared unharmed, but there was a darkened spot on her clothes in the middle of her chest. It looked like she took a mighty big hit.

Sam rushed forward, meeting Tashi halfway and embracing her. The Guardian seemed taken aback by the gesture, but softened and returned the hug. That's when Sam must have gotten self-conscious, because he suddenly broke off the embrace awkwardly. Vance noted to himself that he would have to talk to the kid about hugging, but now was not the time.

"I saw you get hit with that blue bolt," Sam said to Tashi, as they joined Vance and Jaran.

"The creature turned the energy of Gaia against me," she explained. "Unexpected, yes, but not deadly. Where is the worm now?"

"He has returned to his home in the under-earth. Singing tunes into the creature's spiritual being, bringing him back into harmony with nature, but I am afraid it may not continue to work given Mongo's rage."

"Mongo?" Vance asked.

"It is my name for him," Jaran replied. "This anger is unusual," she added, as she surveyed the damage to the encampment. "He has never acted so violently."

"I sent a bunch of locals heading for the mountains; they're injured and they've seen more than they should have," Vance informed her.

"I will send medical help," the ranger told him. "As for what they have seen—I understand your concern, but they can be trusted. They will not speak of any of this for fear of the worm returning."

"That's comforting, but there's someone else who is just itchin' to blab—" Vance turned back toward Boone, but he was gone. "Aw, nuts." Vance quickly scanned the area, then spotted him on a motorcycle—the silver case strapped to the back. "We have to stop him!" Vance shouted and took off in a sprint.

Boone purposely let the cycle's back tire spin in the dirt, kicking up a massive plume of dust. Vance and Tashi ran headlong into the billowing grime, but Vance was forced to stop when the dirt overwhelmed his mouth and eyes. Tashi fired off her shekchen in the direction of the escaping motorcycle, but Boone emerged out of the dust cloud and pulled away.

"That case—" Sam said. "I think there's video and photos of the worm in there."

"Yeah, I reckon there is. We may be dealing with a massive, uncontainable breach. One that could turn our world upside down."

Less than an hour after the incident in the encampment, Sam London was sitting anxiously at a round wooden table alongside Vance and Tashi in Ranger Jaran's residence. It was a small, red-roofed log cabin in the middle of open grassland. They headed there after the ranger had notified the proper authorities of the destruction, which Jaran blamed on a gas leak. Sam sipped a tart juice that Jaran had served them upon arriving. She said it was made of Sea Buckthorn, a berry Sam had never heard of, but was apparently popular in Mongolia. She added a few drops of honey to it and the resulting taste was unusual—like a sour pineapple. Sam didn't love the flavor, but it quenched his thirst and he was too distracted by the memories of the day's events to be picky. He struggled mightily to forget about the people he saw die, but it was not something easily forgotten. Fortunately, the conversation stole back his attention.

"I am pleased that my request for support was answered, even if a little late," the ranger said, then sipped her own glass of the juice.

"Support?" Vance asked, unsure.

"Yes. I communicated the dire nature of my situation to the DMW. I assume that is why you are here."

"Well, no, actually," Vance admitted. "We're from the DMW, but we just happened to be passing through. The dvergen subway shorted out and the tunnel...well, came up short."

Jaran nodded. "Mongo has the ability to disrupt electricity. It is similar to what humans call an electromagnetic pulse, but Mongo uses a form of Gaia's energy."

"It is fascinating," Tashi chimed in. "I had never felt that type of energy before."

"The energy of Gaia is different in the under-earth than it is above ground," Jaran explained. "It is more pure and more deadly. As you can imagine, it makes Mongo exceptionally dangerous."

"When did all of this start?" Vance inquired.

"The Westerners arrived two days ago," Jaran said. "I did not think much of it at the time. We have many television crews who visit our parks. They had the proper documentation and seemed to be shooting the landscape for a nature video. But then things changed. They had somehow managed to infiltrate the worm's home."

"I'm assumin' that thing lives deep underground?" Vance posited. Jaran nodded affirmatively. "How'd a bunch of humans get down there?"

"A question to which I do not know the answer," Jaran replied. "I am quite certain they had help."

"From who?" Sam asked.

"I do not know," Jaran said. "But I would suspect it was a magical creature of some kind. It is not easy to gain entry to the worm's lair—it is well hidden. There is also the curious case of being imprisoned in my own cabin. It was more than a physical barricade; it was an enchantment. A powerful one. I had to use magic to escape and it weakened me—it is why I was so late in reaching you."

"So they had help getting down there, shot some pictures, and took off. Why is the worm so upset?" Vance asked.

"Perhaps it did not appreciate the unwelcome infiltration of its home. It may have seen this incursion as a threat that could jeopardize its existence," Jaran postulated.

"And all this happened today?" Sam asked. The ranger shook her head.

"They first breached the worm's lair early yesterday," she revealed. "They attempted to get away and made it a few miles outside the park. Mongo followed them, but could not pass through the barrier."

"Barrier?" Sam clarified. Jaran nodded.

"There is a barrier that keeps Mongo within the boundaries of the park. It is a powerful magical fence that I placed here and maintain, following an agreement between Mongo and Phylassos. It was believed to be necessary given the worm's destructive abilities and for other reasons."

"What kind of other reasons?" Vance asked.

"Reasons known to Phylassos," Jaran replied.

"If they escaped the park, why did they come back?" Sam inquired.

"A dust storm forced them to return. Unfortunately, it led them to that resort and exposed them to Mongo's attack," Jaran explained. "What do you know of this Boone Walker?" The ranger asked Vance.

"Boone 'Wildman' Walker?" Sam asked, recognizing the name. He had seen Boone's monster hunting show numerous times. Before Sam knew the secret, each week he would watch with anticipation, hoping Boone would uncover a mysterious creature. Unfortunately, the host always came up empty.

"Boone and I go way back," Vance revealed.

"You do?" a shocked Sam asked. "I didn't know that."

"That's because it's not something I like to talk about," Vance told him. "Boone's daddy saw me get carried off by Rupert the Bigfoot when I was a kid. He couldn't see the creature, of course, so he suspected it could camouflage itself and went about trying to trap it. He tried and failed. Until one day he attempted to smoke them out. He set a fire in the woods...the smoke could be seen for miles. Boone and I were in school at the time, but when that kid spotted that swirl of black smoke, he knew. He took off for the park and I followed, fearing the worst. I got there just in time to keep him from trying to save his dad. Mister Walker had gotten caught off guard by how quickly the fire spread and was surrounded by flames. As I held Boone back, and saved his life by the way, he saw something he wasn't supposed to."

"What?" Sam eagerly asked.

"It's not in the official report of the incident, but Rupert tried to save Boone's father. He picked him up and carried him across the fire line, singing his own fur in the process. Boone saw it happen. Rupert placed Mister Walker on the ground outside the flames and ran off, as Boone rushed to his dad's side. But it was too late."

"He died?" Sam clarified, with a pang of sadness. Vance nodded.

"The DMW covered up the circumstances, but Boone never forgot. Him and his momma moved away soon after and he decided to devote his life to proving his father wasn't crazy."

"And he finally has," Sam concluded.

"Appears that way," Vance said. "Watchin' what happened to Mister Walker was something awful. It was the first time I saw a man die and it's something that sticks with you. It messed me up right good," Vance revealed. "So I know what you're going through, Sam. If you want to talk about it, let me know. I found that helpful for me."

"Thanks," Sam replied. He didn't want to talk about it, he just wanted to forget it. But above all else, he wanted to continue the real mission; namely, finding his mom before it was too late. This potential exposure put that in jeopardy—they needed to handle this quickly if they had any chance of locating Ettie. "How can we help?" Sam asked Jaran.

"I do not know," she answered sincerely.

"Well, I need to contact HQ and make sure they're aware of the very real possibility of a major disclosure," Vance said. "We need a plan in place to try and keep this genie in the bottle. There won't be any negotiation with

Boone—he's a man on a mission, but we might be able to head him off at the pass somehow. Course, if we can't get ahold of that footage, we'll have to discredit it."

"You mean lie?" Tashi clarified. The tone of her voice indicated her disdain.

"If it saves lives? You bet," Vance countered. "As for that worm out there, we need to find a way to calm it down."

"It is driven by rage and blinds any who attempt to communicate with it," the ranger explained.

"I experienced this," Tashi noted. "I saw only a searing flash of red when I tried to speak to the creature telepathically."

"It communicates through color," Jaran revealed. "When I sing, I mentally project soothing colors and I believe the singing reinforces these messages. It's enough to calm the creature for a short time, but if you were to help, we might calm it down enough to—" Jaran's face suddenly went pale and the ranger fell from her chair.

Vance rushed to her side, as did Tashi.

"What's wrong?" Vance asked, as he helped her to a sitting position.

"Mongo is attempting to beach the barrier once again," she said in a strained voice. "My life force is entwined with it. As the barrier weakens, it draws energy from me to strengthen itself."

"Perhaps I can help," the Guardian said, as she laid hands on Jaran. The color in the ranger's face returned and she slowly smiled.

"That is helping," she said, then closed her eyes for a long moment. She exhaled a deep, protracted sigh. "Mongo has abandoned his attempt...for now." Her eyes opened and she looked to Tashi. "Thank you."

Tashi nodded and helped Jaran to her feet.

"Can you call the worm?" Sam asked, eager to keep things moving.

"I can sing a song that will summon it," she replied. "Why?"

"I think we should try that," Sam declared. "Call the worm here and see if we can talk to it and calm it down. Do you want to start singing outside or—?"

Jaran eyed him, skeptically, as did Tashi.

"A word, please, Sam London," the Guardian said. She grabbed his hand and led him into the hallway.

"Why are you in such a hurry?" she asked, facing him.

"I just want to help," Sam told her. "It's important that we do, isn't it?"

"Yes, but it is dangerous," she asserted. "And you appear to be throwing caution to the wind."

"I know it's dangerous. But we need to act quickly. So let's act," Sam said. Tashi gave him an inquisitive glare. He asked, "What?"

"What are you scheming?"

"Scheming? Nothing. And that's not very nice of you to think of—"

Tashi cut him off. "Speak plainly, Sam London. Do not cower from truth. And do not try and manipulate friends like pawns on a chess board."

"I don't know what you're talking about, Tashi," Sam told her, even though of course he knew; he just didn't want to get into it now. It would only slow things down and upset her.

"Do you think I am so oblivious as to not recognize that our subway should never have passed through here on our way home? Where were you and Doctor Vantana taking us?"

"It's not important right now," Sam assured her. "What is important is calming that monster down before it escapes. I will answer all of your questions afterward, I promise. But let's just make sure Mongo doesn't destroy the world first."

"We are going home after this," Tashi said firmly.

"Yeah, fine…whatever," he replied, as he headed back into the main room. Time was ticking away and he didn't need to waste any trying to persuade Tashi. They would simply have to convince her later. She'd understand, he believed. What was an extra hour or two detour in the grand scheme of things? Surely, she would see that it was worth it.

* * *

Thirty minutes later, Tashi, Sam, and Jaran were outside of the ranger's cabin. Tashi's shekchen was fully charged and Jaran was preparing to summon the worm. Vance emerged from the cabin, looking frustrated.

"I couldn't get a hold of anyone at HQ," he revealed.

"How's that possible?" Sam wondered.

"It is the worm," Jaran explained. "It prevents communication—it is likely why my distress call was not received by the DMW."

"Whatever it is, I don't like being cut off like this, especially with what we know. We need to get home," Vance asserted. "Are y'all ready?" He asked. Jaran and Tashi nodded. "Okay, then. Let's see if we can have a chat with Mongo."

Jaran began singing. It was the same type of singing she did earlier. Both guttural and high-pitched at the same time. But this song was different from the one at the encampment. The lower tones sounded more overpowering.

She continued for at least a minute and everyone was on edge, especially Sam. He suddenly experienced a major bout of second thoughts. In his zeal to quickly remedy the situation, he hadn't totally considered the myriad of ways this plan could go horribly wrong. After all, the last time this creature made an appearance, it murdered people. Sam glanced toward Vance—seeing him unarmed and vulnerable. He saw Tashi, gripping her shekchen, which had proven ineffective on the creature.

Unfortunately, Sam London's second thoughts came a second too late. Mongo breached the earth in front of Ranger Jaran's cabin, erupting out of the ground and sending a shower of dirt raining over them. Half of its body shot into the air and twisted downward to face the group. Jaran raised her voice and Tashi closed her eyes.

"I am attempting to communicate with it now," the Guardian announced. Jaran nodded and closed her eyes, as well. Her voice shifted and the melody now sounded like the one from the encampment—the song that had calmed the worm.

At first, the plan appeared to be working. The creature's movements were less jerky and it began to settle back into its hole until just the first quarter of its long body, along with its head, was exposed.

"It is pushing back," Tashi reported. Sam could hear the stress in her voice—not a positive sign.

Jaran's voice cracked and the worm's demeanor changed instantly. It let out a squealing roar and the ground shook beneath their feet.

"Break off!" Vance called out to Tashi. "We have to protect Jaran!"

The earthquake grew stronger and knocked Jaran off balance. Her singing came to an abrupt halt, and that was when everything went from bad to catastrophic. The creature's tail emerged from the ground behind the ranger and she began to slide towards the widening sinkhole. She tried to use her wings to fly, but couldn't seem to flap them fast enough. Tashi raced to Jaran's side, grabbing her hand and pulling her to safety. And then the worm shot back out of its hole. But it wasn't coming for Jaran or Tashi or Vance.... It was coming for Sam.

It happened so quickly there was little Sam could do to protect himself. He saw Tashi fire off a blast at the creature, but it didn't even flinch. He saw Vance running toward him, but he would never make it in time. Sam turned to run but the worm grabbed hold of his shirt with its teeth, yanking him backward. Sam screamed in terror as the monster rose up and then reversed into the earth. The sudden freefall took Sam's breath away and the sunlight flickered out of view. What little breath he could muster went to crying and then hyperventilating. His chest grew heavier as they plummeted downward...until breathing became impossible. He felt dizzy and nauseous. The lack of oxygen finally caught up to Sam London, and he lost consciousness in the jaws of the Mongolian death worm.

Chapter 10

CYNTHIA SALAZAR

Threats and tactics of intimidation did not go far with Cynthia Salazar.
DMW employee Bob Ferguson knew this the moment he confronted the
reporter outside the Department of Interior building in Washington, D.C.
When Bob warned Cynthia that her investigation must come to an end,
she narrowed her eyes and smiled broadly. "I knew you'd say something
like that."

Today would be moving in a vastly different direction than all of Bob's
previous days with the DMW (which numbered over twenty thousand).
Sure, there had been surprises that popped up here and there over the years,
but this day was taking on a very dangerous and worrisome trajectory.

Since the DMW's inception, the secret government agency had its share
of tenacious journalists who grew too curious about a creature sighting or
incident and became determined to dig deeper, but these previous episodes
proved easy to handle. The DMW didn't condone or encourage pressuring
reporters into ending their inquiries; rather, it had become a master at dis-
tracting them. The department had powerful friends in the government

and media (some were even mythical creatures hiding amongst humans). Journalists who expressed an interest in the mysteries lurking within national parks were suddenly given high-profile assignments they had been longing for, or learned they had nabbed their dream job halfway across the country. Soon, whatever interest they had in a strange local story dissipated as, in their minds, they were now poised to report on something bigger and more important to the world. Those who couldn't be distracted were simply labeled conspiracy theorists and marginalized, but that response was rarely necessary.

Unfortunately, Cynthia Salazar could not be tempted, distracted, or diminished. She was a journalist on a mission who wouldn't give up until she exposed the truth—she was a lone wolf, which is the most dangerous kind. Of course, the irony was that while Cynthia Salazar could be considered a metaphorical lone wolf, Bob Ferguson actually was one. Bob was not human; rather he was a dwayyo, a creature who had its origins in German folklore, but was more recently associated with the Blue Ridge mountains of Maryland. The dwayyo as a species resembled an upright wolf. It was covered in fur, had a snout, and also a tail, but it wasn't what some might categorize as a werewolf, since it wasn't a shapeshifter.

Much like the cynocephali, the dwayyo appeared human to anyone without the sight. They had chosen to allow their species to integrate into human society because they believed it would help protect them from their mortal enemies—a monstrous, dragon-like beast known as the snallygaster. Fortunately for the dwayyo, their gamble had worked. The snallygaster was relegated to a hidden area of the Blue Ridge mountains, which had been designated as Catoctin Mountain Park.

Bob had sought out work with the DMW after his own encounter with a snallygaster that nearly saw him returned to Gaia. He was rescued by a DMW ranger and Bob felt a responsibility to repay his life debt by committing to work for the DMW for a lifetime. Considering that dwayyo could live hundreds of years, this was a significant vow. Bob didn't seem to mind. He enjoyed his work with the department and though he did envy the work of the rangers on the front lines, his incident with the snallygaster had left him skittish to the idea. Toiling away in the offices of the DMW headquarters was relatively safe for Bob Ferguson...at least it had been.

Today, Bob was thrust into action outside the protective walls of the DOI building and he was understandably nervous. He knew Cynthia didn't possess the sight, but she had already had multiple brushes with the mythical world. Concerned she might be tempted to dig deeper, the DMW had begun tracking her movements weeks ago. Bob had been assigned to keep an eye on her, which he did from the comfort of his office chair, but now things had gotten out of hand. Bob needed to act and so he decided to confront the reporter. The DMW had to learn the extent of what she thought she knew, so an appropriate course of action could be determined.

"And why should I follow your advice and end my 'investigation?'" Cynthia asked with a smirk.

"Because you are going to get yourself arrested, Miss Salazar," Bob answered matter-of-factly.

"Arrested?" Cynthia replied with surprise. "For what?"

"Harassing a government employee in the course of his duty," Bob told her. She gave him a sideways glance.

"Really?"

Bob nodded. "I'm afraid so."

"And what branch of the government do you work for, exactly?"

"I'm with the Department of the Interior," Bob informed her and gestured to the building.

"No, Bob, you're not," Cynthia countered. "You work in the DOI building, sure, but there is no record of you in any of the employment databases. Why is the government hiding you? Or does the Department of the Interior suddenly have a need for secret agents?"

"They're not hiding me, Miss Salazar. And do I look like a secret agent?" Bob replied. "Your databases are wrong. And I think it's time for you to return to California before I follow up with the authorities. This is the sort of thing that could really hurt a person's career."

"Are you threatening me?"

"No, no, of course not," Bob fumbled. "I'm just—"

Cynthia interrupted, "Well, that's too bad, Bob, because I'm going to threaten you and I'd feel less guilty if you did it first."

"Threaten me? With what? More stalking?" Bob responded with a suppressed chuckle.

"Public exposure," Cynthia declared with a deadly serious tone.

The threat to go "public" was the ace in the hole for any journalist seeking to uncover some hidden truth or conspiracy. Bob knew this was inevitable. It was clearly a card she was keeping in her back pocket and was prepared to play to further her cause.

"What would you be exposing?" Bob inquired with his own smirk. "That my name didn't show up in the employment database? Stop the presses! You've stumbled upon a shocking revelation. Pulitzer-level, no doubt."

"Cute, but no. What I'm referring to are the creatures you're hiding," Cynthia told him in just above a whisper. "I know about the D-M-W."

Bob kept his cool, calm demeanor, but on the inside his heart—which tilted right from the center of his body, unlike a human—felt as if it leapt over to the left. How could this reporter know about the department? Nothing in the DMW tracking of her thus far indicated she had stumbled upon this information.

"I'm sorry?" Bob replied with his best puzzled expression.

"I have a source who has confirmed it all and would like to meet you, Mister Ferguson," Cynthia revealed.

Miss Salazar's admission began to fill in some blanks for Bob. He had been made aware of the encrypted communications that Miss Salazar was receiving these past few weeks. The department—working with cooperating individuals at the National Security Agency—had yet to trace the origin of the contact, nor could they eavesdrop on the conversations. That was highly unusual and Bob had a sneaking suspicion there was magic involved. Whatever the case, whoever it was she was talking with was likely the source she was now referring to. But Bob had to continue playing this out.

"I don't really have time for this nonsense. Have a good day, Miss Salazar," Bob told her, but as he turned to step away. Cynthia reached out and gently grabbed his arm.

"Meet us at the foot of the statue on Theodore Roosevelt Island in one hour. Come alone and tell no one, or I won't be able to prevent my source from exposing everything," Cynthia warned.

"Which is nothing," Bob retorted, shaking her loose.

"Are you willing to take that risk?"

"There is no risk if—"

Cynthia interrupted, "My source said I should also mention that they will be arriving by subway at White Oak Canyon falls in Shenandoah

National Park. I honestly don't know what that means, but the source said you would. One hour, Mister Ferguson. Alone."

And with that, Cynthia Salazar turned and walked off. She might not have understood the significance of White Oak Canyon falls, but Bob sure did. There was a dvergen station behind those falls. If the source knew this, then the situation was more serious than Bob imagined.

He contemplated contacting Phylassos directly. In the aftermath of the case known as "The Selkie of San Francisco," which had Bob executing a rarely used protocol (to prevent exposure of the secret) without Phylassos's approval, there was a magic red button installed in the DMW offices that would immediately signal the gryphon if a similar dire situation arose in the future.

Bob didn't believe this current predicament rose to that level, at least not yet. Instead, he concluded that this was his moment to shine—to step out from behind the safety of his desk and do his part to save the secret, once again.

He arrived at the park an hour later to meet this "source" and perform his sworn duty.

SL003-720-30

SOURCE: PR

DATE: ████████

Dedicated as a national memorial and park in 1967, Theodore Roosevelt Island is an eighty-eight-and-a-half-acre natural preserve that sits in the Potomac River. It features over two miles of hiking trails and a memorial plaza celebrating the 26th U.S. President, Theodore Roosevelt, who is considered one of the greatest proponents of the national park system. The centerpiece of the island is a seventeen-foot-tall statue of Roosevelt, which is joined by fountains and twenty-one-foot granite tablets that are etched with famous quotes from the conservation-minded president. Access is limited to a footbridge that crosses the western bank of the Potomac.

The island does not currently accommodate any mythical creatures, given its relatively small footprint and proximity to the Washington, D.C., metropolitan area.

Bob Ferguson stood at the base of the giant Theodore Roosevelt statue and looked around, trying his best to appear patient, even though he was anything but.

"You made it, Mister Ferguson," Cynthia called out, as she emerged from one of the paths that led into the woods. "I guess I made an impression."

"I'm simply curious," Bob replied. "I believe that, despite recent claims, you are a competent journalist and so I want to find out who this fraud is that has been trying to con you."

"Aren't you the ones doing the conning?" a voice said from behind him. Bob spun to see a man walking towards him—a man that Bob instantly recognized as Boone Walker, the reality show star and self-proclaimed monster hunter who had a complicated past with the department. He carried a silver case as he joined them. "Bob Ferguson, am I right?" he said, extending his other hand. Bob didn't shake it. Boone smiled and looked to Cynthia. "Well done, Miss Salazar. Nice to finally meet in person." Cynthia nodded but appeared surprised.

"I didn't realize it was you—" the reporter said.

"Oh, I see, you two have never met," Bob concluded. "Having second thoughts, are you, Miss Salazar? I don't blame you. You couldn't have found a bigger fraud than the monster hunter who has never found a monster."

"All good things come to those who wait," Boone said. "Has anything I told you turned out to be untrue?" he asked Cynthia.

"No," she responded.

"Fortune favors the bold, Miss Salazar. Like old Teddy here," Boone said, as he gestured to the statue. "A real forward thinker. I wonder if he actually knew what was roaming these parks. There are tales that he hunted a bigfoot. So many stories of these creatures over time—are they all just lies?"

"Haven't you proven that time and again?" Bob snarked.

"You know my name is Boone, right?" Bob shrugged.

"You mean it isn't 'Wildman?'" Ferguson quipped. Boone gave Bob an angry look that wiped the smirk off the dwayyo's face.

"There is an old family story that says we're distant relatives of Daniel Boone. That if you shook my family tree hard enough, old Danny would come crashin' to the ground. It's why my father was named Daniel and why he named me Boone. Fascinating fella that Daniel Boone. He also claimed to have seen a bigfoot. Rumor is, he even managed to kill one. I always tended to think that what happened to my dad was payback."

"Your dad?" Cynthia asked. "What is this all about, Mister Walker? I thought we were—"

Boone waved her off dismissively. "Today, all of that changes. Today, we begin to expose the truth to the world and everyone will see I was right. And so was my father."

Bob studied Boone during this exchange and realized—like Cynthia—he did not have the sight. So the threat was relatively contained thus far,

Bob concluded. Maybe Boone was guessing about the dvergen subway; there were rumors about those tunnels. It might have been a shot in the dark to persuade Bob to meet. Whatever the case, Bob decided he no longer needed to entertain the ramblings of Boone Walker.

"I think it's time for me to get back to work. The best of luck with your career, Miss Salazar. Mister Boone, I hope you find what it is you're looking for."

"I already found it. And it's right here," Boone tapped the silver case.

"Let me guess, you have grainy, obscured pictures of something suspicious," Ferguson suggested, mockingly.

Boone smirked and replied in an ominous tone, "Oh, no, Bobby boy. This ain't pictures."

Sam London's eyes opened slowly, as if they didn't care to see the world again. Perhaps it was the fear of what he might find or the exhaustion from burning so much adrenaline, screaming in sheer terror. His head pounded like a road worker was bearing down on it with a jackhammer. His stomach felt as if it had floated upward in his body and settled close to his heart. He was nauseous and lightheaded and that was just his physical condition. His psychological state was far worse. Sam felt instantly vulnerable and scared and anxious and angry. He was upset that he had allowed this to turn in such a terrible way. Sure, he was still alive, but what if that meant he would be forced to consciously endure more horrors?

Sam's blurred vision began to sharpen and the throbbing headache began to subside, albeit just slightly. He apprehensively took in his surroundings and found that he was lying on a jagged, rocky surface. It was akin to obsidian, a dark, glassy volcanic rock that had lines of glowing blue energy running through it like thin, narrow arteries that webbed out in every direction. As Sam shifted his eyes to follow their course, he saw he was in a large cave. The streams of energy spread throughout the walls of rock, which were pocked with holes like Swiss cheese. Sam concluded that these holes must be entrances and exits for the death worm. Sam scanned the area for a sign of the creature and spotted it a few dozen yards away, pressed up against the cave wall. It appeared to be asleep. That was a momentary relief.

Sam noticed another area of the cave that was filled with random objects, like a human garbage dump. Perhaps these were items the worm had collected over time. In the middle of the cave was a flat, circular structure made of large stones. Sam climbed to his feet and cautiously approached the formation for a better look. As he got closer, he noticed that within the arrangement of stones were sticks and other foliage—a ring within a ring. Sam moved further to see what was at the center of this display when he froze at the sound of a sudden, deafening shriek. The worm was not only awake, it was looming over Sam. He quickly backpedaled from the creature, reversing into the garbage pile where he tumbled onto his backside. The worm stopped its charge, retreating to the ring in a protective manner.

Sam's heart raced and his body felt numb. He didn't move a muscle in fear a simple flinch might compel the worm to attack. He didn't understand why he was there. Did the worm want to eat him? Not knowing what this monster's plan was, nor seeing any possible means of escape or ways to defend himself, Sam was paralyzed and a prisoner to his increasingly ter-rifying thoughts. He held out little to no hope for a rescue mission—how would anyone find him this far underground? Even if they could, how would they fend off the death worm while attempting to make an escape? The worm had already shown time and again that it could not be stopped. The whole experience was frightening to the extreme, but it was made infinitely worse when Sam noticed—among the garbage—a scattering of pictures, likely torn from a book. A book about birds. One of the illustrations was of swans on a lake. It was all the reminder Sam needed to send him into a deep, debilitating depression.

Being here inside this cave cemented what he refused to accept. The mission to save Ettie had taken many turns and each seemed to send them further away from the goal. This most recent one would likely be the final, damning twist to his story. He may have mythical blood in his veins, but he was just as powerless as he had always been.

The despair that was building up inside him was similar to the hopelessness he felt on the shores of Lake Baikal. That immense sorrow had been slightly diminished by Doctor Knox. In his wink Sam saw possibility, but in this moment, Sam felt all of that possibility fade away completely. The heartache, the grief, the overwhelming regret and sadness erupted like a volcano. Instead of lava it was the searing pain of tears that flowed down his cheeks.

The water that ran from Sam's eyes was the last remnant of hope that those eyes would ever gaze upon his mother again. He would have given anything to bring her back, but the universe had other plans for Sam London. The boy who saw the gryphon in Death Valley was now in the lair of the death worm...and he was utterly broken. His sorrow consumed his fear. He was no longer afraid of what might happen; he felt the desolation of what had already occurred. There was no escaping that reality, just as there was no escaping his current situation. This deluge of emotion was the final barrier to acceptance.

In the throes of this emotional storm, Sam had become oblivious to his surroundings. But something suddenly caught his teary eyes. The Mongolian death worm was now just feet away, gazing down on him. Sam had no more energy to recoil in fear. He simply clenched his eyes in anticipation of whatever would come next.

Several seconds passed and Sam was pretty sure he was still sitting on the ground, up against that pile of garbage. He opened one eye to glimpse what the hold up was...and then opened both. The worm was still in front of him, but now it was even closer. And that wasn't all. It had a towel in its mouth—a ratty, stained white towel that it dangled inches in front of Sam's face. It nudged its head towards Sam, as if offering the filthy cloth to him.

What was he supposed to do with the towel? Did the worm want him to clean himself before he ate him? Like having to wash a piece of fruit or a vegetable before partaking? Sam knew one thing: If staying dirty would make him unappetizing to the worm, he was about to get as dirty as humanly possible. Dirtier than the time he went two weeks without a bath just to save a temporary tattoo on his arm of his favorite superhero. In retrospect, he probably could have gotten away with cleaning his entire body except his arm, but he didn't want to chance it. Sam eyed the cave to see if there was a spot of mud or dirt he could roll around in—a real challenge to the worm's sensitive palate.

The worm, likely sensing Sam's apprehension, moved closer still, but Sam remained rock still. That's when the worm did something totally unexpected. It used the towel to dry the tears from Sam's eyes.

Sam was touched. "Thank you," he told the worm, as the creature dropped the towel at Sam's feet. It tilted its head, as if trying to understand. Sam repeated, "Thank you," but this time he motioned to himself on the "thank," and then towards the worm on the "you."

The worm took this action as an invitation to touch him. It's chin—or whatever it was—brushed Sam's open palm. Sam could feel the short hair-like bristles on the worm's skin. They felt like thousands of independent fingers, each stroking his hand with their own distinct intensity. Suddenly, Sam's mind's eye was inundated with a flash of color.

BLUE.

But it was more than just a color...it was a feeling: intense sadness. This was an emotion that Sam could identify with and understand. It was a feeling of separation and heartache. This was a duplication of the emotions he was currently experiencing. Did the worm sense these feelings and deliver them back to him? If so, Sam didn't know what the purpose of such a communication was, but he did know he didn't enjoy feeling that way. He reflexively retracted his hand. The worm lingered for a few seconds, then moved back to the center structure.

When it laid down near the rocks, it let out a whiny groan similar to the calls of humpback whales. It was also a vocal resonance that seemed to perfectly match Sam's emotional state. Sam began to wonder if he was understanding the worm. Was it expressing Sam's emotions or its own? Sam's eyes went to that circular set of stones, then back to the picture of the swan from the book.

Sam began frantically pulling the pages of the book together. As they started to form, his realization crystallized. The pages were from a children's book. Not only that, but everything around Sam—the great big pile of garbage—was made up of items a human parent might need. There was bedding and toys and even a mobile with little monkeys. Sam stood up, armed with a new sense of understanding and stepped towards the worm. The worm took notice and flinched, but Sam held out his hand as he approached.

"It's okay," Sam said in a gentle voice. When he reached the circular formation, the worm rose up in a protective manner. "I just want to see," Sam said, gesturing to the circle. "I want to know."

Sam craned his head to catch a glimpse inside the structure. He saw the branches and foliage he caught sight of earlier, but this time it struck him differently. Now it looked like a nest. And within that nest was a small circle of blankets. Sam noticed an indentation in the center of the top blanket, indicating that something once sat there, but was now gone.

Sam instantly knew why the worm was so angry...and so sad all at the same time. He could appreciate this level of hurt and frustration. The worm hadn't been duplicating Sam's emotions; the creature was a mother sharing her own. She had something stolen from her—something precious and irreplaceable. In that moment of realization, Sam accepted his new objective: a new wrong that had to be made right. It might be too late for Sam London to save his mom, but perhaps it wasn't too late for the Mongolian death worm to save her child.

"It isn't much of a stretch to claim a picture is fake, when it really is fake, Mister Walker," Ferguson replied. "Someone prancing through the woods in a bigfoot costume isn't evidence."

"See?" Boone said to Cynthia. "What I've got is far better than some photos. It's irrefutable."

"What is it?" Cynthia asked, sternly. She was tired of playing games.

"I thought you'd never ask," Boone quipped. He walked over to a stone bench, and Cynthia and Ferguson followed. Boone set the case down, then inputted a code in the digital keypad near the case's handle. There was a loud click.

"Just so you don't get any ideas, Bob, this case is rigged. If you put in the wrong code, try to break it open, or if anything should befall yours truly, the contents will be incinerated."

Boone Walker opened his silver case, finally revealing what was hidden inside. Problem was, Cynthia had no idea what she was looking at. The case was filled with wires leading to small pouches of red liquid. Cynthia assumed they had something to do with Boone's failsafe. In the center of the case was a translucent box and inside the box was the strangest creature Cynthia had ever laid eyes on. It was some sort of worm, only bigger. It was at least a foot in length with red skin that rippled along the length of its body. It wiggled and squirmed in its see-through prison, then it opened its mouth—the only sensory part Cynthia recognized—and let out a shriek.

"What is that?" Cynthia asked, unable to look away.

"You want to tell her, Bob? Or should I?" Boone asked Ferguson. Cynthia instantly noticed that Bob Ferguson was pale white, as if he had seen a ghost. "You're speechless. I understand. Well, Miss Salazar, you are looking at a Mongolian death worm. The baby version."

"Baby..." Ferguson repeated with a mix of surprise and fear.

"But the death worm is just an old folktale," Cynthia said, as she shifted her eyes back to the creature.

"So are selkies and gryphons," Boone responded.

"Is it...dangerous?" Cynthia asked, as she moved in for a closer look. The worm appeared to notice her looming over it. Suddenly, a large blue wave ran over the length of its body. A burst of what appeared to be electricity erupted out of the creature's head and illuminated the box. The flash startled Cynthia and she leapt back.

"Its bark is worse than its bite," Boone said with a chuckle. "But its momma is a different story. Killed three of my crew. She ate one whole and the other two she melted with acid."

"Acid?" Cynthia replied with concern.

Boone nodded. "She can spit it. Heckuva thing. Dissolved a truck with them still in it."

Cynthia recoiled at the thought, then suddenly realized: "And you stole her baby?"

"Sure did," Boone responded with zero remorse.

"Why would you do that?" she asked.

Boone eyed her, puzzled. "Evidence, remember?" he said.

Cynthia realized this, but she was having a hard time with the notion that Boone would snatch a baby from a monster...a monster that might come looking for it.

"But haven't you put us all in danger?" she asked.

"I hope so," Boone told her. "This little guy is our two birds. Proof these creatures exist and leverage. Either old Bob here plays ball or I flip the switch on the case and little baby worm goes poof."

"You would kill it?" Cynthia inquired. Things were taking a very unexpected turn. She didn't like the idea of killing an innocent creature simply to get a story. Using a life as a bargaining chip in some negotiation was clearly unethical and could seriously undermine her report.

"In a heartbeat," Boone replied. "But it doesn't need to come to that."

"Bob just has to what? Admit that this DMW exists and that these creatures are real?" Cynthia posited.

"That's part of it," Boone told her. "There's something else that Bob needs to give us."

"I don't know what you want, but I can't give it to you," Bob quickly declared.

"Sure, you can. Now you know the stakes. If you want that critter to keep on living, you're going to escort me and Miss Salazar into the heart of the DMW. And not just the offices," Boone clarified, then shut the case.

"What then are you talking about?" Ferguson asked.

"I'm talking about that big ol' vault you're hiding in there," Boone said. "Yeah, I know all about that too. You're gonna take us to it or the worm here is gonna go boom. I imagine humans killing one of these little monsters could be problematic for you people."

"I don't think you understand the gravity of what you're doing, Mister Walker," Ferguson replied. "The lives you're putting in danger..."

"Is that a 'no?' Cause then I'll just go ahead and press the button and test your theory," Boone told him defiantly.

Cynthia leaned in. "You didn't tell me about any of this," she whispered angrily. "Why do you need to see this vault?"

"Because I do. And if you want to be the reporter who exposes the greatest secret known to man—the one who changes the course of history—then just follow my lead. I brought you this far, didn't I?" Boone asked. "Don't get skittish now. We're almost there."

"I don't know. This doesn't seem right," Cynthia replied. She knew they were on the verge of revealing something extraordinary, but her conscience was nagging her.

"Is it right that they've been conspiring to keep the truth from the world? Was it right when they allowed my father to die because of their lies? The whole town thought he was crazy, but they knew he wasn't," Boone pointed Bob's way for emphasis. "My dad knew the truth and now everyone will. The ball is in your court, Bob. Either you take us to the Vault of Mysteries or this little fella dies."

Tashi of Kustos had failed once again. This was not a feeling she enjoyed nor one she wanted to recreate. First the kooshdakhaa had kidnapped Sam and turned him into an otter—a circumstance from which she was barely able to rescue him—and now the Mongolian death worm had snatched him up and disappeared underground, right in front of her. She simply couldn't move fast enough to stop it and hadn't anticipated that the creature would pay Sam any mind. She was wrong...and perhaps fatally so. When the worm plucked Sam off the ground, Tashi abandoned Jaran and bounded forward.

"Sam!" the Guardian exclaimed, racing for the creature. The worm dove back into its hole and Sam's screams grew more distant with each passing moment. Tashi's protective instinct kicked in and she acted without a second thought. The Guardian leapt in after him.

She was freefalling down a pitch-black hole with no end in sight—the light above disappearing after just a few short seconds. Tashi tried to prepare for landing and gripped her shekchen, ready for a fight. Suddenly, her momentum ceased, but she hadn't reached the bottom yet. She felt a pull on the back of her shirt and peered upward, lighting up her shekchen to see what happened. It was Jaran. The ranger was hovering above her, wings flapping steadily, as she clenched onto Tashi with her talon feet.

"If you wish to rescue your friend, this is not the way," the ranger told her. "Come, we'll make a plan." And with that, Jaran flew Tashi back up through the hole and placed her on the ground.

"I understand why you did that, but let's not try to play suicidal hero again, got it?" Vance said.

"Suicidal?" Tashi replied. Perhaps Doctor Vantana had forgotten that she was immortal.

"I know you think you're invincible, but I don't reckon that gryphon blood will protect you from being melted with acid," the doctor noted.

Tashi considered that. "You make an intriguing point," the Guardian told him. "But if I must risk my life to save Sam, I will do so."

"Oh, I know. I saw what you did back in Alaska," the doctor said.

"Exactly, now if you'll excuse me, I am going to go find him before it's too late."

"Hold on, Guardian," Jaran requested. "I do not believe Sam is in danger. Do you sense him still?"

"What do you mean?" Tashi asked.

"You have a bond with Sam London. Even I can sense it. Would you not know if he was dead?" Jaran asked.

Tashi thought about that a moment. Her bond with Sam was magical in nature, much like her bond with Phylassos. She would feel if the gryphon had died and so it was likely she would sense if something happened to Sam; she didn't sense anything of that sort.

"You are likely correct. I believe Sam is still alive."

"I concur," Vantana added. "That's how I'm keeping it together. I don't reckon the worm is trying to harm Sam. I think he wants to use him as some kind of bargaining chip."

"Perhaps," Jaran replied. "Or he's bait."

"A trap?" Vantana said.

"A possibility we must prepare for," Jaran responded. "Based on our last encounter, we may want to consider a different approach."

"Agreed. We're going to need an army," Doctor Vantana announced.

"An army of who exactly?" Tashi asked.

Vance smirked. "Bigfoot."

* * *

An hour later, Tashi was gazing down into a hidden valley at a village of six-foot-tall humanoid creatures with reddish brown fur.

"Those are not bigfoots," she observed.

"Technically, no. They're almas. Or almasty if you're talkin' about just one. They're a bigfoot-human hybrid unique to this region," Doctor Vantana explained.

These almas looked to be in the midst of a celebration. The village was filled with music and dancing and sporting events.

"What makes you think they will help us?" Jaran inquired.

"Just a hunch," Vantana told her.

Jaran led them to the valley floor, where a small group of almas immediately approached. They stopped a few feet from their unexpected guests and eyed them suspiciously. Then the taller one with violet eyes sniffed the air in one long inhalation that ended with a giant toothy grin. The almasty lunged forward and embraced Doctor Vantana. The doctor peered back to Tashi and Jaran, wincing from the hug.

"Having bigfoot blood has its advantages," he said in a strained voice. The other almas joined their counterpart and the doctor was now surrounded by the creatures and caught in a giant group hug. They heard a crack and Vantana's face went pale. "I think that was a rib."

When the almas finally released him, he collapsed to the ground. Tashi rushed to his side and put a hand on him, healing his rib as she helped him to his feet. "Thanks," he whispered. "Almas are ten times stronger than humans and very enthusiastic."

"Welcome home!" the violet-eyed almasty said, before adding, "You are family." The creature then looked to Jaran, "You are Ranger Jaran. It is good to see you. Who is your companion?"

"This is Tashi. She is a Guardian," Jaran explained.

Violet's eyes went wide. "A protector of the gryphon?"

"Yes," Tashi answered. The almasty let out a high-pitched noise that sounded as though it was rapidly rolling his tongue on the top of its mouth. He embraced Tashi and she felt the creature's strength, but easily endured it.

"You are most welcome here," Violet said as he separated from the Guardian. "Phylassos is family. He protects us so we may enjoy this gift of life."

"I have a favor to ask of you," Doctor Vantana told the creature.

"And it will be granted! But first come and join us," Violet replied, as he turned and headed toward the village.

The doctor looked to Tashi and Jaran, then nudged his head to follow.

Walking deeper into the almas village, Tashi saw it consisted of large yurts, clustered together in groups of five. She also noticed more evidence of just how strong the creatures were. Two almas children tossed a large boulder between them like it was a ball, while an adult almasty carried a fully grown tree, then snapped it in half with its bare hands.

"Their strength is impressive," Tashi told Vantana.

"It's why I hope they'll help us."

"Do they all live in this valley?" she asked.

"They all settled here after the gryphon's curse," Jaran explained. "Phylassos protects their valley from humans' prying eyes. You might conclude that they are frustrated by such confinement, but it's quite the opposite."

"So they are contained, like the yeti?" Tashi asked, referring to the big-foot-like creatures that made their home near Kustos and were the sworn enemy of the guardians.

"Yes, but unlike the yeti, this is not a punishment and they don't see it as such. There were creatures who enslaved and exploited them before Alexander's folly," Jaran revealed. They passed a large group of almas dancing and the ranger smiled. "This celebratory atmosphere reminds me of the Naadam festival."

"Naadam?" Tashi echoed.

Jaran nodded. "An ancient Mongolian celebration that features three games." The ranger gestured to different areas of the village that were the sites of three sporting events. "Horse racing, archery, and wrestling. The almas see these daily celebrations as a way for them to relax from the day's work and enjoy life with their family," Jaran explained. "They are a very gracious race."

As Tashi noticed multiple generations of almas laughing and smiling, her thoughts wandered back to Kustos. She wondered what her parents were doing and how the village was faring. Guardians didn't party like these creatures, but they did have fun at times. And they shared an extraordinary connection to each other—a connection Tashi suddenly felt the absence of.

The trio, led by the violet-eyed almasty, eventually reached the center of the village. The almasty addressed the crowd in a loud, booming voice.

"Dearest kin, we have guests to welcome," the almasty announced. "A relation from afar and his companions."

They were instantly swarmed by dozens of almas, who reached out to touch them, as if they never had visitors before.

"I rarely come to this place," Jaran mentioned to Tashi. "It is not often they have guests."

A burly almasty grabbed Doctor Vantana by both shoulders and declared, "You smell like family. Let's wrestle!" The almasty snatched up Vantana's hand and practically dragged him off. Tashi quickly followed.

"We actually haven't come to wrestle. We need help…" Vantana tried to tell the almasty, as he winced from the painful grip.

"Help after wrestle," the burly almasty said.

"I am not going to bring you back from the dead again," Tashi told the doctor, as she hurried after him. "They believe you are one of them. That you possess equal strength."

"I'm well aware of that, but wrestlin' is about more than just brute strength," the doctor contended. "Plus, if I don't accept the invite, it'll be considered rude. And we gotta get them on our side," the doctor added.

They reached the wrestling match area, which consisted of a large ring, encircled by logs. Doctor Vantana's would-be opponent was already in the center of the ring, waiting.

"I just have to avoid dying and make a decent show of it," he told her.

"I have already expressed my concerns," Tashi told him.

"Yeah, yeah," he waved her off. "Here goes." The doctor stepped into the ring and faced off against his opponent, who was grinning with excitement.

Unfortunately—or fortunately, depending on one's perspective—Doctor Vance Vantana didn't make it past the pre-match, goodwill handshake. The burly almasty inadvertently pulled the doctor's arm right out of its socket and nearly ripped it from his body. Vantana instantly passed out. Tashi moved in and snapped the arm back into place, then healed him of the pain—of which there was a significant amount—but he was still not entirely conscious. The crowd of almas went silent, likely confused by the doctor's sudden injury. Ranger Jaran flew to the center of the ring and tried to explain.

"You must excuse your brother. He is distracted by tragedy. His son is in great danger and his mind is not on games or celebration."

"His son?" Vantana's opponent asked. Jaran nodded. The violet-eyed almasty stepped forward.

"His family is in trouble?"

"Yes. Much trouble. His son was taken by the death worm," she revealed. There were whispers among the almas. "We have come here to seek your help to rescue him."

"His son is like our son," the violet-eyed almasty said. His assertion was met with nods and verbal affirmations. "Of course we will help save him. Almas always protects family."

Communicating with a creature who could only express herself in colors that were sent telepathically was understandably difficult. Sam had made his best effort to interpret the many colors the worm sent to him by deciphering the feelings they evoked when they were received. He had so far deduced that red equaled anger—that was an easy one—blue meant sadness and despondence, orange was warmth and a feeling of welcome, purple seemed to be frustration, green was friendship and tranquility, yellow was a sense of caution and concern, white appeared to communicate a lack of understanding or uncertainty, and black, well, Sam hadn't figured out what black meant. It flashed when Sam asked what the creature's goal was in bringing him there. Sam speculated that perhaps black was simply the worm's way of not saying anything or avoiding the question.

Sam had gotten good at sending colors back to the worm. He would concentrate on a color to trigger an emotional response in the worm that helped to further confirm Sam's color-to-emotion conclusions. Unfortunately, despite Sam's effort to translate and duplicate the worm's telepathic language, he was still stuck in the worm's lair. He was hoping he would be able to use his limited comprehension of this color-based communication to persuade the creature to return him to the surface, but it was much too complex of a message.

Exasperated by his lack of progress, Sam rummaged through the worm's collection of baby-related items and found a few crayons. He grabbed a page from one of the kid's books and returned to the worm in the center of the cave, where he then attempted to draw out his proposal. He drew himself as a stick figure, then followed with drawings of Vance, Tashi, and Ranger Jaran. But Sam was an awful artist and his pictures looked like a pumpkin-headed giant, an old woman with a cane, and some sort of giant bat with legs. The worm's flashes of white became increasingly more blinding.

Sam was abandoning his artistic attempt when he noticed dozens of hairy humanoid creatures pouring into the cave from one of the holes.

The worm was instantly alerted to their presence and spun around. She stretched and rose up to her full height. The hairy creatures formed a line at the end of the cave and didn't advance. They were joined by Ranger Jaran, who flew in from the hole, carrying Vance and Tashi. She put her two passengers down and landed beside them.

"Get away from that thing, Sam!" Vance shouted. Sam could sense the worm growing angry, her mind colors increasingly tinting toward red. Sam quickly stepped between the worm and the others.

"Wait!" Sam demanded. "She doesn't mean us any harm. She needs our help."

"She?" Jaran repeated.

"Yes, Ranger. Mongo should probably be Monga."

"It's a girl?" Vance asked.

Sam nodded. "A mom. That silver case Boone Walker had? Maybe it didn't have footage of the death worm in it. Maybe it had her baby. That's why she's so upset."

"We have never known of the death worm to have offspring," Jaran told them. "She is centuries old, but has never birthed a child."

"That explains the worm's aggressive behavior," Tashi said. "She is trying to protect her young."

"Exactly...and we can help," Sam told them. "We just have to tell the worm what we want to do."

"And how do you reckon we do that?" Vance inquired.

"First off, I think you should all back up, so she doesn't feel threatened," Sam suggested.

"All right, but we're storming in at the first sign of trouble." Vance motioned to the almas to step back towards the cave wall, as he, Tashi, and Jaran did the same.

Once they retreated to a less intimidating distance, Sam touched the worm on her tail and sent flashes of green and orange to communicate warmth and friendship. The worm calmed herself and lowered her body. She nudged her head toward the group and sent Sam a flash of orange.

"She's sending a message of welcome," Sam explained. The worm screeched and Sam looked up to her. The creature nudged her head toward the group once more, then screeched again. Sam looked to the worm, then the group—she appeared to be gesturing toward Jaran. The color went from orange to black in Sam's head, as if she didn't know what to say or wanted to say it to the ranger. "I think she wants to talk to you, Ranger Jaran," Sam told her.

"I may be able to communicate more complex messages," she said, before stepping forward cautiously. The worm didn't flinch, but the color she was sending to Sam changed from black to blue. A deep blue that swirled with purple. Sadness and frustration...and then Sam noticed there were ripples of energy passing over the worm's skin, from her tail to her head.

"What is it? What are you doing?" Sam whispered to the creature. She responded with blackness. Sam instantly felt a sense of dread, but it was too late to do anything.

The Mongolian death worm released a massive burst of energy that hit the unsuspecting ranger in her chest and sent her body flying backward. She slammed into the cave wall and crumpled to the ground. The worm recoiled then spit several wads of acid against the opposite wall of the cave. The rock dissolved and the worm sprung from her spot and escaped through the newly formed hole.

A horrified Sam raced to Jaran, as did Vance and Tashi. She was badly injured and barely conscious. She grabbed Sam's arm.

"The blast weakened my magic...the barrier has fallen...the worm is free." Her voice cracked with panic and there was terror in her eyes.

Chapter 12
COMPROMISED

DEPARTMENT OF MYTHICAL WILDLIFE

WASHINGTON, D.C.

REQUEST FOR PROPOSAL (RFP) NO. 2

CLASSIFIED VAULT PROJECT

The Department of Mythical Wildlife (DMW) is seeking proposals for professional services required for a DMW construction project. The DMW is seeking to hire qualified engineers to construct a vault, which will be located beneath the DMW offices within the Main Interior building at 1849 C Street, NW Washington, D.C., 20240. The successful proposer(s) shall perform all services required under any contract resulting from this request for proposal (RFP) in a satisfactory and proper manner, as determined by Phylassos, in accordance with the design standards set forth by the gryphon.

SCOPE OF SERVICES

The DMW has elected to construct a chamber beneath the DMW offices for the purposes of storing classified materials. This RFP seeks to identify a qualified group of engineers to assist the DMW with the performance of these referenced professional services. Due to the nature of the proposed facility and the mission of the DMW, all services must be completed in secret and all documentation, architectural blueprints, and mechanical specifications shall remain classified. Any divulgence of the existence of this project to unauthorized parties will be considered a gross violation of the Phylassos Accords, punishable by death for human or return to Gaia for mythical creature.

The scope of work will include, but is not necessarily limited to, the following services:

1. The construction of a 54 x 68 cubit chamber.
2. The depth of said chamber shall measure 50 cubits.
3. The chamber will be carved out of existing bedrock.
4. Walls of the chamber, including floor and ceiling, will be constructed out of orichalcum at a thickness of 4 cubits.
5. Preliminary design plan shown below, adapted from existing Gutzon Borglum plan intended for Mt. Rushmore (repurposed at Phylassos's request).
6. Plans will call for a spiral staircase of marble that will lead up to the vault entrance, which will be constructed in the ceiling and remain the only opening to the chamber.
7. Entrance door to be circular, cast in solid orichalcum, and hinged.
8. Two anteroom living quarters shall be required and separated from the main chamber.

9. A cage constructed of orichalcum with dimensions of 7 x 7 x 7 cubits. Ceiling and floor to be solid orichalcum. Orichalcum bars on remaining four sides to be placed 10 cm apart. Location within vault TBD.

In his many years of working for the Department of Mythical Wildlife, Bob Ferguson had never brought visitors inside the Department of the Interior building, never mind the DMW offices. To allow unsanctioned humans or mythical creatures into headquarters would be considered a massive breach of security and highly illegal in the eyes of the gryphon. Yet here Bob was, escorting two humans who were not only unsanctioned but had clearly nefarious intentions. Unfortunately, Bob didn't believe he had a choice. He knew there was little he could do to stop Boone Walker from killing the worm while at Roosevelt Park, but inside the DMW might prove a different story. There were tricks hiding up Bob's sleeves. But first he needed to get them on his own turf, and that meant getting them past Department of the Interior security.

Luckily, Bob was able to whisk them through without any hiccups, even avoiding having Boone's silver case inspected. He did this by leaning heavily on his "Special Projects" classification. Though some might assume that the Department of Mythical Wildlife operated under the auspices of the Department of the Interior's Office of Law Enforcement and Security (OLES), it was actually categorized within the "Special Projects" division and was given a wide latitude.

Many DOI employees—along with those interested in this aspect of government—assumed the "Special Projects" division monitored and supported classified department business. Of course, they would never have imagined that this business involved mythical creatures. Instead, it was believed that there were activities happening within certain national parks that might require high security clearance. One such example could be found in Catoctin Mountain Park, a national park located in northern Maryland. The park was the site of Camp David, the famed presidential retreat, which had been used by American presidents since 1942. Any park business related to this secret retreat would require security clearances and thus be relegated to a special division in the Department of the Interior.

Ironically, the park many believed Bob was associated with was also the home of the snallygaster. At Phylassos's urging, the snallygasters had agreed to keep the peace with the dwayyo and dedicated themselves to the guarding of the president's secret compound, among other undisclosed assignments. The dwayyo kept their distance from their enemies, as just being within a few yards of each other would ignite a battle. DMW scientists had yet to find a way to reverse this instinctual behavior.

Once through security, Bob led his unscrupulous companions across the checkerboard-patterned tile and over the bronze Department of the Interior seal that lay in the center of the lobby floor. It featured the Interior Department's iconic buffalo symbol.

"If old Vancey could see me now," Boone remarked with a smirk.

"Ranger Vance Vantana?" Bob inquired.

Boone nodded, "Yup."

"Are you talking about Ranger Vance Vantana?" Bob asked again.

Boone narrowed his eyes suspiciously. "I just said I was. What are you getting at?"

"Nothing. I didn't hear you the first time," Bob replied, then continued toward the elevators.

Truth was, Bob had heard Boone just fine, but when Boone spoke Vance's name, the DMW official realized he had an opportunity. His DMW badge was in his pocket and he had stealthily slipped his hand into the pocket to activate the device. By saying Vance's full name aloud, the badge would then route any message directly to the ranger. Of course, it wasn't like Bob could blurt out "help" in this situation. Luckily, the badges were able to transmit more than just voice. Bob methodically—and quietly—tapped out a message via the device in Morse code. He had learned Morse back in the early days of the DMW as a way of transmitting messages to DMW rangers stationed at distant outposts. The code consisted of dots and dashes that corresponded to the alphabet and could be communicated through audible flights.

```
DMW CORRESPONDENCE
TO: RANGER VANCE VANTANA
SENDING PARTY: BOB FERGUSON
DATE/TIME FILED: ███████████
```

```
-.. -- .-- / -.-. --- -- .--. .-. --- -- .. ...
. -.. .-.-.- / ...- .- ..- .-.. - / .. -. / -..
.- -. --. . .-. .-.-.-
```

When they reached the elevator, Boone stood toward the back of the car with the silver case gripped firmly in hand.

"Come on, Ferguson, I ain't got all day. And neither does this little fella," Boone said, as he tapped the case.

Bob sighed, then stood in front of the elevator control panel to obscure the humans' view. He placed a key into the keyhole—the one the elevator repairmen used to manually control the elevator. He turned the key to the left and pressed out the access code using the floor buttons. The doors closed and the elevator began to descend.

The floor indicator above the doors froze at "B" for basement, but the car kept descending for a few more moments. When it finally halted, the doors opened to reveal a long, narrow corridor, which ended at an office door—the only door on this sub-basement level. Bob stepped out and the others followed.

"A secret floor?" Cynthia Salazar asked, as she eyed her surroundings.

"There's a hidden floor between the fifth and sixth levels, as well," Boone noted. "But this one's not on the original blueprints, that's for certain."

They finally reached the unmarked DMW office door and Bob hesitated. He knew this situation was snowballing. This was historic territory—the moments that followed could change the world forever and likely not in a positive way. Normally, no creature's life would be worth exposing the mythical world, but Bob knew the danger posed by the Mongolian death worm. If the creature's only child was killed by a human, who was driven to do so by an emissary of the gryphon, they were all in big trouble. Bob was processing the weight of this moment when Boone nudged him.

"Let's go, pal. No stalling and no tricks."

Bob grabbed hold of the ornate buffalo-adorned doorknob and turned it. The door unlocked and creaked open, allowing the trio to step into a short hallway that opened up into a larger office. Boone pushed Bob aside to move deeper into the room. He peered around and became instantly agitated.

"I said no tricks!" he repeated with vehemence. "Don't toy with me, Bobby. I've got no patience for any more of your lies."

"What are you talking about?" Bob asked, quizzically.

"Take me to the DMW offices."

"This is the DMW office," Bob assured him. Cynthia had now entered the main office area and was eyeing her surroundings.

"This place looks like it hasn't been touched since the nineteen forties," she observed.

"It's all original," Bob touted. "I keep it in tiptop shape."

Bob prided himself in retaining the original furnishings and refused any entreaty to renovate. For one, it would require bringing in workers with special clearance and two, Bob just enjoyed the environment the way it was and had always been. Like wolves, dwayyos had den-like instincts, and this office had become his work den during his tenure at the DMW. He was comfortable in it and safe. It contained everything he needed to be an effective administrator for the DMW. Of course, he wasn't the only DMW employee who wasn't a ranger in the field. The department employed many scientists and researchers who spent their time studying mythical creatures and understanding their behavior, as well as developing tools to help rangers perform their duties to the best of their abilities. But the main research and development division of the DMW was not situated in the basement, rather it had been relocated to the floor between the fifth and sixth floors of the DOI building. This "hidden" floor was long thought to be reserved for mechanical equipment, and that was partly true—and made for a solid cover story, but it was also home to the DMW lab—the "eggheads," as Doctor Vantana liked to call them. There was one other room in the basement DMW office, and Bob was hoping he wouldn't need to reveal it just yet.

"Where's the observatory?" Boone Walker asked. So much for that secret, Bob thought to himself.

The dwayyo had one last chance to turn things around: hit the Phylassos panic button.

"I just have to unlock it—the key is in my drawer," Bob explained, as he moved towards the desk.

"Don't take another step, Bobby," Boone told him, his hand on the briefcase button. "No way you would be that easy to convince." Boone turned to Cynthia, "He's probably got some kind of button back there to call in the cavalry. Ain't that right, Bobby?" Ferguson didn't answer and confirmed Boone's hunch. "No more games. Show us the observatory."

Ferguson sighed. Things were about to get exceedingly dangerous.

Sam London was still in a daze of shock, guilt, and immeasurable regret when the almas carried him back to the surface. The bigfoot-like creatures had interlocked their long, hairy arms and passed him back up the tunnel, along with Vance, Tashi, and a weakened, barely conscious Jaran. The worm's attack on the kinnara was so devastating that Tashi couldn't completely heal the creature in the cave without rendering herself incapacitated. And Sam never saw any of it coming. He was the worm's bait. The creature used him to lure Jaran in so she could strike and bring down the barrier. Sam understood the worm's motivation, but he never expected her to attack Sam's friend. He felt foolish for trusting a Mongolian death worm—just the thought of it now sounded absurd.

As Sam planted his feet on land once again, he reflexively shielded his eyes from the blazing sun—it seemed a thousand times brighter than what he remembered. The almas laid Jaran on the ground and backed away.

"I'm sorry," Sam told her, as he kneeled down beside the creature. "I didn't know...I thought I could tell what—"

"It is not your fault," Jaran interrupted, weakly waving her hand. "This is all my doing. I am her caretaker—and the caretaker of all creatures in the park. I should have known the worm was protecting her offspring. That explains her erratic behavior. I failed to protect that child. A once-in-a-millennia miracle it must be. Now I fear that my failure will be catastrophic to the world."

Tashi moved to Jaran's side, placing her hands on her.

"Are you certain it will not weaken you further?" the ranger asked.

"I am re-energized," Tashi assured her.

Jaran's body strengthened but Sam could see that recent events had taken a toll on her heart and mind. She stood up and sighed, then looked to the almas gathered nearby.

"I thank you for your help," she told the creatures, before turning to Vance. "We must alert Phylassos to the breach. The worm's electromagnetic interference should have subsided by now. I only hope he can find the creature before it's too late."

"Ranger Vance Vantana," a voice called out.

Sam immediately looked to Vance, who was pulling his DMW badge from his pocket. The device was now chirping out a series of short and long beeps.

"It's working!" Sam exclaimed. But Vance just held the badge in his hand and didn't bring it to his mouth to speak. "Aren't you going to answer it?"

"It's not that kind of message," Vance explained. "This is a one-way deal."

"It's just a bunch of beeps," Sam said.

"Not just any bunch of beeps. It's code. Morse code," Vance revealed.

"What is the message?" Tashi asked.

"That we may already be too late," Vance said, as he looked to Jaran. "The DMW has been compromised. We need to get to D.C., ASAP."

"Compromised. By who?" Sam wondered.

"I reckon Boone has something to do with it," Vance replied.

"Can the creature sense the whereabouts of her child?" Tashi asked Jaran.

"Possibly," Jaran answered. "She has always been the only one of her kind. The creature is mysterious."

"If Boone has the baby and he's in D.C., then—" Sam began to say.

"Then we'll be dealing with a massive exposure," Vance interjected.

"That is not all you will be dealing with," Jaran said.

"What do you mean?" Vance asked.

"Why did Boone choose to steal the worm's offspring?" she posited, as if working out the answer in her head. "He had help, we know this. So why the worm?"

"Because she's visible without a serum?" Sam suggested.

"They could have exposed a mythical sea creature if that was the goal," Tashi concluded. Sam had to agree—that would have been much easier. "They must have had an objective beyond simply exposing the secret," she added.

"Like attack the Capitol, or hurt the President?" Sam speculated.

"No, I don't believe so," Jaran said, then shifted her eyes to Vance. "Doctor Vantana, do you know of the Vault of Mysteries?"

"I've heard of it," Vance said. "Why?"

"There is a reason that Phylassos had me create a barrier that would confine the worm to this place," Jaran revealed.

"I thought it was because she was dangerous," Sam surmised.

"Many creatures are dangerous," the ranger countered. "But the worm represented a very special kind of danger."

"You mean..." Vance began, seeming to have made a shocking deduction. Jaran nodded.

"The Mongolian death worm is the only creature on Earth who can breach the walls of the vault. And if she did so—"

"We're talkin' global Armageddon," Vance interjected.

"Why?" Sam asked, suddenly unnerved. Global Armageddon sounded pretty bad. "What's in the vault that's so awful?"

"I don't really know for certain, to be honest," Vance replied. "It's above my pay grade. But I have heard stories about it...stories I can't confirm."

"What do these stories tell you?" Tashi inquired.

"That the Vault of Mysteries is sealed and impenetrable for a reason," Vance explained. "That it contains some of the most powerful mythical objects ever created. Phylassos had to hide them. Store them somewhere they could not be reached."

"To protect humankind?" Sam wondered.

"To protect humankind, mythical kind, and Phylassos himself," Jaran said. Vance's eyes darted over to the ranger with concern; she met his gaze. "Now you understand the gravity of our situation. These events have placed the gryphon in extraordinary danger."

"Like I said, we need to get to D.C. And right quick."

"How?" Sam asked. "Is there another dvergen station close by?"

"It is not close, but it may be our only option," Jaran reported.

"Family?" An almasty called out. They all turned to the creature, who was gathered with his brethren a few yards away. He pointed toward the horizon with a hairy finger. "There is a storm coming. We best take shelter. The children first."

Sam and the others looked to the distant sky to see what had the almasty so concerned. At first, Sam assumed the almasty was referring to a dust storm, as those were a frequent occurrences for this part of the world, but Sam didn't spot any clouds of sand; rather, he spied storm clouds gathering in the distance. Sam had never seen clouds roll in that quickly before, nor had he seen ones quite as dark. In just a few seconds, nearly all of the daylight had been snuffed out, leaving only an eerie blue glow across the landscape.

"There is a force that does not want us to leave this place," Jaran reported.

"Mother nature?" Sam responded. Jaran shook her head. Vance sniffed the air and peered upward.

"Ain't nothing natural about that," his dad said.

There was a sudden, deafening clap of thunder that shook the ground. The almas took defensive positions, as if anticipating an attack. *From what?* Sam wondered. *The rain?*

"Everyone, to the cabin!" Vance shouted, as he scooped Sam up in an arm and made a break for the ranger's house. He was practically dragging Sam across the ground in his haste.

"I can run!" Sam told him and wriggled from his father's grip, then, beelined for the cabin. Halfway there and Sam still didn't feel any drops or see any massive tornados heading their way. He looked back toward the looming clouds and saw a mass of darkness emanating from the sky. It appeared to be showering, but it wasn't water droplets, it was a wave of squiggly lines.

Odd, Sam thought. And then Vance lunged at him with his knife in hand. "What are you—" Before Sam could complete the question, he was splattered with a dark blue liquid. Vance had sliced apart a creature of some kind. Sam looked down to see it was a long black snake with a distinct yellow stripe. "What the heck is that?!" He screamed in horror.

"Sky serpents!" Jaran yelled. "Don't let them wrap themselves around you!"

Sam spotted a few of the almas being dragged to the ground, as multiple sky serpents wrapped themselves around an arm or a leg, slowing them down enough for other serpents to join the attack. Fortunately, Tashi was hammering the little monsters with bolts of Gaia's energy, which caused them to stiffen and release their victims. Sam finally reached the cabin and took cover under the porch overhang.

The distance between the hole that led to the worm's lair and the cabin wasn't far, but it was far enough to allow the sky serpents to do their worst. The storm of snakes was not letting up; in fact, it seemed to be growing heavier by the second. If things weren't bad enough, Sam noticed that these creatures posed more of a threat than constricting their enemies—they could spit fire, too! Soon, more of the snakes were erupting with bursts of flame from their fanged mouths, like miniature dragons. Sam watched as an almasty struggled with several of the snakes, attempting to keep them from constricting his leg, but as he tried to pull them off they hissed fire, singing the hair on the almasty's hands. Luckily, another almasty saw his compatriot's battle and came to the rescue, yanking the snakes from his body and pulling them apart, blue-black blood sprayed outward.

Sam's hand went reflexively up to his face—he realized he still had the snake blood on it. Grossed out, Sam used his sleeve to wipe away the remnants. He noticed several of the serpents on the ground near the cabin—they weren't injured, but suddenly disappeared, as if absorbed by the Earth...

"They die when they hit the ground!" he shouted to the others. "They're being returned to Gaia. It's a suicide mission!"

His friends heard him and began tossing the creatures to the ground. Vance had been slashing away at the serpents with his knife, but was now simply helping to cut them from some of the almas who were struggling. Tashi began firing upward at the serpents as they fell from the clouds—that paralyzed the snakes and sent them plummeting to their deaths. Jaran had taken to the sky and was collecting the squirming monsters in fistfuls, then propelling them to the ground.

"Take shelter!" Vance ordered, as they retreated towards Sam's position. Sam opened the cabin door and Vance, Tashi, and Jaran rushed inside.

"Come on!" Sam said, as he waved the almas in, but the creatures stopped on the porch—a few began climbing up the side of the house to swat away the deluge of serpents.

"Go on," an almasty told him. "We will keep them from you."

Once inside, Jaran addressed Vance in an anxious tone.

"This storm will not subside long enough to get all of you to the station."

"There has to be a way," Vance contended. "I can call for help. There are other rangers in the DMW who could get there in time."

"We've already run out of time," Jaran countered. "And no other rangers can face the worm. Sam can speak to her, the Guardian can protect the vault."

"And you can sing to her," Vance said. "But the problem is, getting us all there."

"I am not coming," Jaran told him. "But I will get you there."

Jaran pointed her open palm toward the floor near the rear wall of the cabin. A trickle of blue glimmering light began to emanate from her hand. It reminded Sam of the Gateway to Gaia that he saw Phylassos and Marzanna create in Alaska. But Vance told him only two powerful magical creatures could open one.

"You can't do that by yourself," Vance said. "Even Phylassos can't manage it."

"It can be done, but with a heavy sacrifice," she explained.

"You will be returned to Gaia," Tashi stated, matter-of-factly.

Jaran nodded. "I shall return from whence I came." Her words echoed those of the Maiden Council when they rendered Ettie's verdict.

"There has to be another way!" Sam exclaimed.

"There is too much at stake. We cannot look back," the ranger told him, and she gently touched his face with her other hand. "You have a good heart, Sam London. The worm listened to you before, she will listen again." Jaran then directed both of her hands to the floor and the trickle of blue became two steady streams. She made a slow arcing motion with her arms, forming a small gateway. Sam could immediately tell that expending this much magic was having an impact on Jaran. She appeared to be phasing in and out of existence—her body slowly vanishing right before Sam's eyes. Jaran's entire life force was being poured into opening the portal.

There was a sudden shattering of windows, as the serpents began crashing themselves into the glass, joined by a pounding on the roof. The creatures were now breaking through to the floor above.

"I can't hold it," Jaran said weakly. "Go!" she ordered, her body now barely visible.

"Come on!" Vance shouted as he grabbed Sam's arm and led him through the gate. Tashi followed right behind.

As soon as they passed through the gateway, Sam peered back and got one last look at Ranger Jaran. The ghostly figure met his gaze and smiled.

Then she faded out of existence and the gate disappeared.

Chapter 13

VAULT OF MYSTERIES

CLASSIFICATION 470 (PERSONNEL RECORDS)

LARES FABULOSUS CREATURAE

ACTIVATION DATE: ████████

The lares were the Guardian deities of ancient Rome who protected many areas habited by humankind until the curse.

The lares were often depicted as jovial, happy sorts—not unlike nymphs—who were relied upon by Roman citizens to aid in the various aspects of their lives and communities. As such, there were lares of all types, including those who protect sailors (lares permarini) and ones who safeguarded farms (lares rurales).

Although considered deities, they were in reality magical beings who took pride in aiding the weak and the vulnerable. The beings often operated within an established physical boundary, but their purview could also be restricted to a fixed purpose or objective. In other words, the lares's magic could only be used for their distinct purpose or within the confines of their boundaries.

Post Alexander's folly, the lares chose to integrate into human society and took on roles in the areas of human life that best fit their protective nature. There are many police officers, soldiers, nurses, and other similarly employed humans who are descendants of those original lares. A special group of lares were recruited by Phylassos at the founding of the DMW and given the purpose of helping the department fulfill its mission. They were known as the lares fabulosus creaturae and they were stationed in the DMW headquarters in Washington, D.C., where they oversaw all interactions between human and creature, as well as creature and creature.

The lares fabulosus creaturae accomplished their mission via magically enhanced technology in the DMW observatory. The observatory featured monitoring stations that were specially designed to enable the lares to keep a watchful eye on the goings-on at the various parks within the United States National Park system. The lares's eyesight allowed them to see at a microscopic level, an ability that was utilized in the creation of the DMW's unique surveillance system.

The strange, otherworldly DMW observatory was unlike any place Cynthia Salazar had ever been. Up until the moment Cynthia found herself in the massive, domed room, she had remained skeptical of Boone's wild assertions. For one, Boone wasn't exactly a pillar of reputability. He was ethically-challenged at best, vengeful and unscrupulous at worst. Sure, she had seen that creepy worm in Boone's silver case, but maybe that was some bizarre government experiment gone awry. Yet now she was in the proverbial belly of the mythical beast and all remaining shreds of doubt were torn away. This was real. This was historic. And boy, was it scary.

So excited at the once-in-a-lifetime prospect of exposing a world-changing secret, Cynthia had not anticipated another feeling that was stifling her enthusiasm: apprehension. This agency had been established for a reason and what if that reason was to protect humanity by keeping them in the dark about these creatures. Could their intentions be noble enough to warrant the hiding? Cynthia didn't love the idea of secrets remaining secret, but she was growing concerned that exposing this particular secret would put lives in danger. Cynthia had always weighed the pros and cons of any investigative report that would uncover previously unknown information, but rarely did her work involve the potential of physical harm coming to humans or creatures. This was uncharted territory in more ways than one. The irony of the situation was not lost on Cynthia. For a person who lived for secrets, she had now stumbled upon one so big, she was fearful of exposing it.

Boone Walker had already mentioned in passing how three of his crew members were killed trying to steal the baby worm and, based on Ferguson's reaction, this development did not bode well for anyone. Cynthia believed in being a force for good, but the ethical deviations taken by Boone—to which Cynthia was now an accessory—had left the question of good and bad a touch vague. She was admittedly more reckless with people's secrets back in her youth, but with experience came an understanding of personal responsibility in her reporting. She had tried to limit her targets to those who deserved to be exposed for their corrupt or devious activities. She wasn't sure this "Department of Mythical Wildlife" fit that bill. There was also that odd aside from Boone, prior to their entry into the Department of the Interior building. He pulled Cynthia close—an aggressive move the reporter did not appreciate—and whispered to her with urgency.

"If anything happens to me, the story doesn't have to die here," Boone told her. "Get yourself to Dry Tortugas National Park. We have powerful allies in this fight."

"What do you mean 'if anything happens' to you?" Cynthia asked anxiously. "What would happen?"

"I don't know, but we need to be prepared for all possible outcomes," Boone said. "Just head there. With the weapon or without."

"Weapon?" Cynthia quickly followed. "What weapon?" This was the first she was hearing of a "weapon," and it only amplified her inner ethical struggle.

"You have to trust me, Cynthia," Boone said firmly.

"Trust you?" Cynthia replied, incredulously. Boone hadn't earned her trust just yet, especially with the secrets he was keeping. "I don't know if I—" she stammered, but Boone gripped her tighter and his whisper turned threatening in tone.

"We cast our lots together. Don't you ever forget that," Boone reminded her. "There's no turning tail and running now. I've lived my whole life since I was thirteen for this moment and nothing—*nothing*—is going to stop me from getting the truth out. You, Cynthia Salazar, are my insurance policy."

Boone Walker's words now echoed in Cynthia's head as she stood in the DMW Observatory. Between his veiled threats and the extraordinary sight of this room, for the first time in her professional life, Cynthia was feeling as if she might be in over her head. She tried to find some small sense of peace by allowing her reporter instincts to kick in. Her eyes immediately surveyed her surroundings, but she couldn't quite comprehend what she was seeing. It was like stepping into the future and the past at the same time. The space was cavernous and circular, and resembled a science fiction version of ancient Greek architecture. It appeared to be constructed of pure white marble, except for one area of wall that was exposed rock. The room reached up several dozen feet to a domed ceiling. There was a soft, white light that was evenly bright across the entire space, but Cynthia could not determine the source.

Cynthia felt eyes on her and gasped when she saw approximately thirty or forty young men and women staring at her and Boone. They were dressed in light beige lab coats with forest green pants. The coats sported patches that looked—from a distance—to be similar to the Department of the Interior logo. They were obviously workers with the DMW, Cynthia concluded, and their work stations were unique, to say the least. Each one of these workers stood at their own circular station that was made up of marble, akin to the columns of Greek and Roman antiquity—just much smaller. Atop each column was a miniature park. It sounded like a strange thing to say, but Cynthia couldn't find a better way to describe these displays. These were not holograms—they were miniature recreations of national parks. She was too far away to be certain but she could have sworn she noticed distinct landmarks, including El Capitan in a mini Yosemite National Park and the soaring redwoods of Redwood National Park, as well as several others. But the oddest thing she observed was that they all seemed to be real. The miniature representations weren't intricately detailed models; they were living, breathing reproductions done on a Lilliputian scale. She noticed wind blowing through the trees and flocks of birds soaring above.

"Mister Ferguson, who are these humans and what are they doing in my observatory?"

The voice came from a man who was standing on the far side of the room. He was slightly older than the other workers and similarly dressed, but his collar sported gold stars. He stood with his hands clasped behind his back in front of the only area of wall that wasn't white. It was a cut-out that exposed the underlying bedrock, but that wasn't all. It was part cave painting, part topographical land survey, and—like the miniature parks—it also appeared to be alive. It included the entire continental United States, as well as Alaska, Hawaii, and U.S. territories in both the Atlantic and Pacific oceans.

"Well, sir, I—" Ferguson started to answer the man, but Boone cut him off.

"Let me handle this, Bobby," Boone chided. "I'm guessin' you're the boss man in this observatory." The man eyed him, without answering. "Well, boss, I have a unique authorization to be here and it's right in this case."

"He's stolen the death worm's child," Ferguson told the supervisor.

"And you've let him bring it here?!" the supervisor replied incredulously.

"In his defense, he didn't have a choice. Either he did what I told him or this baby goes boom," Boone said, gesturing to his case. The supervisor began walking toward them.

"I don't know who you are, but you clearly have no idea what you have done."

"On the contrary, I know exactly what I'm doing."

"The Mongolian death worm will be able to track its offspring and it will attempt to retrieve it," the supervisor explained in a condescending manner. Boone just grinned.

"I'm counting on it, chief."

The supervisor narrowed his eyes, then looked to one of his workers.

"Alert the Mongolian Ministry. Ranger Jaran must be made aware that the creature will breach the barrier."

The worker stepped over to a part of the wall that displayed over a hundred symbols, which Cynthia determined represented various government agencies around the world. She spotted the United Kingdom symbol, which denoted the Agency for the Welfare of Mythical Beasts. She had suspected this secret was global, but this wall confirmed it. Beneath each symbol was a telephone handset on a switchhook, ostensibly put there for immediate, direct communication with foreign governments. There were also old teletype machines—automatic typewriters that could send and receive information like a telegraph. The worker was reaching for the Mongolian phone when Boone bellowed.

"Hold it—no one is doing anything without my permission, you got that?" Boone eyed the supervisor. "Don't force me to make this situation worse than it's about to become." The supervisor seemed skeptical of Boone's threat, but Ferguson snuck his colleague an affirming nod. Boone's attention turned to the massive seal on the floor of the observatory. It was in the center of the room, approximately fifteen feet in diameter, and made out of a gleaming reddish gold metal that Cynthia didn't recognize.

But most importantly, Cynthia finally laid eyes on the symbol of the Department of Mythical Wildlife and it featured a gryphon! The reporter felt a sense of vindication amid the oddness of this day. After all, Cynthia Salazar's journey began with Gladys Hartwicke's claim that she saw a gryphon in Death Valley and now it appeared she had been telling the truth.

"I'm guessin the vault is beneath this seal?" Boone said with an eye to the supervisor. The supervisor remained stone-faced and Boone smirked knowingly. "Now we wait."

"I assume you have taken the proper precautions, Mister Ferguson," the supervisor said.

"If you're referring to him hitting that button back in the office, that'd be a 'no,'" Boone informed him. The supervisor looked to Ferguson with a dead stare.

"Collateral damage may be unavoidable at this point. The cost is too great," the supervisor stated soberly. "You have no choice." Ferguson nodded, understanding. Boone, who was now standing a few yards from Ferguson and Cynthia, was sensing that this interaction was problematic.

"Need I remind y'all that I can—" He didn't have a chance to finish his thought. Bob Ferguson leapt like a cat across the distance. Cynthia was stunned by the superhuman speed and agility of the mild-mannered office worker. He tackled Boone and growled, attempting to wrestle the case from him. "If you do this, you will trigger its destruction," Boone struggled to say. Ferguson didn't seem to mind and was on the verge of overpowering Boone when the entire observatory began to rumble. It was a sudden, violent earthquake that sent the workers staggering. Cynthia lost her balance and lunged forward to grab onto one of the park pedestals. Alarms began to sound and lights flickered on the map. Washington, D.C., was lit up like a Christmas tree.

The seal cracked as a rupture zigzagged across its face. Several more ruptures branched out from the main fracture. The rumbling grew in intensity and the seal exploded into shards. Chunks of marble and fragments of the solid metal seal sprayed outward like shrapnel. Boone and Ferguson were thrown in opposite directions, while Cynthia tumbled forward and quickly found herself sliding towards the collapsing center of the floor. The monster that had emerged was a horrifying giant worm—the baby's mother, no doubt. Cynthia screamed in terror as she slid to what she presumed would be her death.

Sam London had no time to mourn for the fallen ranger and friend; as soon as the Gate of Gaia closed the ground beneath Sam began to shake. Tashi had already placed a healing hand on him so he wouldn't lose his lunch, but all the shaking wasn't helping. Sam looked to Vance, who was surveying the scene.

"Where are we?" Sam asked.

"We're in the DMW Observatory," he replied. "It's the agency's command center."

Sam noticed dozens of people in this circular room—they were all scrambling as the shaking increased. He spotted Boone at the center wrestling a half-wolf man. It was total chaos...and then it went from chaotic to horrific. The Mongolian death worm burst through the floor and the room began to cave in, revealing a structure beneath them.

"Ducem lares," Vance called out to a man standing near a giant map that was carved into the wall.

"Doctor Vantana, we could use your assistance," he said before turning to the other workers. "Lares, form a perimeter for containment!" The workers and their leader quickly gathered in a circular formation around the hole. Sam, Vance, and Tashi were positioned just within the boundary. The lares joined hands and put their heads down. A blue wave of energy shimmered up from the floor, over their bodies, and rose above their heads, closing in a dome.

"What is that?" Sam asked.

"It's like the barrier Jaran created for the worm," Vance explained. "Can you two try and communicate with that thing? I'm going to find Boone."

Sam and Tashi advanced toward the hole, the edges were a twisted mass of metal and rock. Sam spotted a woman sliding down a portion of collapsed floor and raced forward to grab her hand. He caught it and, fortunately, Tashi caught him before he was also dragged down. They helped the woman back to the edge. Sam instantly recognized her.

"You're that reporter," Sam said.

"You're Sam London," she responded in surprise.

"Sam!" Tashi called, then gestured to the worm, who had found Boone and was prepared to finish him. "Do you need to touch the worm to project to her?" she asked.

Sam shook his head. "I don't think so."

He closed his eyes and could immediately sense the worm's fury. Sam was seeing all red and tried to counter it with green.

"Think green!" he called out to Tashi.

A few moments of concentration and Sam began to see the red slightly fade. He also wasn't hearing the worm shriek or the sounds of more of the floor collapsing.

"It's working!" Sam heard Vance yell.

Sam opened his eyes and the worm had turned toward him. Sam sensed a flash of green, an acknowledgement of friendship and warm feelings, but that was all. The red returned and Sam instantly felt the anger of the worm. She turned back to her target, but Boone had disappeared. She reared up and shrieked, sending a blast of energy toward the barrier, but the lares's magic simply absorbed the hit. Sam spotted Vance pulling the half-wolf man from beneath the debris. He rushed over, with Tashi and Cynthia following.

"She won't listen anymore," Sam reported.

"Where did Boone go?" Vance asked.

"He's in the vault," the wolf creature told them in a strained voice. "He's got her baby in the case and it's rigged to explode."

"Where's the Phylassos button, Bob?" Vance asked. Bob? Sam realized that the half-wolf man was Bob Ferguson of the DMW home office.

"It's at my desk. In my office. I tried, but..." Bob revealed, feeling guilty.

"Well, we can't get through that barrier until this mess is contained. The lares have a duty to the DMW that will take precedence over us contacting back-up," Vance explained.

"How on Earth are you going to contain this?" Cynthia asked. "You're just one guy with a couple of kids."

"We've handled bigger crises than this," the ranger told her, then turned back to Ferguson. "What does Boone want from the vault?"

"I don't know," Bob replied.

"He mentioned something about a weapon to me," Cynthia interjected. "But that was it."

Vance nodded. "What kind of weapons are down there?" he asked Ferguson.

"I don't have a list of objects held in the Vault of Mysteries," the DMW official explained. "But rest assured, if there are weapons kept in there, they're in there for good reason."

"I reckoned as much," Vance responded. "Are they protected in any way?"

"There is a caretaker from what I've heard and there is a failsafe."

"What do you mean 'failsafe?'" Vance asked.

"Defensive measures that are triggered if the vault is breached," Ferguson replied.

"What kind of defensive measures are we talking about?" Vance inquired. "If I'm going down there after him, I need to know."

"Perhaps that is one," Tashi said, while gesturing.

Everyone followed her pointed finger to see the Mongolian death worm battling a monstrous creature that looked like a cross between a vulture, dragon, and octopus. The hideous beast had a long, sharp beak, hooked talons on the ends of its multiple octopus-like appendages, and a single eye in the middle of its head. The body was scaly and sported two wings of greenish skin that sprouted out of its back. The tail was lengthy, thin, and shaped like a sharpened arrow at its tip, which the monster darted around in lethal fashion. The creature was clawing at the worm and appeared to be causing damage to her. The worm countered with a few energy blasts and a shot of acid, but missed the wily flying monster.

"What is that thing?" Sam asked, stunned by the sight.

The creature let loose a howl that sounded like a thousand train whistles from the depths of Hell. Bob Ferguson slowly rose to his feet, his face now the portrait of pure terror.

"It's a snallygaster."

Chapter 14
THE WORM'S TURN

It was like any other day for Kunibald when he took over his shift as caretaker of the Vault of Mysteries from his brother, Kunibert. Kunibald was a diminutive, bearded kobold whose kind originated in Germanic folklore. Although there were different types of kobolds, Kunibald was the type associated with mines and metal-working, so he felt right at home in this claustrophobic underground chamber. Given the mundane duties of vault caretaker, Kunibald and his brother simply used their time in this place to sleep. It was the ideal occupation for a family-oriented mythical creature like Kunibald, since it allowed him to spend his awake time with his wife and children. Getting on a day/night schedule wasn't necessary for those who lived in Agartha, the under-earth city that Kunibald and Kunibert called home. Although the center of the Earth—Gaia—provided a source of illumination, it wasn't timed like the sun, rather it remained constant. That meant Kunibald's sleeping regimen could be easily adjusted to ensure his family was on the same schedule.

One might assume that sleeping on the job would be problematic—especially for a job related to security—but the kobold were light sleepers and if anything were to happen they would become instantly aware, given the vault's unusual construction. However, the fact was, nothing ever happened. The vault was the most secure structure on Earth and though there had been threats made against it in the past, nothing ever materialized to be of any concern. At the time of its creation, Phylassos sought a creature that was uniquely suited to work in this type of environment. Fortunately, the kobold were creatures who could phase through solid rock, including orichalcum. There were concerns the creatures could not be trusted with a room full of the world's most powerful objects but there wasn't much they could do with them except admire them. Though the kobold could phase through the structure, the objects couldn't. It was also noteworthy that magical objects could not pass into Agartha, which would further discourage any attempted removal.

Phylassos had relocated Kunibald and Kunibert and their families to Agartha for this exact reason. The kobolds were over-earth creatures by nature, which meant that when living above ground they were covered by the gryphon's curse and invisible to humans. But living among their mythical brethren would potentially expose them and their loved ones to threats or blackmail by over-earth influences—the contents of the vault were inordinately valuable to those with nefarious intentions. Understanding the danger involved, the kobolds agreed to leave their homes for Agartha.

Over time, Kunibald had gotten to know all of the objects that were kept in the vault, but there was one item he knew the best and that was because it was more than just an inanimate object. It was a mace known as the Sharur, and it dated back thousands of years to ancient Sumer in

Mesopotamia. Maces were long, bat-like clubs with bulbous ends, which were used to bludgeon enemies, but the Sharur was much more than just a blunt force weapon; it was highly magical and purportedly had the power to destroy entire armies. In fact, its name meant "Smasher of Thousands." However, the magic imbued in the Sharur gave it more than the ability to lay waste to kingdoms; it also bestowed it with sentience. In other words, the mace was a living entity that could take and think and even reason, albeit in a limited fashion. The Sharur's extraordinary powers were documented in the "Exploits of Ninurta," a Sumerian poem about the god Ninurta's defeat of the demon Asag, a triumph made possible by the Sharur.

Kunibald had found these battlefield victories hard to believe. Ever since he knew the Sharur, the legendary weapon sounded more like a pacifist than a tool of epic destruction. Perhaps it was guilt catching up to it, Kunibald speculated. Whatever the case, the Sharur seemed to regret and often lamented its one-time warlike nature. The kobold wondered if the Sharur's frequent consternation and its newfound conscience was only as strong as the creature who wielded it. Despite its sentiments, the Sharur would likely have to obey its master, and that was whoever happened to be holding it. Luckily, the weapon had avoided having a master since being interred in the vault.

When it wasn't begging Kunibald for information about the outside world, it would fly around the chamber and yammer away about ancient warriors and legendary beasts. In the early days, Kunibald didn't get much sleep with the mace's constant jabbering, but soon they came to an understanding and the Sharur focused its need on companionship to the earlier hours of Kunibald's shift.

It was just past noon on an ordinary Monday when a sleeping Kunibald was awoken by his bed shaking. The shaking was joined by an increasingly loud and violent rumbling that sounded like the vault was caving in on itself.

"Kunibald!" the Sharur shouted, as it hovered above him. The mace spoke quickly in a deep, nasally sounding voice. "What's happening?!"

"How should I know?" the kobold answered gruffly. He planted his feet on the ground and stood up but had to grab the wall to keep from losing his balance. "An earthquake?" he wondered aloud.

"But it's getting louder and closer," the mace replied. The weapon was right, Kunibald concluded. This was not a natural phenomenon.

Kunibald stumbled to the central hall of the vault and toward a pedestal that sat near the upper part of the chamber, close to the living quarters. The pedestal held a three-dimensional representation of the vault—it was a similar magical technology that was used above him in the DMW observatory. Surrounding the model was a shimmering blue aura, but there were now ripples cascading through the glow—matching the growing rumble beneath Kunibald's feet. And then the unimaginable happened: the blue aura simply disappeared, entirely.

"*Heiliger Strohsack!*" Kunibald quietly exclaimed. Unfortunately, it was loud enough for the Sharur to hear, who immediately panicked.

"What happened to the magical barrier, Kunibald?" the Sharur asked, practically hyperventilating.

Kunibald could not answer this question quite yet, but he knew there were very few things that could lead to the failure of the magical barrier put in place by Phylassos to protect the vault. How it happened didn't matter—what it could lead to was of utmost concern. Without that protection, the vault and its contents were in extreme jeopardy. It was time to prepare defensive measures, but the shaking had reached such a fevered pitch that just standing upright was becoming increasingly more difficult. Kunibald turned toward his target—the cell at the far end of the vault. He was poised to make a run for it when he noticed wisps of smoke erupting out of the floor in the center of the vault. Black and crimson colored vapors rose up off the orichalcum surface in a circular pattern. Kunibald eyed the development with trepidation—it was sitting between him and one of the vault's most important defensive measures. And then the circle of smokey strands turned into a rush of billowing gas and the floor melted inward.

The Mongolian death worm emerged from the hole and screeched in deafening fashion.

"What is that monster?" the Sharur squealed in horror.

"A death worm," the kobold answered, frozen with fear and resignation. He and his brother had been briefed on the weaknesses of the vault and the death worm was considered the structure's gravest threat. Of course, they were assured it would never be a problem, but now here it was shooting up through a seemingly impenetrable foundation and extending its body toward the ceiling.

"What are we going to do?" the Sharur replied.

"You are a weapon of mass destruction," the kobold reminded him. "Drive the beast back down into its hole." Kunibald hadn't been looking the mace's way, and then turned to find it gone. Kunibald shook his head in disappointment, "Coward," he said to himself as he sprung into action.

The kobold bounded forward, racing toward the opposite end of the vault's central hallway. He barely managed to avoid sliding into the hole; fortunately, the worm didn't seem interested in him or the contents of the vault. It was slamming its head against the top of the domed ceiling—the location of the sealed, hinged door to the DMW Observatory. Kunibald reached the other end of the vault and stopped short, directly in front of an unlit area of the hall. The darkness was like a veil that kept whatever lay beyond it hidden from view. The Kobold turned and pulled a lever on a nearby column. A loud clanging noise followed that caught the worm's attention. It peered toward Kunibald, then shifted back to the ceiling and spit out a massive red glob—acid! The acid immediately began eating away at the door to the vault and the kobold tried the lever again in frustration. Did it work properly? What was taking so long? Finally, a creature stepped out of the darkness, taking the kobold by surprise. He stumbled backward, falling on his backside.

Kunibald had never needed to release the snallygaster before, so seeing it outside its specially constructed cell was unnerving. The creature had made a deal with Phylassos to help protect the vault to avoid a return to Gaia for having attacked a fellow mythical creature. It was kept in a state of magical suspended animation until the lever was pulled and the magic lifted.

Meanwhile, the acid from the worm was eating away at the ceiling. It wasn't enough to melt through, but it severely weakened the structure. The worm slammed its head against the door and the ceiling began to fracture. The snallygaster flew toward the monstrous worm, while Kunibald headed back to find—and possibly use—the mace. He got as far as the base to the stone steps leading to the ceiling's door.

The dome began to crumble, large chunks of orichalcum rained down. The worm breached the DMW Observatory and Kunibald looked up to see a piece of stone hurtling toward him. He couldn't move fast enough.

He heard the worm screeching as his ears rang from the impact, and the world went black.

"Now that is one freaky looking beast," Vance Vantana thought to himself when he spotted the snallygaster. He had read about these critters and saw a few drawings of them, but looking upon the real deal? Well, that was a different story. He immediately recognized the problem with Ferguson being a dwayyo. Vance turned and grabbed Ferguson by the shoulders. The half-wolf, half-human had frozen like a statue. He showed all the signs of a possible fight or flight response—Vance concluded it would have likely been flight.

"Listen to me, Bob," Vance told him. The creature's eyes were wide, his hair sticking up on end. "I understand your kind's history with them things, but I need you to focus for me."

"That's not just any snallygaster, Doctor Vantana," Ferguson stammered. "That's the one who nearly killed me."

"And I'm sure you're having a heckuva time processing all this right now," Vance replied. "But this area is not stable. You have to get everyone back towards the barrier. As soon as the lares stand down, get back to your office and hit that big Phylassos button of yours, are we clear?"

Ferguson managed a nod. "What are you going to do?" he asked, concerned.

"As long as that monster has the worm distracted, I'm going to stop Boone," Vance explained.

"I'm going with you," Sam announced.

"Absolutely not," Vance responded.

"I would offer my assistance," Tashi said. "But I think it best if I remain by Sam's side."

"Agreed," said Vance.

"I'm not a baby that needs sitting," Sam retorted, clearly annoyed. "I want to help."

"Help by staying put and trying to communicate with the worm," Vance told him, then placed his hand on his son's shoulder. "I almost lost ya in Mongolia, remember? I'm not going to let something like that happen again." Sam nodded reluctantly, and Vance turned back to the center of the room where the worm was still engaged with the snallygaster. The two creatures were continuing their battle, oblivious to the goings-on below. Vance spied the staircase that spiraled down from the now smashed opening and into the vault. The area around it was still crumbling and if the battle raged on much longer the entire floor of the observatory would likely collapse. He knew the only way to stop the worm was to retrieve the creature's offspring and hand it over, but to do that he would have to find and neutralize Boone. Vance dropped onto the stairway and descended into the vault.

The stairs were partially collapsed, and the constant movement of the worm was making it increasingly precarious. Vance had to leap several feet across missing steps until he reached the bottom. He immediately spotted an unconscious kobold lying on the vault floor. He tried to rouse him to no avail.

"You've lost, Vance," a familiar voice said. Vance looked up to find Boone standing a few feet away, the silver case in hand.

"Don't do this," Vance implored. "The consequences to humanity would be devastating."

"Like they were for my father?" He replied with narrowed eyes. "You ain't special, you know that? I have as much of a right to know about these creatures as you do. And so did my daddy."

"Your daddy was trying to kill them," Vance reminded him. "Now I'm sorry about what happened to him and how it happened. But this—what you're doing now—won't bring him back. It will bring about chaos and destruction and death. Please...let's work this out."

"I've already worked it out," Boone informed him. "And once I deliver on my side of the bargain, I'll get everything I want and more." That sent a chill up Vance's spine. It sounded as if Boone was confirming that he was working with someone and the weapon he sought was likely going to wind up in the hands of this third party.

Suddenly, the vault shook and more of the ceiling began to crumble. Vance dodged the falling rock and attempted to use the melee to make a move on Boone, but his rival was expecting it and swung the silver case, connecting with Vance's chin. Vance fell backward into a pile of rubble and smashed his head on a jagged piece of orichalcum. Vance reflexively grabbed the back of his head as the pain surged through his body. He could feel a warm trickle of blood stream down from the wound, and his sight blurred as the pain doubled, then tripled. Boone appeared to be standing above him, smirking. Vance tried to stand and his world began to spin. Gravity promptly took hold and yanked him back to Earth.

"Boone..." Vance called out in a strained voice, as he reached out a hand. Boone shook his head.

"You had your chance all those years ago. And now? Your time is up; mine is just beginning." Boone looked upward and shouted a series of words that Vance recognized as Sumerian, an ancient language from Mesopotamia. His conversational Sumerian wasn't stellar but he did recognize one particular word Boone uttered—Sharur. Could it be possible? Vance wondered. Did the Vault of Mysteries hold the legendary mace of Ninurta? Vance was growing more lightheaded by the second and struggled mightily to keep his eyes open. Through the pain and blurriness, Vance spotted an object fly through the air and land in Boone's hand. Vance's sense of dread was instant and overwhelming. Boone Walker now wielded the "Smasher of Thousands."

"Are you my new master?" A voice spoke from the mace.

"Yes, I am," Boone replied.

"What is your command, master?" the mace asked. Vance watched as an immense grin broke out across Boone's face. It wasn't like a kid in a candy store. Oh no. This was a kid who had just bought all of the candy stores in the world.

Every last one.

"Cernunnos!" Sam declared, as Tashi corralled him, Cynthia, and Ferguson closer to the lares's magical barrier. Tashi immediately scanned the room—was the creature here in the observatory?

"Where?" she asked, as she twirled her shekchen in her hands. She couldn't imagine this situation getting any more dangerous or chaotic. The death worm was fighting with a snallygaster, the floor was collapsing, the human Boone was in a vault filled with deadly magical objects, and now that insufferable green monster was here as well?

"No, not here," Sam admitted. "When he had me in his lair, he was trying to recruit me to retrieve something for him in exchange for helping me find my mom. What if he is behind all of this? Boone clearly had help."

Tashi considered it. "Ranger Jaran did say there was magic involved in keeping her in her cabin," the Guardian recalled. "Marzanna is a powerful witch who is in league with Cernunnos."

"And the sky serpents? Someone sent those," Sam added, before turning his attention to Cynthia Salazar. She was—understandably—in a highly agitated and frightened state. "Miss Salazar, did Boone talk about a creature named Cernunnos?" She had a hard time pulling her eyes from the worm but finally looked Sam's way.

"What?" she asked, distracted.

"Did Boone tell you he was working with a creature named Cernunnos?" Sam repeated.

She thought for a moment. "No, but he did say we had powerful allies and that I was supposed to take the weapon to some national park if anything happened to him."

"Do you remember what park?" Sam asked.

"Tortugas, I think? Dry Tortugas?" she replied. "I've never heard of it."

"It's in the Gulf of Mexico. Off Key West," Ferguson chimed in. "It falls under Ranger Sprite's authority."

"This speculation is not helpful in our current predicament," Tashi said. "We need to communicate with the worm, try to calm it down again. Can you convince the snallygaster to stop its attack?" the Guardian asked Ferguson.

"If it was given the mission to protect the vault by Phylassos, I doubt it would listen to anyone, never mind me—its mortal enemy," Ferguson responded. The ground beneath them began to shift back and forth, violently, and everyone turned their attention to the monster battle. The worm had snatched up the snallygaster in her maw and was shaking it wildly.

"What is it fighting with?" Cynthia asked, her expression confused. "I don't see anything."

Tashi had forgotten that the reporter did not possess the sight.

"It's invisible," Sam told her, then quickly added, "It's complicated." Sam eyed the fight, "The worm is going to kill that creature. We have to do something. We have to try and help it."

The worm let out a deafening screech and hurled the snallygaster to the ground. The monster flopped onto the stone floor, badly wounded and now a sitting duck for the worm to finish it off. Sam leapt up to try and help, but Tashi put her arm up to block him.

"Let me go! I can save it!" Sam insisted.

"He's already going," Cynthia said, pointing with an outstretched, shaky finger. Tashi spotted Ferguson dashing across the room towards the snallygaster.

"The worm is going to blast it!" Sam shouted, gesturing to the creature. The death worm had begun to generate a surge of energy in her body. Ferguson finally reached the snallygaster and grabbed hold of the creature, attempting to pull it out of harm's way.

"Ferguson!" Sam yelled. "Look out!"

But Ferguson couldn't move the snallygaster quickly enough. The worm released a blast that grazed Ferguson's torso. He yelped in pain, then slumped onto the fallen snallygaster. With a roar, the worm slipped back into the vault.

"We have to warn my dad!" Sam said, as they raced over to Ferguson's side. Tashi turned the DMW official over and found him alive, but dazed.

"I can help," she told him and prepared to put her hands on Ferguson to heal him. He waved her off.

"Later," he whispered. "Get inside the vault and do what you can to put a stop to this." Tashi nodded. She turned to find Sam and Cynthia already at the edge of the hole. Sam was starting to climb down, as Tashi bounded over.

"My dad!" Sam shouted and pointed toward the bottom. Tashi was about to follow when Cynthia grabbed her.

"I'm coming too," the reporter said.

"It is not safe. You would be putting yourself in great danger," Tashi informed her.

"I helped create this mess, I can help clean it up," she said.

"You're only human," Tashi told her. She was extremely vulnerable. No magic, no training, not even the sight.

"And Boone's human, too. Maybe I can talk some sense into him." Cynthia moved past Tashi and started down the crumbling stairs, hugging the wall.

When Tashi and Cynthia reached the bottom, they found Sam crouched down next to Vance, who appeared unconscious.

"He's bleeding," Sam reported, revealing a gash on the back of his dad's head. Tashi quickly leaned over and put her hand on the wound.

"I cannot heal him completely at the moment," she told Sam. "To do so would weaken me for a time—and we cannot afford that. I will stabilize him." Tashi could feel the pain as she absorbed it into her body. She raised her hand as soon as she could no longer feel the flow of blood. "He will be okay. We must find Boone."

"He's there—" Cynthia announced, pointing to the far end of the vault.

Boone Walker stood with a weapon in his hand—a mace—and the silver case in the other. The death worm was looking over him, her entire body now inside the vault. Tashi stood and headed toward Boone. Sam and Cynthia were right behind her.

"Somebody better tell this worm to back off or its kid is a goner," Boone demanded.

"That case with the baby worm is rigged to destroy anything inside it," Cynthia explained to Tashi and Sam in a hushed tone.

"So if the worm attacks him—" Sam began to say.

"It might accidentally trigger the case to kill the worm's offspring," Tashi concluded, to which Cynthia nodded.

"Uh oh," Sam said, pointing to the worm. She was charging up again to release another blast. Boone must have noticed. He placed the mace in front of his body.

"Sharur, you will protect me from harm," Boone announced.

"Yes, my master," the mace replied.

"Did that thing just talk?" Sam nudged Tashi.

She shrugged. "I suppose it did," she replied. The weapon's ability to talk was the least of their problems. Given its internment in this chamber, it was likely the mace was extremely dangerous.

The worm erupted with a shot of energy that headed straight towards Boone, but it never reached its intended target. The mace absorbed all of the energy.

Boone was still standing.

"I like that," Boone chuckled.

"Boone!" Cynthia shouted, as she charged toward him.

"Miss Salazar!" Sam yelled after her. "Don't!" Tashi had no idea what the reporter was thinking, but her actions would likely get her killed.

"Good to see you're still alive," Boone said. The worm turned toward Cynthia for a moment and she immediately put her hands up in a defensive manner. "I see you're taking up with the enemy," Boone added with a hint of annoyance.

"I'm not with them," Cynthia insisted, as she slowly edged toward Boone. "You think they're going to let me go after this? You were right. We're in this together now. No turning back. But we have to get out of here."

"I'm glad you saw the light," Boone said with a smirk.

Did this woman not realize who the enemy was? Did she think that Boone was someone to be trusted? Tashi quietly charged her shekchen, preparing to fire at both of these criminals. She glanced toward Sam to see him reaching out to touch the worm.

"What are you doing?" she asked in a hushed tone.

"I'm going to try and calm it," he replied. "If it kills Boone or damages that case, things are going to go from worse to world-ending."

Tashi nodded in agreement, but didn't believe anything Sam did would improve their situation. Tensions and emotions were simply too high at this point. The Guardian was gaming out possible scenarios while Cynthia spoke to Boone. She conversed quietly with her compatriot, but Tashi could still hear them.

"There's a barrier above us that we can't pass through," she informed him.

"What did I miss?" A voice said from behind Tashi. It was Vance—his hand on the back of his head and his legs a little wobbly. Sam spotted his father and rushed to embrace him.

"It looks like that reporter has betrayed us and they are preparing to escape," Tashi reported. Vance nodded, as Tashi continued, "There isn't much we can do as long as he holds that case."

"Or that weapon," the doctor added quietly.

"What is that thing?" Sam asked.

"An ancient Sumerian mace that's incredibly powerful. Boone is now its master." Vance shouted to his rival, "You're not getting out of here alive, Boone. Not unless we help."

"I'll be just fine, Vancey," Boone chided. Then he spoke to the weapon. "Sharur? Fly us out of here."

"As you wish," the weapon answered.

"How is this going to work exactly?" Cynthia asked.

"Just grab onto me," Boone told her.

"If that thing is going to fly us out of here, one of us needs to be holding it with both hands," she insisted. "Give it to me."

"No can do," Boone told her. "You hold onto the case and me."

Boone handed the silver case over and the worm lurched, but didn't attack. It appeared to be taking stock of the situation, as if it understood the stakes and was being extra cautious. Cynthia gripped the case and moved to grab hold of Boone.

"How do I ignite the explosive inside it if we get separated?" she asked.

Boone pointed to a switch on the handle. "As long as you keep your hand on that it's fine, but if you release it—boom. You ready?"

"No, I'm not," Cynthia replied. Then she turned and ran towards the others with the case. The worm shifted toward her, ready to strike. Tashi looked quickly to Sam and luckily he already had his hand on the creature.

"Green!" Sam shouted.

Tashi immediately projected the color green to the worm to help calm her.

"Now that was a dirty thing to do," Boone snarled. "But I don't need that anymore. Sharur? Get us out of here!" The Sharur attempted to take flight with Boone, but the worm suddenly turned to face them. She extended her body and caught Boone's foot in her mouth...severing it from his ankle. Boone squealed in pain then angrily swung the Sharur toward the worm. The head of the mace connected with the creature, striking her head like an anvil. A massive burst of blue energy exploded upon contact, sending a concussive blast that lit up and shook the chamber.

When the dust settled the vault was even more damaged than before. Tashi quickly scanned the area for Sam and found him next to the worm, Vantana by his side. The creature wasn't moving and her skin was no longer pulsating. In fact, its color had changed to a sickly, pallid gray.

"I think she's dead," Sam said, tears in his eyes. "Can you do anything?" He asked Tashi, but she shook her head. Tashi's healing abilities would not work on the worm.

"Where's Boone?" Cynthia asked, looking around. She was still clutching the case. Tashi spotted the human stuck beneath a large pile of crumbling rock. He was barely conscious and reaching for the Sharur, which was just a few feet away. Tashi raced forward and grabbed the weapon.

"Sharur," Boone whispered, calling for the mace. Tashi could feel it trying to leave her hand, but she maintained a firm grip and planted her feet. Boone looked up and saw Tashi. "Sharur," he repeated, a touch stronger now. The mace tried again to leave Tashi's hands, but now she had clutched onto a crevice in the stone floor. Soon, the mace had her body stretched out, desperately trying to return to its master. Tashi clenched her eyes in pain—it felt like she was going to be ripped apart. A frustrated Boone attempted to get out from under the rock.

"Don't move!" Vantana warned him. Tashi didn't understand until she realized that Boone was in a precarious spot. His movement would likely set off a chain reaction that would lead to an avalanche of debris crashing down on him. "Just stay still," Vantana told him. "I can help you."

"Like you did the day my father died? I don't think so," Boone replied with pained defiance. He shifted, pulling himself from the rocks. A slight smile was forming on his face, but it never had a chance to materialize. A deafening rumble filled the chamber and a section of the vault collapsed. Boone Walker was instantly buried under several tons of orichalcum. The Sharur stopped pulling on Tashi and she dropped it to the ground. She noticed her arm had torn at the shoulder. It was bleeding, but slowly knitting itself back together. She caught Doctor Vantana's solemn expression.

"It was his choice," she told him, but he didn't nod.

"Let's get the worm out of here," Cynthia said, holding up the case. "If I keep hold of the handle I think it will be okay to open." Tashi nodded and pried it apart, while Cynthia kept her hand on the switch. The baby was inside...and, miraculously, still alive.

"It's okay!" Sam declared, triumphantly. He reached in and removed the small encasement that was holding the creature. Sam eyed it a moment, then saw how to open it up. As soon as he did, the baby worm sprung from the translucent box and wiggled toward its mother, but when it got close it must have realized something was wrong.

The worm began to screech. The sounds were piercing and caused Doctor Vantana, Sam, and Cynthia to immediately cup their ears with their hands. Every time the creature vocalized Tashi noticed a spurt of energy rippled across its body, until its entire body was glowing. It was generating energy, much like the mother worm did before she released a blast. The energy continued to travel across its tiny body and then it touched its head to its mother. As soon as it made contact, the waves of energy began leaving the baby worm and entering its mother's body. At first, the blue ripples only spread an inch or two on the mother worm's skin, but with each successive screech the energy grew and the ripples spread further.

"What's it doing?" Sam wondered aloud. He got his answer just a few moments later, as the mother worm's massive body twitched. And twitched again. The twitches grew stronger and more controlled until the Mongolian death worm rose up from the ground and groaned. The sound echoed throughout the chamber and Sam whooped and cheered.

The mother bent back down and pressed her head against her baby. The baby squirmed into one of the folds of skin on its mother's body and the giant worm wriggled toward the hole in the chamber floor. Tashi received a sudden and sustained flash of green and orange and then the creature disappeared into the earth.

"Perhaps someone can fill me in on what happened," a gravelly voice said. Tashi spotted a kobold walking toward them. "I am Kunibald, the caretaker here."

"It's a heckuva story, but everything is right as rain now," Vantana assured him.

The creature glanced around. "It does not look that way, Ranger," he said. "The vault is exposed and how am I to believe you are not the cause of this destruction? Perhaps in league with that worm?"

"The man responsible is buried under a great big pile of rubble over there, Kunibald," Doctor Vantana told him. "We're the good guys, I can assure you."

"Excuse me if I do not believe you without confirmation," Kunibald said.

Tashi noticed Cynthia looking around nervously and remembered she didn't have the sight, so the kobold was a disembodied voice. Vance must have realized it, as well.

"I reckon you're mighty confused right about now," Vance told her.

She nodded. "Confused and incredibly ashamed for my part in all of this," she said. "I know I can't undo what I've done, but I'd like to help, if possible. I promise that I won't speak of this. I think I can understand why it has to be kept secret."

"Kunibald? You want some help picking up the joint?" Vance asked. The kobold grunted what sounded like an affirmation, then muttered under his breath about how this just had to happen on his watch. "She's going to need the sight, but with everything she's already seen it's sort of a moot point. Let's see how things are going topside."

"Before you three can leave, I must secure all of the artifacts and ensure nothing is missing," Kunibald said.

"What do you mean 'three?'" Tashi asked the kobold. "There are four of us."

"I see three," Kunibald replied. Doctor Vantana spun around.

"Where's Sam?"

Tashi felt a pang of concern, as she scanned the chamber. There was no sign of Sam. She also noticed something else was missing from where she had left it.

"Where is the Sharur?" she asked.

Chapter 15
SHIFTING FORTUNES

When trees talked, Ranger Woodruff Sprite of Everglades National Park listened. As a mythical wood sprite, the ranger had the ability to communicate with plants and trees, and he did so often. Truth be told, Woodruff secretly preferred the friendship of foliage over animals, including humans. Trees were quiet observers who loved to listen, and when they did speak, it was always with great import. They were wise and even-keeled. Rarely did they ever grow agitated or upset, so it was a surprise to Ranger Sprite when the gumbo-limbo trees he was chatting up one lazy spring morning bristled with worry.

Trees in the northern part of the park were sending urgent messages to the gumbo-limbo trees, who in turn rustled their branches. The sounds of the leaves brushing against each other formed a language of whispers. They spoke to Sprite and he listened intently.

"Danger," the trees communicated. "Danger is coming. Creatures. They are coming for Woodruff."

As the ranger absorbed this unexpected news, he heard movement in the woods. It was growing closer and was soon joined by the snarling sounds of what Sprite immediately identified as barghests, monstrous beasts that were best described as a wolf-bear hybrid with massive jaws. Sprite quickly scaled the closest tree to get a better vantage point and spotted the creatures a few hundred yards away in the dense forest. They were closing fast and weren't alone—the barghests were being led by woodwoses, wild men of the woods who were antagonists of the gryphon. They were far from their home across the Atlantic, but were apparently unconcerned with violating the gryphon's law.

Sprite descended the tree and headed for the swamps to try and lose his pursuers. As he bounded through the park, he tapped his DMW badge.

"DMW headquarters," he spoke in a breathless voice. He wasn't used to getting this much exercise at his advanced age—he stopped counting after one hundred and fifty. There was no response from HQ. He tried again and still nothing. *Very curious*, Sprite thought. But the woodwoses were gaining on him and he needed to shift all of his attention on his escape.

Sprite entered a thick mangrove forest and slipped behind several red mangroves with their strange, spindly roots that stretched out above the surface like fingers gripping the earth. He waded into the waist deep water and removed his shirt and hat, submerging them in the swamp. He then clutched onto the closest mangrove and altered his body pigment to match the colors of the root system. Wood sprites possessed a camouflaging ability, but Woodruff rarely utilized it in his capacity as a DMW ranger. For a second, he wondered if his body would recall how to do it. Fortunately, instinct kicked in and it worked perfectly, allowing Sprite to seamlessly blend with his surroundings. Such visual trickery might fool the woodwoses, but the barghests had noses that were a hundred times more sensitive than a bloodhound. He was banking on the smells of the swamp to throw them off. But just in case they didn't, Sprite decided to ask the mangroves for some assistance.

"Confuse them, please?" Sprite whispered, as he pressed his hands against the tree. The trees didn't reply, but they shifted their branches in unison, blocking the path to Sprite. Their movements were so subtle the ranger's pursuers didn't even seem to notice they were being intentionally misdirected. The snarls of the barghests began to fade in the distance, as Sprite sighed in relief.

As the ranger paused to consider his next course of action, he heard a bubbling gurgle up from behind him and the ground began rising beneath his feet. When he attempted to move, he slipped and was now straddling the mystery thing that was lifting his body. He tried to get off but now seemed stuck on the object. The bubbling grew louder and stronger, then the head of a horse breached the water's surface. It had red eyes and a mangy black mane. Sprite immediately recognized it as one of the most feared creatures in Scottish folklore—the each uisge, a malevolent horse with a penchant for murder—and not just any kind of murder, but violent, sadistic deaths.

Once on an each uisge, a person could not climb off. The creature's hair had an adhesive property that enabled it to keep a rider on its back. After capturing its prey, the horse would dive into the water, drowning the victim then tearing them limb from limb. Understandably, the creature was not allowed to "quench" its blood thirst under the gryphon's law, so like many evil-intentioned creatures, the each uisge had its violent instincts tamped down by Phylassos. Sprite wondered if perhaps that magic had worn off.

The ranger knew that struggling to get off the beast was a pointless endeavor. It would only exhaust him and give the monster an advantage. Sprite relaxed and the each uisge dove back down. Wood sprites could remain submerged in water for a much longer time than humans, but he hoped to trick the beast into believing him dead. Once it attempted to pull him off and finish its attack, Sprite would be poised to escape.

But the opportunity never arrived. The horse did not appear concerned with Sprite, rather it was swimming out to sea. After a short time, the creature emerged from the water, allowing Sprite to breathe. Sprite determined that the creature was heading southwest.

"Where are you taking me?" the ranger asked. The creature didn't respond. Sprite yanked at its wet mane. "Where are you taking me?" he demanded. The each uisge let out a shrieking whinny then reared its head back, slamming it into Sprite and knocking the ranger out. As his world grew dark, Sprite wondered if he'd ever open his eyes again or if the only thing they found of him would be his liver—that was, after all, the calling card of an each uisge.

* * *

Sprite eventually woke up with his liver intact, but he was no longer at Everglades National Park. As his eyes slowly focused, he found himself in a kneeling position in a large grassy area enclosed by massive brick walls. He knew this place—it was Fort Jefferson on Garden Key in Dry Tortugas National Park. The park was comprised of a seven-mile archipelago of seven islands and was mainly known as a bird and wildlife sanctuary. The centerpiece of the park—and its most visited area—was the fort, which was an unfinished fortress that dated back to 1846. It consisted of six brick walls measuring up to 477 feet high, plus a parade ground courtyard in its interior, a visitors center, lighthouse, and barracks that were only partially left standing. The park sat about sixty-eight miles west of Key West in the Gulf of Mexico.

Though it fell under Ranger Sprite's jurisdiction, he rarely had reason to visit—one, because it required a boat or seaplane ride and two, it was not used as a habitat for any mythical species. It was, however, home to hundreds of mythical species at the moment. There were redcaps, woodwoses, barghests, and other creatures of the nefarious sort gathered together.

Sprite was grabbed by the hair and forced to look upward. He was instantly eye-to-eye with a fiendish creature that he had grown to despise.

"If it isn't the gryphon's loyal walking stick," Cernunnos said with a sneering grin. "I trust your trip here was terrifying? The each uisge tends to have that effect."

"You've gone too far this time, Cernunnos," Sprite told him, as he jerked his head from the creature's grip.

"I haven't gone far enough, ranger. At least not yet," Cernunnos told him. "The reckoning has come. Enjoy your last hours while you can."

Ever since the revelation that Henry Knox was Phylassos, the mythical world had grown increasingly tense. It was as though Chase the cynocephalus's attempt to destroy the gryphon's claw—though unsuccessful— had emboldened the enemies of Phylassos. Sprite had come to learn that Cernunnos was behind Chase's rebellion—it appeared to be a way of testing the gryphon's strength and undermining his authority by proxy.

For centuries, Phylassos ruled as a sort of benevolent dictator. Creatures both feared and respected him. Of course, it was fear that kept the evil ones in line. But now? Cernunnos had stood up to the gryphon, presenting himself as an appealing alternative—a creature who professed to be more loyal to his kind than the gryphon. But Cernunnos wasn't stupid—he had always known that he could not take on the gryphon himself, nor with an army of redcaps. His bristling overconfidence gave Sprite pause. *What did he have planned this time?* the ranger wondered, anxiously.

Cernunnos paced in front of the crowd before the mass of monsters split down the middle, creating two columns. Cernunnos stopped and looked down the newly created aisle. Sprite craned his neck and spotted Marzanna, Cernunnos's sorceress, heading toward him. When she reached her "Lord," as she called him, the two exchanged words that Sprite could not discern. Whatever it was she told him, it seemed to both surprise and please Cernunnos.

"Let him approach," Cernunnos bellowed towards the entrance of the fort. The mass of creatures turned in unison to see who the mysterious "him" was. Sprite could only catch fragmented glimpses, but it looked as if there was a human approaching.

A small human. A child?

Two redcaps were escorting Cernunnos's guest, and Sprite squinted in the dusky light to discern the human's identity. As soon as he did, his eyes went wide and his jaw dropped in shock.

It was Sam London! The boy who helped save the gryphon's claw, the son of Vance Vantana and Odette the swan maiden. Sprite had gotten to know Sam on case #SL002-130, "The Selkie of San Francisco." After Odette was returned to Gaia, Vance had taken a leave of absence from the DMW and Sprite had assumed Sam would have, as well. So why was the boy here, of all places?

"Sam?" Sprite called out. "Have they kidnapped you? Does your father know? Where is Tashi?" Sprite would have continued shouting questions, but a woodwose walloped him in the back of his head. Sprite fell forward, then raised his eyes and looked to Sam for a response. The boy shifted his gaze to Sprite, but his guise was cold.

"I wasn't kidnapped, Ranger," Sam said, matter-of-factly. "I've come here willingly to meet with Lord Cernunnos."

Sprite noticed Sam was carrying something in his hands—a large mace. An odd thing for a twelve-year-old boy to have.

"I have to confess, Mister London, when Marzanna informed me that you were here, I didn't believe her," Cernunnos said, then gestured to the mace. "Is that what I believe it to be?"

"It is," Sam replied. "The legendary Sharur. The smasher of thousands. Fresh from the Vault of Mysteries." Cernunnos smirked, then narrowed his eyes.

"I wonder how it came into your possession," the green giant mused.

"It is what you wanted me to retrieve for you, isn't it?" Sam asked. "That day in Scotland. This is what you were referring to?"

"Perhaps," Cernunnos replied apathetically. "But if memory serves, you declined my offer and I retracted it in Atlantis. Yet here you are. A strange and suspicious development, don't you think?"

"No, I don't. The Sharur could lay waste to this island and everyone on it, but here I am and here you still are," Sam said. "The same can't be said for Boone Walker."

"Who?" Cernunnos responded.

"Give me a break, your lordship," Sam told him. "I've had a rough couple of days. I was nearly eaten by the Mongolian death worm, killed by fire-breathing sky serpents, and almost turned into an otter for all eternity. So let's get real for a minute. I know you were helping Boone. I know Marzanna was involved because of the spell on Ranger Jaran's cabin. And I also know it was probably you who sent the snake storm that led to Ranger Jaran's return to Gaia. You turned to him because I turned you down. Well, guess what? He failed. But I didn't."

Cernunnos stepped forward. He eyed Sam for an extended moment, like a predator trying to determine how best to eat its prey. He suddenly lurched forward, eye-to-eye with Sam, who reflexively flinched but held his ground.

"What happened to Boone?" the creature snarled.

"It was quite a plan, Cernunnos, I'll give you that," Sam admitted. "Free the death worm, lead her to the vault, then have your guy collect the prize? It was risky, reckless, and almost successful. But you made one fatal mistake."

"Enlighten me," Cernunnos said.

"You never accounted for us," Sam revealed. "How could you? We weren't supposed to even be in Mongolia. It's sort of funny, actually."

Cernunnos stood and stared down at the boy with murder in his eyes. "Funny?"

"Not ha-ha funny, just funny in the way things sometimes work out. Your refusal to help me find my mom led me on my own path. A path that just so happened to lead through Mongolia," Sam explained. "So if you had helped me then, we wouldn't be here now. Hilarious, right? You would probably be preparing to overthrow the gryphon or planning how you would enslave mankind. I'm guessing that was the ultimate goal. Why else would you need a weapon like this?"

"You still haven't answered my question," Cernunnos noted.

"Oh right. Boone Walker. Unfortunately, he couldn't let go of the past and things ended badly for him. I am curious about one thing, though," Sam said.

"I am growing tired of this conversation," Cernunnos responded with a dismissive wave of his hand. "So unless you have a point or an offer—"

"That's exactly what I'm curious about," Sam told him. "What did you offer him? He was highly motivated. I mean, he almost caused a disaster of apocalyptic proportions. What was he getting in return for selling out his entire species? I'm sure you didn't mention that little nugget of information when you sold him on the deal."

"Humans are simple creatures," Cernunnos replied with an emphasis on "simple." "They are guided by emotion, by an irrational and senseless attachment to the corporeal. So foolish. Naïve. Like children," Cernunnos explained.

"Are you going to tell me or insult me?" Sam retorted.

"Boone was led by those all-too-human flaws, but he also possessed another motive. One I could understand," Cernunnos revealed.

"He wanted everyone to call him 'Lord?'" Sam quipped. Sprite chuckled at this and got another smack to the head by his minders.

"Vengeance!" Cernunnos roared. His booming voice echoed through the fort. "But he thought too small, his human brain not capable of much else, I suppose. He just wanted the 'sight.' And he wanted to tell the world we existed. He wanted the credit, can you imagine?" Cernunnos laughed at this. His minions laughed, as well, likely out of loyalty. The green monster continued, "A perfect illustration as to why humans are the lesser species. Why *they* should be hiding from *us*. For centuries, the gryphon has kept us from realizing our destiny—taking our rightful place. Mister Boone would have enjoyed his last few moments on Gaia, reveling in his 'credit,' seeing the real world. Before it would be ripped from him and his kind forever."

"Jeez," Sam explained. "That doesn't sound like a very good deal."

"Enough of this tediousness. You came here with the mace and you came here alone, why?"

"You should know why," Sam replied. "You have something I want and I have something you want."

"Ah, yes. Of course," Cernunnos replied with a knowing grin. "You wish to know where your mother is before her soul is gone forever. Another human who can't let go of the corporeal."

"I guess not," Sam said. "When I was in the vault, I saw an opportunity. A chance to save her."

"And what of your father and that irksome Guardian? Did they see the opportunity as well?" Cernunnos asked, glancing around suspiciously.

"Of course not," Sam replied. "It's why I'm here by myself. For myself. There's an old human saying, 'better to ask for forgiveness than permission.' As a kid, I have found that to be a very reliable piece of advice."

"And I'm to believe you are prepared to betray the gryphon and humankind?" Cernunnos responded in an incredulous drawl. "After your sanctimonious display in Scotland?"

"I know it's hard to believe," Sam conceded. "I can be a bit of a goody two shoes sometimes. Not as much as Tashi, of course, but it happens. Unfortunately, as much as I don't want to admit it, you were sort of right."

Cernunnos cocked his head in sudden interest. "Sort of?"

"I don't owe the gryphon anything," Sam declared. "He is responsible for what happened to my parents, for making me miss out on a father, and for sending my mother back to Gaia. As for my fellow humans, I ask that you don't eliminate us. It would create a serious imbalance. Look what happened in the Valley of Ten Thousand Smokes. Maybe just clip our wings a bit, cool?"

Cernunnos contemplated it and grinned. "Cool."

"Great," Sam said. "Now where's my mother?"

Sprite couldn't believe what he was hearing. Sam London was going to commit treason against the gryphon and doom humanity? What was he thinking? Sprite knew that grief was a powerful motivator, but would it really drive Sam to something this heinous? Betray Phylassos? Defy his father? Ranger Sprite lived a relatively relaxed existence: he rarely allowed himself to get worked up over anything nor was he one to blow things out of proportion. But what he was witnessing at Dry Tortugas's Fort Jefferson was about to blow up to an unimaginable proportion. He could not sit idly by and watch Sam make the single worst mistake in history.

"Sam!" Sprite shouted. "Don't do this! He cannot be trusted. Your mother wouldn't have wanted this!"

"I'm sorry, Ranger, but Phylassos has left me no choice," the boy replied with a deadly seriousness that left Sprite feeling instantly and utterly dispirited.

"The next time the stick speaks, silence him for good," Cernunnos ordered his minions. They wrenched Sprite further down on his knees, until he was practically kissing dirt.

"I'm waiting, Cernunnos," Sam said.

"Hand over the mace and I will fulfill my end of the bargain."

"No way, Jose. Mom first, mace after," Sam insisted.

"Or I could simply have Sprite here eliminated while you watch," Cernunnos offered. "Hand me the Sharur, and I will tell you what I know."

Sprite raised his head and watched as Sam considered the terms...and then he handed the mace to Cernunnos. Sprite sighed and slumped down in defeat.

"Well?" Sam asked.

"Of course," Cernunnos replied. "I keep my promises. And I promised to reunite you with your mother. She is part of Gaia now, so let me help you join her." Cernunnos turned to his redcap army. "Kill the boy and that wretched walking stick."

"You sneaky green bean!" Sam yelled. Before the woodwoses could follow Cernunnos's order, Sprite scrambled to his feet and raced out to Sam.

"Oh, Sam," Sprite said. "Why did you have to go and do that?"

"Because," Sam responded in a hushed voice. "I needed to stall."

Sprite was considering Sam's unexpected response, when the boy suddenly shouted out: "Sharur!"

Chapter 16

THE BATTLE OF FORT JEFFERSON

Vance Vantana wasn't the most well-behaved tyke growing up. He was willful, stubborn, mischievous, and, as his father would say, "too clever by half an hour." That last phrase was of his father's own creation and meant that young Vance was just smart enough to convince someone of anything for a short while. However, once they had a moment to clear their heads and ruminate on Vance's request, argument, or proposal, they'd realize it was unwise, risky, or just plumb crazy. By then, he had usually already succeeded in whatever endeavor he was perpetrating. His dad would often say how he was looking forward to Vance having his own kid someday, so he could experience all the delights and difficulties that come with fatherhood.

If only his dad could see him now, Vance thought.

It was certainly true that Vance Vantana's experience with fatherhood had begun in an unorthodox way. Given their unasked-for estrangement, Vance simply didn't know his son as well as most fathers knew their children. Sure, they had gone on adventures with each other, and nearly died together on several occasions, but it wasn't like Vance had been around since Sam London's birth. So it was understandable that Vance felt a pang of dread and disappointment at realizing his son had run off with the Sharur. Vance knew he had caused his own father a hefty number of headaches, but this was a five-alarm fire of a migraine. Calamitous on a global scale.

Given the level of determination Sam exhibited in relation to saving his mother, Tashi believed he decided to use the weapon as leverage in procuring information on Ettie's whereabouts. Vance couldn't discount her assessment as possible, but he wasn't yet ready to accept it. He enlisted the others to search the vault and the hole the death worm created in the floor for any sign of Sam or the Sharur. In the process, Vance couldn't help but notice several intriguing vault items—one of which would come in quite handy if things were to go south right quick.

"If your child stole it and declared himself to be the Sharur's master, he will be so until he dies," Kunibald explained, as they searched for the weapon. "But that mace does have a mind of its own. Now that it's out of this vault, who knows what it is capable of. It's been imprisoned for some time."

Vance nodded, understandingly.

After an exhaustive search—and Kunibald finally accepting the realities of his situation—they headed up to the observatory, unsure of their next steps. The lares had already lowered their magical barrier and were back at their posts, trying to salvage what they could. Vance spotted the supervisor, who was frazzled but in control.

"You didn't happen to see a kid with a four-thousand-year-old magical mace come through here?" Vance asked.

"As a matter of fact, he came through right after we dropped the barrier and headed into the office," the supervisor reported.

"Vance?" a voice called.

Vance spun to see Bob Ferguson on the ground, near the snallygaster. The creature wasn't moving and had turned a shade of pale blue.

"This guy needs some help," Bob said.

Tashi stepped forward. "I can try," she said, as she kneeled down and put hands on the creature. The healing was slow—and looked especially painful for the Guardian, no doubt a result of the snallygaster's unusual anatomy. The creature's wounds healed partially and its color returned. Vance noticed that Bob was holding one of the snallygaster's octopus arms in a consoling manner.

"You two aren't going to suddenly try to murder each other, are ya?" Vance asked.

Bob shook his head assuredly. "Not a chance. We've put all of that behind us. He's grateful for me risking my life to save his. And he's also pretty angry about what happened. He'd like to help punish whoever it was that caused this mess."

"Understood," Vance said. "How about you show me this button you've got to signal Phylassos?"

Bob stood and nodded, excitedly. "You bet."

"Supervisor?" Vance called out. "Miss Salazar would like to be of some help to you. She'll need a serum."

The supervisor considered it a moment, looked around at the destruction, then nodded his approval.

"No questions asked," he said.

"Of course," Cynthia assured him, as she stepped forward.

Vance, Tashi, and Bob crossed the observatory and entered the outer office. Bob headed for his desk when a voice spoke up and startled the trio.

"No need to push a button to reach me."

Doctor Henry Knox was standing in the hallway that led to the office door. He was neatly dressed in a beige suit with a tie and was holding his hat in his hand.

"It has been an eventful day for the DMW," Knox added.

"That's the understatement of the year," Vance quipped.

"Indeed, and I'm afraid it will be even more eventful if we don't move with haste," Knox said.

"So you know about Sam and the—" Vance started.

Knox nodded. "Despite my protests, your son has put himself in great danger. But if his plan works, it will do quite a lot of good."

"So he wasn't going to—" Vance began.

"Betray me and the department?" Knox completed the ranger's thought. "Gosh no. He's your child. He shares your sense of duty."

Vance smirked with a hint of pride. He was relieved to hear that Sam hadn't gone and done the unthinkable. But that triggered Vance's other parental instinct.

"You said something about great danger?"

"Yes. Out of the frying pan and into the fire, as they say. Let's go help him extinguish the flames."

* * *

Less than an hour later, Vance found himself on the back of the gryphon with Tashi, flying at an incredible velocity, thousands of feet in the air. They made their way from Falling Waters State Park to Dry Tortugas National Park, after having hopped a dvergen subway in Shenandoah National Park. According to Doctor Knox, Sam had taken much the same route after he hit the special gryphon button in Ferguson's office and summoned Phylassos. Knox appeared moments later to learn what the trouble was and Sam filled him in on the way to the dvergen station. Apparently, once he reached Falling Waters, the Sharur flew him to Dry Tortugas. *That must have been quite a ride,* Vance thought to himself—he was glad he wasn't there to witness it, as it sounded much too dangerous. Of course, flying on a gryphon wasn't exactly a picnic either. Tashi had to keep her hands on Vance the entire time so he could withstand the oxygen deprivation and the force of the winds. It was painful, but worth it if it meant reaching Sam quicker. He looked over to his right to check on Bob Ferguson, who had joined them—and was riding on the back of the snallygaster. It was nice to see them getting along so well, considering the age-old rivalry.

The gryphon flew low as they made their approach toward Fort Jefferson, gliding just a few feet off the water's surface. They had to come in undetected, just in case Sam was in the midst of completing his mission. They took cover near the Harbor Light lighthouse that was on the southeast side of the fort and gave them a great vantage point for the goings-on in the courtyard.

They arrived just in time to hear Cernunnos readily admit to major crimes against the gryphon. Vance appreciated Sam's determination to see this case through to its proper and just conclusion. He also marveled at his son's superhuman capability to stall. This was a trait Vance had seen Sam utilize in their two previous cases to great success—here in Fort Jefferson, facing Cernunnos, Marzanna, and an army of malevolent mythical creatures, the kid shone once again. Vance cringed a little as he watched Sam give up the Sharur, but he took comfort in what Kunibald said about the mace's connection with its master. When Sam shouted "Sharur!" and called back the weapon, it was their signal to strike.

The cavalry charged in and took the enemy by surprise. Phylassos swooped down over the courtyard and tilted his body to allow Vance and Tashi to slip off and join Sam and Sprite. The snallygaster followed suit, letting Bob off to reunite with his friends. Cernunnos's soldiers froze as the awesome sight of the mighty Phylassos spooked them. Cernunnos didn't even flinch. He stood defiantly in the face of the gusts of wind generated by the gryphon's flapping wings.

"Just in time," Sam told his dad.

Vance glared at him. "Remind me to ground you if we survive."

"You have committed countless crimes, Cernunnos," Phylassos announced, his booming voice shaking the fortress walls. "Against me, against your fellow mythical creatures, and against humanity, as well as Gaia herself."

"What I do, I do for the good of my kind," Cernunnos responded, unrepentant.

"You have usurped my authority."

"How could I? You surrendered that to humankind ages ago."

"Your insolence, your defiance, your wickedness…. It ends here," Phylassos declared. "I have allowed your criminality and shameless disregard for our law—"

"Your law," Cernunnos interjected in a derisive tone.

"You will order your allies to stand down," the gryphon directed him. "And then you will surrender and be punished."

"I will never surrender to you, gryphon," Cernunnos said with a sneer. He addressed his army, "Did I tell you to hold? Kill them! All of them!"

Cernunnos raised his staff high in the air and massive green vines sprung from the earth. These gargantuan tentacles grabbed Phylassos and pulled him down, slamming his body into the ground. The impact rocked the earth and sent up a billowing cloud of dust. In just seconds, Phylassos was completely ensnared in the vines and struggling to break free. The surprising show of power by Cernunnos energized his army, who shouted their approvals and charged Vance and the others. Meanwhile, the barghests were leaping up to snap at the snallygaster, but the creature was wily and managed to stay airborne and counter their attack.

"Sam? How about you use that Sharur and get us out of this mess?" Vance suggested.

"I can't," Sam replied. "We had a long talk and, well, he's sort of a pacifist now. He did some pretty awful things back in the day."

"You're serious?" Vance responded, incredulous. Sam nodded.

"Thank you, Sam," the Sharur chimed in. "I appreciate you respecting my wishes to remain a non-combatant. Don't worry, Doctor Vantana, I will defend my master from all enemies."

Great, Vance thought to himself, as he pulled his knife and faced the converging army. Tashi was already firing at the creatures—paralyzing them with bolts from her shekchen. Bob was holding his own, as well, tossing the little monsters back as they attacked. Sam was seemingly untouchable—the Sharur wasn't joking when it said it would protect him. Every creature that lunged for Sam was sent soaring back by a massive blast of energy from the mace. Sam was grinning wide, as he held it aloft. Things seemed to be handled here, so Vance looked to see how Phylassos was faring. Unfortunately, the gryphon was still on the ground, covered in those constricting vines, which now had help from Marzanna's sorcery.

Vance looked to Sprite. "Any chance you can communicate with those vines? Maybe convince them to ease off?"

"I will see what I can do, but Cernunnos's and Marzanna's magic is strong," Sprite reported.

"I'll take care of old greenie," Vance said. He had been clamoring for a rematch with Cernunnos for some time. Vance pulled his knife, got a running start, then launched himself at the creature, but vines sprung from the earth and caught him mid-flight. He was pulled to the ground and flipped onto his back. The vines constricted and Vance fought mightily against the pressure.

"I'll give you this much, Vance Vantana," Cernunnos said, as he stepped toward him. "You are tenacious. Stupid, but tenacious." He snatched Vance's knife from the ranger's bound hand and pointed it at him. "How fitting," he said, before lunging at Vance.

This was it, Vance thought to himself. He didn't love the idea of dying from his own blade, but when the tip of the knife finally made contact with Vance's chest, it stopped. Cernunnos appeared confused by this turn of events and tried again, but once more the tip of the blade stopped on contact. Vance was grinning, as Cernunnos pushed with all of his strength.

"We could do this all day," Vance quipped. "Or at least until the chimera serum wears off." A sudden look of realization filled Cernunnos's face. Knox had brought it with him when he returned to the DMW office, no doubt thinking it might come in handy. Luckily, the experimental serum worked as hoped and, more importantly, it caught Cernunnos by surprise.

Vance took advantage of his enemy's loss of focus. He pulled himself from the vines and walloped Cernunnos in the jaw. The chimera serum made Vance's skin as dense as rock, so the blow he delivered to the green giant sent Cernunnos reeling back...and bleeding. A stream of red trailed down from the corner of his mouth. Vance stalked him and struck again; this time a punch to the gut. Cernunnos groaned in pain and fell to his knees. Vance balled up his fist, then grabbed onto one of Cernunnos's antlers, pulling his head upward to look in his eyes. Vance felt an unfamiliar urge building up inside of him. But it wasn't steeped in vengeance or even an odd sense of justice; it was driven by a sudden and rapacious thirst for blood.

"I can see it in your eyes, Ranger," Cernunnos said. "The chimera has more than impenetrable skin. It has an insatiable desire to murder."

Cernunnos was right, Vance realized. And the urge was difficult to suppress. Penelope had hoped she could isolate only the skin strength characteristics of the creature, but this feeling in Vance said differently. He quickly looked up to see how the battle was going, his eyes went blurry as soon as he looked away from his "prey."

He saw Tashi firing her shekchen at Marzanna, Sprite trying to speak to the vines, the snallygaster fighting back against the barghests, and then he saw Sam, wielding the Sharur. He was reminded of how proud he was of his son. He had been through so much yet never faltered. Vance felt the urge to kill begin to weaken. His sight clearing. He held onto this feeling—the love he had for his child. It would be just enough for him to counteract the serum's adverse effects, but he wasn't sure how long he could hold out.

Fortunately, with Cernunnos weakened and Marzanna held at bay by Tashi, Sprite coaxed the vines to retract and free Phylassos.

The gryphon's emerald eyes glowed as he rose up and roared, sending a shockwave through the fort. Cernunnos's army staggered and fell backward. Instantly, two pillars of blue energy shot up from the ground beneath Marzanna and Cernunnos, the two trapped within columns of Gaia's life force. Marzanna attempted to reach past the energy field, only to retract her hand, screaming at the searing pain. Phylassos then surveyed the armies of Cernunnos, who were starting to get back to their feet.

"Stand down, brethren, and perhaps you will survive this day," the gryphon informed them. The redcaps and woodwoses glanced at each other, unsure how to respond.

Phylassos turned back toward Cernunnos, when Vance spotted a barghest breaking off from his pack. He charged the gryphon, leaping into the air.

"Phylassos!" Vance shouted in warning, but the gryphon didn't even bother to face his attacker. His eyes sparkled once again.

The barghest was only feet away from Phylassos when he simply disappeared. His body surged with blue energy then exploded into a dazzling display of twinkling blue light. The tiny specks of energy dissipated in mid-air and transformed into dozens of fireflies that swarmed together then flew off into the night. The barghest had returned to Gaia in one of the most awesome displays of power Vance—and likely anyone else present—had ever witnessed.

There was an instant hush in the fort, as Cernunnos's minions recognized the gravity of this event. They saw the raw power of the gryphon and likely concluded that they picked the wrong horse. Every last one of them dropped to their knees and bowed their heads in reverence. Phylassos would not have to warn them again.

"Cowards," Cernunnos muttered from his cylindrical prison.

"For a creature who forever professed to being enlightened, it is your hate that has led you to this defeat," Phylassos said. "A blinding hatred of those you consider inferior."

"On the contrary, mighty Phylassos," Cernunnos countered. "It is not hatred of humans that guides my hand, nor is it arrogance or ego that fuels this fight. I simply seek justice for my kind. Someone must protect them. You know this curse cannot sustain. The day will come when you must choose your side, gryphon. I have chosen mine."

"It does not have to be that way," Phylassos told him. "It can be like before."

"I wonder, is it humanity that is blind to us, or you that is blind to humanity?" Cernunnos asked. "You elevate these insects to our level and in so doing diminish us, trivializing our greatness and relinquishing our authority. You will punish me, just as you have punished so many others—those who also saw what was to come, and those who refused to be shackled any longer. But no matter how many of us you silence, our voices continue to echo, until those singular echoes become a booming chorus. It won't be long now, gryphon. Claw or not, this charade is coming to an end."

"I thank you, Cernunnos," Phylassos replied. It was a response that Cernunnos clearly wasn't expecting, given his narrowed, suspicious glare. "I have often thought about this moment when I would be forced to pass judgment on you. Yes, I have known for centuries that this day would inevitably come, even back when we might have considered each other friends. I always hoped that perhaps you would choose another path, but your nature would never have allowed it. Yet how does one punish a creature so misguided? What is the ultimate consequence for their supremely evil actions? Perhaps it is to end their existence?"

"Of course," Cernunnos replied. "The return to Gaia, your enemies gone in the blink of your eye. Just as you prepared for this moment, so have I. I am not so arrogant to believe there was no possibility I would fail...and pay the ultimate price, as you deem it. But returning to Gaia is not so much a punishment as it is a completion of a cycle. A reunification. It may not have come at the time of my choosing, but I welcome it nonetheless."

"I have no intention of returning you to Gaia, Cernunnos," the gryphon revealed.

Vance found this surprising and disappointing. He didn't wish death on anyone, but Cernunnos's crimes certainly rose to the level of a justified return to Gaia. This was not a singular problem with this creature, rather it was an ongoing nuisance that had put millions of lives at risk. Surely, he would need to be imprisoned for all eternity at the very least.

"I don't know what trickery this is, gryphon, but I remind you I am not Alexander. I am not weak like a human," Cernunnos maintained.

"Not yet," Phylassos replied. "Returning you to Gaia would not change your heart, nor is it, as you have said, a punishment. Your actions require a more unique response. One that better serves you and is an example to the creatures who share your thinking and heed your call. You, Cernunnos, will be stripped of your magic and live as a human being without any knowledge of the mythical world." Every creature gathered released a collective gasp.

"Even you do not wield that kind of power," Cernunnos sneered.

"You are correct," Phylassos admitted. "It would take two powerful magical creatures to generate such a transformation. Marzanna?"

The sorceress was understandably startled to hear the gryphon speak her name in this context. She looked to him from her own cylindrical prison. Vance had had a few encounters with Cernunnos's most loyal and powerful acolyte. She was a true believer who had demonstrated her willingness to do the horned creature's bidding without fail. Her devotion to Cernunnos was militant. Vance had come to conclude that she had played a major role in ensuring that Ettie found her wings, which then led to her return to Gaia. Her fingerprints also appeared to be all over the incidents in Gobi Gurvansaikhan National Park, which led to Jaran's return to Gaia. All in all, Marzanna was a nasty piece of work, so it was shocking that Phylassos would call on her help in this moment.

"You have been a faithful servant of Cernunnos," the gryphon said.

"Lord Cernunnos," she corrected him, haughtily.

"And we see the strength of that allegiance even now," Phylassos added. "But loyalty has its limits."

"Not mine," she snarked.

"You have no doubt sworn to protect his life with your own?" the gryphon asked.

"Gladly, as have all who follow him," she answered.

The gryphon nodded with understanding. "As I suspected," he said. "And so I give you the opportunity to do so now. To fulfill your oath. To prove this loyalty."

Marzanna eyed him, skeptically.

"Do not listen to his false promises," Cernunnos interrupted.

"I make no promises," the gryphon claimed. "For you, Marzanna, and the followers of Cernunnos, have committed countless crimes against my law and your fellow creatures." Marzanna was poised to interject, but Phylassos had anticipated her defense. "It does not matter if you see these violations as noble or necessary. The consequences are the same. But I offer you a choice. Help me and you and all who have followed Cernunnos will not be returned to Gaia on this day. Help me and Cernunnos lives. Refuse and all shall face punishment."

"We are prepared to meet our fate and be one with Gaia," she said defiantly.

"Very well," the gryphon replied. "Then you have doomed your leader to share the same fate." The gryphon's eyes sparkled and the blue column of light that surrounded Cernunnos grew brighter, almost blinding.

Cernunnos pushed his hands against the walls of this cylindrical prison and howled, resisting his return. His body began to fade, as the blue light consumed him. The howl turned to a roar as the pain likely grew unbearable.

"Wait!" Marzanna cried out. "Stop this! Spare him!"

The gryphon's eyes returned to their normal, solid state and Cernunnos's body became solid once again. He collapsed inside the column of light.

"If I help you, Lord Cernunnos lives?" she asked.

"Yes," Phylassos answered.

"But as a human...without his magic?"

The gryphon nodded. "His magic will be kept waiting for him"

"How long must he endure this wretched form?"

"For as long as it takes for him to learn what it is to be human," Phylassos explained.

"No," a pained Cernunnos whispered.

"I will help you," Marzanna told the gryphon.

"You would betray me?" Cernunnos stammered.

"I will save you...and save us all," she replied.

"Come forth, Marzanna," Phylassos said. The column of light that imprisoned the sorceress suddenly dropped.

She stepped toward the gryphon, tentatively.

Phylassos drifted back to the earth, as the flapping of his wings slowed then stopped. The ground trembled when he touched down. He reached out with his front left paw, turning the palm upward.

"Give me your hand," the gryphon said. Marzanna placed her pale, delicate hand on top of the gryphon's palm. Phylassos's claws peaked out and wrapped around it. "Understand this, sorceress, if you or any creature interferes with Cernunnos, you will all be returned to Gaia. He will live with no knowledge of the mythical world or magic. And when the time comes, he will be returned to his true form."

"And who will make that decision?" Marzanna asked, peering up at Phylassos.

"I will," he answered.

"And I am simply to trust you?" she countered.

"As I am trusting you," the gryphon responded.

Marzanna eyed him, unsure of his meaning.

"You will be the keeper of his magic. Now let us begin."

The gryphon's paw closed in on Marzanna's hand completely. At that moment, the blue light of Gaia that was surrounding Cernunnos grew brighter. Cernunnos was lifted off of his hooves and was now floating within the column of light. The energy passed over his body in waves. Ring after ring of brilliant blue light shot up through the column and each time it crossed from the ground to Cernunnos's antlers, the creature changed. It was subtle at first. Vance noticed his green skin began to lighten. Then his hooves became feet, his body shrunk, his antlers disappeared. Soon, Cernunnos was not the magical creature Vance had come to know or so many had grown to fear. He appeared totally human, of average height with blondish red hair that fell to his shoulders. And then the human Cernunnos slowly faded from view and the blue column of Gaia's energy vanished.

"What have you done?" Marzanna exclaimed.

"He has been sent to live among humans," Phylassos said. "But his whereabouts will be known only by me."

The gryphon released Marzanna's hand and she stumbled back, weakened by the interaction. Phylassos gestured to Cernunnos's staff, which now lay on the ground. It glowed with an aura of blue light. Vance had come to learn that Cernunnos's staff was a magical object that could change forms. Often it could be found as a reddish-yellow snake with curled ram horns that wrapped itself around Cernunnos's neck. But here the creature had taken the form of a long staff that channeled Cernunnos's magic. The staff had a snake head at its tip, which also sported ram horns.

"His magic and his very essence have been secured inside his staff," the gryphon revealed. "It is under your care now, Marzanna."

The sorceress stepped toward it, then kneeled down to pick it up. It crackled with energy and she handled it gingerly, as though she was concerned she might damage it. Marzanna raised her other hand to the sky, sending a stream of red light into the night, and a mass of flying creatures descended on the fort. Gargoyles. Hundreds of them. But they didn't attack, rather they picked up the army of redcaps, woodwoses, and barghests and flew off into the darkness. Marzanna mounted one of the larger gargoyles, then looked back to Phylassos.

"You best keep your promise, gryphon," she warned.

"And you best heed my authority," Phylassos reminded her. "Do not test me or you will lose everything."

Marzanna nodded and took flight.

"How did you know she would help?" Vance asked, catching the gryphon's eye.

"Marzanna's blind devotion was not borne solely out of her sense of duty," Phylassos explained.

"You mean—" Vance began to say.

"She loved him?" Sam interjected with surprise.

The gryphon nodded, affirmatively. "Indeed, she does. But he could not see it, nor would he have understood it. Perhaps, in time, he will."

"So you weren't condemning him," Vance suddenly realized. "You were saving him."

Chapter 17

THE SWAN MAIDEN

The tragedy at the DMW and the events leading up to it had been a wake-up call for Cynthia. She always believed that exposing the truth was of paramount importance and that, in the end, it would all work out for the best. The ends would justify her means. But this time she had gone too far and left a path of death and destruction in her wake. Now she was trying to pick up the pieces by helping to pick up the literal pieces of the nearly decimated Vault of Mysteries.

Of course, there was a part of her that was reeling from the wonder of it all. Since receiving a serum in her arm from the observatory supervisor, she was suddenly able to see the kobolds—the small human-like creatures who guarded the vault. Kunibald had grown increasingly ornery in the hours since the others left to help Sam London. He spent much of the time mumbling to himself and tossing rocks and debris this way and that.

His brother, Kunibert, who had arrived for his shift and was shocked by what he found, only made things worse. He reveled in poking fun at Kunibald. "I never had a breach on my watch," Kunibert quipped at one point. "Wait until mother and father find out you messed up worse than I ever did," he chided. Kunibald did not appreciate the jibes and threatened his brother with physical harm several times, but that only managed to encourage Kunibert to continue the ribbing.

Cynthia was busy cleaning the living space that the kobolds used when on watch. It had emerged relatively unscathed, but was caked in dust and small bits of debris. She had just finished wiping down a large chest of drawers, when she felt eyes on her and looked up to find both kobolds standing a few feet away and staring. It was creepy.

"Uh...everything okay?" Cynthia asked.

"You know it is not 'okay,'" Kunibald said.

"I do?" Cynthia replied.

The kobolds both nodded.

"We know you have it," Kunibert informed her.

"Have what?" Cynthia asked, genuinely confused.

"Item number thirteen is unaccounted for," Kunibald told her. "Empty out your pockets, human."

"Wait, is this about that mace?" Cynthia said. "Because it wouldn't fit in my pockets."

"This is not about the Sharur," Kunibald revealed. "No more tricks."

"Guys, I didn't take anything," she insisted. "If I had, do you think I would stick around here to get caught?"

Kunibert looked to his brother. "It is true that a thief would likely not linger at the scene of the theft." Kunibald stroked his chin and narrowed his eyes, then nodded, as if convinced.

"Can one of you please tell me what's going on?" Cynthia asked. "What's missing? What is item number thirteen?"

"It does not matter to you what it is; what matters is that it is danger-ous," Kunibald explained, gruffly.

"I thought everything in here was dangerous. Hence the whole sealed vault thing," Cynthia replied. "The mace was dangerous, right? So how dangerous is this item thirteen? More? Less? Are we talking end of the world here?"

Kunibald shook his head. "It is not like that. The item is not a weapon but can be…harmful."

"If it was taken," Kunibert said, thoughtfully, "I can promise you that whoever took it does not understand what they have done to themselves. The consequences of such short-sightedness are…unpleasant."

"Unpleasant?" Cynthia responded, as she contemplated the kobold's statement. From what she could currently gather, this item—whatever it was—would prove more detrimental to its possessor than to the world. Did that mean it would make whoever possessed it sick? Or maybe give them severe pain? But how wouldn't they realize it was a problem, almost imme-diately? And what would compel them to take this item in the first place? Like any good journalist, Cynthia felt the urge to dig for more information. "How big is this item? What does it look like?"

"It is contained inside a small box, but even that cannot prevent its magic from affecting those who handle it," Kunibald explained.

"You said 'it' is contained inside a box. What is 'it'?" Cynthia asked. The kobold brothers just eyed her and didn't answer. The reporter rolled her eyes, "Classified, I get it. I'm guessing that also means you can't tell me what kind of magic we're talking about? The whole magic-is-real thing is still pretty new to me, so any help understanding it would be appreciated."

"Magic comes in various forms and many degrees of power. It is the manner in which a creature—or object—can repurpose or focus the energies of Gaia," Kunibert explained. "This item manipulates Gaia's energy in one of the most powerful ways possible."

"Hence why it is kept locked up in here," Cynthia concluded.

"That is correct," Kunibert said.

"How do you know someone even took it?" she asked. "If it's small, look around—this place is a mess. It could be anywhere. I mean, in case you forgot, there's a great big hole in the floor. Couldn't it have fallen in there? Or have gotten buried under a bunch of rock?" Cynthia suggested.

Kunibald considered her words, then Kunibert leaned over and whispered to his brother. Kunibald waved him away.

"You have made a valid point, human," Kunibald admitted. "Perhaps we jumped to conclusions in assuming you absconded with it. Our assumption was understandable given the nature of the item. But it may indeed still be on the premises. We will conduct an exhaustive search before investigating other possibilities."

"Great," Cynthia said, pleased she could help ease the kobold's concerns. "Where should we start looking?"

"I'm afraid this is where you take your leave, human," Kunibald told her. "We have eliminated you as the thief, for now. So it is best that you leave. We cannot have you finding it before us."

"Seriously?" Cynthia replied, surprised by their decision.

"Seriously," Kunibald said.

She looked to Kunibert, who shrugged.

"Well, okay, then. I hope you find it," she told them.

"As do we," Kunibald said, soberly. "Otherwise, I take great pity on the creature who now holds it in their possession."

Once Marzanna and Cernunnos's army were whisked away by a flock of gargoyles, Sam joined the others in the center of the courtyard, the Sharur firmly in hand. His dad immediately pulled him up into a great big hug, then scolded him without missing a beat.

"I am both proud and perturbed," Vance said. "I appreciate what you did for the cause, son, but the risk was way too high. Plus, you gave Tashi quite the scare."

"I was not 'scared,'" Tashi insisted. "Nor was I surprised by your actions. You have displayed a total disregard for your safety and the safety of others in your quest to save your mother."

"Well, I wouldn't go that far—" Sam responded, defensively.

"Need I remind you what occurred in the Gates of the Arctic or Mongolia?" Tashi asked. "Because in Alaska you nearly—"

"No, you don't need to remind me," Sam interjected, ceding the point and feeling guilty.

"Is anyone injured?" Phylassos asked the group.

"My pride is wounded," Sprite quipped. "I thought I was going to be returned to Gaia for sure. I'm guessing I missed a lot."

"You don't know the half of it," Vance remarked.

"I assume headquarters was compromised in some fashion?"

"Big time," Sam confirmed.

"Speaking of which, I should probably head back to D.C.," Bob Ferguson announced. "There's a lot of clean-up to do."

"It looks like I'll be needing to make some decisions regarding the vault," Phylassos remarked.

"Sorry I wasn't able to prevent that," Bob said, sheepishly.

"You were placed in an impossible situation," Phylassos told him. "I appreciate your efforts and I'm especially delighted that you and the snallygaster were able to overcome a difficult past and quell your instincts. You are both an example for your kind."

"It wasn't easy," Bob admitted in a whisper. "But Sid and I made our peace." Bob patted the snallygaster on its head and the creature let out a short, high-pitched whistle. "Ready?" Bob asked the monster. The creature nodded, then Bob climbed onto its back and gestured toward Sam. "I should probably put that someplace safe." Sam gripped the Sharur protectively.

"Phylassos?" Sam addressed the gryphon. "Can we talk in private?"

"Of course, Sam," he replied. "I'll see to it that it's returned," the gryphon informed Bob, who nodded and took flight.

Sam walked to the far side of the courtyard with the Sharur and the gryphon followed. Once they were out of earshot of the others, Sam spoke to the mace.

"Go ahead, Sha," Sam said. "Tell him." Sam let go of the mace and it floated in the air in front of the gryphon.

"I don't want to go back to the vault," it said. "I've changed. I've been rehabilitated."

"And I believe him," Sam added. "We had a lot of time to talk after we left D.C."

"I'm sure you did, but the Sharur is an extremely powerful weapon," Phylassos explained. "You have only seen a small glimpse of what it is capable of. If it were to fall into the wrong hands—"

"I know," Sam interjected. "But what if we could ensure that Sha was no longer a threat?"

"And how would we do that?" the gryphon inquired.

"By setting him free, but with conditions," Sam suggested. "The magic that binds the Sharur to its master is similar to the magic that binds a jinn or genie to its master. That means the master should be able to set it free. So what if I set it free on the condition that it takes a magical oath to not harm anyone ever again. It can defend itself, but it can't intentionally hurt humans or creatures. Its freedom would be forfeited if it did so and the punishment would be self-destruction."

The gryphon considered Sam's proposal. "Would you agree to such an agreement?" Phylassos asked the Sharur.

"I most certainly would, mighty Phylassos," the Sharur replied.

"And what will you do with this freedom?" Phylassos asked.

"I will stay with Sam and maybe help him in his work with the DMW. I do know a lot about the mythical world," the Sharur said.

Phylassos shifted his eyes from Sam to the Sharur. "I am getting the distinct feeling you two have thought a lot about this." Sam nodded affirmatively. "All right, then," the gryphon relented with a smirk, as Sam grinned. "But you must speak the words carefully, Sam. You are creating a binding, magical oath and it must be precise."

"It will be," Sam maintained. He had already practiced this with the Sharur and was ready to deliver. "Sharur, Smasher of Thousands, Weapon of the great Ninurta, as your master I grant you a conditional freedom. If you agree to these conditions, you will be immediately unbound from your pledge of submission to any master from this point forward. The first condition is to never intentionally harm a creature, human or otherwise.

Another condition is that you must always abide by the gryphon's law. If, at any time during your existence, these conditions are not met, you will self-destruct. You do have the right to defend yourself if threatened and you may also use your abilities to blend into the human world. Do you accept this new magical oath that comes with your conditional freedom?"

"I accept this conditional freedom and the magic that binds it."

"Then I, your master, hereby set you free!"

The Sharur zipped up into the sky and released a loud, whooping cheer. It even let loose with a few fireworks that exploded in the air in a dazzling display of color and light. The weapon zoomed back down to rejoin Sam and Phylassos.

"Congratulations," the gryphon said. "Please do not make me regret this day."

"I sure won't," the Sharur insisted.

The three returned to the center of the courtyard where Vance, Tashi, and Sprite were waiting. Phylassos explained to them the Sharur's new freedom and both Vance and Tashi were skeptical—especially with the idea that the mace would be living with Sam.

"How's that gonna work, exactly?" Vance asked. "People might get curious about a floating, chatty mace."

"The Sharur can disguise itself," Sam explained. "It doesn't shape shift, but it can project other forms around itself. We've talked about what the ideal form would be and well...Sha? You want to show them?"

"Sure thing!" The Sharur answered, excitedly. In a flash of light, the mace winked out of sight and was replaced by a bird. A large, grey parrot.

"An African grey parrot," Sprite observed with a knowing grin. "The smartest bird in the non-magical world."

"Exactly," Sam said, as the disguised Sharur flew over and landed on Sam's shoulder. "No one will think it's weird for a parrot to talk."

"I can blend in," the parrot squawked.

Vance shook his head, incredulous. "Now all Sam needs is an eye patch and a peg leg."

Even Tashi laughed at that.

* * *

After a short trip via seaplane from Fort Jefferson to Panama City, Florida, Vance, Sam, Tashi, and the Sharur headed up to Falling Waters State Park in Chipley, Florida. The park had the only dvergen subway station in the state, located inside the waterfall known as Falling Waters Sink.

During the time spent in both the plane and the car, Sam noticed that his dad was abnormally anxious. He was fidgeting a lot and seemed to be thinking hard about something or other. Sam asked if everything was okay and Vance insisted it was fine. Sam wondered if it was a side effect of the chimera serum, but Vance claimed the serum was only designed to provide a temporary enhancement and had since worn off. As they were settling into the dvergen subway car, presumably to head home, Vance announced a sudden change in plans.

"I need to head back up to D.C., so we're going to take a detour," he informed them. "Sam, you'll be staying with my parents for a few days. It'll be a great opportunity for you to meet and get to know them."

"Wait," Sam interjected. "Why are you going back to D.C.?"

"I have some business I need to handle, but I'll be back quick as lightning."

"What kind of business?"

"The kind that's none of your business," his dad replied with a wink. "No big deal, just DMW-related stuff."

"Why can't we go with you?" Sam asked.

"It's quicker if I do it alone," Vance contended. "Plus, I know your grandparents are going to want all the time with you they can get."

"They know about me?" Sam asked; he had forgotten he even had grandparents. He never knew his mom's parents and she hadn't spoken of them.

"Not yet," Vance admitted. "But they're going to find out sooner or later, so why not sooner? I've got an explanation worked out. Your grandma is the skeptical one of the pair, but I think she'll just be grateful to have a grandchild, and she won't ask too many questions."

"What about Tashi?" Sam, asked.

"I can find a wooded area to—" the Guardian began to say.

"You're not staying in a tree, Tashi," Vance told her. She had once lived in a tree in Benicia Park when she was keeping watch on Sam during his first case. "My mother will love having a girl in the house. They don't know anything about the DMW and what-not, so we'll stick with the foreign exchange student cover story for now." Tashi nodded in agreement. "Just make sure your parrot doesn't get too chatty there, matey," Vance added, gesturing to the Sharur in its animal disguise.

"Sha will be fine," Sam assured him. "Now that you're reinstated, are you going to be away more often?" Sam asked.

Before they had departed Dry Tortugas, Phylassos granted Vance a full pardon for his crimes against Cernunnos. The gryphon felt it was more than justified in light of the treasonous activities of Cernunnos, and Vance's efforts to save the Mongolian death worm, the DMW, and the world.

Sam hadn't given the prospect of Vance being more involved in the DMW much thought until this moment. He had successfully pushed aside all contemplation of the immediate future to avoid feeling sad. But his father's announcement had conjured up a feeling of loneliness in Sam, which then reminded him of his mother's absence. According to Pinga, Ettie's soul would be lost at the end of the new moon cycle—a cycle set to end that evening, which was a fact Sam had avoided acknowledging.

"We'll talk about it later," Vance assured him; then, programmed the subway's navigation console and the machine rocketed from the platform.

* * *

They arrived in North Carolina at a dvergen station that sat behind Linville Falls, which was located in an area known as Linville Gorge Wilderness. The gorge was inside Pisgah National Forest in the Blue Ridge mountains of Western North Carolina. It was a dense green forest that sprung from mountainsides with a twisting river that cut through the landscape and created a lush valley. Vance had arranged to have a National Park Service SUV waiting and they all hopped inside.

They were on a highway headed toward Sam's grandparents' cabin in the Great Smoky Mountains when Sam noticed his father getting anxious once again. He was muttering to himself, as though upset about something, and shaking his head.

"What's wrong?" Sam asked.

"I don't know what I was thinking," Vance said, but it seemed mostly directed at himself. He slammed his hand on the steering wheel. "I'm losing it," he said.

"Why do you say that?" Sam inquired, concerned by his father's state.

"There's a dvergen station closer to the cabin," he replied with a sigh.

"Why would we not go there?" Tashi asked.

"That's what I'm asking myself," Vance said. "It's like I didn't even remember it existed. Not only did I set the navigation console for Linville, I arranged for the car. All the while I knew there was one closer."

"But you forgot," Sam concluded.

"But I didn't really forget. It's hard to explain," Vance contended. He continued muttering to himself about his forgetfulness and needing to get back up to D.C. as soon as possible. Sam didn't understand the connection between those two things and dismissed Vance's memory issue from a lack of sleep. They were both exhausted. In fact, Sam could hardly keep his eyes open much longer. He drifted off as the car headed west on highway US-19. Unfortunately, his stomach woke him up about an hour later. Amidst all of the happenings of late, Sam had ignored the need to eat. His belly growled angrily with hunger.

"I'm starving," he informed Vance in a groggy voice.

"Yeah, I could use a bite myself," his dad replied. "We'll stop at the next town."

As they continued down the road, Sam kept his eyes peeled for a sign indicating the next possible food stop. He spotted one in the distance and when it came into focus, Sam's heart nearly leapt out of his chest.

"Stop!" He exclaimed at the top of his lungs. Vance hit the brakes and the car skidded to the side of the road.

"What? What happened?" Vance exclaimed. "Did I hit something?"

Sam didn't bother to answer, he simply pointed and Vance followed the gesture to the road sign. It read: "Welcome to Marshall, North Carolina."

"Marshall? Is that not the name of your dad?" Tashi said. "Fake dad, I mean."

"Yes, it was," Sam replied. "She's here," he declared. "She has to be here." It was a leap, for sure, and Sam half-expected Vance to chalk it up to coincidence, but his father's face told a different story. His mouth hung open and he narrowed his eyes, as if working things out in his head.

"I think you're right, Sam," Vance said haltingly. "Let's go have ourselves a look-see."

Sam was so excited he could hardly sit still. As Vance maneuvered the car down the town's main thoroughfare, Sam's head was on a swivel. He was eyeballing every person he could see, hoping to spot his mom.

When they passed a state courthouse, Vance spoke up.

"I know this place," he confessed. "I've been here. Ettie and I were going to get married at that courthouse, but Sprite insisted on getting us to Atlantis before we were found."

"If she's here, we have to find her quick—we're running out of time," Sam said. "We need a plan."

"Yoo hoo," the Sharur chimed in.

"What is it, Sha?" Sam asked, as he turned to the parrot that was perched on the back headrest.

"I know everyone thinks I'm just a weapon, but one of my primary functions in service to Ninurta was surveillance. He would send me to scout ahead," the Sharur revealed. "While you all come up with a plan, I'll do reconnaissance."

Sam looked to his dad for agreement and Vance shrugged.

"Not a bad idea," he said. "We can get something to eat while he's doing his thing, and figure out next steps. Everyone knows everyone in towns like these. And she would be new, I reckon. We can start at that diner and ask around," Vance suggested, pointing at a small restaurant on the main drag.

Even with the surge of adrenaline, Sam was feeling faint from lack of food. He agreed with Vance and his dad pulled the car up in front of the diner.

"We'll be inside there," Sam told the Sharur. Sam pulled a photograph of Ettie from his pocket. It was the one from Fontana Lake—he hadn't had a chance to remove the fake "Marshall" from it, but it was the picture he loved the most of his mom. He simply folded it in half, so he could only see her. Sam showed it to the Sharur, "This is Ettie. Come back the second you find her."

"Got it!" the parrot announced, then flew off. As the Sharur took to the sky, Sam felt something he hadn't felt in quite some time: hope.

* * *

The door to the diner jingled as Sam, Tashi, and Vance entered. The waitress was helping another table but heard the chime.

"You can sit anywhere," she shouted from across the room without looking their way.

The trio grabbed a table near the window, so they could keep an eye on pedestrians. Sam quickly scanned the menu—he was so hungry, everything looked good—but he was also aware of what they were up against. And time was running out.

"What's our plan?" he asked the others.

"Do not look at me," Tashi told him. "I have made my position on defying the will of Gaia well known." Sam sighed and shifted his attention to Vance, who pursed his lips.

"Well, we can show her picture around, maybe go ask the police," he suggested.

"Morning," the waitress greeted them, as she arrived at the table. "Can I get y'all something to drink?"

Sam, Vance, and Tashi all looked up to give the woman their drink orders and were instantly speechless. The waitress at the diner in the town of Marshall, North Carolina, was none other than Ettie London.

Chapter 18

TAIL OF THE DRAGON

*I soon found myself head over heels in love with this girl...
But I was afraid to begin, for when I think of saying anything to her, my heart would begin to flutter like a duck in a
puddle; and if I tried to outdo it and speak, it would get right
smack up in my throat, and choke me like a cold potato.*

A Narrative of the Life of David Crockett,
—of the State of Tennessee, 1834.

For Vance Vantana, seeing Odette the Swan Maiden in a diner in North
Carolina was like seeing her for the first time all over again. It was a rush of
emotion that left Vance confused as to whether he should be shouting for
joy or crying tears of happiness. He was reminded of the words his ancestor Davy Crockett wrote about the moment he fell for the love of his life.
Vance's heart was indeed fluttering like a duck in a puddle and he couldn't
seem to speak or move, for that matter. It was a glee-induced paralysis. Sam,
on the other hand, did not suffer the same immobilizing condition. He leapt
to his feet and impulsively threw his arms around the waitress.

"Mom!" Sam exclaimed, tears in his eyes. Ettie, whose name tag identified her as "Renee," recoiled with surprise.

"Whoa, there," she said. "Do I know you?"

Sam sputtered and Vance attempted a rescue.

"No, ma'am. You're just the spitting image of someone we know. Sam?" Sam stood there like an Easter Island statue...that was wide-eyed and trembling.

"I'm sorry. They say everyone has a twin, right? I guess we know yours," Sam said as he dropped into his chair. He looked like he just wanted to crawl under the table and stay there.

"Your mom?" Ettie replied.

Sam hesitated, then replied. "No. A friend whose name is Mahm. M-A-H-M."

"That's an unusual name," Ettie said.

"Yeah, it's Swedish, I think."

Vance felt for the kid. Seeing his mother after everything that happened and she had zero idea who he was—a strange turn of events for certain.

"What's your name?" Ettie asked. Sam finally looked back up at her.

"Sam," he told her. "Sam London."

"London? I've always wanted to go there," she confessed with a smile. "So what can I get for you, Sam London?"

"What's good here?" Sam asked.

As Ettie revealed the diner's best eats, Vance and Sam smiled broadly. Their enthusiasm must have been infectious because pretty soon she couldn't stop grinning either.

"You two might just be the hap-hap-happiest customers to ever walk in this place," she told them, then stepped away to put in their orders. Once she was out of earshot, Tashi addressed Vance with narrowed eyes.

"Doctor Vantana, why did you choose the dvergen station that would lead us to drive through this town?"

"I told ya, I don't have the foggiest. I reckon I simply forgot."

That answer didn't seem to satisfy her.

"The odds of us coming upon Ettie in this manner are astronomical," she reported. "Your forgetfulness appears very specific and favorable to this chance meeting."

"What are you getting at?" Vance asked.

"There is something more to this," she replied. "Perhaps something magical, even."

"Maybe it's the luck of the gryphon—we did spend a lot of time around Phylassos," Sam said. "And the time I met him in—"

Tashi interjected, "That was your first time encountering a gryphon. Whatever luck you experienced was temporary and would not be duplicated."

"Well, I don't know how magic works; all I know is that we're here and we found her. That's the only thing that matters now," Sam insisted.

Tashi didn't respond but was clearly suspicious.

Truth was, Vance had more he could have said and it had to do with the reason the ranger needed to get back to D.C., but now was not the time to bring it up.

"Knowing her location is just half the battle, Sam," Vance informed him.

"I know and we're running out of time," Sam said, anxiously. "How can we bring her back for real?"

"According to Pinga," Vance began, referring to the Inuit goddess he met on Xanadu, "To return Ettie's soul to her body will require us to take her to Gaia."

"You mean like 'the' Gaia?" Sam asked. Vance nodded.

"The one and only."

"Talking of this is putting us in danger," Tashi noted. "Miss Bastifal was correct when she warned you of subverting the will of Gaia."

"How do we get there?" Sam asked, ignoring Tashi's concerns.

"Sam London—" Tashi began, winding up a scolding.

"Agartha," Vance said quickly, before Tashi could unleash. "We have to go to Agartha."

"Doctor Vantana!" Tashi exclaimed, shifting her fury to the ranger. "The under-earth is no place for a human or a half-human. It is dangerous and forbidden."

"Just because no human has been there and back doesn't mean it's forbidden. Dangerous as all get out, sure. But not forbidden," Vance maintained.

"You are flouting the will of Gaia," Tashi reminded him. "There are consequences. Consequences you do not understand nor ones I can protect you from."

"I know you're not on board with this, Tashi," Sam told her. "And maybe you never will be, but if there's a way, I'm going to try, no matter the consequences."

"I agree," Vance said, then clarified. "Mostly. Like Tashi, my priority is your safety. If it's starting to look—"

Sam interrupted, "Right, of course. I understand. Now how can we get to the under-earth?"

"There are only a few entrances scattered around the world. Fortunately for us, there's one relatively close to us in Kentucky. At Mammoth Cave National Park."

"So we just have to get her to Mammoth Cave, get through the entrance to the under-earth, and then find Gaia, right?" Sam asked.

"First we find Agartha, the city within the world," Vance explained. "From there we will have to find a guide who can take us the rest of the way. But the truth is, I've never been there. No human has—or no human has gone and returned, that is. And the mythical creatures who have been there, they ain't talkin.'"

"Can we take a subway to the cave?" Sam asked.

"We can. There's one not too far north that should work," Vance said.

"And what do you suppose we do with this human formerly known as Ettie London?" Tashi asked pointedly. "Tell her she needs to accompany us to the center of the earth so we can give her back the memories of a life she doesn't know existed? Would that not be a violation of the gryphon's law?"

"Not if you put her to sleep," Sam said. "We take her—unconscious—to this Agartha place and ask Gaia to restore her real self. If Gaia refuses, then we bring her back here and she has no memory of what happened." Sam grinned, proud of his solution.

"But this is who she is now," Tashi replied. "She is just as much her real self as she was prior to her return to Gaia."

"I don't believe that and I don't think you do, either," Sam told her firmly. "Here's the thing, Tashi. I'm doing this, whether you think it's a bad idea or not. And I'm asking you—as my friend—to help me. I know the chances of pulling it off will increase a ton with you by my side. Will you? Please?"

Tashi appeared conflicted and Vance could understand why. Guardians were warriors who pledged their lives to the gryphon, but Tashi was different. By healing Sam, she had pledged her life to both him and the gryphon. Her world had expanded beyond the confines of Kustos, and she was expe-

riencing life as a human that—as much as she resisted it—included complicated emotions like friendship, loyalty, and compassion.

"I know why you are motivated to bring your mother back to this world,
but I also know the danger," Tashi explained in a soft voice. "I know I can
seem rigid when it comes to the rules of the mythical world, but those rules
keep us safe...keep you safe. That is my charge. But if you insist on this
course, then I shall help you, if only to protect you along the way."

"I understand," Sam told her with a small smile. "Thank you." Tashi
nodded. "Now how do we get her outside and into the car without people
thinking it's a kidnapping."

"Kidnapping?" A voice said with surprise. Ettie had returned with food.
"I hope everything is okay," she said while doling out the plates.

"It's fine. We were just talking about us kids napping. I'm super tired,"
Sam told her.

"Y'all might want to save room for cookies. They're really good here
and you strike me as a kid who loves cookies," Ettie said, directing her comment to Sam.

This made him grin about as wide as humanly possible. If there was
one universal truth about Sam London it was his love of cookies. It was an
appreciation that even helped save the gryphon. But most importantly, it
was a love his mother knew quite well. Even Tashi acknowledged the coincidence with an eyebrow raise.

"Totally!" Sam confirmed.

"Great," Ettie replied. "If you need anything else just—"

SLAM!

The diner window rattled from a massive impact that reverberated
through the restaurant and wrested every diner's attention. Vance looked

over to find the Sharur in parrot form, dazed and teetering on the edge of the window's ledge. The ancient weapon clearly had not seen the glass and careened right into it.

"Oh my goodness!" Ettie exclaimed. "The poor thing," she said, as she rushed outside. Vance, Sam, and Tashi followed. Vance paused before exiting to address the concerned patrons.

"It's just a bird, folks. It'll be okay," he told the crowd, who seemed comforted enough to return to their food and conversation.

When he got outside, he found Ettie leaning down to check on the parrot. The Sharur, or Sha, as Sam liked to call him, shook off its haze and flew to Sam's shoulder.

"You found her," he said.

Ettie gasped. "It talks?" she replied. "And...you know it?"

"It's my pet," Sam told her. "He knows a few words."

"Sorry!" Sha said. "I didn't see the glass and I was in a hurry—"

"That's more than a few, I'd say," Ettie noted.

"Sha?" Sam addressed the parrot. "This is the waitress from the diner..." He was trying to signal to the Sharur that he needed to cut back on the chattiness.

Sha suddenly squawked—it was a terribly awkward and fake squawk, but at least he tried.

"Trouble. Squawk!" Sha said. "Trouble over there. Squawk! Big trouble. Squawk!" Sha continued. The parrot nudged its head up the road and Vance followed his gaze, but didn't notice anything to be concerned about.

"Trouble?" Vance replied, unsure. "I don't see—"

"Sky. Squawk!" Sha added.

Vance's eyes wandered upward and he caught sight of what the weapon was referring to...and it was most definitely trouble. Large black birds were gathering on the buildings and power lines. There looked to be hundreds of them and their numbers were growing by the second. Vance knew immediately what they were, but it was Tashi who verbalized it.

"Bennu."

The birds that were gathering en masse in downtown Marshall were not of the ordinary variety. Sam recognized that glaring reality immediately. First off, they were entirely black in color, even their beaks and legs. The lack of color variation meant that when they were grouped together they appeared like a mass of darkness. They were also big—two to three feet in length, with a pointed beak, long neck, and a feathery black crest that swept back off the tops of their heads.

As nightmarish as they looked, nothing could compare to the bone-chilling sound of their call. The birds let loose in unison with a vocalization that was a bizarre and disquieting cross between a seagull and the roar of a wild, vicious beast. The noise didn't just sound terrifying; it filled Sam with a sudden, almost debilitating sense of fear. It echoed through the small town and rattled the windows of the storefronts. Pedestrians stopped and looked around for the source. Others emerged from stores and buildings to investigate the awful sound.

"What was that?!" Ettie exclaimed, her hand to her chest. "It scared me half to death."

"They already know what you're planning, Sam," Tashi informed him quietly. "Now do you understand why I protested? No one knows what they are capable of and you've drawn their ire."

"Spilt milk at this point," Vance quipped. "Might as well dump the whole carton. It's now or never."

Sam agreed. Why wait for the bennu to attack? If they were going to act to save Ettie, now was the time.

"Tashi?" Sam said, gesturing to his mother, who was still processing the noise. We have to get out of here, fast."

Tashi sighed, then nodded.

The Guardian stepped toward Ettie and placed her hand on her shoulder. Sam knew from experience that Tashi's healing ability could be used in reverse in a sense. On his first case with the DMW, Sam needed to sleep to meet Phylassos in his dream and Tashi was able to draw enough energy from Sam to send him into a deep sleep. It was no different with Ettie—one moment she was awake and alert, the next she was falling back, unconscious. Tashi caught her and Vance swooped in to assist.

"Let's get her in the car, before someone makes a fuss," he said, as he led Tashi to the SUV. Sam opened the back door and they placed Ettie on the seat. When Vance slammed the door shut, the bennu called out again. It was even more startling than before. Sam felt the sound vibrations pass through his body and reverberate in his bones. He froze for a moment and noticed Vance did, as well.

"Everybody inside!" Vance demanded.

Sam got into the back with Sha, while Tashi took the passenger seat. Vance slipped behind the wheel and started up the engine.

"Looks like we're going to have to take a different route out of town," Vance announced, as he hung a U-turn in the middle of the street.

Sam looked out the back window and spotted the black cloud of bennu now pursuing them. The birds were on the move...and closing fast.

The Guardian Tashi would later note in a case debriefing that she felt as if her actions assisting Sam London in his quest to save his mother were not completely rational. She had become suspicious of Doctor Vantana and the coincidences that got them to this point in the journey. She believed there was something else going on—a magical force that was compelling these events—but it was a fleeting thought that she pushed aside at the time. Perhaps the push was coming from the very same force that was provoking her suspicion. She justified her efforts as those of a friend and protector, who had little choice but to help a cause she did not fully believe in.

As for the bennu, the creatures didn't appear to care about anything but stopping the will of Gaia from being thwarted—even if it meant endangering the lives of those around Ettie. Although these creatures were invisible to humankind, they apparently didn't consider themselves bound by the gryphon's law and acted without concern for exposing the secret.

"The bennu will overcome us, eventually," Tashi reminded Vance, as the SUV sped down the highway with its siren wailing and lights flashing to help clear traffic. He had managed to keep ahead of the creatures, but they were making incremental gains. "What is your plan to evade them?"

"We'll try to lose them at the Tail of the Dragon," Vance assured her.

"Tail of the what?" Sam quickly chimed in from the backseat.

"Dragon, but not the mythical kind," Vance revealed. "This is a roadway. One of the most famous in the world. Three hundred and eighteen curves in eleven miles. And I happen to know it like the back of my hand."

As Vance hit the accelerator and weaved in and out of traffic—barely outrunning the birds, he explained that this "Tail of the Dragon" was a popular road in the Great Smoky Mountains that straddled North Carolina and Tennessee. Though he was confident that the sharp turns and foliage would allow them to outmaneuver the bennu, Tashi had her doubts.

The entrance to the "Tail of the Dragon" was marked by a metal dragon statue. Vance sped past it and towards the first curve. It became quite obvious to Tashi that Vance's plan was not going to work as intended. The birds were simply too smart to be lost so easily. They were nimble and intuitive and the curves on the road were beginning to give them an advantage. Every time Vance had to slow down to turn, the birds gained.

"Um, Dad," Sam said, as he peered through the back window. "This isn't working."

Suddenly, one of the birds caught up with the SUV and was flying next to Tashi's window. When she peered over, the bird looked right at her, its eyes pitch black with a fiery red dot as a pupil. It squawked and the noise shattered the side window. Doctor Vantana swerved reflexively and nearly careened off the road.

"I concur," Tashi said, before she fired at the bennu and hit it. The bird was tossed backward but quickly regained its bearings and continued its pursuit.

"I'm not done yet!" Doctor Vantana declared, as the SUV skidded around another sharp curve. It felt as though the top-heavy vehicle was going to tumble over.

Tashi decided to help matters. The Guardian opened the passenger side door and began to climb up onto the roof of the car.

"Are you crazy?" Sam asked. "Get back in here!"

"I'm going to attempt to slow their pursuit," she explained.

"This seems like a really bad idea," Vance told her, as he kept his eyes on the road.

Tashi didn't like to qualify ideas as good or bad—rather she preferred to judge them on whether they were a success or failure, and failure was never an option.

Tashi pulled herself onto the roof, struggling against the rushing wind. She held onto one side of the car roof, while she got her bearings. Lying on her belly, she slowly climbed to her knees and fought to maintain her balance. Soon, the Guardian was standing tall on the roof of the SUV, as it took sharp, hairpin turns. She leveled her shekchen towards the bennu and began firing. A few were hit and fell away for a moment; then, the birds got smarter. She'd fire and they'd collectively move out of the way. With each shot, a hole would form in the black mass of bennu, and the blast would simply pass right through.

"That's not working," a voice said. She immediately noticed the Sharur was flying alongside her.

"It is this mode of transport," Tashi complained. "They have the advantage of flight."

"You're right," the Sharur squawked. "Maybe I can help." And with that, the parrot returned to the vehicle. A few seconds later, she heard Sam yell up to her.

"Hang on tight!"

Tashi spun around and dropped to her belly, grabbing the sides of the roof. The SUV sped up and the math wasn't difficult to calculate—there was no way Doctor Vantana would be able to make the approaching turn at their current velocity.

"You are going to flip this vehicle!" she shouted to the ranger, but the vehicle continued to increase its speed. Tashi's eyes went wide as Doctor Vantana didn't even bother trying to make the corner. The car simply drove straight towards the edge of the road, left the Tail of the Dragon and launched off a cliff.

Chapter 19

GRAND, GLOOMY, AND PECULIAR

As the SUV plummeted to the ground, Vance Vantana had a momentary thought of the secondary variety. Granted, they were running out of options to escape the relentless bennu and the Sharur insisted its plan would work, but now the car was hurtling toward the ground at breakneck speed with his son and his wife in the backseat, and a Guardian of the Gryphon's Claw clutching onto the roof. They were just a few feet from certain death when the car finally leveled out and rocketed upward, clearing the tree line and disappearing into the clouds. Sam let loose an extended "Woohoo," and Tashi opened the passenger side door and slipped back inside. She glared at Vance.

"A warning would have been courteous," the Guardian said, irritated.

"My apologies for that, but I had to call into HQ to clear the airspace and ran out of time," Vance reported. "For the record, it was the Sharur's idea." He gestured to the Sharur, which had transformed back into his natural weapon form and was pressed up against the roof of the car, which was now dented outward due to the pressure it was applying to hold the car up.

"Technically, it was Tashi's idea," the Sharur noted. "But I am the only one who can fly, so..."

"Road or sky, it hasn't seemed to slow them down," Sam said, hooking a thumb to the rear. The bennu were still in pursuit. The black mass of birds rose up from beneath the cloud cover and was closing in on them once again.

"Little known fact about me," the Sharur began, "Not only am I the most destructive weapon ever created, I'm also the fastest."

And with that, the SUV shot forward with tremendous acceleration. However, given the mace's position on the roof and the manner by which it was flying the car, the force pitched the vehicle at a downward angle as it sped forward. Vance lurched forward and, luckily, the seatbelt engaged before he went through the windshield. The others quickly found themselves at the mercy of their seatbelts as well.

Vance shifted his eyes to the sideview mirror to find that the bennu were still on their tail, but they were falling further behind. He watched patiently until they blinked out of sight, then sighed in relief.

"Speed is our best hope now," he told them. "I don't think they'll follow us into the cave."

"And you know where we need to go once we get inside?" Sam asked.

"I can get us to the doorway to the under-earth, what happens beyond that? Well, there's a first time for everything."

"And a last," Tashi reminded him.

SL003-720-40

SOURCE: PR, AR

DATE: ███████████

Comprised of roughly eighty square miles in Central Kentucky, Mammoth Cave National Park is much more than just above ground hiking trails and picturesque streams. The park is best known for what lies beneath it—the longest cave system in the world. It has been reported that approximately 412 miles of the cave have been explored at the time of this report and that it reaches a depth of 379 feet with five levels of passages. Evidence of human activity in the cave dates back six thousand years. These early inhabitants of the cave were known as the "Archaic Ones." At some point these "Archaic Ones" abandoned the passages and, although human scientists cannot account for their disappearance, the DMW is aware of the true history involving these beings. Such information remains classified and it is for this reason that certain parts of the Mammoth-Flint Ridge cave system are sealed off to any individuals who do not have approval from the DMW.

Since its rediscovery by a European settler in the nineteenth century, the cave system has mystified and intrigued humans. Tourists have come from far and wide to explore the passages and marvel at the beauty of the limestone formations. The earliest maps of the passages were drawn by Stephen Bishop, an African-American slave who acted as a guide to tourists. Bishop was the first to cross what is known as the "Bottomless Pit," which opened up a new area of exploration. He famously referred to the cave as "grand, gloomy, and peculiar," and it is likely Mr. Bishop knew just how peculiar, if he had ventured into some of the now secret areas.

With high public interest, competing property owners, and poor upkeep, the U.S. government decided to get involved. In 1924, the Mammoth Cave National Park Association was created to go about acquiring the land necessary to create a national park and the Civilian Conservation Corps began work on constructing the facilities that would be needed, including housing, roads, communications systems, trails, and restrooms. Mammoth Cave National Park was formerly dedicated as the twenty-sixth park in the system in 1946.

Establishing Mammoth Cave as a national park was a critical part of the Department of Mythical Wildlife's early mission. Though the DMW went about securing the parks that already included mythical creatures, it also sought to protect other areas that would either become homes for displaced creatures or were vital to helping protect the secret. The latter included Mammoth Cave.

Soaring through the air in a sport utility vehicle by way of a magic talking mace would be an extraordinary experience for most everyone, including Sam London, but Sam's mind was too busy playing out scenarios of how they would manage to save Ettie. As he gazed out the window of the SUV, he wasn't marveling at the fact it was a flying, rather he had his eyes on the horizon. The sun was setting and it was like a giant orange hourglass, reminding Sam that Ettie's time was running out.

Sam didn't want to entertain the possibility that they wouldn't make it before the moon rose, but he couldn't help but contemplate how they might deal with failure. Perhaps they could simply befriend this new version of Ettie and hope she enjoyed their company. Or maybe they could convince her she had amnesia and had forgotten about them. Vance must have noticed the consternation on his son's face.

"Don't worry, Sam," his dad told him. "I think luck is on our side on this one. We'll make it." Vance winked at his son, then looked ahead.

His words certainly calmed Sam. There was a confidence in his voice that gave him a brief respite from his anxieties. It did sort of seem like luck was on their side. From Vance's mistake in choosing the "wrong" dvergen station to stepping into that diner, perhaps the universe had chosen to throw Sam London a bone.

"Why would 'luck' be on our side?" Tashi inquired, delivering a suspicious side eye to Vance.

"Relax, Tashi," Vance told her. "It's a good thing, right?" Tashi didn't appear satisfied with his answer. Her eyes lingered on Vance, until he purposely changed the subject. "We're approaching the park. Sharur, touch us down near that loop of road right over there." Vance gestured ahead.

"Sure thing, Vance," Sha replied.

The SUV slowly descended toward the spot. It was dusk and the park had been emptied of tourists per Vance's request. The landing was a bit rough, as the Sharur dropped the SUV a few feet from the ground.

"Let's move," Vance ordered, as he opened the door.

Sam climbed out of the car and found himself in a heavily wooded area that was looped by a narrow roadway and sat inside a shallow valley. There was a small wooden pavilion at the bottom of a set of stairs, which led to another set of stairs and a path that ended at two rusty metal doors. Tashi got out of the car and helped Vance pull the still unconscious Ettie from the backseat. The Sharur transformed into parrot form and perched itself on Sam's shoulder.

"I'm going to scout above the tree line and make sure we're in the—" Sha began to say, but Sam had already looked toward the horizon and saw the dark cloud of bennu rise up over the trees.

"They're coming!" Sam announced.

Vance quickly carried Ettie to the pavilion with Sam and Tashi close behind.

"If they catch us, they will return us to Gaia," Tashi told Sam, before looking to Vance and adding, "You they will likely just kill."

"I've been dead before," Vance quipped. "I don't feel like dying again."

When they reached the cave entrance that was built into a concrete structure embedded in the hillside, Sam opened the creaky double doors, revealing a staircase that led to a single door with a small, vertical, narrow window. They all entered the stairwell, as the squawks of the bennu grew louder.

"Shut those doors," Vance ordered. Tashi closed them, but they had holes where knobs should be—meaning the bennu could easily pass through.

The creatures smashed into the metal doors with a loud clang. Their repeated strikes multiplied quickly until they sounded like machine gun fire–each hit denting and shaking the metal doors. A few found the holes and Tashi quickly fired her shekchen to drive them back.

"We cannot hold them here forever," Tashi reported.

"We need to get further inside," Vance said. Sam and the Sharur headed through the single door at the end of the first stairway. Vance followed, then

Tashi slipped down the steps and through the doorway. She shut it just as dozens of bennu slipped through the holes in the main doors and swarmed the short stairwell.

"They will get through here in seconds," Tashi said, gesturing to the single closed door.

"I can help," Sha said, then turned itself back into a mace and pressed itself against the metal door. "Go!" The magical mace exclaimed. Tashi looked to Sam, unsure. "Go on," Sha insisted. "They cannot return me to Gaia."

"The weapon has a point," Tashi said, then stepped down a long stairway with Sam and Vance.

At the end of this second stairway was another door, which they closed as well. The trio—or quartet, including Ettie in the arms of Vance—hurried around a bend and into a large passageway. It was dimly lit and seemed to go on forever.

Although they had no time for sightseeing, Sam caught glimpses of the interior of the cave, which was at once awe-inspiring and unsettling. The latter was due to the quiet eeriness of the space.

They continued down a long passage that Vance referred to as Cleveland Avenue. It led to the "Snowball Room," a cavern with bulbous chunks of gypsum that dotted the ceiling. They continued past an area with picnic tables and bathrooms and into a place Vance called "Mary's Vineyard," named for the formations that looked like grapes. At this point, Vance veered left down a narrow unlit passage with stairs. That passage led to a fork and Vance headed left. Sam and Tashi followed and they soon reached an underground river. There was a small rowboat waiting and they climbed inside. Vance laid Ettie down, then moved to the front of the boat, where he switched on an electric lantern. He picked up a long oar from inside the boat and used it to push off from the rocky platform.

"This is the Echo River," Vance noted, as he guided the boat through the dark passage. "Back that way is the River Styx," he added, gesturing behind them. "Ironic considering where we're headed."

The boat continued along for a minute or two, when suddenly Vance pushed off the bottom with the oar and directed the boat toward a cave wall.

"Dad! Look out!" Sam exclaimed, as he pointed to the fast approaching wall.

"You should know how we roll by now," Vance quipped...and the boat passed right through the wall. It was an illusion of some kind that Sam surmised was either magical in nature or created with hidden projectors.

The river opened up into a cavernous chamber, which the lantern could only partially illuminate. Tashi helped supplement the low light by firing up her shekchen. The inside looked like a castle formed from rock. Massive spires of limestone shot up from the water towards the ceiling. Vance maneuvered around the spires and towards another passage.

"Hang on," he cautioned. Sam grabbed onto the sides of the boat, as it entered the tunnel and immediately tipped downward.

The boat rode down a small rapid that dropped it with a splash into another cavern. This one was shorter in height and the walls were smoother, reminding Sam of the dvergen tunnels. *Had this part of the cave been carved by hand?* Sam wondered. They drifted up to a narrow rocky shoreline that jutted out from a cave wall. The wall sported a door-sized silver panel in its center. Sam grabbed the lantern as he climbed off the boat with the others.

Vance walked to the panel and pushed on a rocky protrusion on the adjacent cave wall. The panel slid open with a long creak, revealing that it was at least a foot thick and hiding a wood elevator that wasn't much more than a box with a cable mechanism at the top. Once inside, Vance shifted the old fashioned control handle clockwise and the elevator lurched, then began to descend.

It finally came to a sudden and abrupt halt. There was no elevator door here, rather it was just an opening to another cave.

"Stay close," Vance warned.

They stepped into a narrow passage. The lantern Sam was holding provided just enough illumination to see a few feet ahead. The passage led to a larger chamber, and Sam raised the lantern to get a better look, but the light flickered then shut off. They were instantly thrust into darkness, but Sam noticed a faint glow in the distance.

"Wait, there's a light up ahead," Sam announced and headed for it.

"Sam, don't!" Vance yelled.

But Sam was already reaching out for the glowing orb when Tashi fired up her shekchen and illuminated the chamber. Sam quickly discovered that the glowing orb of light he was reaching for was attached to a massive beetle. The monstrous bug was at least four feet long and made a deafening clicking noise as it leapt into the air and landed on Sam. He fell onto his back and struggled against the giant insect, its pinchers just inches from his face and snapping. Tashi fired a shot from her shekchen and nailed the creature. It sailed across the room, slammed into the cave wall, then scampered into the darkness.

"What the heck was that?!" Sam exclaimed, jumping to his feet.

"Headlight elator," Vance told him. "A species of click beetle that has bioluminescence."

"It was huge!" Sam said, shivering from the sheer creepiness of it.

"Nature works a little differently down here," Vance reported. "Some people believe it has something to do with the proximity to Gaia. We don't know for certain. No one comes down here to do much scientific study. At least, not anymore."

"Why not?" Sam asked, already predicting the answer.

"In the early years of the DMW, they sent a few people in. Problem was, they never came out," Vance revealed. "The humans, anyway."

"And the mythical creatures?" Sam wondered.

"The ones who did return refused to talk about it," Vance revealed. They were fearful that if they spoke about what lies beyond this, the guard wouldn't let them pass through again."

"Guard?" Sam inquired with concern.

"You didn't mention a guard before, Doctor," Tashi said. "What kind of guard?"

"No one knows—or at least, no one's talking," Vance replied. "Whatever it is, it guards the gateway to the under-earth and one must have a good reason to be allowed to pass."

"And if you do not have a good reason?" Tashi inquired.

"Let's just hope we do," Vance said. "I'm not worried."

"How are you so confident?" Tashi asked. "This guard could be a deadly creature."

"The deadliest creature," Vance corrected her.

"Excuse me?"

"I said we don't know what kind of guard is at the gate, but we do know that it's supposedly the deadliest creature in the mythical world," Vance revealed. "It doesn't matter—"

"I believe it does matter," Tashi told him. "Because I do not believe we have good reason—at least not in the eyes of those that protect the will of Gaia. And I imagine this creature—whatever it is—is also a protector."

Sam didn't much like the sound of any of this, but he also was trying his best to keep focused. Time was ticking.

"Can we just go and find out?" Sam said. "We don't have long before it'll be too late, anyway."

"Sam's right," Vance asserted. "And plus, I have a secret weapon."

"What kind of weapon?" Tashi asked, as Vance started toward the entrance to another passageway.

"I inadvertently borrowed something from the vault," he admitted. "Something magical."

"I knew it!" Tashi declared. "All of this? It was far too coincidental."

"I didn't realize I still had it until after Fort Jefferson," Vance told them. "And I haven't used it—at least, not intentionally. This object—I think it works whether you want it to or not. I thought keeping it sealed in its case was enough to prevent it from doing what it does—"

"Which is what exactly?" Tashi asked.

"It helps things go the way you hope, in a sense," Vance explained.

"Does it manipulate behaviors and events?" Tashi inquired.

"I don't know how it works.... Point is, it works. And it helped us get this far. Hopefully, it'll take us the rest of the way," Vance said, then headed into the passage.

Sam followed his dad, and Tashi brought up the rear. She was clearly annoyed by his admission, but anything that helped the cause was okay by Sam. The passage they were in serpentined, and scurrying creatures could be heard all around them—probably more of those terrifying beetles, Sam speculated. The passageway eventually opened up into a cavern, whose walls emitted a faint blue glow. Sam recognized it as the same phenomenon he experienced in the cave of the Mongolian death worm—veins of Gaia's energy. These blue streams webbed out across the walls, ceiling, and floor and all led to the other side of the cave, where there was an intricately carved archway that led to a smaller chamber. There were two large columns on either side of this space, and above was an arcing band of sculpted rock. In the middle of the arch was a diamond shaped cutout that held a fiery red-orange gem. But it was what lay beyond this archway that took Sam's breath away…and not in a good way.

There was a creature—if you could even call it that—inside the separated chamber. It was a gruesome beast that looked like an amalgamation of several animals smashed together into a mutated mass of flesh and bone. Its flesh was so thin and emaciated that you could see the animal's organs, as well as the blood pulsing through its arteries. The skin was covered in pustules that were erupting copious amounts of yellow pus. A slimy green mucus seeped out of what looked like the creature's nose and dripped down to where it joined with a brownish-hued saliva. The beast was the size of a Clydesdale and had borrowed parts from a veritable hodgepodge of creatures, including a camel, warthog, hairless cat, and a goblin shark—a particularly monstrous animal Sam had once seen on a nature show. Like the goblin shark, this creature had a protruding jaw of sharp jagged teeth and a long snout. It also featured a misshapen, yellow horn that sprung from the top of its head. It was too awful to look at for more than a moment and Sam quickly turned away, utterly disgusted.

"Ewwww, gross," Sam whispered. "I'm seriously going to throw up."

"Maybe the rumors got bungled and they meant to say the homeliest creature," Vance remarked. "That thing is uglier than a mud fence—and I reckon even its momma would agree."

"What are you both talking about?" Tashi asked, incredulous. Sam noticed the Guardian was looking the creature's way but her face was lit up. She was smiling, broadly. "That creature is the most beautiful animal I've ever seen."

"You're joking," Sam said. "It's hideous."

"It is no such thing," Tashi insisted.

"Hold on now," Vance ordered. "What exactly do you see, Tashi?"

"I see a shimmering, majestic unicorn..." the Guardian revealed with breathless wonder. "Its body is a different vivid color every time I shift my gaze. Like a crystal refracting the frequencies of light. A truly magnificent beast. Do you not also see it too?"

"You don't want to know what we see," Vance told her.

"Yeah, I wish I could unsee it," Sam added.

"I've heard rumors of this," Vance posited. "To those who are pure of heart, unicorns appear as their conventional depiction in folklore—magnificent creatures. But to those who aren't, they look like that thing."

"I'm just a kid," Sam countered. "I'm pure of heart." Vance flashed him a side eye.

"You ever squash a bug just because?" his dad asked.

"Maybe," Sam replied with a guiltless shrug.

"She hasn't," Vance said, gesturing toward Tashi, who was staring lovingly at the unicorn. "Ugly or not, I think we can agree that it is deadly." Vance pointed to the area surrounding the creature and Sam noticed what was scattered about wasn't rocks...it was skulls and bones and complete skeletons. "I guess we know why no one returned." Sam swallowed his fear and spotted their goal directly behind the unicorn.

"Is that a—" Sam began, pointing to a large circular disc in the ground that glowed blue and resembled a perfectly round puddle of still water.

"Gate of Gaia by the looks of it," Vance completed Sam's thought. "The gateway to the under-earth."

"So we just need to get past that thing," Sam said, considering their next steps. The unicorn suddenly became aware of their presence, as if Sam's pronouncement had nudged it. The creature shifted its head toward them and snorted. It bared its fangs and its jaw protruded farther from its mouth. Man, this animal was freaky. And the stench...Sam caught a whiff of it a moment after it looked their way. It smelled like an outhouse at high noon on the hottest day of summer. Tashi breathed it in and exhaled with what Sam could only describe as delight.

"What a beautiful scent," she declared. "This creature is a wonder for all five senses."

"Here's what I think the plan should be—"

Before Vance could finish his sentence, Tashi bounded forward without hesitation.

"Tashi!" Sam called out, but she was already at the unicorn. She reached out to pet the creature, lightly stroking its head. But all Sam could see was Tashi's hand running across a pitted, pus-laden mane of ratty black hair. "Ugh, don't touch it!" Sam exclaimed. "You're not allowed to touch me with those hands ever again."

"You're speaking nonsense, Sam London," Tashi replied. "Atu means us no harm. She is happy we are here."

The unicorn stretched its neck and snatched one of the skulls up in its jaws. It bit down, crushing it, then started chewing. Sam was horrified.

"Uh...what do you see it doing right now, Tashi?" Sam asked.

"It's eating sunflowers. They're surrounding her. The most perfect, vibrant sunflowers," the Guardian reported. Sam looked to Vance, who raised his eyebrows.

"Does it know why we're here?" Vance asked. Tashi nodded.

"She does," the Guardian replied. "She will let us pass." Both Sam and Vance sighed with relief. They moved toward the creature, as Tashi continued to pet its grotesque body. When they crossed under the archway, Tashi turned to Sam.

"Do not forget to thank the creature, Sam," Tashi told him. Sam eyed her a moment, unsure of her meaning. Then he looked to the unicorn and managed a subdued, "Thank you."

"Pet it," Tashi instructed, gesturing to the animal.

"Seriously?" Sam asked, furrowing his brow.

"Sam London! You will show your gratefulness to this majestic creature, this instant!" she demanded. "She is an ancient animal that was chosen by Gaia to protect this portal. It is an honor to be in her presence," the Guardian said, before adding, quietly, "You should be bowing to her. Now go on and show her you are grateful."

Sam swallowed, then looked to Vance, who shrugged.

"I don't reckon it's going to eat you," Vance whispered.

"That's encouraging."

"Just go on and get it over with," Vance told him. "Close your eyes if that makes it easier."

"You will be showing your gratefulness as well, Doctor," Tashi informed him.

"Pardon?"

"Pet and thank the unicorn for allowing us to be in its presence and for letting us pass," she directed.

"But I'm holding Ettie," Vance countered. It was true—he didn't really have a free hand, as he was now carrying Ettie in both arms.

"Give her to me. I will carry her," Tashi asserted, then stepped forward and scooped Ettie up from Vance's arms. Sam smirked at his dad. "You can always just close your eyes."

His father sighed and approached the unicorn with Sam. The creature grunted loudly and they both jumped back.

"She will not harm you," Tashi assured them. "You are acting like infants."

Sam reached out and placed his hand on the creature in the safest spot he could find—one that didn't appear to be seeping or infected. But even then, the creature's skin was sticky to the touch. When Sam dragged his hand across the unicorn's body, petting it, his hand was soon coated in a grungy slime that he wiped off on his pants—pants that he would no doubt be burning when he returned home. Vance followed suit, but inadvertently triggered a giant pimple on the unicorn. Like a crusty, pink volcano, it exploded and sent a spray of yellow pus onto Vance's face. He gagged and scrambled to scrape it off with his shirt as best he could. It was totally gross, yet he somehow managed not to puke. Sam nearly did just watching the eruption.

"She must like you," Tashi noted. Vance glared at her in disbelief. Tashi noticed his expression, then added. "She covered you in glitter!"

"Gli—" Vance was about to verbally explode, but Sam touched his arm and shook his head. Vance nodded and calmed down—this was not the time to argue.

"The unicorn wishes me to go first," Tashi said, then walked to the portal and stepped inside.

"Wait!"

But she had already vanished through the gate, leaving Vance and Sam alone with the unicorn. It instantly spun around and snarled at them. *Uh oh*, Sam thought. It lunged, but one of its front hooves slipped on a skull.

"Quick!" Vance shouted and they both leapt into the gate.

Sam was freefalling through a black void. He was trying to get his bearings and right himself when his momentum suddenly stopped...but he hadn't hit the ground. He felt like he was floating, and when his eyes adjusted he saw a magnificent city before him. The buildings appeared to be carved from rock and minerals of varying, vibrant colors. They were massive spires of stalagmites, but with openings akin to windows that were lit from within. Sam noticed the lighting of the under-earth was surprisingly bright. The entire city of Agartha glowed with a warm hue that radiated from beneath—it looked to be built on a bed of rose quartz with a miniature sun shining through it.

Sam was so entranced by the awesome, other-worldly sights of the city and its strange source of illumination, he almost didn't realize that he was flying. But the more amazing part was how.

Sam London had wings.

Chapter 20
RETURN FROM GAIA

Sam London could fly and it was everything he dreamt it would be.
The instant he became aware of his wings he put them to the test. He rocketed up, dove down, twirled and spun and reveled in every exhilarating superhero-kind-of-moment. His sense of freedom was transcendent. The wings didn't feel alien to him. It was as though they were simply part of his body, like an arm or a leg. Flapping these feathered appendages were second nature and reflexive, akin to breathing. Sam surrendered to the thrill, the rush, and the absolute joy that had suddenly become available to him. He had willed this metamorphosis as he fell from the gate, a survival instinct kicked in and had transformed Sam, both literally and figuratively.

Sam had never felt more like himself than in this form. So enthralled with his new found ability, Sam didn't immediately notice what was happening around him. And then a strange, airy voice that fluctuated in timbre brought him back down to earth—or the under-earth, as it were.

"The moon rises, child. The swan maiden's time is dwindling."

Sam glanced over to the source of the voice and saw an ethereal being standing on a white, glowing disc. The figure was tall and thin with long limbs and wispy fingers. It appeared to emit a radiance of light—a permanent aura of silvery white.

"Who are you?"

"Nergal. I am an Archaic One. A being of the under-earth, an oracle of Gaia."

Sam instantly snapped out of his happy fog and got his bearings. He was hovering above a ledge that jutted out from a mountainside of reddish-hued rock, which looked out over the city. He descended and landed softly on the plateau.

"Nice wings," Tashi said with a smirk. He immediately felt self-conscious and that triggered a tingling feeling on his back. The wings instantly receded into his body—this ability really did operate like an innate reflex. He hoped he might have time to experiment with how he could will his transformation, but he suddenly realized someone was missing.

"Where's my dad?" Sam asked, scanning the area to see if he had missed him.

"I do not know," Tashi replied. "Did he enter the gate?"

"Yeah. We both did. At the same time," Sam told her. "You left us with that monster. It was going to eat us."

"You are being dramatic, Sam," Tashi said.

"I'm being serious," Sam insisted. "You were like hypnotized by that thing. It was chomping on skulls up there."

"The unicorn has an ability to entrance those pure of heart," the ethereal being chimed in, now floating just beyond the edge of the ridge. "But it can also trick those who aren't. It is a protective instinct, a way to dissuade those seeking to do it harm or those looking to enter the under-earth without a worthy reason."

"So it isn't the deadliest creature?" Sam clarified.

"No, it most certainly is," the being replied. "But it would only kill if left with no other choice."

Sam nodded. That was somewhat reassuring. If Vance was stuck up there with that creature, it hopefully didn't see him as a threat. But Sam still wasn't sure why he never made it down. Tashi must have sensed his lingering question.

"I think it was because of that magical object he had," she speculated in a whisper, as she leaned over to Sam. "The unicorn told me to leave my shekchen, as magical objects are not allowed to pass through the gate."

"Why not?" Sam wondered.

"For the same reason you were able to grow wings," the being answered. "Magic is amplified the closer one gets to Gaia. A Guardian's shekchen would be too dangerous to wield in the under-earth. Your powers were strengthened enough to manifest themselves before maturity."

"So once I leave this place..." Sam began to say.

"So will those abilities," Nergal revealed. "But they will appear in time."

Sam nodded, understandingly. "Can you help me bring my mom back?"

Nergal shook his head. "That is up to Gaia. Only she can decide what is right and just."

"And how does a person ask Gaia for this?"

"You must be in her presence," Nergal explained.

"Is she there—in Agartha?" Sam asked, gesturing to the glowing city in the distance.

"The great under-earth city of Agartha lies near to Gaia. Near enough to power our world and lighten our days, but you will need to go closer," Nergal explained. "There are places—ancient places—that were once used to divine her wishes. There you can ask for what you seek. But be warned, what you ask defies her will. It has never been done, nor do I believe it should."

"Then why did you grant us permission to enter here?" Tashi asked Nergal.

"A wise question, Guardian," Nergal replied. "For if it was only up to us, you would not be here. But the Archaic Ones allowed passage out of respect to the king of all mythical creatures."

"Phylassos?" Sam asked, surprised.

"The gryphon came to us in a dream days ago. He believed there was an injustice done to you, Sam London. One he felt responsible for, but one he could not resolve," Nergal explained. "He believed you might succeed in bringing the swan maiden here to attempt to right this perceived wrong. He assured us he would not interfere and we agreed to allow you a chance, if you managed what we concluded was near impossible. How did you find her and avoid the bennu?"

"Sort of a long story, but—"

"Magic was involved," Tashi confessed. "Not from the gryphon, but something powerful helped us find this new incarnation of Odette." Nergal considered it and nodded.

"It seems that perhaps the universe has conspired to aid you in your quest in other ways as well, Sam London," Nergal told him.

"Other ways?" he asked, unsure of Nergal's meaning.

"Simply passing through the gate with Odette would not have been enough. To reach Gaia we must venture deep inside the earth. It is a long journey and we would have reached it far too late for what you seek."

"Would have?" Sam replied, but Nergal likely didn't hear him, as the being was now floating toward the mountainside. He placed a glowing hand on the rock that was webbed with iridescent blue veins—Gaia's energy. A moment later, the ledge shook beneath Sam and he nearly lost his footing.

Gargantuan chunks of mountain broke off and crumbled down into the serpentine valley below. A fissure opened up in the mountainside and Sam's mind was suddenly inundated with flashes of orange and green. The colors were so vibrant, so vivid that they triggered their corresponding emotions in Sam. He felt a surge of positive energy overwhelm him and he reflexively smiled. The Mongolian death worm had arrived.

"The worms are among the most ancient of creatures. A true elder of the under-earth that is capable of taking us to Gaia in time," Nergal explained.

"It will help us?" Sam asked.

"It insisted," Nergal revealed. "The worm can sense much beyond our understanding. Your link to it is eternal, though you may not realize it. The worm knew when you made contact with Odette and the bennu came for you. She wished to thank you for helping to reunite her with her child by helping however she could to reunite you with your mother."

This revelation touched Sam. He concentrated on the color that best reflected this joy and gratefulness. It was a blazing yellow that shone like the sun. The worm responded in kind and Sam felt an immediate sense of calm. She emerged completely from the hole and set down on the edge of the ridge. Sam noticed the worm's baby was tucked into one of the grooves between the segments of its mother's body.

"We must hurry," Nergal declared, as he slid into one of those same grooves along the worm's skin.

"For protection during travel," the being explained.

Tashi stepped forward, then placed Ettie over her shoulder. She climbed onto the worm and tucked Ettie into a groove, before slipping into the one next to her. Sam was the last to board. He grabbed onto one of the large coarse hairs that sprung from the worm's skin and pulled himself up. He settled into the same groove as his mom, so he could keep an eye on her.

It should be noted that under normal circumstances, Sam London would be thoroughly disgusted at the mere thought of crawling into a fleshy, pink furrow of the segmented body of a monster worm, but desperate times, as the saying goes. He tried to keep his eyes on the prize, metaphorically speaking, of course. His real eyes were closed as soon as he tucked himself into that squishy, damp, musty groove. It felt like he had been rolled up in a wet towel that was left on the floor of the bathroom for a few days, maybe even weeks. Sam knew that odor, since he would often subject his own bath towels to the same treatment, much to the chagrin of his mother.

Once the worm took off, it was like being blindfolded and strapped to a deafening rollercoaster that jumped the tracks. Sam's digestive organs seemed to float up into his chest cavity, where they remained for the duration of the trip. The sound of rock crumbling away from the worm's body as it dove into the earth was tremendous, like a continuous, terrifying avalanche.

When the worm's forward momentum came to a slow stop, Sam instantly saw flashes of green—the worm was communicating safety. The furrow opened and light hit Sam's closed eyes. He opened them and squinted from the brightness. His vision adjusted, and he saw Tashi looming over him, offering her hand. He took it without a word and she pulled him from the groove. Sam slid down the side of the worm and found his mom was already there, lying down on the ground on lush, green grass. It was easily the most vibrant shade of green Sam had ever seen. It was almost surreal, as if painted on a canvas. He scanned the area and took in his extraordinary surroundings.

He was standing at the end of a long cavity in the earth that was structured like an ancient Greek or Roman temple. But this "temple" wasn't built out of marble or limestone; it appeared to be made out of plants and trees of every kind. The sides of the cave were lined with soaring trees, Gaia's version of the columns seen in ancient architecture. These trees were as massive as the redwoods that populated the bigfoot habitation zone of Redwood National Park. They stretched high into the air, and sported branches that reached out across the cave, creating a ceiling of leaves at their peak autumn colors...but these colors were constantly changing. It was a moving, vivid canopy of reds, oranges, purples, and yellows. The ground was covered in scores of flowers that also changed color at will and rivaled those found in the Swan Maiden Sanctuary. They were in a continuous cycle of blooming, giving the ground—like the canopy—the illusion of movement.

Sam was joined by Tashi—carrying Ettie—and Nergal. They paused at the base of steps formed by thick tree roots, which led into the temple's columned hall.

"Gaia awaits us beyond this point," Nergal announced, then walked up the steps and entered the hall.

Though the ground was blanketed in those constantly blooming flowers, they receded with every step the trio took, creating a series of grassy stepping stones that appeared only when needed. Sam also noted that the leaves on the trees rustled every time Sam took a step forward, as though they could sense and feel his touch. Sam continued to follow Nergal and peered ahead to catch a glimpse of what might be waiting in the distance, but there was nothing to see except more trees and fields of ever-changing flowers. It appeared as if the hall was infinite, and when Sam looked back to the entrance, it was no longer visible.

Sam was about to ask Nergal how much further they would need to go, when the Archaic One suddenly stopped walking.

"Is this it?" Sam asked, stopping and glancing around. It didn't look any different than the area to the front or rear of them.

When Nergal didn't answer, Sam reached out to tap his shoulder. But before Sam could make contact, the ancient being turned to face them. His eyes were now glowing blue—sapphire spheres devoid of pupils. Sam stumbled back in surprise. The voice that emerged from Nergal was not the same as before. It sounded like several female voices speaking in unison, their vocal resonances just barely different to detect the distinction.

"Greetings, Sam," the choir of voices spoke. Nergal, who had been completely expressionless up to this point was grinning broadly. It was a disarming smile, one that made Sam feel instantly comforted. He quickly deduced that Nergal had been possessed by Gaia. "It is nice to meet you and you, as well, Tashi of Kustos. Though we have already known each other since your lives began."

Tashi suddenly fell to her knees and bowed her head in deference.

"It is my honor, Gaia," she said, her voice shaking. This was the first time Sam had heard Tashi sound genuinely nervous. He realized he should probably be bowing, as well. He moved to kneel, but Gaia touched his shoulder and shook her head.

"There is no need to genuflect in my presence," Gaia told him. "We are not kings or queens, nor do we require your veneration." Sam nodded with understanding, then Tashi peered upward and Gaia motioned for her to stand. Tashi rose to her feet, slowly, and Gaia walked to her. "And this is the shell that contained the swan maiden," Gaia said.

She held out her arms and Tashi handed Ettie's unconscious body over. Gaia turned and the flowers that covered the ground suddenly rose up, forming into a bed. Gaia laid Ettie upon the bed and gently stroked her hair. "Odette is how we knew her. She served your world for us. Magic exists in the over-earth because of sanctuaries like that of the swan maidens. These gardens are connected to Gaia, allowing magic to find its way to the surface where it is cultivated and harnessed. It is why the rules that govern the garden are so strictly enforced. Tending the sanctuary is a great responsibility, one that has far-reaching consequences. The verdict of the council was just."

"Just?" Sam asked rhetorically. "She was punished for falling in love. And my dad was punished for simply trying to protect her. And I was punished because I was born. Both my mom and I lost all of those years with my dad. Then she lost her life. That isn't fair or just."

"Sam!" Tashi scolded him.

"What?" he replied. "It's true. It wasn't her fault. It wasn't Vance's fault. If anything, the universe caused these events to happen in this way. If I hadn't followed my dream and gone to Death Valley, I wouldn't have met my dad—and my mom would still be alive. I was destined to go and in that moment I doomed her. But what if I hadn't? If I stayed home and ignored that dream, the world wouldn't be the same. Magic would be used for evil and the gryphon would be dead."

"We understand your feelings, Sam," Gaia said. "We feel them too, as you are part magical and connected to us. It is a connection that goes beyond the physical forms your kind inhabit. Odette is not gone. She is everywhere you look, Sam. Her soul is part of our world. She is present even here and now. One day you too will join her." Gaia plucked a flower from the bed Ettie lay on. "When this flower returns to Gaia, another appears." The flower disintegrated in Gaia's hand and the particles that were left drifted back to the bed. Upon touching the surface, another flower sprouted, blossoming taller than the others. "The body does not have a soul, it is the soul that has a body."

"But we found her. We did it before the new moon," Sam said. "That means she can be returned. Her soul can return to this body."

"What do you think of this request, Tashi of Kustos?" Gaia asked.

Sam immediately looked to Tashi with anxious eyes. He already knew how she felt about it, but would admitting it to Gaia harm Sam's chances of getting his mom back? Tashi avoided his pleading gaze.

"I believe Sam never properly mourned his mother," the Guardian answered.

"But I have," Sam interrupted.

"You have not let go, Sam," Tashi replied firmly. "It is your human side that clings to the notion that Ettie's spirit is better in a body than in joining with Gaia and enriching the world."

"She deserves a chance to live as she had hoped to live—with her husband and her son," Sam insisted. "Maybe it is the human part of me that wants her back. But I'm just righting a wrong. To be honest, I didn't even think I'd make it this far. I thought I was going to die in the worm's cave. I had given up on finding her before we saw Marshall."

Tashi faced Sam and placed her hands on his shoulders. It was an unexpected move from the Guardian and caught Sam by surprise. He quickly met her gaze and her sympathetic eyes calmed him for a moment.

"I know you care deeply for her. I care deeply for my own parents," she said softly. "But there are rules to our world. Certain realities that, no matter how painful, must be accepted."

"No," Sam said defiantly, and stepped back so Tashi's hands were no longer on his shoulders. Her arms dropped awkwardly to her sides. "Pinga told my dad that we could save her. I'm here to do that." Sam shifted his attention to the possessed Nergal. "You are Gaia, the very life force of the earth. I was told you can restore my mom's soul, can you do that or not?"

"It is possible," Gaia answered.

"Then please do it," Sam replied.

"There is a cost," the being revealed.

"I know," Sam replied.

"A balance must be kept," Gaia explained. "You cannot take from Gaia without giving. To restore your mother's soul to this body would create an imbalance."

"So this cost would restore the balance," Sam reasoned. Gaia nodded.

"It can."

"But it must not happen," Tashi insisted.

"Why not?" He was growing more than a little frustrated with all of the caginess.

"Because it demands a sacrifice," Gaia answered. That word got Sam's attention. What could one give in exchange for Ettie's soul? Ettie's body was here, Sam just wanted her spirit, her life force back where it belonged. And then he had a realization.

"Take it," he said, firmly.

"No, Sam—" Tashi protested.

"My magic, right? That's what we're talking about?" Sam asked. "If you take my magic from me, it will keep the balance."

Gaia nodded. "Both you and your mother will become completely human."

"Sam, you do not even yet know the strength of your powers," Tashi told him. "Destiny brought you to Death Valley and led you to save the gryphon and the world. We do not know what the future holds. But your magic will protect you when destiny calls again. It is who you are."

Tashi's words gave Sam pause. He couldn't disagree. The moment he grew wings and took flight was unlike anything he'd ever known or imagined possible. It was like being reborn. As if he suddenly realized who he was and finally had the chance to live as his true self.

For so long, Sam had believed there was nothing special about him. Nothing that helped him stand out. Nothing he was good at. Then the gryphon appeared to him in a dream and changed everything. It was true that he helped save the gryphon and save the world. That he saved Princess Iaira and her kingdom. Just in the last few days, he helped the death worm reunite with her child, averted a world-ending catastrophe, and helped bring Cernunnos to justice.

But he had done all of this without magic. It was his curiosity. His determination. His sense of right and wrong guided him in his time with the DMW. He was suddenly reminded of the words of an old friend who had returned to Gaia after sacrificing himself to save Sam.

"It's not who you are that makes you special, it's what you do," Sam said aloud. "I want to do this."

Gaia grabbed hold of Ettie's hand and reached out her other hand toward Sam.

"Take my hand and know this, Sam London," Gaia's tone turned serious. "There is no reversing this decision. You will no longer be a magical creature. That part of you will be returned to Gaia, leaving only the essence of you that is human. As such, you will be vulnerable to all that threatens this fragile form."

Sam moved to grab her hand, but Tashi grabbed it instead.

"I cannot allow this to happen," she declared. "I am sworn to protect you. It is my duty as a Guardian. An oath I took when I healed you and gave you back your life."

"It is not your decision," Sam reminded her.

"Yes, but I do not think you realize the consequences of your choice. The danger you will be placing yourself in. As your friend and protector, I must stop you."

"A friend would understand why I have to do this," Sam asserted.

"I do understand," Tashi insisted. "But that doesn't change my reasoning. Your mother would not want you to let go of the magic she gave you. Especially if it might save your life. She gave her life for you. She understood the stakes. Let us leave this place, before you make a mistake that cannot be undone."

"The only mistake I've made was bringing you down here," Sam said, more harshly than he intended. "I just...I should have known you would try and stop me. I'm sorry I got you involved."

"I am trying to help you," Tashi stammered in reply, surprised by Sam's tone.

"I know that's what you think. And I know you took an oath and that you're bound to me. I'm sorry for that and for all the trouble I've been. How about this? I officially release you from your oath, Tashi. From everything. Thank you for healing me and protecting me and putting up with me, but you don't have to worry about me, anymore. Consider yourself free."

"Sam, please," Tashi pleaded.

Sam could see she was upset. Her eyes were watering. Perhaps he crossed a line, he admitted to himself. He was frustrated and upset. He could apologize later. Right now he had more important things to do and his time to do them was disappearing.

Tashi caught his eye and said, slowly, "I'm doing this because I—"

"Have to, I get it," he interrupted. Tashi was now holding his hand with both of hers. Grasping it, tightly.

"No, that's not it—"

"My life is my own, Tashi," Sam said, cutting her off again. "I know you mean well, but my family is everything to me. I love them and would do anything for them."

And with that, Sam shook off Tashi's grip and grabbed Gaia's hand. Upon his touch, Gaia looked upward and blue light poured from her eyes, then enveloped her body. Sam felt the surge of energy enter his hand then travel up his arm. It quickly overwhelmed him. His muscles seized and a tingling sensation took over. Like pins and needles all over his body. When the energy of Gaia left his body, the pain was excruciating—it was as though he was being pulled apart. Like every cell in his body was torn from him. And with this searing pain came a crushing sense of despair, a paralyzing fear that made him want to cry. But the agony was just too great and so he screamed at the top of his lungs. At least he thought he was screaming.

There was no sound emanating from his mouth. When the final remnants of this magical energy was gone, Sam saw the blue light disappear and he collapsed to the ground. He felt cold and alone and immeasurably sad. His world was spinning and his eyes went dark...and then he felt something on his forehead. A kiss? A voice whispered in his ear. Tashi. Her three simple words echoed in his head.

"Goodbye, Sam London."

Chapter 21

CASE CLOSURE

Cynthia Salazar was home, but nothing felt the same, because Cynthia Salazar wasn't the same. Upon returning to San Francisco from Washington, D.C., the tenacious reporter struggled with re-assimilating to her old life.

She had promised her bosses a spectacular story—her biggest ever— but now she had to backtrack. She claimed her leads didn't pan out and that her sources dried up. She tapped into her dormant drama skills and acted embarrassed and crestfallen by this turn of events, even agreeing to let her bosses count her vacation days for the time she was away. She didn't do her ambition any favors, but the higher-ups bought her excuses and stopped asking questions. She had uncovered the world's greatest secret, but she couldn't tell a living soul...and that was okay. Cynthia knew the stakes and was happy to bear the burden.

She had only been back a few weeks when her boss called her in for a meeting. She attended, nervously, believing they might be looking to let her go after her non-story. It turned out that veteran anchorwoman Peggy

Peggleman was retiring and they wanted Cynthia to take over her spot. She had to wonder if the DMW might be behind this promotion. The timing was suspicious and when she contacted Bob Ferguson about it, he feigned ignorance and congratulated her.

"You're certainly very deserving," he told Cynthia. "The DMW has much to be grateful to you for. Perhaps we will be calling on your help again in the future."

* * *

Ironically, the very first story Cynthia covered as anchor on the evening newscast was the death of reality show star Boone "Wildman" Walker. He was reported to have been killed in Mongolia, while searching for the fabled Mongolian death worm. Witnesses said the star suffered a fatal injury when a yurt collapsed on him in a remote resort of a Mongolian national park. According to the accounts, Boone was rescuing people from a fire that was ignited by a propane explosion. Local law enforcement claimed Boone saved several people before meeting his demise, and they hailed him as a hero.

The DMW had done him a great service by putting out this false hero story, but it made Cynthia squeamish to cover it. She knew the cold, hard truth and had to keep her mouth shut. She wondered what other stories she had reported on or heard on the news that were influenced by the DMW. The whole experience made her more skeptical of everything she saw and read. She was reminded of what Ferguson told her—that perhaps they would be calling on her in the future. She didn't know how she'd feel about helping to hide or bend the truth at their request. Though it was against her nature, Cynthia certainly understood the justification. But how long could this go on? At what point would humanity be ready to see the world as it really is? And was there anything she could do to help pave the way?

She tried her best to push all thoughts of the DMW and the existence of mythical creatures aside and focus on the reality that most people knew. Ferguson had given her an antidote of sorts that removed her ability to see mythical creatures. She didn't love the idea, but understood its necessity. She couldn't be sure she wouldn't flip out if she came upon a mythical creature when she was out and about, especially when she learned that some are encouraged to live among humans. Just seeing Bob Ferguson in his natural half-man/half-wolf form was shocking enough.

After her second night of anchoring the eleven o'clock news, Cynthia got home a little after midnight and was looking forward to going straight to bed. She entered her one-bedroom apartment and locked the door behind her. She flipped on the lights in the foyer, put her purse on the credenza, then reached down to take off her shoes.

"Don't be frightened," a voice called out from nowhere.

Cynthia was immediately frightened; in fact, she was in the process of removing her shoes, so she was balancing on one foot, and the shock of the voice sent her hopping backward and screaming. She stumbled into a coat rack, which tumbled onto the credenza and knocked over a vase of flowers. The vase crashed onto the floor and shattered, sending a flood of water across the foyer. When Cynthia attempted to regain her footing, she slipped on the slick hardwood surface and fell forward. Her face was inches from slamming into the floor when her body froze in mid-air. Someone had caught her—but there was no one there. She was floating.

"My apologies for surprising you," the voice said.

"Kunibald?" she asked, recognizing his voice.

"Yes, it is me," he confirmed.

"Are you holding me up right now?"

"I am. Is that all right? I didn't want you to get hurt because of me," he said. Cynthia climbed to her feet and eyed the mess. She headed to the kitchen and grabbed paper towels.

"You scared the heck out of me, Kunibald," Cynthia told him. "Next time, leave a note or something—or have Bob text me that you're going to visit."

"No one else knows I'm here," Kunibald confessed in a guarded whisper. That admission intrigued Cynthia.

"Really? Why are you here?" she asked, as she wiped up the water. "And where are you right now; I don't know what direction I should talk towards."

"I'm over here by the table," he said. Cynthia looked to her kitchen/dining room table that sat to the front of the main room. She couldn't see him, but at least she could speak in his direction. "I'm here to follow-up on the missing magical item."

"You didn't find it?"

"I'm afraid not. It was definitely taken from the vault," the kobold told her.

"And you still think I might have taken it?" she asked as she finished sweeping up the glass. She disposed of it, then walked back into the room and sat at the table.

"I had entertained that possibility," Kunibald admitted. "After I learned you received your recent promotion, I thought that might be an indication you possessed it, but after what just happened with your fall and the vase breaking, I now know you do not have it."

"What is it, exactly?" Cynthia inquired.

"It's a four-leaf clover," Kunibald revealed. "The oldest one known to man or mythical creature."

"So it's like a lucky charm? That's a real thing?"

"It is a real and magical thing," Kunibald revealed. "The older the clover, the greater its power. Is there anything you can tell me about that day? Any possibility you might have seen the culprit?"

"I honestly don't remember seeing anyone steal anything, except the boy and that mace, of course," she told him. "But there weren't that many of us there..."

"No, there were not," Kunibald agreed. "And now that we've eliminated you as a suspect, I believe I know who is responsible. And it will make things...complicated."

"Can't you just go to the person and take it back?" she asked.

"It's possible, but tricky," Kunibald said. "It is easier if they give it up, willingly. But they would not be motivated to do so for good reason."

"What do you mean? They would just want to keep it, to continue having really good luck?" Cynthia posited.

"I believe the individual who took it did so for a very specific, some might say, noble purpose," Kunibald explained. "It wasn't theft in the traditional sense and he may not have even 'used' it, but likely doesn't realize that simply possessing it—whether it is in its case or not—does not make a difference. And now it would be too late."

"Too late for what?"

"Once you possess such an item, parting with it can be dangerous," Kunibald said.

"How so?"

"When a person who has possessed and benefitted from a four leaf clover gives it up, they will experience a surge of bad luck," the kobold explained. "The amount of bad luck is directly proportional to the strength of the magic, which in this case is extremely high given the age of the clover."

"So they could die?" Cynthia inquired.

"No...it wouldn't kill the person, but everything that could go wrong, will. And in a very immediate way," Kunibald responded. "The person would become the unluckiest person in the world. And that could lead to catastrophic consequences for anyone close to him."

"Him?" Cynthia replied. "That ranger took it, didn't he? Vance Vantana."

"That is my conclusion," Kunibald said. "And I fear for him. For the DMW. For his family. And for the misfortune and misery that now lies ahead."

Sam London was awake a moment before his eyes opened. He suddenly became aware of the world again—not of his immediate surroundings, but of life, itself. He was alive. He had survived. Sam couldn't hear anything or anyone and he was lying down on something soft and springy. He could also feel his head on a soft, raised surface, and there was something on his body. He grabbed it. A blanket?

Sam's eyes popped open and he was surprised by what he found. He wasn't in the under-earth, he wasn't in the garden of Gaia, and he wasn't in the cave with that hideous unicorn. Sam London was in his bed in Benicia, California.

He shot up to a sitting position and scanned his room. The sun was peeking through his window and the clock by his bed said it was 8:36 in the morning. But what morning? How long had he been asleep? He didn't see Nuks around and his bedroom door was closed. He wasn't entirely certain he wasn't still dreaming, but things looked real enough so far.

When he climbed out of bed, he noticed he was in his pajamas. He didn't recall changing; in fact, he didn't recall much of anything. His last memory was of clutching Gaia's hand and experiencing the agony of having his magic ripped from his body forever. That's what it felt like—a surgical removal without anesthesia. It was the worst, most awful feeling that Sam had ever felt. Just thinking about it made him uncomfortable—like his body was recalling and reliving the pain. He could sense that something was missing from him now. It was hard to describe, but he didn't feel complete. He knew it was gone, but his mind and body hadn't quite accepted it. There was an emptiness that didn't exist before and a sorrow that accompanied it. But then Sam suddenly remembered why he gave it all up.

He was out of his bedroom in an instant.

Sam's excitement was too overwhelming—he couldn't find out if his sacrifice had worked fast enough. He darted to his mom's bedroom, but it was empty, the bed perfectly made. Then he heard muffled voices coming from downstairs. He spun around and headed for the steps. The smell of breakfast hit his nostrils and stopped him cold. There was something so comforting about that smell. Home. He could detect the scent of toast and the sweet smells of melting butter and eggs and the fluffy warmth of pancakes. He was moving slowly now, savoring the scent like he was tasting it with each step. He had no idea what might await him downstairs but he wanted to relish in this moment.

The muffled voices became clearer and it turned out to be just a single voice. Vance. Who was his dad speaking to, he wondered. The curiosity was too much to bear and he leapt over the last two steps to get to the bottom, landing with a pronounced thud that jingled the glasses on the table.

"Well, look who's finally awoken," his dad said with a grin so wide his eyes and nose seemed to disappear. Sam was about to talk—to say his first words of the day and ask his burning question, when a voice spoke up from behind him.

"Good morning, Sam."

Sam froze in place. The sound of that familiar voice sent his heart racing, practically pounding out of his chest. His breaths turned rapid and short as his stomach suddenly felt like it was hosting a mass migration of butterflies. Was it her? Was it really her? Or was he simply imagining it? Vance must have noticed the eager anxiousness in Sam's expression because he caught his son's eye and nodded, assuredly. Sam pivoted, slowly, and when he finally got all the way around, there she was.

Odette London stood before him in a flowered dress looking just as he remembered. A wave of happiness washed over him. Ettie opened up her arms and Sam fell into them.

There was a time—not so long ago—when Sam London would be embarrassed by Ettie's over-the-top displays of affection, especially when she dropped him off at school. In fact, he had made it a mission to persuade her to ratchet back the endless hugs and kisses, often saying things like "C'mon, Mom, I'm not leaving on a hundred-year voyage."

In the days after Ettie's return to Gaia, Sam would think back on those moments with regret. He realized why she was so affectionate. She knew her time was fleeting—just like everyone else—but perhaps she had a deeper, unconscious understanding of how quickly her life with Sam could be upended. When she was gone, all Sam wanted was one more chance to hug her and to express how he felt. He was always so worried about how he would look in front of other kids that he missed out on what was most important. Now he had a second chance and he wasn't about to blow it.

"I love you!" Sam declared so firmly the sentiment could be heard resonating from his voice.

"I love you, too," Ettie whispered in his ear, as they embraced.

Sam burst into tears, but these weren't sad tears—no way. These were big fat drops of pure joy parading down his cheeks. Ettie was crying as well. They held onto each other for what seemed like forever, but that still wasn't long enough. Sam suddenly felt two other arms wrap around him and his mother and squeeze.

"Our first official family hug!" Vance declared. Sam's cheeks were starting to hurt from smiling so much. After a moment, Vance broke off. "Uh oh. Pancakes are burning." He headed into the kitchen to tend to breakfast, but Sam remained with his mom. She gently cupped his face in her hands.

"Thank you for what you did for me," she told him. "I am sorry you had to do that."

"I'm not," Sam replied firmly.

"I probably would have told you not to," she said with a smile.

"That's what Tashi said," he admitted.

"She's right. But I'm grateful. Incredibly grateful." She hugged him again. "We have a lot to catch up on, don't we?" Sam couldn't form words yet, so he nodded his agreement. "Letting a shapeshifting raccoon dog masquerade as you? Nearly sacrificing yourself to save Ta Cathair? Missing all of that school? You're grounded for life, young man." Sam's eyes widened, until his mom finally grinned and winked. "Got you."

"Yep. You sure did," Sam replied with a sigh of relief.

"Get it while it's hot," Vance announced. He placed a platter of pancakes on the table, along with buttered toast, scrambled eggs, bacon, and hash browns. Sam's stomach growled angrily as he sat down and quickly reached for the food.

"Hang on," Vance said. "This is our first meal as a family. I reckon a blessing's in order. We've got a lot to be grateful for."

Sam nodded in agreement. The three bowed their heads and Vance spoke a short but thankful prayer.

"How did we..." Sam asked after his father finished up.

"Get home?" Vance replied. Sam nodded and began stuffing his face with food. "Dvergen subway. Tashi carried you. I carried your mother. Even the Sharur was helpful."

"Where is Sha?" Sam was suddenly reminded of his new companion.

"He's a trip," Ettie said with a smile.

"You two met?" Sam asked.

"We did. He's quite a talker," Ettie told him. "He's out exploring—in parrot form, of course. He was cooped up a while in that vault, I guess, so he's enjoying his freedom. He'll be back soon."

"And Nuks?"

"Foraging with Nuiko," Vance told him. "I haven't heard from Tashi since we got back, but I'm sure she'll want to know you're awake."

"How did you deal with the unicorn?" Sam asked. "When I went through the portal, I realized you were still stuck up there with that thing."

"I guess I got lucky," Vance said. "The more important question is: what are we going to do today? Our first family day."

Sam hadn't even thought about it. He looked to his mom, who looked to Vance and shrugged.

"I don't know. What would you like to do?" she said.

"I'm so glad you asked," Vance replied with a grin.

Sam's dad excitedly rattled off possibilities, including national parks, forests, and seashores. Not surprisingly, they all had a park ranger theme. As his father spoke, Sam was suddenly and lucidly present. This was a moment he could never have imagined but always hoped might happen. He was with his mom and dad. They were finally all together. The most rewarding part of it was seeing the way his mother's face lit up. For as long as Sam could remember, he sensed a sadness in Ettie, as if there was something missing from her life. But that was no longer the case. In fact, he had never seen her so happy and that was the one thing he wanted more than anything.

As Sam ate breakfast with his family, he considered all of the possibilities that suddenly became possible. He couldn't wait to tell Tashi. To share with her this feeling and to express that, despite what happened, he was grateful for her. His time in the garden of Gaia was still fuzzy, but he had the feeling he owed her an apology. He was sure she'd understand. After all, the future had never looked brighter or happier for Sam. He was certain he made the right choice.

Sam recalled how different he felt after parting with his magic. He had sensed that he was incomplete without it, as if the removal of this mythical part of his being had left a hole in him. But sitting around the table with his parents, the emptiness was now overflowing with love. And that was all the magic Sam London ever needed.

EPILOGUE

It was still light out when Sangmu had finished her day's chores. It was that magical hour when the orange sun began to set behind the snow-topped mountains, illuminating the sky with vivid shades of yellow, red, and purple, casting a golden glow on her small village. The colors of Gaia were an extraordinary sight and a reminder of its great beauty—it was always humbling for Sangmu to be in its presence and witness the wonders it created.

With a little time before dinner, she headed into the village center where preparations were being made for the coming contests. Her people did not hold many celebrations, but this wasn't a typical celebration. This was a tournament of champions, which pitted the village's warriors against each other to find the greatest of all.

No one knew what to expect from this series of contests, as they were last held over two hundred years ago. Only the village elder remembered the previous tournament and, as village elder, only he had the power to call for another, which he had done to the village's surprise just a week earlier.

The announcement had sent the village into a flurry of whispers as to who might take part and who might triumph. Sangmu was not especially excited to see this contest for her own personal reasons. She believed—rather, she knew—that the greatest warrior in the village would not be present to compete and so any winner would be illegitimate.

Sangmu reached the center of the village, ready to help clear the space for the construction of a tournament arena, when she noticed a crowd gathering at the entrance of the village. A friend in the throng caught Sangmu's eye and waved her over.

"Sangmu," the friend called out. "Come quickly!"

Sangmu moved swiftly toward the gathering and began to hear the murmurs of the crowd. The content of these murmurs surprised her and propelled Sangmu to push through the villagers, who noticed her presence and parted to let her pass. She reached the front and stared out across the valley floor.

In the distance, a figure was walking toward the village. *Could it be?* she wondered. Sangmu suddenly found herself walking to meet the figure. The walk turned into a run. Sangmu was, like the rest of her kind, not an overly emotional type, but she was a mother. There is a very special bond that a mother shares with her child. Her eyes were moistened with joyful tears as she called across the frozen landscape.

"Tashi!"

When Sangmu of Kustos reached her daughter, she immediately threw her arms around her. She was surprised by the strength of Tashi's hug. They lingered for a moment, holding each other, and when they parted, Sangmu looked into her daughter's eyes.

"It is wonderful to see you here. In this world." Tashi had only visited them in dreams of late given her distance from the village.

Tashi nodded. "It is nice to be home and to see you."

"How long do you have with us?" Sangmu asked, knowing her daughter's responsibilities to the gryphon in the human world.

"As long as Gaia wishes," she replied. "I will not be returning to Benicia." This confused her mother.

"What about Sam London?" Sangmu asked.

"Sam London has his family. And I have mine," Tashi said, matter-of-factly. "Our time together is complete."

Sangmu wasn't sure she understood what Tashi meant or the implications of her return, but she was happy she was home. She took her daughter's hand and they walked together to the village and the waiting crowd.

Tashi, Guardian of the Gryphon's Claw, had returned to Kustos.

The End.

Sam London will return in "The Tengu of Tokyo."

DMW FILE CLASSIFICATION

DMW case files are presented in the following format: #XXXXX-XXX-XX.X. This ten or eleven-digit code consists of both letters and numbers.

The initial series of letters and numbers represents the investigating ranger and the case number involving that ranger. These particular files are associated with Sam London (SL). As this is Sam London's third case the files are designated as 003.

The second series of three numbers indicates the applicable DMW offense code. In this instance, offense code 720 is used. This code encompasses those crimes defined as "Unsanctioned Operations Involving DMW Employees." In the department's use, "Unsanctioned" relates to any and all operations that are not under the immediate direction, jurisdiction, or auspices of the Department of Mythical Wildlife. These operations may also lead to or involve other crimes that undermine or subvert Phylassos' Law.

The final number pertains to the section of the file for those files with multiple sections. Numbers that appear after the section and are separated by a period indicate subsections.

SUBJ: This is the subject or subjects of the section.

SOURCE: This notes the source or sources of the information included in a particular section. These sources are designated by an abbreviation. Below is a list of relevant abbreviations:

SA: Special Advisor

MC: Mythical Creature

ODB: Operational Debriefing

MR: Medical Records

SR: Surveillance Records

BG: Background Investigation

WS: Witness Statement

PR: Public Record

AR: Agency Record

DATE: This is the date on which the incident or inquiry took place.

FORMS: In some instances, case files include forms used by DMW personnel to record information from witnesses or intelligence sources related to an investigation. For example, FD-204 is an Investigative Report that consists of all supporting documentation for a DMW case, including relevant information originating from human law enforcement agencies.

SPECIAL CLASSIFICATIONS: Files that are administrative in nature are given a classification code in the 400s. For example, classification 470 is reserved for personnel records and 480 for employee medical records. Specific file numbers of these records have been withheld due to privacy concerns.

CIPHERS: The communications of the DMW are highly classified; as such, they must often be encrypted for protection. The decryption methods are not reproduced here for security reasons, but they are presented in coded form, in the spirit of their original source. These reproductions use a Caesar Cipher, which can be denoted by a cipher key of XX-X.

The first two characters in the cipher key will be either RS or LS. These letters indicate a Right Shift or Left Shift in the English alphabet from the encoded letter. The third character will denote the number of places shifted. For example, a cipher key of RS-5 indicates a shift to the right of five letters. In this scenario, an encoded letter "M" when decoded is the letter "H."

To learn how to decode the cipher used in Sam London's third case, visit www.mythicalwildlife.com.

PARKS TO VISIT

Catoctin Mountain National Park
Maryland
United States of America
https://www.nps.gov/cato/index.htm

Dry Tortugas National Park
Florida
United States of America
https://www.nps.gov/drto/index.htm

Everglades National Park
Florida
United States of America
https://www.nps.gov/ever/index.htm

Falling Waters State Park
Florida
United States of America
https://www.floridastateparks.org/parks-and-trails/
falling-waters-state-park

Gates of the Arctic National Park
Alaska
United States of America
https://www.nps.gov/gaar/index.htm

Gobi Gurvansaikhan National Park
Mongolia

Great Smoky Mountains National Park
Tennessee and North Carolina
United States of America
http://www.nps.gov/grsm/index.htm

Katmai National Park and Reserve
Alaska
United States of America
https://www.nps.gov/katm/index.htm

Killarney National Park
Ireland
https://www.killarneynationalpark.ie

Mammoth Cave National Park
Kentucky
United States of America
https://www.nps.gov/maca/index.htm

Redwood National Park
California
United States of America
http://www.nps.gov/redw/index.htm

Shenandoah National Park
Virginia
United States of America
https://www.nps.gov/shen/index.htm

Theodore Roosevelt Island
Washington, D.C.
United States of America
https://www.nps.gov/this/index.htm

Yosemite National Park
California
United States of America
https://www.nps.gov/yose/index.htm

Support America's National Parks:
National Park Foundation
Official Charity of America's National Parks
http://www.nationalparks.org

MEMORANDUM

Date: (▮▮▮▮▮▮▮)
To: DMW Rangers & Administrative Personnel
From: Dr. Vance Vantana
Subject: Creatures linked to Case SL003

The following is a list of the mythical wildlife connected to Sam London's third case. At my request, the department's forensic arts division has provided illustrations for reference.

Adlet
Origin: Alaska
Known Abilities: Enhanced strength and senses
Favorite Food: Humans (or each other!)
Comments: Kind of like werewolves,
but smarter and hungrier.

Almas
Origin: Mongolia
Known Abilities: Super strength
Favorite Food: Khuushuur

Comments: Wrestle at your own risk.

Ant-Lion
Origin: Greece
Known Abilities: Strength in numbers
Favorite Food: Picnics and people

Comments: You're going to need a stronger bug spray.

Bennu
Origin: Egypt
Known Abilities: Unknown
Favorite Food: Unknown

Comments: Can you say persistent?

Dullahan
Origin: Ireland
Known Abilities: Capturing souls, causing nightmares
Favorite Food: Can you eat with a detached head?
Comments: Bring gold.

Each Uisge
Origin: Scotland
Known Abilities: Adhesive skin
Favorite Food: Humans (but not their liver)

Comments: The ride of your life. Literally.

Kinarra
Origin: Asia
Known Abilities: Magic, Höömei
Favorite Food: Sea-Buckthorn Juice

Comments: Ultimate karaoke partner.

Kooshdakhaa

Origin: Alaska

Known Abilities: Shape-shifting

Favorite Food: Human souls and fish sticks

Comments: Don't let him touch you!

Snallygaster

Origin: United States

Known Abilities: Instilling terror?

Favorite Food: Take a guess

Comments: As mean as it looks.

Tornit

Origin: Alaska

Known Abilities: Super strength, heightened senses

Favorite Food: Seafood and any food they see

Comments: Large and in charge.

ACKNOWLEDGMENTS

It's time to acknowledge all of the people who helped make all of this possible, worthwhile...and fun!

Tiffany and Valentina for the love, encouragement, and giggles.

Dolores for all the support, including the whole giving birth thing (seems important).

Lacy and Dabney for always looking out for me.

Anthony Ziccardi and Permuted Press for believing in the adventure.

Krista Vitola for once again sharing her extraordinary editing talents.

Heather King for masterfully managing the process.

Anika Claire for taking it to the next level.

Alana Mills for helping me look smart.

Kevin Keele for sharing his incredible artistry.

Chris McClary for his amazing design...and friendship.

And to all the others I don't have enough room to thank but have contributed to everything I do: thank you!